AN HEIR OF FROST

ELISE KOVA

Silver Wing Press

An Heir of Frost

ELISE KOVA

This book is a work of fiction. The names, characters and events in this book are the products of the author's imagination or are used fictitiously. Any similarity to real persons living or dead is coincidental and not intended by the author.

Published by Silver Wing Press
Copyright © 2023 by Elise Kova

Cover Artwork by Polar Engine
Developmental Editing by Rebecca Faith Editorial
Line Editing by Melissa Frain
Proofreading by Kate Anderson

ISBN (paperback): 978-1-949694-61-1
ISBN (hardcover): 978-1-949694-60-4
eISBN: 978-1-949694-56-7

Also by Elise Kova

A Trial of Sorcerers

A Trial of Sorcerers
A Hunt of Shadows
A Tournament of Crowns
An Heir of Frost
A Queen of Ice

Also set in the Air Awakens Universe

AIR AWAKENS SERIES
Air Awakens
Fire Falling
Earth's End
Water's Wrath
Crystal Crowned

GOLDEN GUARD TRILOGY
The Crown's Dog
The Prince's Rogue
The Farmer's War

VORTEX CHRONICLES
Vortex Visions
Chosen Champion
Failed Future
Sovereign Sacrifice
Crystal Caged

Married to Magic

A Deal with the Elf King
A Dance with the Fae Prince
A Duel with the Vampire Lord
A Duet with the Siren Duke
A Dawn with the Wolf Knight

Loom Saga

The Alchemists of Loom
The Dragons of Nova
The Rebels of Gold

See all books and learn more at:
http://www.EliseKova.com

for those who feel like home

Table of Contents

THE
MAIN CONTINENT
VANGAR
GRAYSTON
SOLARIN
"THE CAPITAL"
RIVEND
MOSANT
THE GREAT IMPERIAL WAY
OPARIUM
TIX
THE
SOUTH
LYNDUM
PACA
LEOUL
CR
SHAN
THE FINSHAR
DELTA
HASTAN
THE
EAST
CYVEN

THE CRESCENT CONTINENT
THE BARRIER ISLANDS
THE WEST
MHASHAN
GRAYSTON
QUI
XIA
TIX
NORIN
LAU
SILME
YON
ORE
THE CROSSROADS
ANTO
POHEAT
THE PASS
DAMACIUM
SORICIUM
LAKE IO
THE WEST
ALDA
THE NORTH
SHALDAN

EFER
DOLARIAN
M
VARGA
BALLAST
DANT
OFOK
WARICH
RISEN
VENMIR
MER
EMPIRE OF
CARSOVIA
LUTH
FRANHURT
REPUBLIC
OF QWINT
LOSOG

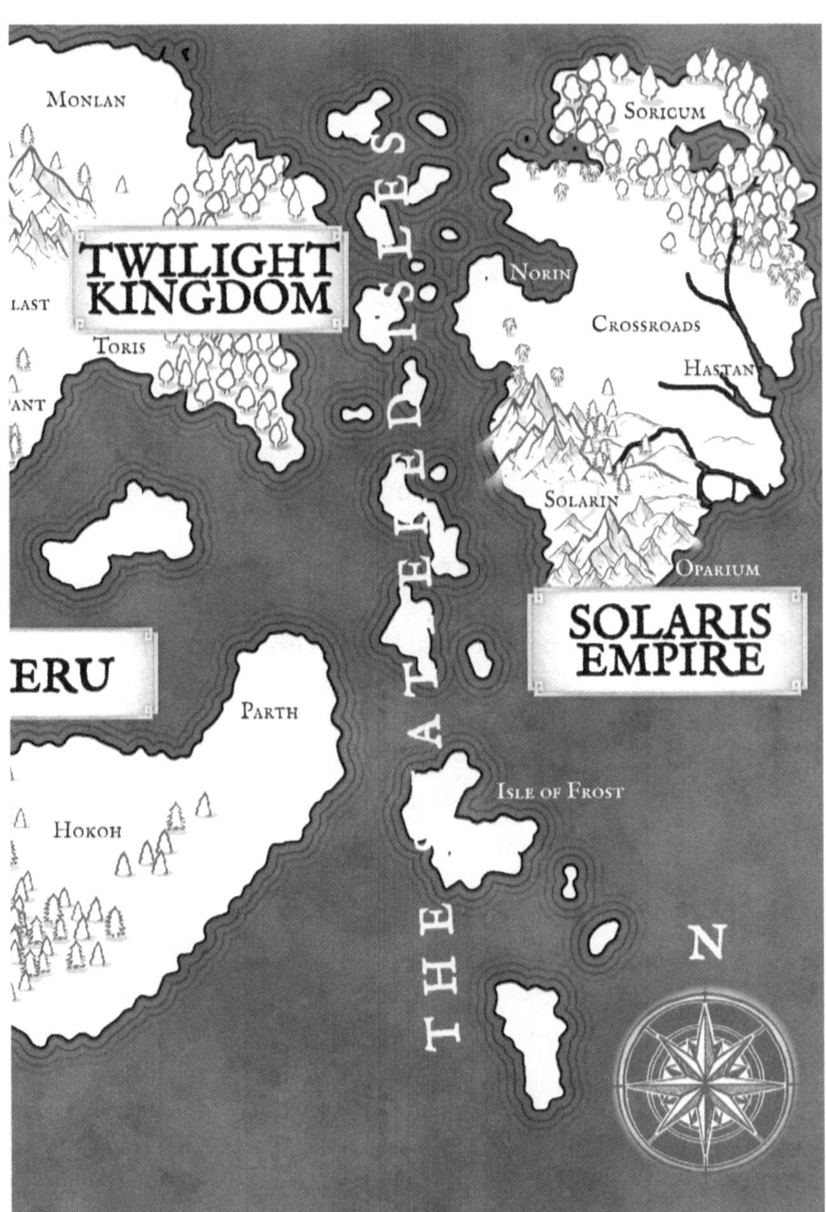

MONLAN
SORICUM
TWILIGHT
KINGDOM
LAST
NORIN
TORIS
CROSSROADS
ANT
HASTAN
ERU
SOLARIN
OPARIUM
PARTH
SOLARIS
EMPIRE
ISLE OF FROST
HOKOH
THE SHATTERED ISLES
N

**Need a refresher on what happened in the
previous books?**

Head over to this page of my website...

https://elisekova.com/a-trial-of-sorcerers-summaries/

... to read a full summary of what happened in the previous
three books to make sure you're ready to continue Eira's
adventures!

CHAPTER

ONE

THE TOWN OF Warich burned in the distance. The fires had only grown as they'd slipped away from the death and chaos, sailing down the river that cut through Meru. The Pillars were putting their fearsome might on display for all to see, sending a message that would rock the very foundations of five kingdoms for years to come.

But Eira's focus wasn't on the distant carnage. Or the fact that the boat that she had escaped on with her friends was presently sailing in the *opposite* direction of where they had been intending to go. Or the countless pains that were still setting in following their frenzied flight from the coliseum.

None of that mattered.

The entire world had condensed in a second, reduced to the woman standing before her.

She was about Eira's height and also of narrow frame. Hair as fine as moonbeams and nearly the same platinum shade cascaded over her shoulders, perfectly straight and catching the slightest breezes as if she were some kind of ethereal specter. Eyes the same color as the ice in the deep mountains narrowed slightly as she tilted her head back, looking down her nose.

"Hello, Eira."

All Eira could do was croak in response. She opened and closed her mouth, several times, but no words formed. Her mind was empty—a void where all thoughts had once been.

This was some kind of hallucination, brought on by a day that just wouldn't end. Her family might have just died. The leaders of her empire probably perished in a ball of fire. Cullen had been stabbed through trying to save her. Everything she thought she knew was crashing down around her. *This couldn't be real.*

"Nothing to say before you die?" A slight smirk stretched across the woman's face, curling thin lines into her cheeks, as though this particular expression of smug confidence was one she had repeated thousands of times, to the point that it was forever etched onto her visage.

"You—you're…"

The woman's gaze shifted slightly, looking over Eira's shoulder. Eira had completely forgotten Ducot was just behind her at the helm. "They always blubber, don't they?"

Whatever reaction Ducot had wasn't vocal, so Eira missed it.

"You're Adela," Eira whispered, finally mustering two thoughts together.

"Yes." Adela shifted her grip on the cane. It was made of ice, the same as her right arm and left leg, judging from the icy boot that extended out from beneath her pant leg. "I know who I am. But the real question is, do you know who *you* are?"

Before Eira could respond, Adela moved. It wasn't sudden, or quick. She practically strolled across the deck to cover the gap between them. But Eira didn't even try to flee. She just…watched as the deadly woman who had been little more than a blank slate in her dreams approached.

Adela came to a stop a step from her. Reaching out with her hand of ice, she gripped Eira's chin, turning her head left and right. Eira was reminded of how the merchants inspected livestock fresh off the boats in the market of Oparium. But the whole dreamlike oddity of the situation had her allowing it to happen. It dulled the biting chill of Adela's fingers.

As Adela conducted her inspection, Eira did the same. Their hair was of similar shade. Eira's perhaps a touch more golden, but Adela's silvery hue could be from age, or the moonlight. Their noses were different; Eira's had a bit of a bulb at the end of hers compared to the sharp point Adela's narrowed into. But their eyes…

It was like looking into a mirror.

The part of her that had been wondering for months tried to reach out. Would Adela's magic feel like her own? Eira attempted to extend her magic, forgetting it was no longer there. The ghost of her former power provided her with the illusion of magical pulses she knew should be there. But they weren't real sensations.

Her magic was gone. She'd sacrificed it trying to bring down Ulvarth by closing his channel. Little good it had done. He'd orchestrated the downfall of the royals with such thoroughness that he didn't even need his power.

The cold from Adela's hand was finally reaching the bone of her jaw. Eira fought chattering lips. Her magic was no longer there to fend off the cold, either.

Adela released her and stepped to the side, rounding her. "You said she was a Waterrunner."

"I did," Ducot answered.

"She shivers." Adela's voice from behind had a chill racing up Eira's spine.

"You have that effect on people." Ducot had the same tone as when he reported to the Court of Shadows. He was working with Adela—*for* her. The whole time he was at the court…everything he asked Eira about Adela, everything Eira had told him of her history, her fears…

The searing betrayal was the only thing that could cut through the cold that frosted the very air around Adela and sharpen Eira's senses enough to bring her back to the present. Eira blinked, as though she were waking from a dream. The empty deck stretched before her.

"Where are my friends?" she demanded, voice firmer and more even.

"You should be more worried about yourself than them." Adela finished her sharklike circling, coming to a stop again before Eira.

"What have you done with them?"

The pirate queen merely smiled that same mischievous,

borderline-sinister smile in reply. It oozed control, like Eira was a new toy to play with.

Eira wasn't about to go from one madman's game to another's…even if the woman moving the pieces of this new board might be her mother. She glanced over her shoulder, back at Ducot. There was another man next to him now. A draconi took his place, assuming the helm from the blind man. Ducot stepped back and sat, leaning against the railing, no doubt to catch his breath from the exertion of having to sense the water around them constantly.

"They were your friends, too," Eira seethed at him. "Or was that also a lie?"

"Relax," Ducot said dryly. There wasn't any animosity in his voice; he sounded as he always had. Even though Eira felt the sting of betrayal, he clearly did not seem to think anything had changed between them. "They're fine. Just sleeping."

"Where?"

"Where else? In the hold," Adela answered, drawing Eira's attention back to her. "I won't harm them so long as I am not given a reason to. My business is squarely with you, Eira Landan."

"Why?" Eira ignored the odd, prickling sensation that ran up her arms at the sound of Adela saying her name.

"I wanted to see the woman who was claiming to be me."

"*Be* you? I never—"

"I have heard the rumors spreading like wildfire. Some even say that I am walking the lands of Meru again, reborn." She slipped some hair over her shoulder. "I must admit, I am constantly flattered by the new tales they make up about me." Her preening turned back to intensity. Her fingers tapped across the top of her chin in quick succession. "But when those rumors are also about *you*, I find myself less inclined to enjoy them."

"I didn't start or perpetuate any of the rumors," Eira said firmly. "In fact, it would've been far more convenient for me if they hadn't begun at all."

None of this was how she'd imagined meeting Adela would

unfold. Not that Eira had any kind of clear imagining before this moment. The pirate queen was a legend. A scary story told to kids to make them oblige. She'd hardly ever seemed real, even despite Eira having spoken to people who had encountered her.

But, if she were honest…part of her might have been holding hope that their meeting would've been the slightest bit different. Warmer, perhaps? But that would've been too much to hope for from the pirate queen known for ice ships and biting frost.

"Now you insult me by saying association is an inconvenience?" Adela's expression didn't look insulted in the slightest. "You don't think I know how much sway my name has? The fear it strikes into the hearts of men?"

"I'm sure you know the terror your name inspires, and so do I; I grew up in Oparium. Except I never *wanted* that reputation." She motioned backward to where Ducot still was. "Just ask him. I never spread the rumors."

"Ducot has kept me well-informed."

If Adela was here, now—if she had been watching her—it all meant that she'd finally come for Eira, right? Why else send Ducot to be close to her? Why keep such close tabs if not to rescue Eira from the Pillars?

Her thoughts jumbled with every possibility, every hope and fear merged. Each seemingly more impossible than the last, adding to the surreal nature of the moment.

"If you've been following me, then you should know—"

"What I want to know is what made you think you could get away with it." Her expression shifted. The coy, wicked smirk she'd worn gave way to something far, far more sinister. "Even if you did not spread the rumors yourself, you enabled them by imitating my magic."

"I…I admit that I have been using your magic. But—"

Unlike before, Adela now moved with speed and murderous intent. Her cane arced through the air, transforming into a frosty rapier by the time it hovered underneath Eira's chin. The weapon was purely for show. Eira knew all too well how deadly Adela's magic could be with a single look. She'd been in grave danger from the moment she'd met Adela's eyes.

"Tell me who your man or woman on the inside is and I *might* be inclined to let you live."

"Excuse me?"

"You have surprising resources for someone so young, I'll give you that." There was a gleam of what looked like pride in the pirate queen's eyes. "Under other circumstances, I might have been proud that you'd managed to infiltrate my ranks enough to learn my magic. Might've even asked you to join my crew."

Exhaustion slipped into Eira's palms, pulling her down, causing her shoulders to slump. This woman…might be her mother. And Eira had managed to disappoint her within minutes of meeting her. Laughter slipped through her cracks, coming out as almost a bark.

Adela, for her part, remained poised, the rapier perfectly still. Though her eyes did narrow slightly at Eira's admittedly strange shift in demeanor.

"I don't have anyone 'on the inside.' *You* taught me how to use your magics."

"Excuse me?"

"I have your journals."

Adela's pose eased. The rapier slipped slightly away from Eira's throat. Adela's expression relaxed with what Eira could only assume was recognition.

"You *have* them?" Adela breathed. Not "had." Eira's words had been chosen intentionally.

Eira nodded now that the rapier wasn't so close to her chin. "Well, I did…they're back there." She pointed to Warich.

Adela swooped the rapier down—it was a cane once more that seemed to extend from the palm of her icy hand. "Reverse course. We return to Warich. We can unload the rest of the cargo there as well."

As soon as Adela had issued her command, the vessel banked hard. Eira noticed another ship sailing near them doing the same.

She wondered just how many of the small boats making their way upriver were under Adela's control.

"Eira, with me," Adela commanded, walking to the front of the boat. In a daze, Eira followed. "I had planned to kill you for the transgression of using my name but—"

"You'd kill your own daughter?" Eira blurted. It wasn't how she had intended to broach the subject, but none of this was going according to her imagining.

Adela stilled. She slowly turned her face to Eira. Her brow was furrowed in confusion, but her eyes were alight with cruel amusement. A quiet *hrmph* sounded like every last person who had ever laughed at Eira in her life.

"My…*daughter*?" Adela repeated.

"Yes, I—"

"Foolish girl. I have no children."

TWO

I HAVE NO CHILDREN.

The night was collapsing around her. The stars blotted out from a darkening sky. Her vision tunneled and her ears rang. All Eira could see was the smoldering town in the distance. An angry spot at the edge of her horizon. As if the world was burning down around her…

No children.

The angry flames were a cold Eira had never felt before. The last flicker of hope, of finding something—some kind of meaning, or purpose, or explanation for the yawning hole that had opened within her following the discovery of the vast unknown that haunted her past—extinguished. All that lingered was the smell of smoke and a darkness as complete as the pit. As cold as the lake Marcus had died in. The chasm within her that had been created with her parents' revelation only grew wider. Pulling her in. It'd never be filled.

"Are you sure?" Eira desperately tried to find that spark of hope one more time.

Adela stared at her incredulously. "I believe I would know if I had conceived and birthed a child."

It had been a foolish question. Of course Adela would know if she had given birth. But if Eira wasn't Adela's, then whose daughter was she? Who would've left her on her parents' doorstep with the mark of Adela as a baby? Where did her magic come from and why was it so, *so* similar and suited to Adela's?

Although, all Waterrunners' magic was similar. Maybe their overlapping talents meant nothing at all. Maybe, after finding the journal by a twist of fate, Eira had been hunting for meaning that was never actually there.

"I would never allow the risk of an offspring to myself or my legacy," Adela added coolly, as if the mere idea of a child was utterly unpalatable to her.

Did she offer that addition because it was true? To be cruel? Or…perhaps Adela was lying. That could've been some way of her hinting that Eira could actually be her daughter, but Adela couldn't risk saying so.

The questions and uncertainties spiraled with her, further and further down into the abyss of her own making. Adela was either oblivious to Eira's turmoil, or didn't care.

"Glad we've cleared that up." She added, under her breath, "My child, *really*," with a small chuckle. Even though Eira's body was cold all over, she wasn't numb. Not yet, at least. And the words still stung. "As I was saying, I had been planning on killing you. But you can buy your life—at least a bit more of it—so long as you make yourself useful to me."

"I've found myself rather partial to living." Eira's mouth was moving, words were forming—they were even cohesive, miraculously. But it felt like someone else was the one behind them. Her mind was in a distant place. It had been jolted from her body by the events of the day. The scales had tipped out of balance; everything had all added up to be too much.

"Most are." Adela shifted her weight with an air of smugness. Eira got the sense that this was a tactic that she'd used many times. But, for once, Eira didn't have the strength to fight, or even care, at someone so blatantly using and manipulating her.

Perhaps *because* it was blatant was why it didn't bother Eira, unlike the people around her who tried to lie and be subversive time and time again. Or maybe it just didn't matter anymore. Her parents. Her uncle. Vi and Taavin… Her friends…

She gripped the railing at the bow and sank to her knees, physically holding herself up from toppling over into the river. The weight of the world was compressing her. Collapsing with each passing moment onto her shoulders. Everything was lost. Her eyes burned.

"Really, you crumble that easily?" Adela snorted at Eira's pain. "To think anyone believed you could've been me reborn."

Eira didn't fight. She just hung her head between her arms and allowed the tears to spill from her eyes, onto her bloodied knees and pants that still held the dust and smoke of the arena. She was so immeasurably tired. She could sleep for a thousand years and still wake exhausted.

"Let my friends off the boat." Eira's voice was weak and cracking. She looked up at Adela, who still loomed. "When we dock back at Warich, let them go." The ship was speeding along at a good clip; they'd be back soon. "As you said, your business is with me—not them. They shouldn't be kept here."

Adela thrummed her fingers against the railing in thought. She leaned forward. "What makes you think I would ever do the honorable thing?"

"Nothing," Eira admitted.

"Remember who you're dealing with before you ask ridiculous questions." Adela straightened and headed back across the deck, where she began to give instructions to the crew of where to dock and what would be happening. There was a pulse of magic and a bird flew from their boat to another before turning back into human shape.

Eira didn't move. She continued to kneel on the deck. Her arms fell limp at her sides and she stared listlessly ahead.

She knew she should be listening, trying to overhear some kind of useful information, but her ears just rang. She had to formulate a plan…some kind of direction. She had to at least try to *see* her friends and ensure they were in one piece. But Adela's voice was already in her mind, Eira could already hear what she'd say: *What makes you think I'd let you see them?* Eira pressed her eyes closed, tears continuing to fall. She buried her face in her palms.

It was her fault. She'd told Deneya to send the knights back to Risen. She'd allowed her uncle to go to the royals rather than her parents. She'd studied from Adela's books even when everyone had told her the dangers, starting with Alyss at the very beginning of it all.

Every major downfall could be traced back to a decision that she had made.

The vessel coasted to a stop just down the banks of the river from Warich. A dirt road ran along the water into the town. There was more movement behind her, but Eira remained stuck in her stasis.

"Come on, up with you." Ducot grabbed her bicep, trying to hoist her.

"Don't touch me." Eira jerked from his grasp, glaring up at him. Ducot's expression was hard, closed off. "Don't pretend like we're still friendly."

"Do I need to send someone else with her?" Adela asked from halfway down the deck.

"No, I can get her to comply," Ducot called back, then knelt. His tone shifted, voice going low. "If you want to make it through this alive, you need to come with me."

For a brief second, Eira saw the man who had led her to the Court of Shadows. The man she had put her faith in, blindly following into the night. Then the pirates on deck came back into focus.

"I don't even know you," she hissed.

"Well then, it's nice to meet you. I'm Ducot, the man who's trying to save you and your friends' skins." He grinned, scars pulling at the corner of his mouth. Eira wondered if the story she knew about them was even true. Perhaps he got those scars from some mission Adela had sent him on. Eira trusted nothing when it came to him anymore. "If you want to see tomorrow morning then follow my lead."

"Is she refusing to release the magic on her lockbox?" Adela asked, folding both hands on top of her cane. "We can force that, if necessary."

"No, she agreed to release her magic." Ducot stood. "Didn't you, Eira?"

Release the magic on her lockbox? What was Adela talking about? Eira pushed off the deck, fighting against everything that was trying to force her back down. She'd passed the brink of exhaustion, mental and physical, yet somehow she continued to move. It was as if her body was trying to spite her with a will to survive that refused to quit. If not for herself, then for her friends. She wouldn't let them down.

"I'll do what you need," Eira agreed tiredly.

"Good." Adela studied her from head to toe as she approached. "The girl is about to collapse. Someone mend her wounds."

A pirate stepped forward as a hulking man threw a rope ladder over the side of the boat. The movements barely registered for Eira as she was more focused on the Lightspinner quickly mending her various ailments. *Adela was healing her.* That meant she wanted her alive, which counted for something… *Right?*

When the pirate was finished, she stepped away and Adela tapped her cane on the deck, summoning everyone's attention back to her. "I would like this to be quick and clean." She narrowed her eyes at the three other pirates who were now present. "You all know the rules while on Meru."

They all nodded, Ducot included.

Two of the pirates descended. Ducot gave Eira a small push in the center of her back. "You next."

Eira did as she was told, Adela watching her the entire time. She regarded the pirate queen from the corners of her eyes. When Adela smiled thinly at her, Eira didn't bother hiding her inspection any longer.

This was the woman Eira had been hunting for. Now, Adela had found her. The pirate queen had obviously left her ship, the *Stormfrost,* behind in deeper waters to come halfway into Meru… for Eira.

That had to mean something. Adela's decision to go to such lengths to pursue her must be more than merely because of some rumors. There were secrets Adela was keeping about her, she was certain of it.

Eira swung herself over the railing, climbing down the rope ladder. At the bottom, she splashed down into the thick mud and reeds of the riverbank. The water and muck came up to her shoulders and she swam for the shore, where the other two pirates were trudging up.

Ducot landed into the water with a splash not long after. Ripples pushed out from him, his magic physically moving the water as he followed behind. When Eira's feet hit solid ground, she slowly trudged up to the other pirates. Instinct had her attempting to summon magic to wick the water from her. But none came and she was left to drip, shivering from cold…and from fear.

She had always had her magic to depend on and to protect her. Now it was gone and Eira had never been more vulnerable. She had never given much thought before to how Commons might feel in a world of sorcerers. Now she wondered how they went about their entire existence feeling so exposed.

"Good luck, Ducot," one of the two pirates said. He was human, wearing nothing but a vest. Black tattoos ringed the brown flesh of his arms and were painted across his exposed chest. "Looks like a mess back there."

"You'll soon learn that anywhere this one goes ends up a mess." Ducot clasped Eira's shoulder and gave a friendly shake. She broke free as subtly as possible. She was playing along for survival—her own and her friends'. Ducot wasn't counted among her circle any longer.

"I give her three days." A pale, lanky pirate smoothed back his brown hair, pulling it into a ponytail. A gap between his front teeth whistled slightly as he spoke.

"Three? You're generous, Fen." The other pirate chuckled.

Fen shrugged and started walking down the road. Ducot followed him, leaving Eira no other choice than to do the same. She tried to bring her exhausted mind back into focus. They were going back into a burning town overrun by Pillars, because Adela wanted her journals back. The same journals Eira had studied from when she had magic, which she no longer had. And Adela had come halfway across the known world to find Eira... The more she thought about it, the less sense it all made.

Eira shook her head. Her relationship with Adela could wait. The best thing she could do was focus on the present and let the rest be what it would be. One foot, then the next. She had to keep going for her friends. Once they were safe, she'd figure out if she still had the strength to continue searching for answers with Adela.

Men, women, and children continued to flee the burning town with soot-stained and tear-streaked faces. They were so focused on getting away that most of them didn't pay Eira and the three pirates any mind. At most, their unlikely quartet were the recipients of a confused look or two. But the people were too worried about their own survival to have the will, or energy, to concern themselves with anyone else.

By the time the four of them reached the edge of Warich, the roads were mostly empty. Everyone who was going to escape had already made it out. Smoke was heavy in the air, beginning to sting Eira's eyes.

Fen slowed to a stop and pulled a small, cracked watch from the pocket of his trousers. "She told me to give you two an hour."

"Should be more than enough time," Ducot said confidently.

"Assuming *she* doesn't give you trouble." Fen nodded in Eira's direction.

"She won't," Ducot spoke for her. Eira continued to stay silent. He glanced her way. "Come on, then."

Eira followed him into the blood and chaos of Warich. The other two pirates went their own way, splitting up to take care of business unknown to Eira.

The town she'd come to know through her limited explorations with Alyss, Cullen, and Ducot was upended. Most of the smoke and flames were centered on the coliseum. But the explosion had sent burning debris throughout half of the town, starting fires across multiple buildings. More were catching fire; no sorcerers were staying to put out the flames. Cinder and ash filled the air. An eerie silence had settled on the town. There were no screams, no wailing. Other than the crackling of wood, and a distant clamor of some structure falling, the town was as silent as a grave.

So she was jolted when Ducot finally spoke.

"The fire and smoke are impacting my magic. I need you to be my eyes."

"Why would you escort me if you couldn't navigate?" Her tone was flat, dull.

He stopped. "Well, I couldn't *see* the state the town was in, could I?"

"Adela could." Just the mention of the pirate queen had Eira's head spinning. Adela was here and Eira was her prisoner.

"She trusts us to know what we can and can't do."

"Trust must be nice." Eira folded her arms. Though she still continued looking around. The streets were still mostly empty… but every now and then she saw a curtain pulled aside in one of the houses. People locked up tight, riding out the storm that had descended on their formerly sleepy town. Praying the fires didn't come for them.

"Would you have preferred me to tell you when we first met that I was practically raised by the pirate queen you resembled? That, oh yes, my loyalties really lay with her. I can imagine how well *that* might have gone over." Ducot's milky eyes never met hers as he spoke.

"You deceived me."

"I neglected to tell you something about myself that, frankly, had no relevance until this tournament's beginnings," he countered with a slight frown. "Adela had me working with the Shadows on Meru long before any of us even knew you existed." Ducot glanced over his shoulder. "We can keep talking, but we should keep moving. You heard Fen, we only have an hour."

"Until?"

"Until Adela decides we're dead or too inept to be in her employ. Either way, she leaves without us."

Taking my friends with her. Eira began walking again, assuming the lead. "What else did you lie to me about?"

"I never outright lied," Ducot continued to protest.

Eira glared at him, but opted not to explain her expression. "You said you were raised by Adela? I thought your family was murdered on the edge of the Twilight Kingdom."

There had been a time, back when they were still sneaking in and out of the Court of Shadows, that he had explained his history. He had spoken of a settlement on the outskirts of the Twilight Kingdom's forest. Of an attack by Ulvarth when he was still the leader of the Swords of Light.

"They were." By Ducot's tone alone, she knew he was telling the truth. Even despite all her doubts and questioning of his intentions, she could hear it in his voice. "What I neglected to tell you was that the reason we would dare form a settlement on the outskirts of the forest where we were vulnerable to the zealots of Yargen is because we wanted to be closer to the water—closer to where the *Stormfrost* might come."

"You were all pirates?" Eira hesitated at a corner, looking up and down the street before turning.

"The majority, and those of us that weren't actively on her payroll knew what the rest of us were and did."

"But Adela—"

"Never harmed the Twilight Kingdom, unlike most others," he interrupted. "She was good to us, as she is to most of the unwanted wretches of the world."

"But you said you joined the Court of Shadows right after to avenge your family." Eira hastily crossed the street. She was making a point of heading generally parallel with the river.

"No, *you* said that," Ducot corrected.

Eira thought back to their conversation, racking her memories. He had told her of his family. Of Ulvarth's attack. Rebec finding him clinging to life.

Then she had said, *So you vowed vengeance and joined the Court of Shadows then and there*. Ducot had nodded…but hadn't said anything else. The conversation had shifted.

"Okay, but you nodded in agreement," she muttered under her breath.

"What I told you about Rebec finding me was true. As was my need for vengeance. But what could a boy do against a madman like Ulvarth? I needed time. And Rebec *did* offer to take me in… but I knew I had somewhere to go and refused to follow her then and there. She assumed that 'somewhere' was back to the Twilight Kingdom. Rebec told me to seek her out when I was older and ready."

"You did, and joined the Court of Shadows as a double agent."

He nodded. "I was there to observe. Not to meddle, and not to harm Meru. If anything, the opposite."

Eira slowed her pace. They were nearing the docks, and judging from the distant shouting, there was still some kind of chaos unfolding. The idea of running to find her family, or Olivin, crossed her mind. But Eira pushed the notion away. Her family was either dead or somewhere she wouldn't be able to get to. As hard as it was not to run to them, she had to focus on the people she could still help—and those people were back on a boat controlled by Adela.

"Why would a pirate—one of Adela's, no less—*not* harm Meru?"

He shrugged. "If I knew, I would tell you. She's instructed all of us who set foot on Meru's soil not to do anything that would harm the well-being of Meru. No murdering, pillaging, stealing, or any of the usual piracy."

Deneya's words came back to her. *Adela hasn't been seen along the coast for a long time*. Perhaps Adela truly had lost interest in Meru. Which made it even more mysterious as to why she had defied all odds to come back for Eira. Her earlier suspicion that maybe Adela wasn't being entirely truthful returned unbidden.

Ducot must have heard the increasing noises of the town

growing around them, too, because he came to a stop. "Listen, Eira…I never wanted to mislead you. But I *couldn't* tell you. She's already going to be cross that I allowed you on her vessel."

"Didn't she want to see me?" Eira asked softly. His answer could crumble her theories of Adela's return to Meru and the meaning behind it.

"Adela was very, very curious about you the moment word got out. She hasn't come this close to Meru in decades. Something really shook her years ago and she's made it a point to never come back."

"What was it?"

"No one knows." He shook his head. "The important thing is, the rumors of you did burn a hole in her brain. You've wormed into her thoughts and that's why we're both still alive. But Adela isn't a charitable woman. That's why I told her the lockbox you kept the journals within was sealed shut with your magic, and so *you* needed to come. You need to start proving to her now that you have strength and utility."

"You didn't tell her my magic was gone?" she whispered.

"Not yet. I wanted to give you a chance to prove yourself first."

"And what if I don't prove myself?" Eira asked.

"I think you already know the answer to that."

She swallowed thickly. "Right. We should get going then; our hour is ticking away."

"One more thing." Ducot reached out his hand toward her. The smoke must really be interfering with his senses because he only grabbed air. Eira took his hand, their fingers clasping together firmly. "Will you still trust me?"

She studied his face. Every scar had become familiar. His milky eyes that never quite saw her, and yet looked right into her. The emotions that she had first felt when he revealed his true alliances began to dull. He was right, what could she have expected from him? And it wasn't as if he'd ever done anything to harm her. In fact, the opposite. Even up to this very second he was trying to look after her.

And, besides, she'd seen the way Noelle looked at him. She couldn't betray one of her best friends by not giving her paramour a second chance.

"I do," Eira admitted, ready to follow him once more into the unknown.

"Good, because I really didn't want to have to do this by force."

"Like you could."

"You know, you and I should actually spar sometime." He released her hand. "See who really is stronger."

"I doubt I'll put up much of a fight without my magic." The words stung and the weight of their truth pulled them down.

Ducot frowned slightly. "If anyone is going to be able to help you heal…whatever happened to your magic, it will be Adela."

He might have a point. Whatever Eira had done was impacting the channel from which she drew her power. Adela's crew could heal her physical wounds with their Lightspinning, but Meru's magic couldn't touch magical afflictions. If there was any hope of fixing it, she needed a skilled and powerful Waterrunner…just like Adela.

"If she's willing to help me," Eira said.

"Prove your worth to her. She rewards strength and loyalty."

"All the more reason to keep moving." Eira reached for his hand again. "It might be easier if we make a run through the docks. Hopefully we'll look like just two more people fleeing."

"In champion's clothes?"

She stared down at herself. Exhaustion must be hitting her. How else could she overlook something so obvious?

"Take off your shirt."

"Now is not the time for such scandalous acts." He curled in on himself, popping a knee and touching his collarbone like a dainty courtier flustered by a suggestive remark.

"Oh Mother above, can you be serious for a second?"

"Only for one second, then I get bored of it."

"So I've learned."

"Then why do you expect anything else of me?"

Eira pulled at the sleeves of her tunic, yanking at the tears and seams. With a grunt, she ripped off one sleeve and then the next. Then she pulled at the side seams from the bottom hem, taking them halfway up to her waist. Twisting, she teared the fabric horizontally to make a rough, sleeveless shirt that just reached her naval. "Our most identifiable clothing are our tunics. Without them, and moving quickly, we should be able to avoid recognition."

Ducot finally relented, pulling off his tunic. Scars crossed his body, down his neck and over his shoulder. Ulvarth's brutality was written on his skin and Eira wondered just how he had the strength to continue fighting against that madman when he'd already endured so much at his hands. More likely, his resolve was cemented because of the brutality he'd endured.

"It's bad, isn't it?" Ducot rubbed his shoulder.

"It's nothing to be ashamed of." Eira knelt and ran her hands through the ash piling on the edge of the street, teasing it through her hair, dulling the gold.

"Do you think…Noelle would mind them?" A soft dusting of rose crossed his cheeks. Eira had never seen the usually self-assured, overtly suggestive at times Ducot seem anything less than his confident persona. But they all had their insecurities, their doubts.

"I don't think Noelle would be bothered in the slightest." Eira patted his arm because he couldn't see her smile. She hoped he'd hear it in her voice. "If anything, I'm sure she'd find them rugged and tough looking. Probably would be *more* attracted to you because of them."

He chuckled but it didn't sound as sincere as it usually was. "You're probably right."

Eira had little doubt he was just agreeing with her for the sake of putting on a brave face and his usual confidence. But it was good he *could*. Sometimes, these things were a matter of telling yourself one thing until it became reality.

"But you're never going to have the chance to find out if we don't keep moving."

"I know." He shifted, taking her hand once more. "Lead the way."

Eira held onto him tightly, taking them into the thick of the smoke and chaos of the docks.

There were still people trying to flee onto the few remaining vessels. Others, who did not look like Pillars, had decided to capitalize on the chaos. They threw rocks through the windows of storefronts and fought with shopkeepers on the streets. Eira tripped over herself at the overwhelming compulsion to help up a bloodied and beaten man thrown down by a group of looters.

She had always imagined Meru to be…better than this. The gorgeously illuminated manuscripts she'd pored over had painted pictures of an idyllic world where magic was plentiful and powerful. Where the people had all they wanted and lived joyously underneath their sage, beloved queen. That this land was exempt from the blood and conquest and infighting that plagued every page of Solaris's comparatively short history.

Except, it wasn't. *They* weren't.

Meru was a land of people just as Solaris was. From top to bottom. They fought and squabbled as much as Solaris had, if not more. There was awfulness every step of the way, outlining the gilded images Eira had constructed in her mind.

Fortunately, they didn't run into any Pillars at the docks. The ones that had chased them not long ago had left. But their absence almost made Eira more alarmed. *Where were they?* She knew they had to be on the move. Was there more business here in Warich? Or had they already begun heading back toward Risen?

Before she knew it, she and Ducot were back in the alleyway with the entrance to the secret tunnel Alyss had made. Eira released Ducot's hand and went for the familiar swirl. She paused, running her fingers over the design. It seemed like they had only just been here—the four of them.

Olivin… Her chest tightened and she looked over her shoulder despite herself. As if he would round the corner at any moment. But he didn't.

Had he found his brother, Yonlin? She hoped so. With any luck, they were already out of Warich and halfway back to Risen. No…with any luck, they were headed far from Warich, or Risen, or Ofok. They would go out into the plains and forests of Meru and make a good and peaceful life for themselves in some cute little cottage with breathtaking vistas. Just like she should have done when she'd had the chance.

"Is everything all right?" Ducot knelt beside her. "Alyss didn't seal it up, did she?"

"No. It's fine." Eira hoisted the opening off to the side. "You first."

Ducot went ahead and she scrambled down the ladder after him. With a grunt, Eira pulled the cover back into place.

The tunnel was pitch black. With the cover replaced, she could hardly see her hand in front of her face. Luckily, there was only one path and Alyss's construction was perfect, so there was nothing to trip over.

Ducot paused at the bottom of the short staircase that led up into the Solaris household. He didn't have to say why. He was no doubt doing the same as Eira—waiting, listening, seeing if there were any Pillars above them that would strike the moment they came through.

But everything remained silent.

"Do you think it's safe?" she finally whispered.

"As close to 'safe' as we might get." Ducot took a step up, holding out his hand until it met the ceiling. Then he took another step, hunching over. "Let me up. I'll see if I can sense anything."

Without further explanation, he shifted into his mole form. Eira could see the rippling of reality changing around him. The wiggles that he slipped between as a human and emerged from as a mole. But she couldn't *feel* it. Her magical senses had been well and truly silenced.

The void that had opened in her when she'd learned the truth of her parentage was nothing like the yawning chasm that now was left behind in the absence of her powers. There was nothing where she knew something should be. The sensations she *should be* feeling weighed on her mind, accenting the lack of them.

Perhaps…Ducot was right. The best chance she had at reclaiming her magic was to work with Adela. To prove herself, despite having no magic at present. Surely, fixing her channel would be easy for a sorceress of Adela's caliber.

Or she could find her uncle. Eira's heart hammered at the thought of her parents and uncle, making it hard to keep her hand steady when she scooped up Ducot. The entire time she was opening the trapdoor above them—just a crack so Ducot could slip through—her mind was back in the arena.

The remnants of the arena were so close. Just a short passage through from the village. She could make a quick detour and see what was left. Venture through the tunnels to get back to the docks again using the same passages she found the first time. Assuming the Pillars weren't still there…

There was nothing left for her at the arena. Eira knew it without needing to go. She'd seen—survived the explosion. The chaos that followed consumed every spectator and royal alike. No one would still be in that place. No one alive, anyway. But perhaps, if her family had perished, she could find their bodies and offer them a proper Rite of Sunset. Her eyes stung. She owed them that, didn't she?

The trapdoor opened above her without warning, casting hazy light on her dark thoughts. Ducot was there, holding it open.

"It seems clear," he whispered. "At least in here. I still hear noises outside."

"Let's move quickly, then." Eira scrambled up.

Ducot eased the trapdoor closed behind her. "Here I was thinking we should take as much time as we possibly could to potentially attract their attention, just to make this a bit more interesting."

"I'm rolling my eyes at you." She wasn't, in fact.

"You do that a lot."

"You're right. You should constantly assume I am and save me the breath." Knowing there weren't any Pillars in the house, Eira moved quickly up the stairs, not worrying about any creaking floorboards. Though, Alyss's construction had none.

She paused in the doorway of her room, staring at her familiar things, the bed—still unmade from waking earlier that day. The trunk left open. Clothes strewn about... All Eira wanted to do was curl under the silken bedding they'd been gifted from the draconi and pretend to not exist for a while. To sleep for a month and hopefully wake and discover this was nothing more than a nightmare.

"Are the journals not here?" Ducot asked, hovering uncertainly.

"No, they are." Eira moved to her chest. "Everything is just as I left it. It's a bit surreal to see."

"I'm surprised they haven't ransacked Champion Village yet." He leaned against the doorframe, looking neither at her nor down the hall. She was certain his magic was pulsing across the house, keeping watch for any Pillars who might approach, even if she couldn't feel it.

"It's not like we have much here. None of us could bring too many things with us."

"Yes, but *your* things are still here. And, for whatever reason, you are one of Ulvarth's least favorite people."

"Don't remind me," Eira murmured. An idea had struck her halfway through unloading her suitcase. She stood, squeezing past Ducot and heading for Alyss's room.

"What're you—"

"This will only take me an extra minute."

Alyss had a trunk and a large bag that she kept everything in. Eira dumped out the contents of the latter, quickly picking through for Alyss's essentials. Just as she was about to leave the room, she ran back and rummaged through the chest, grabbing the journal Alyss had procured in the market—the one she'd begun scribbling a story of her own into. Her friend would prefer that over a fresh pair of trousers any day.

Noelle was next. Eira grabbed a few changes of clothes, stuffing them in the bag, but focused on returning sparkling pieces of jewelry to a velvet satchel. Noelle had mentioned on the first day of the tournament that she had been wearing her family's jewels. Either they were sentimental objects, and Noelle would be grateful for them, or they could be used to barter with the pirates. Noelle was as pragmatic as she was focused on honoring her heritage.

Back in her room, Eira added only one change of clothes. She quickly stripped down, changing into her other, most practical outfit.

"Are you…undressing?" Ducot asked uncomfortably.

"First off, I didn't take you to be one to concern yourself with modesty." Eira slipped on a fresh tunic.

"I… You're right," he admitted with a slight grin.

"Secondly, it's not like you can see me, nor are you touching me to find out what's there." Exhaustion might be in her bones right now. But the Lightspinning had healed the worst of her injuries. The dip in the river had washed away most of the blood and the walk shook off most of the muck from the river. With a fresh change of clothes, she felt *almost* like a new person. Enough so to make it back to Adela's boat, at least.

"The idea of touching you in that manner is possibly the most unappealing thing I've ever heard."

"You wound me. Though, the feeling is mutual." Eira paused after stuffing the last of the journals into the bag. The dagger that Ulvarth had given her at the start of the tournament was still at the bottom of her trunk—the one that looked identical to the weapon she'd plunged through Ferro's chest at the ball.

Without a second thought, Eira grabbed it and slipped it through one of her belt loops. She might not have her magic, but now she had *something* she could defend herself with. And Eira had trained with ice daggers enough to understand the fundamentals…even if she'd have to adjust to not having other magic to supplement her attacks.

"Do you have the journals?"

"Yes." Eira adjusted the strap of the bag to go across her body. It was growing heavy, but there was a little room left. "One more stop."

"What?"

"I want to grab a few things for Cullen." Eira made haste down the stairs, turning into the hall and entering Cullen's room without hesitation. Ducot followed, closing the door behind them for good measure.

"We really shouldn't linger."

"I know." Eira went right for his trunk. "But a few supplies aren't going to hurt and we're already here."

Cullen's clothes and effects were as orderly as she would expect them to be. Everything was neatly folded with not one article out of place. He kept his trunk like the rest of his life, and that brought a somewhat sad smile to her face. She didn't see shirts or trousers; she saw all the different little pieces of *him* in their neat and tidy spots. There was nowhere anything extra could be added. Not a shirt into his trunk. Not her into his life.

The idea was a serene sorrow. One she had begun to accept and yet, some part of her still held out hope the world might have had a different design for them. As if she still wasn't ready to let him go. Perhaps it was because she knew part of him had never let go. Her fingers tingled with the phantom sensations of air currents tangling with them. She could still feel the warmth of his forehead as he pressed it against hers, trying with all his might not to kiss her. See life leaving his eyes as he told her he loved her with what might be his last breaths.

Shaking the memories, she continued packing. Eira knew, without hesitation, what he would want for clothes. Without consciously doing so, she'd paid attention to all his favorite outfits. Or perhaps she was selecting the things she thought he looked best in, and might need.

Eira's hand brushed against something cool and round. There, as if placed on a satin pillow made from a shirt, was the metal ball they'd practiced with for hours on end. She could see the outline of them sitting together—him against the wall and her against the foot of his bed.

Those days had been the first time she had thought they could make peace. The first time her heart hadn't felt like it was going to beat so hard it would rip in half around him. That was when she still held the notion that, perhaps, they could find a friendship in the aftermath of all the rushed and messy emotions their love had blossomed from.

As if friendship would ever be possible now. Not after he had taken a sword for her following the explosion. *I love you; I've always loved you*, his words as he lay in her arms, bleeding, echoed through her mind. He had been willing to die for her.

"We need to move," Ducot said. It sounded as if he spoke from a distant place.

Eira inspected the iron ball as though it were an egg, holding all her fragile hopes and dreams. Was Cullen still alive? Had Adela's Lightspinners healed him like they had her or were the pirates just letting him bleed out? She had to get back to him.

"Eira—" Whatever Ducot was about to frantically say was lost as the door to the house slammed open.

"Search the place," an all-too-familiar female voice commanded, as cold as steel.

· CHAPTER ·

Four

*O*LIVIN'S SISTER WAS *here*.

Ever since hearing Wynry's words in the stone she'd thrown at Eira before the start of the tournament… combined with the ordeal of saving Yonlin, and learning of the dark relationship Olivin had with his sister in the process…Eira didn't think she could ever forget the sound of Wynry's voice.

She mirrored Ducot's intense expression. Eira shoved the iron ball into the bag and quickly tied it closed. With a swing onto her shoulders, she was ready to move. Without hesitation, Eira went for the window over where Cullen had sat, pulling it open as silently as possible while the sounds of heavy footsteps filled the hall.

Trusting Ducot to follow, Eira leaped over the window and started back toward the wall that encircled Champion Village. Ducot landed with a heavy thud, the earth crunching under his boots as he raced over to her. Eira adjusted the bag's strap across her body, making sure it was as tight as possible.

They were out in the open. Pillars were sweeping the houses so there was nowhere to hide. They were going to have to run for it.

Ducot started to speak. "Someone's—"

"There's someone here!" a Pillar shouted behind them.

"Coming? I know." Eira grabbed his hand and pressed it against the back wall that encircled the competitors' village. The time for subtlety had passed. "Make us an opening!"

Luckily, Ducot didn't hesitate. With a ripple of magic distorting the air, the stone before them changed its shape from a wall to an archway…facing another building. Eira, still holding Ducot's wrist, took a step and touched it to the wall of the house.

The Pillar jumped from the window, another following.

"Again!" she commanded Ducot.

The Pillar that had first given chase was almost upon them, opening his mouth. He was going to use Lightspinning and she didn't have her magic to stop him. But that didn't mean she was helpless.

She crouched down, grabbed a fistful of the dusty earth, and threw it in the Pillar's direction as he inhaled. It sent him into a coughing fit, disrupting his magic words. Other Pillars burst from the back door of the house, but her deflection had bought them enough time. Ducot had made another opening and Eira led them through.

"Should I close it?" Ducot asked as she dragged him through the house. Eira flipped chairs and pushed over a bookcase behind her, anything to slow them.

"They'll just shatter it with Lightspinning; don't waste your time." Eira burst through the house's front door, emerging onto a familiar street. They were farther down from where Alyss had made the exit of her tunnel, but close enough for Eira to know where she was.

If only she could make them invisible…

"Follow me!" Her body was past the point of exhaustion, but Eira found new limits as she began sprinting. She had to release Ducot for speed, but luckily the street was empty enough that he had no trouble following her by sense or sound.

An explosion rang out behind them—as expected, the Pillars were shattering her barricades. Eira made a hard right, dashing into the alleyway with Alyss's tunnel. The rush fueled her muscles, and she hoisted the circular, stone disk off the opening of Alyss's tunnel and jumped down. Every part of her body screamed as she landed on the hard rock below and Eira bit her lip so hard she tasted blood to prevent herself from crying out.

Ducot was behind her, scrambling down.

"Use the shift," she panted. "Seal it."

His acknowledgment came in the form of his magic, doing just as she asked. The thin ring of light that had shown where the opening was sealed up, vanishing. Ducot slowly finished climbing down, kneeling next to her, breathing heavy as well.

"…where…" Voices were muffled through the thin layer of stone, barely audible.

"Thought…they…here…"

"… searching…they…far…"

Eira held her hand over her mouth, holding her breath, waiting for them to pass. Wiping away blood from her split lips and praying to the Mother, Yargen, whatever god or goddess might be listening against all odds that the Pillars simply…moved on. Eventually, the voices faded, and everything was still.

"Good thinking back there." Even underground, Ducot still kept his voice down. They were taking no chances of something echoing back to the house at the other end of the tunnel.

"I do what I can." Eira pushed herself off the ground. It was harder to stand than before. Even though the Lightspinning had helped mend her flesh, it couldn't cure exhaustion and she was fading fast.

"Impressive that you're still useful without magic." Ducot began climbing the ladder.

The words stung, but they were true. She had no magic, and as hard as that was to accept, she had to, otherwise she'd put herself in dangerous situations expecting her powers to help her get out of them. Eira forced the thoughts away, for now, and rummaged through the bag that she thankfully hadn't lost to produce one of Cullen's shirts and her cloak as Ducot created the tunnel cover once more with a pulse of magic.

"Elegant design…" he murmured. "Down to it being easy to shift."

"Alyss is pretty incredible," Eira agreed as he pushed aside the opening and scrambled up. She tossed up the shirt before climbing behind him. "I know you're bigger than Cullen, but it's better than nothing."

"They're going to be looking for us." He readily accepted the clothing.

"Do you think they've found Adela?" Eira half hoped they had. Delicious thoughts of the pirate queen ending the Pillars then and there filled her.

"For our sakes, let's hope not." Ducot pushed the stone disk back into place.

"Our sakes?"

"If she senses trouble, or anyone knowing she's here, she'll flee."

"Some mighty pirate queen," Eira mumbled.

"I don't know what scared her away from Meru, but it was something significant," he said with a note of severity. "And anything that scares Adela is worth heeding."

"Could it be Ulvarth and the Pillars?"

Ducot shook his head. "Ulvarth was around in my childhood and she had no problem pillaging Meru's coastline then."

"Do you have any idea what it might have been?" The mystery of something scaring Adela that much intrigued her. If it wasn't Ulvarth himself, perhaps it was something, or someone, they could use against him.

He shook his head. "But I do know it's not important right now."

"Agreed, we should keep moving." Eira held out her hand. "Want me to lead?"

"Thanks for the offer, but I'm fine for now. I'll take it if I need to." Ducot motioned for her to carry on.

"Right." Eira started out of the alleyway.

They didn't speak a word the entire way back. The docks were quieter than the last time they'd passed through. But Ducot still took her hand when the smoke got thick. The few people out looked more like looters than Pillars. Still, Eira took a few winding back alleyways after the docks, trying to make sure no one was following them. Once or twice, she thought she saw movement out of the corners of her eyes. But it ended up as nothing.

She breathed a sigh of relief that still tasted like a campfire the moment she saw Fen. Eira never thought one of Adela's pirates could be so comforting by presence alone. But when the alternative was the Pillars, she'd take the pirates.

"I'll have you both know, I waited an extra"—Fen checked his pocket watch—"ten minutes."

"Does your generosity know no bounds?" Ducot asked, panting softly from their speedy trek out of town.

"Only when it comes to you." Fen patted Ducot on the cheek and Ducot waved the other man's hand away. "Right, then, you have them?"

"I do." Eira shifted the bag still on her shoulder.

"And then some, it looks like." Fen had a hungry gleam to his eyes that made Eira keenly aware that Western rubies the size of coins were on her person.

"Nothing for you to be concerned with," Eira said coolly. "Now let's go, we don't want to keep Adela waiting."

"Oh, Adela?" Fen repeated. "I thought those from Oparium still didn't say her name for fear of her *curse*." The way he emphasized the word showed just how ridiculous he found the notion.

"I might be from Oparium, but my heart was never there." Eira kept calm, thinking of what was to come next. Adela would demand the books, and there was nothing she could really do to stop her from getting them. But they were also the only bargaining chip she had with the pirate queen. She couldn't just…hand them over.

"And where is your heart?" Fen asked.

"Wouldn't you like to know?" Eira gave him a sharp look that only elicited laughter. But he didn't press further. So that counted for something. She used the silence for continuing to think of her next moves.

"Oi, Pine!" Fen called with a wave of his hand, drawing over the other pirate that had disembarked with them. "They made it back."

"Pine?" Eira couldn't help but blurt.

"A lot of the crew have interesting names," Ducot said. "Many of us didn't have families. Or, if we did, we don't want to remember or honor them with the names given by them."

"Right…" Eira looked over her shoulder at the mention of family. There wasn't any time to make it into the coliseum, what was left of it. What had happened to her parents? The unknown was a deep-rooted pain. Just when she had thought things were improving with her uncle, and when there could be a path toward peace with her parents, it was all ripped from her. Another thing Ulvarth had stolen.

"You gave them extra time," Pine grumbled as they started into the muck of the riverbank toward where the vessel was still waiting.

"I did no such thing." Fen raised his fingertips to his chest, as if he were scandalized by the mere suggestion.

"Ducot was always your favorite."

"Well, can you blame him? Fen has exceptional taste." Ducot preened.

"Fen has all the taste of a blind man," Pine said.

"Exactly, that's why we get along so well." Ducot waved his hand in front of his face with an over-the-top smile. The three laughed.

Their conversation betrayed deep familiarity. These were bonds that were as established, if not more so, as the ones Eira had with her friends. Ducot had been telling the truth…he was a pirate through and through. These were his allies, friends, and, based on what he'd told her, family. She imagined they'd known him since he was a boy, or even younger than that.

When the water was up to her chest, Eira situated the bag onto her shoulders and head to keep the old, delicate journals dry. She looped the strap down under her armpits and then around her arm, securing it in place. It wasn't particularly comfortable, but it wasn't choking her and the journals weren't damaged.

"Would you like me to hold that?" Fen offered as he was halfway up the ladder. He stretched out a hand. "Here, pass it up."

"No, I have it." Eira started up next, making it a point to show him as much. If she had her magic still, she would've just walked on ice across to the vessel. Perhaps not doing so would give her away? Eira took the ladder one rung at a time. She couldn't spend time worrying about things she couldn't change, just how she would manage them henceforth.

"You gave them an extra ten minutes," Adela echoed Pine, speaking to Fen, as they emerged onto the deck. She sat on a wooden folding chair, leather suspended between the two sides for her comfort. Even though it was of simple make, with her perched upon it, the chair looked as though it were a throne.

"I figured ten minutes was better than not getting your journals back," Fen replied.

"The Pillars attacked just as we were leaving; that's what held us up," Ducot explained.

Adela hummed, eyeing Eira as she undid the bag strap from around her arms, situating it once more on her shoulder. "That bag looks awfully full for just some journals."

"I grabbed a few other things, for my friends and me." Eira didn't see the point in hiding it. "It took no extra time."

"Well then, let's see them." Adela placed both hands on the top of her cane, leaning forward slightly, her knees spreading to the sides.

Eira shifted the bag, but instead of walking farther, she stepped back and thrust it out over the railing. The other pirates moved toward her but Adela stopped them with a slow raise of her hand. The pirate queen tipped her head to the side, inspecting Eira.

"Tell me, what is it you're hoping to accomplish, little Eira?" Her words were like the biting frost creeping across the deck around Adela's feet, stealing all warmth from the air.

"These journals are pretty old, aren't they? I imagine a bit of water would ruin the parchment and ink. You'd lose all of your records."

"I've done just fine without them so far." Adela lowered her hand back down to her cane. She had a slight smile curling the edges of her lips.

"True. But you wanted them badly enough that you wasted time—you lingered here on Meru"—which Eira now knew was significant, thanks to Ducot—"to allow me to go and get them for you. Even if you don't *need* them…no one is above being a sentimental fool, not even you."

"You call me a fool?" Adela stood.

"Don't come closer." Eira held out her other hand to one of the pirates who tried to shuffle toward her, hoping that the idea of her having magic could function, at least somewhat, as a plausible threat. "I will drop it."

"And lose your best bargaining chip?" Adela arched her brows. Eira's heart sank. Something must've shown on her face because Adela continued. "We both know destroying those journals is not advantageous to you. Now, I *could* take them by force. There is nothing you can do that would stop me. But you've intrigued me enough with this little ploy. What is worth so much to you that you would risk the ire of the pirate queen?"

"My friends."

"*Ah*, yes. Speaking of being a sentimental fool…" Adela's tone sounded as though she was scoffing at the notion of being willing to sacrifice for those you cared about, but wasn't this the same woman who had taken in an orphaned Ducot? From the brief glimpses and knowledge Eira had gleaned, she would bet that Adela had more sentimentality than she was letting on.

"You have to know it to recognize it."

Adela's smile grew wider, but her eyes narrowed with annoyance. "You still have not named your price. I grow tired of this game."

"I want you to free my friends and me," Eira demanded. "We have no business with you."

"Eira…" Ducot whispered. She could almost hear what he had said back in Warich. *Adela is the one woman who could help you get your magic back.*

She felt a little nauseous. He was right. Adela could. But it would come at a cost higher than Eira suspected she wanted to pay. She was better off trying to find her uncle, or getting back to Risen, then Solaris. Someone would be able to help her along the way.

The demand seemed to confuse Adela. "Your friends, yes, but you…*you* have no business with me? She who stole my name?"

"I told you that I never meant to," Eira repeated herself from earlier. Though, the way Adela had said *"you"*… Were Eira's suspicions that Adela had been lying earlier about being her mother right? Her want to take her chances by staying warred with what she knew what was best for her friends. But Eira remained steadfast in her decision.

"I know what you said. But I have yet to render my judgment on the matter." The way Adela spoke left little doubt that she was judge, jury, and executioner. Eira prepared a retort but Adela continued before she could get another word out. "Very well. We shall have it your way."

"Really?" Eira asked skeptically.

Adela shrugged. "I am a pirate, but I am also a woman of my word. It is so rarely given; I might as well be."

It was too easy. Eira combed through her thoughts. But doing so was hard. She was tired…very tired. Dawn was nearly upon them and she was going on almost a full day of no sleep.

"Now, my journals, if you please." Adela unfurled her hand, waiting expectantly. "I won't ask again nicely."

Eira pulled the bag back to her and dragged her feet over to the pirate queen. Up close, Adela was even more fearsome. Eira didn't need sorcery to know that murder was in the air. She could only imagine what unfathomable power constantly crackled around her.

"You will let us go?"

"Of course," Adela assured her.

Eira passed the bag into the pirate queen's waiting hand. "Now, my friends—"

"Take her," Adela commanded simply.

"But you said—"

"I said I would let you all go. I never said when, how, or in what state." She leaned forward, looming over Eira, silencing her with the force of her presence alone. "The first rule you must learn, if you're going to ever hope to be in league with the pirate queen, is to be *very* specific in your negotiations."

Eira scowled up at the woman. She balled her hand into a fist and then sprung open her fingers, willing her channel to pop open. But no power came.

And she was far too exhausted, and weak, to fight when a voice behind her uttered, "*Loft not.*"

Against her will, Eira fell into a deep and dreamless sleep.

FIVE

ONSCIOUSNESS FILTERED BACK to her. It wasn't like the last times she had been rendered unconscious with Lightspinning, where she woke with a start. This time, her body clung to the restorative sleep the magic had brought on with all its might.

Sounds came first.

There was the soft creaking of wood. The whisper of water against the hull of the ship as it cut through the river. Heavy thuds overhead and muffled discussions. Others shifted nearby. Some close whispering that Eira couldn't make out.

Then came touch.

The floor underneath her was cold and hard. Damp. Saliva had pooled around her cheek—she must've been snoring.

Forcing herself to crack open her eyes, Eira blinked into the dimness of a cargo hold. Light stood in narrow columns in the center of the space, streaming through holes poked in a grate of the deck above.

Eira pushed off the wooden floor, rubbing her eyes. She felt as if she hadn't been knocked out merely by magic, but by potions and a hard hit to the head as well. It wasn't far-fetched to think Adela would ensure through multiple ways that she was good and unconscious and would stay that way for some time.

A clanking around her wrist distracted her. Eira looked down, blinking at the flat, iron shackle held in place by a small padlock. A design had been pressed into its surface. But it was difficult to make out the glyphs in the low light. She held up her wrist, squinting.

"Oh good, she's awake," Noelle's voice cut through her focus. The oddity around her wrist was no longer even remotely important.

"Noelle," Eira breathed, turning. "Alyss!" She lunged forward. Both her friends were right next to her and Eira's arms flung around both their shoulders, pulling them in tightly. As quickly as she grasped them, she pushed them away, assessing them both from head to toe. It was impossible to stand, the cargo hold was too small, but they seemed as if they were well and in one piece. "You're both alive."

"Judging from your reaction, you have a better idea than we do as to what in the Mother's name happened." Noelle's tone was a bit curt, but any annoyance she felt at their circumstances seemed to be lost to a similar relief Eira was feeling.

"I…yes." Eira explored the small hold with her eyes. Cullen was to the right of Noelle—he still had yet to rouse. Eira shifted to sit closer to him, running her hand down his cheek to rest lightly on his neck. His breathing and heartbeat were steady and strong. The wounds on his body looked equally mended. *Thank the Mother…* No matter what they were, she wasn't ready to say goodbye to him just yet. And she certainly didn't want him to die for her.

Varren and Lavette were stirring on the other side of Alyss and Noelle. They were still filthy from the Pillars' attack on the coliseum. But, true to Adela's word, all of Eira's friends were still in one piece.

"Tell me as far as you remember." That'd give Eira a starting place to fill them in.

"It's not much," Noelle said. "We had just made it on the boat. You went to Ducot…then it all went dark."

"I think I heard a noise behind me?" Alyss pursed her lips, clearly frustrated with herself that the memories weren't clearer. "I can't—" She made a noise of disgust. "—I can't remember anything after that. I assume we got on the wrong boat and the owner attacked us?"

"Not quite…" Eira rubbed the back of her neck, trying to figure out what to tell them, and how. They'd find out everything eventually anyway.

"That doesn't explain *these*, either." Noelle lifted her wrist. Locked around it was the same odd shackle Eira had.

"I have one too." Alyss held out her fist as well.

Was it some kind of pirate branding? Eira kept the thought to herself for the time being. She had to unravel their situation calmly to avoid panic.

"Where's Ducot?" Noelle asked. After Eira's conversation with Ducot, and all she'd seen at the tournament, she was very aware of where Noelle's worries for the morphi man stemmed from.

"He's…fine." Eira hesitated.

"Why isn't he here? What happened?" Noelle grabbed her hand.

Eira had no hesitation about telling them the truth, but she wasn't sure where to start. Just when she thought she'd landed on a good collection of words, Lavette and Varren sat up.

"My head is throbbing." Varren rubbed his temples. "I think I have a lump."

"You hit the deck hard," Lavette said grimly.

"You saw what happened?" Alyss asked.

Lavette shook her head. "I only caught a glimpse of movement, Lightspinning perhaps…" She looked down at her own wrist. Sure enough, the many stacked bracelets of runes that those from Qwint used to summon their magic were gone. In their place was an iron shackle identical to Eira's and Noelle's. Lavette's tone turned bitter. "Well, this is simply *marvelous*."

"They have me." Varren was hunched over, staring at his wrist. His rusty hair fell into his face, hiding the majority of his expression. But Eira could still see his mouth twisting in horror. He drew his hands to his chest, one holding the iron shackle wrapped around the other, and began to rock slightly. "They have me. They found me. They're taking me back. They—"

"Varren—Varren, look at me." Lavette dipped her head and tilted up her face, forcing him to meet her eyes. "What do you see?"

"You. Wood. A ship that's going to take me back—"

"What do you hear?" Lavette interrupted him right as his breathing quickened.

"You. The creaking of the ship that's—"

"What do you smell?" she interrupted faster this time.

Varren's chest continued to heave, but his words became slower. "Damp. Rotting wood. Old burlap…sweat, just like the mine—"

Lavette nodded and held out her hand before he could run away on a tangent again. "What do you feel?"

Varren took her outstretched fingers. His breathing was now under control. Words even. "The wood under me. My damp clothes clinging to me. You…holding my hand." His eyes slowly drifted to her face. Eira could see the inhale he calmed on, emotions back under control. As if he could breathe in the very sight of her.

"Yes. You are here. With me. You're not back in Carsovia. You're not with them and you'll never be with them again."

He pressed his eyes closed and nodded, a little too quickly. "Sorry, it's… I was doing so well…"

"It's all right, you have nothing to apologize for. You've had a lot of reminders this past day." Lavette released him with a sad smile.

"Carsovia?" Alyss asked delicately.

Lavette didn't answer; instead she remained focused on Varren. They all hung in silence as he shifted, clearly gathering the nerve. If he'd been Eira's friend, she would've stepped in and relieved him from the pressure of having to explain whatever it was that was clearly causing him such immense discomfort.

But Lavette apparently had other ideas of what he needed. And, since she knew him far better, Eira refrained from doing anything or passing judgment.

Varren finally found his voice. "I was born in Carsovia. Life there was…difficult."

"I see." Alyss gave a small nod.

Lavette finally stepped in. "These shackles are made in Carsovia at the pleasure of the empress. They're imprinted with runes—not unlike our bracelets—except these markings block all magic."

Noelle scoffed. "We'll see about that." She held out her fist and squinted. Sparks crackled, snuffing almost instantly. There was not even the barest hint of smoke in the air. "No, I'm not letting some stupid bracelet…" she growled, trying again.

"It's pointless," Lavette said plainly as she crawled over toward Cullen. "The shapes on them are a runic art. It's not easy to get rid of them or work around them. As long as they're in contact with our flesh, magic isn't an option."

Eira heard the words, but also couldn't take her eyes off how Lavette knelt by Cullen, holding his face with both her hands, leaning over him. She stroked his cheeks tenderly, almost lovingly. The action seemed in contrast with what Cullen had said of their relationship. With what Lavette had said in the warehouse: *I have no interest in fighting with you over him… Frankly, I have little interest in marrying at all.*

Had feeling begun to blossom in the undercurrents of their relationship? Or was this simply Lavette's nature? She had always seemed like she was even-tempered and, as the leader of the delegation from Qwint, naturally inclined toward looking out for those around her.

"He looks all right, too," Lavette whispered, releasing him and moving away. "Glad we all seem unharmed."

As if sensing the attention was on him, Cullen's eyes cracked open. "What…where are we?" His voice was a rough croak. "Where's Eira?"

"I'm here," Eira said softly. Cullen lifted his hand and she shifted toward him once more, cradling it in both of hers.

"Are you all right?" His gaze never wavered from her, as if

her presence was all the comfort he needed. He was the one who had been skewered at sword point, but her heart felt like it was now bleeding.

"I'm fine; we all are." Relief crashed down upon her like a wave, threatening to crumble the walls she'd built around her emotions. If not for her ironclad resolve, tears might have welled in her eyes. She'd been scared—terrified that he was going to be snatched away by Death without her ever having a chance to speak with him again.

No matter what their future held, it couldn't end there. She wasn't ready for it to. Not when there was still so much between them unresolved and clearly left unsaid.

"Thank the Mother." He relaxed with a soft sigh. Eira resisted the urge to pull him into her arms. To ask him to lay bare the innermost designs of his heart. They needed to sort this out, once and for all. However, now wasn't the time. She didn't move for him again.

"We're not really *all* okay," Noelle said somewhat curtly. "Where's Ducot?"

With everyone awake, now was as good a time as any to try and fill them in. Eira took a deep breath.

"None of you remember anything?" she asked, hoping someone did. They all shook their heads and uttered various noes. "The person who's imprisoned us, whose vessel this is…is Adela Lagmir, the Pirate Queen."

They all stared. No one moved. No one seemed to even breathe.

"I must have misheard you…" Cullen murmured, slowly sitting. "You said Adela? The same Adela who might be—"

"My mother? Yes," Eira finished for him with a grave note. She didn't proffer the knowledge that Adela had already denied being her mother. There were still mysteries there, still things Adela wasn't saying. *There had to be.*

"Better than Carsovia," Varren murmured. "Though only slightly."

"Why is Adela here?" Lavette asked. "Last I heard, she was sailing far to the north. West? Regardless, she hadn't been sighted around Meru—or Solaris—for decades."

"You keep close tabs on the pirate queen?" Eira asked.

"I am an aspiring representative of the republic, should they choose me," Lavette said calmly. "It is my duty to prove my worth to my people through identifying threats to them and ensuring their safety. Qwint has mostly avoided Adela's ire and I would hope to keep it that way."

"Right."

"What about Ducot? Did Adela…" Noelle couldn't finish. "Is he all right?"

"He is." Eira nodded. "He…"

"Then I will get this off of me and they will know my wrath." Noelle slipped out of Eira's hold to fight with the shackle around her wrist. "I will—"

Eira stilled her friend with a hand over Noelle's. "He's one of them."

"What?" She inhaled sharply, going still. Eira could almost feel the numbness overtaking Noelle's body. She watched as every bit of the woman relaxed with shock.

"He's a pirate. One of Adela's."

"You're lying." Noelle forced laughter. "Good joke, Eira, but now isn't the time."

"I'm not joking. He's always been one."

"It's time to stop." Noelle had a warning note to her tone.

Eira's stomach twisted, almost making her sick. Luckily, it had been a long time since she last ate, long enough that nausea wasn't a threat. "His parents were pirates."

"They were killed by Ulvarth," Noelle countered.

So Ducot had told Noelle as much, too. "Yes, they were, but they were outside the Twilight Forest when it happened because they didn't risk going back into the city when working for Adela."

"Eira, stop."

"Rebec invited him to go back to the Court of Shadows, but he already had Adela's crew to return to. He went to the court later, on Adela's orders."

"I won't have you sullying his good name."

"Noelle, I'm only telling the truth," Eira said softly. Regret slowly gripped onto her with an icy touch that *almost* felt like her magic returning. This should have been Ducot's truth to share. But what else could she have told them? It seemed far more cruel to allow Noelle to steep in worry and fear of the unknown surrounding his wellbeing. And, given how hard Noelle was taking things, it was probably for the best that Eira was giving her the brunt of the news; then she would have time to process. Hopefully by the time she saw Ducot next, level heads would prevail. "Listen, Ducot is—"

"You're lying!" Noelle lunged for her. Eira tipped back, Noelle on top of her, grabbing her by the shoulders and shaking. "Stop, stop saying lies about him; I won't stand for it!"

"Noelle, enough!" Alyss moved for her.

Cullen tried to move as well, but fell back down with a hiss. His body still wasn't healed enough to be jerked around.

"If Ducot was a pirate, he would've told me. He would've! He knows…" Noelle stilled, pressing her eyelids shut. She drew a quivering breath. "He knows how much he meant to me. He wouldn't have lied to me. He knew I…I couldn't handle another betrayal."

"He didn't lie," Eira said softly. She gave a small motion to Alyss, holding up her hand in a signal to hold off from ripping Noelle away. "He didn't," she insisted. "He just didn't tell the whole truth."

Noelle opened her eyes—they were now red and shining—and glared down at Eira. "If he kept this from me, it's as good as a lie and he's as good as dead."

The woman eased away, allowing Eira to sit. Noelle stared at nothing, and they all gave her a moment of space and silence to process. The last time Eira had seen Noelle this fiery was when she had been telling off Adam in the Tower. The last man she had held affections for had also betrayed her trust.

Eira resisted reaching out to Noelle. Telling her that she understood. That she, too, had been plagued with awful choices in men that always ended badly. She wanted to tell Noelle it wasn't her fault. And maybe there would be time in the future to say all those things…someday. But now wasn't that time. So Eira kept silent.

"It's all right." Alyss leaned forward, reaching out to Noelle's shoulder.

Noelle slapped her hand away. "Don't placate me. You're always trying to make peace. You ever think that sometimes we *shouldn't* sit quietly? That sometimes we should speak up? We should rage, and throw things, and be just as violent as all the people trying to hurt us!"

"I just—"

"I'm tired of you always butting in where someone doesn't want you," Noelle snapped.

Eira could no longer stay quiet. "Noelle, I know you're hurt but you're not being fair to Alyss."

"Yes, Eira, take her side. The two of you are always inseparable after all." Noelle rolled her eyes.

"This isn't about sides. It's about you misplacing your anger," Eira said.

"Eira, I'm fine, you don't have to defend me." Alyss held up her hands in a gesture of forfeit.

Noelle rolled her eyes at Alyss. "There she is, backing down again."

Alyss looked into the shadows of the hold. Eira almost wished Alyss would get mad and rage right back. She had to stand up for herself.

But Alyss said nothing and Noelle continued. "Can't even defend yourself. Great, we're *screwed* when it comes to the pirates, then. Why don't you try and talk them through not killing us?"

"Noelle, *stop*." Eira's voice was firm, borderline harsh. Lavette and Varren were uncomfortably looking anywhere but the conversation. They clearly knew this squabble wasn't their place to get involved. Cullen seemed too glassy eyed and exhausted to do anything. "Just because you feel wounded doesn't give you permission to attack others."

"You've no idea what I feel."

"Betrayed by a man?" Eira scoffed. "I think I know *exactly* how that feels."

That softened Noelle. "It's not…"

"The same?" Eira could almost hear the two words unsaid and spoke them anyway. "Right, Ducot misleading you a bit about his history really isn't the same as your first love making a mockery of your affections."

"I'm sorry," Noelle said so softly that Eira could barely hear.

Eira should have stopped there, with that, and let it be. Noelle had clearly understood the point. She'd struck a personal note, as Noelle had been there that night when Adam had unleashed his cruelty on Eira.

But Eira didn't stop. "Or the second lover killing your brother. Or the third stealing into your bed the night before you see him dancing with the woman who he knew he was engaged to."

"*What?*" Lavette's soft gasp was the only thing that could jolt Eira from her tirade. Eira looked over at her and Cullen, a cold horror seeping into her. Even if Lavette suspected…or knew… that matter should have been handled with far more tact. Lavette's eyes darted between them but landed on Cullen. "Is this true?"

"I… It… Yes." He lowered his eyes, looking as pathetic as he'd been when he'd come to Eira after the ball. At least he didn't deny it.

Lavette's expression was a mix of disgust and horror. Eira hadn't been expecting it, but the woman turned back to her with almost an apologetic look. Rather than being angry with Eira, she seemed…sympathetic.

"Alyss, I'm sorry," Noelle blurted loudly. It was painfully

obvious she was trying to shift the topic. "Eira was right. I was just…seeing red a moment."

"Firebearers can be a bit volatile," Alyss said with a forced laugh.

"I've heard that," Varren jumped in, too, trying to iron the tension from the air. "Fascinating to see it play out."

It didn't matter. The rest of them could say or do whatever they wanted. But Noelle still shifted uncomfortably, oscillating from rage and awkwardness. Lavette's gaze was boring a hole between Cullen's brows, as though she were trying to extract every last memory from his mind with excruciating precision. Cullen, for his part, wasn't offering denials, or trying to defend himself.

Eira sighed. Lavette deserved to know, didn't she? Even if she did, was it Eira's place to tell her? And even if it was her place… it shouldn't have come out like that.

"Lavette, I—" Eira didn't get a chance to finish. The hatch above them opened, revealing Pine. A terrifying smile crept across his lips.

"Good, the lot of you are already awake. Adela is wanting to see you."

NOELLE WAS A blur as she crawled over to the hatch and stood. Pine had to quickly lean away, nearly toppling back, or else be headbutted. "Where. Is. Ducot?"

"He's—"

"I'm over here." Ducot could barely be heard, coming from what Eira assumed to be the back of the ship, judging from its sway.

"You…little…" Noelle snarled through clenched teeth. She put both of her hands on the deck and jumped up.

"Oh, Mother above," Alyss groaned.

"The fieriness of Firebearers really isn't an exaggeration," Varren appraised with awe. "Thank goodness she's on my side."

Lavette and Cullen were still stuck in their staring contest. Neither moving. *Well, this is off to an exceptional start.* As the only one not stunned, or trapped in surprise or frustration, Eira went to the opening next.

"Wait a minute, I didn't say you could leave the hold," Pine blubbered as Eira pushed him out of the way with a hand on his shoulder, scrambling up in the same motion.

"—lied to me!" Noelle had pinned Ducot against the back railing. The other pirates seemed too amused to step in, allowing her to verbally berate the man.

"Noelle, I—"

"Did you think I wouldn't find out the truth? Did you think me that ignorant?" Noelle and Lavette couldn't be more different in how they were handling difficult news. So many types of rage, and all of them on display. Though, a key difference being Noelle, unlike Lavette, might actually be in love.

"I would never think you were ignorant." The glowing dots on Ducot's brow scrunched in the middle. "It wasn't that I didn't want to tell you, or wasn't going to, it's just that—"

A wave crashed into the side of the boat, rocking it and no doubt drenching their friends still in the hold below as the crest washed across the deck. Adela arrived with fanfare, gliding atop the water. In the sunlight she looked unnervingly ghostly. Her hair so light it was nearly the color of bleached bone. The water collected at her missing arm and leg, solidifying to ice. Adela swept her hand across the railing, collecting the moisture and condensing it into her usual cane.

"I believe that I cannot abide by you accosting my crew." Yet, even as Adela spoke, she wore her usual smirk. Amusement glinted in her eyes.

Noelle looked over her shoulder and her glare briefly transformed into shock—but only briefly. "This is a lovers' quarrel; it doesn't concern you."

Eira blinked. Even Adela seemed taken aback for a second. The pirate queen laughed, tapping her cane on the deck.

"Anything involving my crew concerns me."

Yet Noelle didn't step away from Ducot. "Listen, Pirate Queen, I'm sure you're going to threaten me within an inch of my life—or worse—no matter what I say or do. So you're just going to have to wait a minute while I get this out."

Adela arched her brows as Noelle turned back to Ducot. Her eyes bounced over to Eira, who could only shrug. The whole situation was strange and surreal. But the one thing it emphasized was that Noelle was a force of nature. The woman could stop a hurricane with a stern look if she wanted.

"Now, you listen to me, Ducot, and listen well," Noelle said firmly. "If you have anything else you need to tell me, you do it in the next few days. If I'm still alive, of course. But when I told you I wanted to know you—*all of you*—this is what I meant. No secrets. No lies. No shame."

"I wasn't sure if you would accept this part of me," he said softly, sounding almost scared.

Eira glanced around, wondering if anyone else was as uncomfortable as she was. This felt like a moment that should be only for Ducot and Noelle. But none of the other pirates were bothering to hide the entertainment they were getting from the couple.

"You know, I thought even a blind man could see this…I care about *you*. All of you." Noelle reached forward and took his hand in hers.

"What if you find out something you don't love?"

"Then we'll broach that when it comes." She shrugged. "But I've yet to see something."

"Even that I'm a pirate?"

"Women are usually pretty into dangerous men." Noelle smirked.

"Even my scars?" The whisper was so faint that it was almost lost to Alyss and Varren scrambling from the hold. Lavette and Cullen not far behind.

Noelle cupped his cheek with her other hand and leaned forward. She planted a kiss right on the white, gnarled flesh of his face. "I think they make you look dashing. And really fit with the whole pirate look."

"Well, I do hate to interrupt this touching display…but there is the matter of killing you all I need to get on with," Adela said dryly.

"You really do have a heart of ice, boss." One of the pirates sniffled. He seemed…genuinely moved by Noelle and Ducot's display of affection? What kind of deadly pirate crew was this?

"And you have one of rose petals and feathers, Krut."

"I take that as a compliment." Krut wiped a tear from the corner of his eye.

Adela sighed and ran a hand through her wispy hair. "Men like you and Ducot soften my heart of ice. Fine, *fine,* I can see which way the wind blows. Our captives can stay alive a bit longer."

"You said you would let us go," Eira insisted.

"Once more, I never said when or in what condition." She smiled thinly. "Don't push me, Eira. I am not a woman you want to test."

"I'll see that they learn the ropes," Ducot said quickly, interjecting himself into the conversation.

"Ensure that they do," Adela said with an ominous note. "All of my crew must earn their keep." The pirates shifted. There was some discomfort at the mention of them being part of the "crew" and some approving nods at the sentiment. "Now, Eira, give me your wrist."

Eira held out the hand that had the shackle around it. She could only assume that was what Adela was after, as the other wrist had no reason for the pirate queen to be interested in it.

From a pocket on the inside of her worn, double-breasted coat, Adela fished out a small key. She unlocked the shackle, placing it in a larger pocket on the outside of her coat. The motion seemed to almost challenge Eira to take it.

Adela's fingers remained closed tightly around Eira's wrist, as hard as the iron. The pirate queen leaned in slightly. "Don't get any ideas. I still have your friends under my control."

"I'll stay in line." There wasn't a choice, for now.

"Good, now come with me," Adela said to Eira alone.

Adela's cane collapsed into a puddle of water. The river rose to meet it, flowing over the edge of the vessel and onto the deck. Her leg, and opposite arm, melted as well, becoming one with the water. It supported and lifted her up, carrying her back over to the other nearby boat, which looked no more suspicious than the one Eira was on.

Eira walked over to the railing. She was aware of everyone's eyes on her. Not just on this boat, but the other as well.

"Show me some of that magic that everyone said was mine reborn," Adela called over.

Eira dug deep, searching for any scraps or flickers of power. She only needed a little. Just a bit… If she could close a channel, then she could open one, too. At least her own.

She held out her hand at the water and scrunched her brow. *Rise*, she commanded, *rise as ice. Freeze. Do something!*

But the water did nothing other than continue to lazily lap alongside the ship. The currents were calm. There wasn't even the whisper of power underneath her fingers.

"Eira…" Cullen said softly, full of pity.

"Do not test my patience," Adela warned.

When everything in her wanted to hang her head, Eira stood a little taller. She forced herself to stay upright against the weight of shame. "I can't."

"What?"

"I *can't*," Eira repeated.

The water rose once more at the other vessel and, in an instant, Adela loomed over Eira—the vessel beneath Eira rocking from the currents created by the waterspout that supported the pirate queen.

"I lost my magic," Eira admitted. "I lost it fighting Ulvarth— leader of the Pillars—right before he blew up the coliseum with flash beads. I closed his channel and mine with it."

Eira waited for Adela to mock her, to be disappointed. Flashes of her parents overlapped with the pirate queen. She had failed one. Why wouldn't she fail another?

But instead, Adela smiled, wider than Eira had ever seen. Her eyes gleamed. "*Oh*, you are an interesting one, aren't you?"

Before Eira could respond, Adela made a scooping motion. The water resembled the pirate's palm as it rose. Eira was pulled off her feet by the sudden current. She fell back into Adela's watery, magic hand. They glided across the river to the other vessel. Eira was gently deposited on the deck, in a perfect upright position, left soaked and amazed.

"How did you manage to get just the right upswell of water?" Eira couldn't stop herself from asking. "It was enough to support me, but not enough to make me uncomfortable, or send me flying."

Adela shifted her shoulders, subtly adjusting her stance, the movement like a preening bird. "Many would be horrified to hear you praising my skill."

"Any who wouldn't praise it would be lying." Eira's mind was still on the magic. "It wasn't cold, so you didn't use ice to thicken and strengthen the water at all."

"No." Adela held out her icy hand, her cane growing from her palm.

"Was it a sort of reverse whirlpool under me?"

"Child, it was nothing but power and control." Adela started toward the aft of the vessel. The boat was similar to the one Eira had just been on, except this had a larger cabin space, more of a pleasure barge than a trader's vessel.

Eira knew Adela wanted her to follow, but her gaze was drawn back to the first boat—where her friends still were. If she followed Adela into the cabin, she wouldn't even be able to see them any longer. But she also couldn't do anything from here to help them.

"My friends—"

"I said they would be kept alive, for now, did I not?" Adela stopped with an air of impatience.

"And what about their things?"

"You should know when to stop while ahead, Eira," Adela said coolly, making it clear she wouldn't be pressed on the matter any further.

Eira had no choice but to put her trust in the pirate queen, as wretched as that felt. So she followed behind. The other pirates on this vessel were new faces and they regarded her warily from where they lounged on the deck. Even though none of them were posed in a particularly aggressive manner, Eira could sense danger coming from every direction like invisible daggers hanging in the air.

The interior of the cabin was lavish, though small. It was all queen and no pirate. A short stair down gave enough room to stand. Two lanterns hung from the ceiling to the left and right. One was directly over a small bed piled with furs and quilts. The other was over a desk flanked by two narrow bookcases, dowels running the length of the spines to keep them in place during inclement weather. Though, nothing about this vessel suggested it was made for the seas, and Eira suspected that it didn't face too many violent swells in the river. At the very back, two tall and tufted chairs were positioned on either side of a small table where a stack of familiar journals were set out.

Adela motioned to one of the chairs. "Sit."

Eira did as she was told. "What do you want with me?" In the back of her mind, the question of, *Are you my birth mother?* still burned. Adela had seemed convincing when Eira had first asked, but perhaps…too confident? Adela had made it clear that there were risks to her surrounding having a child, and then there was the matter of keeping Eira alive when all common expectations surrounding the pirate would've been for Adela to kill her… Eira could read into every action Adela took seven different ways.

"Today, I want you to tell me what in these journals you read. We will start there."

"Start?" Eira arched her eyebrows as she reached for a journal, skimming through it. It was one she hadn't had a chance to pore over as much and she set it to the side.

"It is still a few days to Ofok, the current in the river is not fast, and the winds are fairly stagnant." Adela rested her elbow on the table and her chin in her palm, staring listlessly out at the water passing by through the portholes.

"And you will let my friends off in Ofok?"

"Annoy me further and I will be certain not to."

Eira pursed her lips and grabbed for another journal. It opened easily to the pages she'd studied to the point of nearly being able to recite the words scribbled across them. Eira rested it on the table, tapping on the page. "I spent a lot of time studying how to freeze people solid without killing them."

"What did you think of it?" Adela leaned away from the journal after skimming it only for a second.

"I thought it was…dark," Eira admitted. "At first, it seemed so cruel that it would be something I would never use." She slowly looked up from the page, meeting Adela's eyes. The pirate queen's gaze was as passive as always.

"But then you did use it," she finished softly.

"Then I did," Eira echoed. "It is a grim and fearsome magic. But it is also…elegant. The idea of keeping someone alive in a frozen state without harming their internal organs. Of knowing just how far the body can be pushed and how long it can be held… It is a fearsome skill."

"And you did it well, I heard." Adela lifted the journal off the table, placing it in her lap. She flipped through the notes with a nostalgic smile that didn't match at all with the horrors of the magic she was reading about.

"You heard? Ducot?"

She nodded. "And others from within the Pillars."

"You were working with the Pillars, then?" Nausea passed over Eira. Just when she'd thought that perhaps Adela was someone to be reasoned with…

"If I had been working with the Pillars, wouldn't I have sailed you right back to Warich and left you in their hands?"

Eira considered this. "Perhaps you want me to have a false sense of security around you to extract information. I have no guarantee this isn't all a long play at a game I can't yet see the end of. Perhaps the Pillars want me in Ofok for some reason and you wanted to ensure you at least got your journals out of the exchange."

Adela closed the journal with an exasperated sigh. "I am not working *with* the Pillars, but I make it a point to have eyes and ears everywhere. Though, I do commend you for your suspicions. Expect everyone is out for themselves, Eira. Always. That's your first lesson for today."

"For today?"

Adela continued as if Eira hadn't said anything. "Now, to the hold with you. Since I know your channel is closed, there is no need for the shackle."

"But—"

"Crow!" Adela called.

The door promptly swung open, revealing a young woman with raven hair, cut short around her ears. She had light brown skin and an ear that was more gold than flesh from all the cuffs and hoops she wore. "M'lady?"

"Put her in the hold and throw enough scraps down that she doesn't starve."

Eira stood as Crow approached. She could see she didn't have a choice and wasn't about to be manhandled. Shreds of dignity were all she had, but Eira was determined to hold on to them with all her might.

"May I go back to the other boat, at least?"

Adela waved her away. "I can't be bothered to fetch you every morning. You'll stay here."

Every morning? Eira didn't have a chance to ask before Crow was pushing her out with a shove on her shoulder. Adela clearly had plans for her. But what they were…Eira wasn't sure she wanted to know.

The entrance to the hold on this vessel was very similar to the other—a board with some holes bored into it, lifted from where it rested flush with the deck. But the hold itself was much smaller and Eira could hardly sit up. As Crow replaced the opening, Eira was forced to lean back onto her elbows, wedged between crates and sacks.

"Sleep well," Crow said with a smile, even though it was still morning.

Eira lay back and closed her eyes. She folded her hands over her stomach, feeling the rocking of the waves. Ducot was with their friends and he'd done a good job so far in looking after all of them. Eira didn't have a choice but to trust he would continue to do so.

In the meantime, she would do her best to make the most of her time. She focused on the sound of the water lapping up against the hull. *Ebb and flow.* Just like the magic she reached out in search of.

AT DUSK, THE opening to the hold opened once more. Without warning, a mostly empty bucket was turned over. It was a rain of sinewy and fatty discarded pieces of meat, cheese rinds, and the crusty ends of bread—half chewed.

"Enjoy," Crow said cheerfully before replacing the hatch, the latch engaging. The woman didn't immediately walk away this time. She leered from above as Eira propped herself up and rolled onto her side. Crow must have been waiting for Eira to protest at the quality of food, or beg for more. But when she didn't, the deck creaked with Crow's heavy footsteps. Eira could barely hear her speaking to someone else, but the words were lost.

Eira picked through the scraps, sorting by type. She'd eat the meat tonight, what little there was of it. It looked freshly cooked and wouldn't keep. The cheese rinds could survive until the morning. The bread would keep the longest and that would be lunch. They hadn't mentioned feeding her more than once a day so she had to be cautious and make the food last.

She picked up the first knob of meat, pleased to find that it had been cleanly cut—someone had used silverware rather than just digging in with their teeth. She wondered if these were actually table scraps, or if they were only meant to look like it and the pirates were taking better care of her than they might otherwise let on. If her theories about Adela possibly hiding her lineage were correct, then that would make sense…

Slowly working her way around the connective tissue and sinew, Eira ate every bit of meat and fat that was digestible. What little remained she pushed through one of the holes in the opening above her. She didn't want to share her tiny space with rotting food. Hopefully it would get knocked off into the water or a bird would eat it before the morning. She could already imagine Adela having something to say about her "daring to dirty the boat."

The next piece of meat was marginally better than the first. The third far worse. There were only five morsels in total. By the time she was finished, she was far from full, but she refrained from eating her other provisions, instead pushing them as far to the side as she could. Out of sight and out of mind. Hopefully this way the pirates didn't take them either.

Eira lay back down and stared up at the holes above her. Were her friends all right? Were Cullen and Lavette having a much-needed conversation after what had come to light? Even if there weren't feelings of romance there, the situation was murky and Lavette deserved better than that from both Cullen and Eira.

She had to suppress a groan as she cringed inwardly. She hadn't meant to spill everything like she had. Or at all… She'd been working so hard to move past Cullen and the memories they shared. She'd even been doing pretty well with it, all things considered.

Had she been doing well, or merely distracting herself?

Olivin's stormy eyes flashed through her memories. Their night together, walking to the display the Twilight Kingdom had put on. He had been a distraction. But at least she felt like she had made the right decisions when it came to him. She had been more grounded in her approach and kept herself from rushing in with her heart, even if her body had other ideas…

As for Cullen, she was clearly still weak when it came to him.

Eira closed her eyes and sighed. There were so many more important things to worry about than her failed love life. Yet here she was, thinking about both of them. Feeling guilt, and shame… and longing.

At some point, she'd managed to fall asleep. Stomping overhead jolted Eira awake and was followed by the hatch above her being pulled open, revealing Crow.

"Good morning, Adela impersonator," she said with a bitter note. If Eira had any doubts on Crow's feelings toward her, there were no questions now. "The bane of the seas has asked to see you again. I hope you are appropriately honored."

Eira got up without question or hesitation. But she clearly moved too slow for Crow's liking. The woman hooked her arm with Eira's and yanked her through the opening.

"Best not to keep Adela waiting; you've already offended her enough by taking her name."

There was no point in protesting or trying to correct Crow. Her opinions, like much of the crew, seemed to paint Eira as amusement, insult, and a dangerous enemy. It wasn't likely to change until Adela corrected them, if Adela ever did.

Crow led her to the cabin Eira had met with Adela in last time. The pirate queen was situated in her same chair, journals out, just as they were yesterday. Crow left without word, but did give a small shove in the center of Eira's back.

"I trust you were comfortable with your accommodations." Adela made it sound as though Eira was a real guest and not a prisoner.

"I have no complaints." They would fall on deaf ears anyway.

Adela glanced up from the journal she was inspecting to study Eira with equal intent. Eira had never been more aware of someone's gaze than she was as she crossed the room and sat opposite the pirate queen. "I'm surprised to hear it."

"Really? I thought it would be obvious, given the extent of hospitality you go to for your guests. A balanced meal, my own private room, what more could I ask for?" Eira leaned back in the chair, making herself comfortable. Her back ached from sleeping on hard wood, again. But she wouldn't show it.

Adela wore a thin smile. "Indeed."

"But I'm sure you didn't call me here to discuss how I slept."

"Not in the slightest." Adela patted the stack of journals. "You never told me how you came across these. I can only assume my old hideaway was finally discovered?"

"Yes."

Eira didn't need further proof of Adela's astute reasoning, but the pirate queen put it on display anyway. "And since these journals fell into the hands of a young woman, rather than being confiscated by the Solaris crown, it leads me to believe that you did not share its existence with the current leadership of the Tower."

"I didn't."

"Who else knows of its existence?"

"Only one other person," Eira dodged slightly.

"And that is?" Adela continuing to press the matter told Eira that the answer was important for reasons she could only speculate.

"No one important." Eira shrugged. She wasn't about to tell Adela that one of her friends, and one of Adela's other captives, knew of the secret room. It would be too easy for Adela to just kill off Alyss if she wanted to ensure the secret workroom remained hidden.

Adela shifted, putting her right ankle on top of her left knee. "Come now, Eira, we're friends. Are we not? Clearly you're not one to keep secrets from friends."

Friends. Eira resisted snorting. Adela had been as friendly as a viper.

"It was another Waterrunner," Eira lied with ease. "They were killed in the trials before I came to Meru."

"Pity." There was nothing about Adela that made Eira think she found it a pity at all. The pirate queen was blasé about it at best. "How did *you* find it?"

"I can—*could*"—the correction was painful—"hear echoes in objects."

"I've heard of this power of yours." Adela continued to expand on just how many details Ducot had reported about her. "Tell me more."

Eira wondered if the fact that Adela was asking meant that she could not sense and hear echoes. If that was true, then Eira had knowledge of a skill the pirate queen would no doubt deem valuable. "I'll tell you. But first, are my friends all right?"

Adela chuckled. "So predictable. Yes, I've kept to my word, so far, and they are well."

The "so far" had Eira less confident than she might have otherwise hoped, but there wasn't much more that she could do in her current circumstances. So she kept her word as well, hoping that any favor she could earn with Adela would pay off when it came to her friends.

"The echoes, as I call them, are a kind of unintentional vessel. I believe they're made when someone with significant power possesses a strong emotion while having a conversation, activating their power. Or, perhaps, uses their magic when speaking. Either way, the key is that the words are tied in with the magic."

"Much like creating a vessel to capture words intentionally…" Adela mused, stroking her chin. Eira nodded. The practical theory was all there. "And you heard one of these unintentional vessels that led you to my old hideaway?"

"Yes."

"What was it that you heard?"

Eira hesitated, not because she'd forgotten—she could never forget those words—but because she wasn't sure how Adela would take to the truth. What if it had been a secret? Adela's icy eyes continued to stare, breaking down all of Eira's walls.

"I heard you talking about killing the sovereign."

Adela narrowed her eyes slightly. Nerves pulled on the muscles around Eira's spine, making her sit a little taller. Without warning, the pirate queen burst out laughing. She roared so hard with amusement that it nearly rattled the rigging. By the time she managed to calm herself, she was wheezing and wiping tears from her eyes.

Eira sat patiently, waiting for Adela to compose herself. The pirate queen was no doubt someone who didn't appreciate being interrupted. Especially not when she was putting on quite the display.

"I wondered when it would finally come out. But after all these years, I was beginning to think it never would. And if the truth were to come to light, my bet was on his son Aldrik. I heard he was a real chip off the block. Took after his father with all his anger, and lust for power." There was a dreamy quality to her words as her gaze softened and Adela stared at a time long since passed. Eira had heard many things about the emperor. But at worst the critiques seemed lukewarm. Most people liked Emperor Aldrik and regarded him as a just ruler. Though she doubted that Adela would want to hear such an assessment. "But to think, what did me in after all these years was a mere girl. Not that it matters now."

"Did you actually do it?" Eira asked softly. "Were you behind the Mad King? Did you kill Emperor Tiberus Solaris?" She'd heard Tiberus was killed by the Mad King, but Adela seemed to have a hand in everything. Eira would hardly be surprised at this point if history had been told wrong.

"Tiberus?" Adela laughed once more and Eira was waiting yet again for her to compose herself. "No, the sovereign I killed was his father, your current Emperor Aldrik's grandfather, the final Solaris king, King Romulin."

She was so calm about admitting to committing regicide, so matter-of-fact, that Eira stared without any kind of reaction for at least a minute. "The final Solaris king before Emperor Tiberus died of illness."

"I heard that was the official statement from the Solaris crown." Adela shifted and placed both feet on the floor. With a flick of her wrist, she summoned her cane, placing it between her knees and leaning forward. "It would have looked very bad for the royal family to admit that their only heir had fallen helplessly in love with the Pirate Queen Adela, and she'd used that love to slip right under his nose and murder his father."

Eira slowly pieced together a probable story in her mind—what she knew of history, and what Adela was telling her. Emperor Tiberus Solaris was the first Emperor Solaris. He had declared himself such upon ascending the throne following his father's—the last Solaris king, Romulin's—sudden death. Tiberus didn't marry for years following, an oddity for a ruler. But if he was nursing a wounded heart, a betrayal from a former lover who killed his father…

"I grew close to Tiberus. Close enough for him to show me all the hidden passages of the castle—including one that connected his royal wing with the Tower of Sorcerers. Close enough for him to tell me where they kept the royal jewels. Do you have any idea the kind of ship Solaris gold could buy over seventy years ago?"

"One like the *Stormfrost*, I would imagine," Eira said softly.

"Not quite; a little early for my *Stormfrost*. But you're thinking along the right lines." Adela smirked. "Now, tell me more of these echoes."

"What is it that you want to know?" Eira remained cautious about giving any more information than she absolutely had to.

"Everything," Adela said with a smile.

So much for trying to be coy. But Eira relented without a fuss. In part because she wanted to stay in the good graces of the pirate queen. But also because, in a way, it seemed fair. Adela's journals had helped her survive with magics Eira would've never even considered on her own. Eira had never thought about awarding Adela a repayment as a result of her accidental help, but Eira supposed Adela was owed one, in a way.

By the time she left the cabin, any supposed debt was undeniably paid. Eira had shared everything she could think of about the echoes and answered all of Adela's many questions. For her part, the pirate queen seemed pleased enough to allow her to live another day. Saying, as Eira was escorted away by Crow,

"I look forward to speaking with you tomorrow, so I think I shall keep you alive, for now."

The next day was back to the journals. There wasn't even the slightest mention of the echoes. Eira thought about asking if Adela had already tried to listen for unintentional echoes but ultimately decided against it. There was no world in which Adela would tell her. And Eira could assume that the pirate queen would figure out and use that skill soon enough. Eira had to be cautious, and warn her friends to watch their tongues at the first opportunity.

Though, the thought of her friends made her unable to think of anything but them. "My friends, are—"

"They are fine." Adela rested her chin in her palm with a look of amusement. "As they have been the entire time. I hear your Groundbreaker is particularly useful with her skills. Many Groundbreakers struggle with rope—all the little fibers, man-manipulated materials...but I hear she can manage them with little trouble."

"Alyss is very talented." Eira couldn't stop the slight softening of her voice.

"No harm will befall them...yet."

"Such an ominous, lingering 'yet' that you keep reminding me of," Eira muttered.

"I am a rather ominous person." Adela had a wicked smile but it didn't strike the fear in Eira that it might have at one time. On the whole of their interactions, the pirate queen had been more of an aloof or prickly scholar than pirate...or queen.

So long as Eira ignored the kidnapping and captivity that left her stomach roaring and back aching.

"Now, show me something else you studied and how you utilized the magic..."

Eira did as she was told yet again. Their conversations had

begun to focus on the subtle ways Eira had used the magic differently than Adela. She had begun to feel like she was a sounding board for new sorcery ideas and applications.

As the final journal closed for the day, Adela tapped her cane on the floor. "Good work. For your diligent assistance today I will let you live until tomorrow night."

"Your generosity knows no bounds." Eira stood as the door opened. Crow was waiting, as usual.

"Don't forget it." Adela smirked and Eira was brought back to the hold that was now painfully familiar.

That night, as she gnawed on her rations—which had improved somewhat in quality—and stared up at the stars, Eira decided that Adela was a lesser evil than the Pillars. The food was consistent, though still not great, there was the whisper of fresh air when the breezes were strong, and she could see the sun and stars.

A vast improvement over the pit.

And while Adela regularly threatened her life, it lacked the same bite of pure malice the Pillars had. If the pirate queen was to be believed, her friends were also still safe. Perhaps better than merely "safe" if Alyss was literally learning the ropes of the ship…or were they were being treated as servants? Or worse? But something about Adela, the crew, and the whole atmosphere didn't give Eira that impression. Plus, there was no way Ducot would abide Noelle receiving such treatment.

Which brought Eira back to her theory that Adela's kindness was not all simply by chance. Adela was taking pity on her and her friends far more than the pirate queen was known for. There had to be a reason, right?

Eira's prior suspicions about her possible relationship to Adela returned to the forefront of her mind. She would get to the bottom of it, one way or another. She would find the truth without doubt. Whether that was what Adela had already told her, or something more.

The next morning, Eira walked into the cabin with purpose. There was no more shoving from Crow and no more side remarks. The pirate had grown tired of that game, or had been told to cease with the jests.

Eira went to her usual chair and sat, crossing her legs and folding her hands in her lap with an air of authority. Adela took notice of the shift in demeanor with a slight cock to her head and arch of her brows. But she said nothing, and Eira assumed that to mean that she was given the floor.

"This is the fifth day that we've done this," Eira began, keeping her tone level and factual. "Judging from the speed we have been traveling, and the changing landscape, I suspect that we will be at Ofok within the next one or two days."

The banks of the river were becoming sandier and there was the faint smell of salt in the air. The lands around them were becoming marshier and flat. It all heralded the sea, based on Eira's knowledge of Meru.

A knowing smile crossed Adela's lips. "An accurate assessment. I would expect no less from a young woman who grew up around the ships and docks of Oparium, and who took a keen interest in Meru. Your point is?"

Eira didn't recall telling Adela where she had grown up, or about her nearly lifelong fascination with Meru. Now that she thought about it...Pine or Fen had commented on Oparium superstitions. Eira's history had been well-known to even Adela's crew.

Her heart tried to skip a beat at the idea that Adela was informing them all about her for the sake of protecting her. But, for now, she kept her focus. "Before we arrive in Ofok, I want you to help me restore my magic."

Adela settled back into her chair. She rested both elbows on the armrests and pressed her fingertips together, bringing them to her lips in consideration. The air dropped in temperature and Eira fought a shiver. Every creak with the slight sway of the boat was suddenly deafening.

"Why would I do that?"

"Because I'm more valuable to you with my magic," Eira dared to say. It was a bold assessment, but one she'd been thinking about between worrying for her friends night after night.

"You think so?"

"I do. Why else would you be asking me all these questions? You've been gathering ideas for new applications of your powers, or modifications to old techniques. I bet you've never taught anyone some of these skills. Or, if you did, they couldn't master them as I already have." Eira leaned forward slightly, resting her forearm on the table. Her skin prickled into gooseflesh. The chill radiating from Adela was a warning but she pressed on anyway. "If you restore my magic, I can help you in more ways than just hypothetical discussions."

"If I restore your magic, you will use it to try and kill me. Which you will undoubtedly fail in doing, but then I will be forced to kill you. You will be useful to no one dead."

Eira noticed that Adela had yet to deny that she was useful alive. Hope warmed her. "Why would I try to kill you if it would mean my own death? Haven't I shown I'm partial to living by working with you so far?"

"People do foolish things when they feel power is on their side."

"Then I suppose it's a risk you'll have to take."

"'Have to'?" Her tone was slightly amused, rather than offended.

"I will certainly exhaust my usefulness without magic sooner rather than later. At which point, I'm sure your choice will be to kill me then or restore my magic. At least the latter has the opportunity of more direct benefit to you."

"I might release you."

"We both know that's not happening," Eira said flatly. She met

Adela's gaze and held it—a silent challenge. "You have too many reasons not to allow me off your ship alive. As long as my friends disembark by Ofok, in one piece—well, and without shackles—I won't fight whatever you deem my fate to be."

After a long minute of studying her, Adela finally spoke. "You're improving your negotiation skills."

"I'm learning from the best. So, will you do it? Will you restore my magic?" Eira asked, heart hammering so loud that Adela surely must hear the crack in her calm veneer. Adela said nothing. "Unless…you don't think you're capable of it?"

Adela chuckled slowly. "Challenging my skill was not necessary. I do not have anything to prove."

Eira bit the insides of her cheeks, worried she'd overplayed her hand. But…

"Very well, Eira. I will see your magic returned to you. And then you will henceforth use it solely at my beck and call."

EIRA SAT, STUNNED, letting the words seep into her. "You… will?" she whispered.

"Don't seem so surprised. You practically consigned your life to me. I think I came out with the better end of the deal."

Still, it somehow felt like a victory. Every day Adela didn't kill her was a triumph alone. But getting the pirate queen to agree to helping her get her magic back was something Eira never expected would be possible, despite Ducot's initial optimism. Yet another bit of evidence that might suggest she was right—there was more to Adela and her than met the eye.

"It should be a relatively simple matter. We'll first need to collect a vessel with your magic. It'll take a while to get back to Solaris, unless you have one in Risen? Please don't tell me we have to sail all the way back to Warich simply because you overlooked grabbing one."

Eira's racing heart stopped and sank right into the darkest pit of her stomach. Of course…a sorcerer's channel could be blocked using a Waterrunner's magic alone, or sometimes even just through extreme trauma. But to remove that block and open the channel once more for magic to flow easily, a vessel was required. The slightest bit of magic would call to the sorcerer's channel and restore the link to power.

The knowledge had been in the recesses of her mind. So far back that she hadn't remembered it'd be a requisite for restoring her power. Had she just consigned herself over an impossible task? Perhaps that was why Adela had agreed so easily. She certainly had received the better end of the bargain and then some.

"I never made a vessel with my magic," Eira confessed in a small voice.

Adela sighed heavily and pressed her fingertips into her temple. "The Tower of Sorcerers is *still* not having their students make vessels as a precaution?"

"I've never had it recommended to me."

"The fools. I swear, I would run that Tower far better than any."

The mention of running the Tower brought Eira's uncle back to the forefront of her mind. Eira struggled to push him away, but the memory of him and the explosion fed on the hopelessness that was growing within her. The monsters of doubt and sorrow were warring to consume and control, feasting on what little hope she'd mustered.

Adela remained oblivious to Eira's turmoil. Or didn't care. Likely the latter, given how astute she was. "Very well, it will be done the hard way."

"What?" Eira blinked, the statement jarring her from the negative spiral of everything feeling hopeless. "There's a way to restore my magic without a vessel?"

"Child, with enough power and determination there is a way to do *anything*." Adela smiled confidently, borderline arrogantly. But there was something inspirational about the expression. Eira wasn't sure if she had ever met someone with so much blind faith in themselves. "Most sorcerers—most people are only limited because they believe what others tell them when they hear they cannot do something. Your mind will limit you well before your body, and *that* is why it is the first thing others will try to control."

The water flowing past the portholes distracted her. Eira's thoughts drifted just as effortlessly. "I suppose I understand what you mean. I saw it in the Pillars."

Adela leaned forward, holding out her hand expectantly. Eira didn't immediately understand the pirate queen was waiting on her to take it. Trying to conceal her confusion and hesitation, Eira rested her fingertips lightly on Adela's palm. The pirate queen grabbed her fingers and flipped over Eira's hand without warning. She ran her frozen fingertips over the lines on Eira's palm, filling them with frost that quickly thawed in the relative heat of the cabin.

"Tell me of your time with the Pillars." It wasn't phrased as a question. Nothing about Adela was that delicate, or tactful. But the demand wasn't cold or harsh either.

"I was captured because I followed Ducot," Eira admitted. Ducot had probably told Adela as much, but if he had, she didn't say so. Adela remained focused on Eira's hand, leaving her with nothing to do but speak. "Ferro, Ulvarth's son, murdered my brother. He tried to kill me as well, but couldn't…"

Eira told the pirate queen of the trials in Solaris. Of the night Marcus died. For a woman the legends painted as a ruthless killer—so deadly that even the utterance of her name would bring a curse—she was surprisingly easy to talk to. Perhaps it was *because* Adela had that reputation that there was no fear of judgment. If the woman pillaged and murdered for sport, what did Eira have to hide or be ashamed of?

"…and now I'm here." Eira's words were slightly raspy toward the end. Her throat sore. She must have spent at least an hour talking and Adela had done nothing but listen. "There are some other details I overlooked. But I suspect you already know them through Ducot."

"I prefer to get information from the source, whenever possible." Adela reached for Eira's other hand and began the process over again. This time, it was her hand made of ice holding Eira's, sending a chill down her spine. "It's little wonder you've handled my captivity so well."

"I've known hunger, and darkness, and confinement. The Pillars taught me well in those respects." Eira stared past the slow movements of Adela's fingertip on her palm. "At least here I see the sun."

Adela snorted. "Don't give me an idea to take it from you."

Eira quickly shifted the subject. "You said you weren't

working with the Pillars now, but…did you ever work with the Pillars?"

"Once," Adela admitted with a tense expression. She rolled back her shoulders as if suddenly uncomfortable in her seat. "A man sought me out, interested in some goods from Carsovia. A dangerous job and I was a fool to take it with little information."

"What did he want you to get?" Eira asked.

"Something not worth the cost, in the end." She wore a grimace, her eyes clouding with an anger that wasn't directed at Eira. "Once I realized who the man commissioning me was, and his affiliations with Meru, I severed all ties and went back north."

"Why do you avoid Meru?"

Releasing her hand, Adela leaned back. She rested her hands on the armrests of her chair, tapping them almost restlessly. "I made a bargain with someone a long time ago. They demanded I cease sailing anywhere close to Solaris or Meru and I have kept my word ever since."

"Who?"

"Who else? The only person that could make me bend for them…" Adela smirked and answered coyly, "The Goddess Yargen herself."

Eira rolled her eyes and looked back out the window. If Adela didn't want to tell her, she could've just said so. Though, she shouldn't have expected the pirate to bare her soul just because Eira had. She brought her attention back to the present. Adela didn't have to tell her things. She just had to get Eira's magic back.

"Well, can you open my channel?" Eira flexed her fingertips. "I don't feel any power."

"If you wanted this to happen quickly, you should have made a vessel," Adela said with a slightly scolding note. "But, yes, I believe I will be able to open your channel. Though you might not enjoy the process."

"I will do anything to get my magic back."

"Anything?" Adela arched her brows.

"Anything." There wasn't a trace of hesitation in the word.

"Good. Both hands." Adela's waiting palms seemed harmless enough, but like prey before a predator, something within Eira knew differently.

It took actual effort to prevent her hands from quivering as she reached for Adela one more time. Her fingertips slid across the woman's palms. Adela stretched forward slightly, grabbing Eira by her wrists. Eira mirrored the movement on instinct, meeting the ice-blue eyes of the pirate queen. This close, she could see all the similarities and differences of their features. Adela's cheeks were sharper than Eira's, more sunken. Perhaps with age, perhaps as a function of her usual appearance. The bridge of her nose was just as narrow as Eira's; her brow had the same slope.

"Brace yourself, girl."

"What are you going to—" She wasn't given a chance to finish. There was no warning for what came next.

Frost ripped through her.

It raced up her arms and struck Eira square in the chest. With unseen fingers, the cold grasped for her heart. Eira gasped, choking on air. Her lungs spasmed, shuddering. Her body would shiver if her muscles weren't locking from tension the cold placed them under.

Slack-jawed, she stared at Adela, barely breathing. The invisible hands the pirate held on her lungs slowly drew air in and out, squeezing and relaxing. The chill sank down to her toes. Eira's body emitted a faint haze as the cold condensed in the air.

Adela was doing to her what Eira had done to others. What they had talked about only a few days ago, debating better practice of. Eira was being turned into a living ice statue. She wanted to curse at the woman—to spit venom. But Adela had an intense furrow to her brow, her eyes half-closed.

If she could still access magic, Eira suspected she would feel the subtle pulses of Adela's powers through her. Probing. Perhaps trying to force open the channel.

As suddenly as the cold had come on, the magic retreated,

sinking back into Adela's hands. Eira gasped and hunched, half collapsing over herself. Her muscles felt spent, exhausted. The tension they had been placed under made it feel as if she'd run a marathon.

Adela's grip tightened. She pulled Eira, yanking her to the edge of her chair and jerking her head up to face her. Adela's fingertips were no doubt pressing bruises into her skin, but all Eira could focus on was her face.

"I took you for stronger," Adela said briskly.

"I will surprise you yet," Eira said firmly, still working to catch her breath.

"We will see about that." Adela's fingers tensed once more.

Magic flooded her again as frozen, unseen water. Eira was pulled into the icy depths of Adela's control. Eira's jaw locked as she held it shut to keep her teeth from chattering so she didn't risk biting her tongue.

The entire time, she continued to keep her focus solely on Adela. Even if she couldn't speak, or change her expression, she could show with her eyes that she could handle this much.

This much and more. I welcome it, Eira thought with every bit of determination she could muster.

Just when the frost reached her head, her vision becoming tunneled, Adela relaxed her magic. Eira slumped again, though not as much as last time. She'd known what was coming and had been ready for it.

"Catch your breath." Adela loosened her grip. "That's it for—"

It was Eira's turn to grip Adela. Tight enough that Eira's skin fused with the ice of Adela's right forearm. Eira lifted her head slowly, looking through strands of hair that had fallen into her face.

"Again."

"Do not—"

"We arrive in Ofok in less than two days," Eira ground out through clenched teeth, already bracing herself. "*Again.*"

A slight smile crossed Adela's lips. "Very well."

On the sixth time, Adela pulled away and Eira didn't have the strength to hold on to her. She almost doubled over, catching herself by her knees. Eira thanked the Mother for the chair beneath her, otherwise she might be a puddle on the floor.

Adela stood, crossing over to the small writing desk wedged between the bookcases. Eira could no longer see the pirate queen with the curtain of hair framing her face. Her vision was too blurry at the edges to even make it worth trying. She just focused on breathing. On allowing the warmth of the room to sink into her bones and try to expel the chill that now felt like it was a part of her marrow.

A crystal-cut glass appeared in front of her face, held by a frozen arm. Eira dragged her eyes up, meeting Adela's. She took it skeptically.

"It's not poisoned. If I am going to kill you at this point I would give you the respect of letting you know first."

"Careful, or I'll think you actually like me," Eira murmured as she sank back into the chair, bringing the glass to her lips. The amber liquid was heavily spiced with cinnamon, clove, and cardamom. The drink burned all the way down, bringing warmth and instantly dulling some of her aches. Eira tipped the glass slightly, inspecting it. "A warming potion?"

"A very good liquor. The draconi aren't just known for their silks." Adela had a glass of her own and leaned forward to tip it against Eira's. "Good work today."

"Are you close to restoring my channel?"

"Today was merely the beginning of learning your magical inclinations and pathways. There is still work ahead…and much will depend on your ability to reconnect yourself as well. I can't do it all. At a point, it will be up to you to restore your connection on your own. Fortunately, our magics are quite similar…similar enough that I might be able to use my power to call out to yours in place of a vessel. Think of it like a rope—I can swing it in your direction, but you'll have to catch it."

Our magics are that *similar…* Eira took another sip of the liquor. It couldn't be merely chance. Her heart wouldn't believe it.

"Adela—"

"Your Banefulness," Crow interrupted, opening the door to the cabin. Eira hadn't heard Adela summon her.

"Take Eira to the crew cabin," Adela commanded.

"The *crew* cabin?" Crow stole Eira's question.

"Give her a hammock." Adela looked back to the windows thoughtfully. "She'll need it to recover so she won't be utterly useless tomorrow."

Eira stood, swaying slightly. Crow crossed the small cabin in a few steps, wrapping an arm around her waist. Eira glanced over her shoulder once, but Adela was focused on something else… something far beyond the here and now.

CHAPTER

NINE

I *MIGHT BE ABLE to use my power to call out to yours*. Eira continued to repeat the words over, and over, *and over* again. She wanted to commit them to memory exactly as Adela had said them, and how she looked while speaking them. She didn't want time, or hope, to change a single detail.

Crow led Eira to a different hatch at the front of the boat, past her usual spot. They climbed down a ladder, passing through a narrow squeeze where the hold Eira was usually kept in was walled off at their backs. The lower hull of the ship opened up enough underneath where the upper hold was for five hammocks. In the very back of the vessel was a small galley, squeezed into the point. Chests were piled on either side of the ladder.

Two of the hammocks were occupied with pirates Eira only vaguely recognized. Though she couldn't recall if she'd seen them on this deck, or the other ship. One was an older elfin man with brown skin and rows of braids woven closely against his scalp. The other was a young human woman, fair-skinned, perhaps a year or two younger than Eira, wore a patch over one eye and had her black hair tied in a messy bun at the top of her head.

"We have a guest?" The man sat up, his hammock swaying slightly.

"Adela has requested she get a hammock."

"You one of us now?" the woman asked, twisting her head to look at Eira with her good eye.

"She is certainly not." Crow bristled. "Adela merely needed her to recover, lest she be useless to our queen."

"Is joining the crew an option?" Eira asked no one in particular.

That notion of another possibility that wasn't captive or Adela's experimentation had crossed her mind. But she'd assumed—perhaps wrongfully—that Adela wouldn't consider it.

"Let's not get ahead of yourself." Crow pointed to the hammock in the middle on the right-hand side. "You can use that one."

"Am I taking it from someone else?" Eira was too tired to stop herself from dragging her feet over to it regardless of whose it might be. It was a wonder she had been able to grip the ladder on the way down here.

"No, it's just the three of us on this boat," the man said. "I'm Puck and this is Zaila. Crow you know already."

"You just go making friends with absolutely anyone, even our captives." Crow hopped into her hammock with a huff. "Some *fearsome pirate* you are, Puck."

"I'm fearsome when I need to be." Puck had an air of confidence that assured Eira he had the ability to back up the claim. "But Adela clearly sees an opportunity in her if she's trusting her to be down here with us while we sleep."

Trusting her to be down here… Eira had only considered her captivity in terms of keeping her confined—tortured, in a mild way. She had thought Adela would put her with the crew because they could keep an eye one her. She hadn't considered that she could be the one seen as the danger.

"May I ask you three something?" Eira asked, shifting in her hammock. It would be too easy to sink into the canvas and fall asleep. But for all she knew this might be her only time to get information.

"No," Crow said.

"Absolutely," Puck said nearly at the same time. He smiled when Crow rolled over, every movement exaggerated with frustration.

"What's it like being a part of Adela's crew?"

"You're not becoming one of us and that's that," Crow insisted without facing them again.

Puck acted like she hadn't said anything at all. "It's the best life most of us could've ever dreamed of."

"Why is that?" Eira asked.

"She takes the broken ones." Zaila shifted and swung her legs over the lower edge of her hammock, holding on to either side like a swing as she kicked her feet. "Those of us that aren't criminals, are orphans, or would be better off if we had been. We're the outcasts from society. And that's why it makes it all the more delicious to stick a thin, sharp blade right between that society's ribs." A glint to her eyes reminded Eira that they were still pirates. However lovely the sentiment was in some ways.

"Some of us came from fine families and don't have warrants out for their heads…they were just called to the seas. To adventure," Puck said more lightly. "Others have made their families among her ranks."

"Like Ducot." Even though Eira knew it was true, it was still strange to accept after being in the dark for so long.

"And myself." Puck had a warm smile. "By the time we make it back to Black Flag Bay, I suspect my wife will be holding our baby in her arms."

"Black Flag Bay?"

"Oh sure, tell her *all* our secrets!" Crow threw her arms in the air, rolling over in the process to pin Eira with a stare. "Aren't you supposed to be recovering for tomorrow? Less talking, more resting."

Puck continued to ignore Crow's moodiness, something that irritated the woman greatly and only amused Eira all the more. "Black Flag Bay is well-known among sailors. It's hardly a secret," he said to Crow. Then he continued to Eira, "It's Adela's northern hideaway, ever since she abandoned the Isle of Frost."

"The Isle of Frost was abandoned? I always heard the sailors in Oparium speak of it as though it's still there." Eira was grateful she'd grown up familiar with Adela lore now more than ever.

"Adela still holds it with her power," Zaila said. "She keeps it frozen over—wrapped up in a massive glacier like a present for whenever we might be able to return south.”

“She…has a whole island frozen and is able to keep it that way from this distance?” Eira whispered.

“She is the strongest sorcerer to ever walk among us,” Zaila said proudly, as though Adela’s skill was her own.

Eira leaned back into her hammock, the information heavy. Throughout them working together, Adela exploring Eira’s power, she was also keeping an island frozen solid in the back of her mind. And a ship, as well, if the legends about the *Stormfrost* were to be believed. *That amount of control. That power…* “Crow.”

“What?”

Eira shifted enough to face Crow. She looked the woman dead in the eyes and said, “You were right. My power is nothing compared to hers.”

She’d been expecting Crow to snap back with some kind of snide remark. Yet, Crow’s expression softened some and she gave a small nod. “You’re right. It isn’t. But then again, none of our magic is. Now, you need to rest or else she will be cross with us.”

Eira nodded and closed her eyes. She felt a little dizzy, but it wasn’t from the rocking of the ship or swaying of her hammock. Nor was it from exhaustion or Adela’s spiced liquor.

Perhaps they all were right. And, Adela hadn’t been lying. She didn’t have any children. Because…if Eira had been her daughter, she would never have lost her magic. She would’ve mastered the ability to open and close channels without issue.

There was no way Eira was strong enough to be Adela’s daughter. But that wasn’t about to stop her from fighting to be worthy of her training.

Eira worked to catch her breath. It felt as though Adela was pulling out her soul through her fingernails every time she withdrew her magic. The morning had been spent much the same as last night. Freezing and thawing. Eira was all too glad to accept the small glass of warming liquor when it was offered, not caring in that moment for what hour of the day it was.

"You neglected to detail precisely how your channel came to be closed before the coliseum's explosion." Adela sat after giving Eira her drink.

"Ferro…he suspected I could close channels. But I also had reason to believe I could open them more. So I—"

Adela lifted a hand, halting her. "Open them *more*?"

Eira nodded. "I first gain an understanding of the person's channel by becoming accustomed to their magic. Once I can sense it, I can almost place my own power underneath it and then use that to draw more magic from their channel. It's a bit like shifting the flow of a tide, and my power acts as the current."

"You speak as if this is something you've done." Adela rested her elbow on her armrest and leaned forward.

"I have. Twice. I was beginning to get a better mastery of it during the games. But then when I confronted Ulvarth, I attempted to use the magic in reverse to close his channel."

"And closed yours in the process because you had connected your magic with his by hastily establishing this flow you speak of," Adela murmured. Eira nodded and took another sip from the glass. Adela had barely poured her half a finger. But it was enough to nurse as the chills stopped wracking her body. "I don't think I need to tell you that trying to block a channel in that manner was foolish."

"So I've learned." Eira set down her glass. "But I wasn't exactly taught how to open or close channels, and when a religious zealot is trying to murder everyone I've ever loved isn't the best circumstances under which to learn." The thought sobered her. It was Eira's turn to stare out the windows at their side. Thoughts of her family were distant with shock. Or perhaps she had become completely numb instantly whenever they crossed her mind.

It was a different pain than Marcus's death because she didn't know, for sure, if they were dead. She wasn't going to mourn until she did.

But what did that mean if she never found out the truth? Would she live forever with hope? Or would the mourning be a slow, dull ache rather than a sharp stinging wound that could be faster stitched and mended?

"We can work on closing channels once your magic has returned to you." Yet another reference to a future working together. "It's this opening of a channel that I am most interested in."

"You've never done anything like that?" Eira was shocked to hear it. Especially after last night. After learning more of the true depths of Adela's power, and combining that with what was in her journals, Eira thought she could truly do anything.

"No." Adela wore a thin smile and had a glint to her eyes. "Though I now think I would very much like to. Start at the beginning."

The rest of the afternoon was spent with Adela working on her channel and Eira telling the pirate queen all the details of her work trying to learn how to open and close channels. The discussion became intense at one point around the theoretical nature of magic. Adela was adamant that channels flowed one way—from the unknown source all magic drew from. For Eira to "reach in" to a channel would require it to go both ways. Eira disagreed with the theory because she had, in fact, done it.

By the time the daylight was turning orange, Eira was exhausted in body and mind. But oddly delighted. Even Adela wore a slight smile as she leaned back in her chair a final time.

"You have more than earned your right to stay alive today. I'll see you in the morning." She lifted a hand, summoning her cane.

"Wait." Eira held out a hand and stopped Adela from calling Crow. The pirate queen arched a brow at her boldness. "I wanted to ask... May I go back to the other vessel for tonight?"

"You try my good will," Adela said curtly. Though she still wore her slight smile. "Is your life not enough of a reward?"

"You can't really be surprised I'm trying for more, can you?" Eira cocked her head to the side. "Please? I believe you that they are all right. I have stopped asking after them…but I want to see them before Ofok." Before they disembarked and Eira stayed on board, a captive of the pirate queen forever.

Adela said nothing and Eira braced herself for disappointment. The surreal sense of sitting back in her uncle's office overtook her. Waiting for his verdict on her asking for permission to start working in the city, like all her peers had. She struggled but succeeded in sitting tall and remaining calm, not giving in to her nerves and squirming like a girl begging for permission.

"Very well," Adela said, finally. "But you forfeit your hammock for the night. I can't be bothered to send you back and forth at your whims."

· CHAPTER ·

TEN

E IRA WAS ALREADY on her feet with restless excitement. "Yes, of course."

"You would do well to remember this kindness." Adela stood as well.

"I will not forget, Your Banefulness."

Adela leaned back slightly, arching a brow, no doubt taking note of Eira's use of Crow's term of endearment. Eira smiled somewhat sheepishly and strode forward, leading the way out of the cabin. She could've sworn she heard Adela murmur under her breath. But the words were lost to her. Perhaps, when she had her magic back, she could listen for echoes in the room and find out everything Adela said about her when she thought Eira couldn't hear.

"I will bring you back in the morning," Adela said firmly as she came to a stop by the railing. "Be ready first thing when the sun rises."

"Of course." The other boat was adjacent and just behind them. She could see her friends on the deck, sitting in the back of the vessel. Though they had yet to notice her. Eira refrained from calling over, maintaining her composure.

Without warning, Adela flicked her wrist. The river swelled, collecting Eira off the deck and carrying her across to the other vessel. The rocking from the wave alerted her friends, drawing their attention before Eira was deposited—soaking—in front of them.

But her being dripping wet didn't stop Alyss from scrambling over and slamming into her, crushing Eira in a tight embrace. "You're all right!"

"I told you she was!" Ducot was visibly offended.

Noelle was the next person to throw her arms around Eira. Such outward displays of affection were rare from the woman and Eira stood stunned. "We were so worried."

"Noelle?" Ducot grabbed his chest as though he were physically wounded. "You, too, didn't believe me?"

"You are a fearsome pirate who can't be trusted," Noelle said lightly, pulling away from Eira. "It is so good to see you again. We were missing our fearless leader and troublemaker."

"The feeling was mutual." Eira gave them both a final squeeze as they released each other. Her eyes met Cullen's.

He simply stood there with a slight smile. His gaze had gone soft, almost shining. The sunset haloed his hair in gold and outlined his shoulders, as though he were woven by the magic of Lightspinning. He stood as tall and strong as she remembered him, perhaps even stronger, given the swell of his muscles against his shirt, no doubt from his labors on the ship.

The world faded away. The sound of the vessels cutting through the water, propelled by wind, vanished. They were alone on the boat, him and her.

I love you; I've always loved you, his words echoed to her. The last thing he'd said before he took a blade for her. Those words had never received a response. So much still left unsaid surrounding them.

"It's good to see you, Eira," he murmured.

"And you." Eira nodded, trying to keep her voice level and steady. *We should talk,* she wanted to say. But she couldn't pull him away right now. Plus, she wanted time with her other friends, also. And there was nowhere that even resembled the privacy she'd want for a discussion with Cullen.

Eira followed Alyss and Noelle back to where they'd been sitting—where Ducot, Varren, and Lavette were still. Cullen was a step behind. Eira was painfully aware that he had yet to touch her. He returned to his former spot between Alyss and Noelle.

"I take the fact that you're not all confined to the hold as a good sign." Eira sat and pulled her knees up, wrapping her arms around them as she dripped dry.

"We're permitted out of the hold and have been given freedom along the boat, for the most part," Noelle said.

"So long as we're 'good,'" Varren added. He sounded like he hadn't been taking the warning from the pirates as seriously as he potentially should have been.

"Not good enough to remove these." Noelle lifted her wrist and turned to Ducot. "I'm glaring at you."

"I can feel it," Ducot assured her. "At least some of you could have it removed."

"I couldn't!" Noelle lowered her hand as a fist, tapping it into her thigh in frustration.

"Unfortunately, fire is not very useful on boats. The opposite. And you're all still on thin ice with our queen." Ducot shifted closer to her, draping his arm around her shoulders. It was good to see that they had remained on positive terms.

Eira smiled and Noelle rolled her eyes at her. Though a faint dusky blush was barely visible on the russet hue of her skin.

Eira turned to Alyss. "I've heard you were helpful to the crew."

She nodded. "They seemed surprised I could manipulate ropes so well. I told them it wasn't very hard."

"For an expert like you, maybe." Eira nudged her shoulder against Alyss's.

"By the way, thank you." Alyss lifted the journal they'd procured in the market from the deck at her side—the same journal that Eira had grabbed when she'd gone back to Warich with Ducot.

"I told them how you insisted on getting their things," Ducot said.

Eira released tension she'd been holding between her ribs since Adela hadn't solidly said one way or another what had happened with the rest of the contents of Eira's bag. Yet another gesture of kindness from the pirate queen. Adela really wasn't living up to her bloodthirsty and heartless reputation when it came to them.

"It wasn't much to do," Eira said.

"Having my family's rubies is priceless." Noelle reached over to squeeze Eira's forearm.

"Sorry I couldn't get anything of yours," Eira said to Lavette and Varren. "If I'd had more time…"

Lavette shook her head. "We understand. And your teammates have been generous enough to share some of their clothes with us." She pulled at the hem of the cloak she was wearing. Eira recognized it as Alyss's.

"We're all stuck here together, might as well make the most of it." Alyss smiled.

"Speaking of stuck." Cullen met Eira's eyes once more, pinning her with an expectant stare. "How have *you* been?"

"I've been all right." They didn't need to know about her time in the other ship's hold, or about the scraps and initial cruelty. "Adela hasn't hurt me. In fact, she's going to help me get my magic back."

"That's excellent!" Alyss clapped her hands.

"What does she want in return?" Lavette's skepticism was understandable. She was far too astute not to ask.

Eira tried to answer without really answering. "I'm going to help her test out some magic."

"I don't like the sound of that," Cullen said warily.

Eira shrugged. "What choice do I have? It's better to chance it and regain my power."

"What if she wants to experiment with some kind of torture on you?" Cullen frowned.

"She hasn't yet, and I've been completely vulnerable."

"If Adela says she won't harm someone, she will always honor that," Ducot insisted.

Eira had her doubts. Ducot's opinion was likely colored by Adela having been the one to take him in and shelter him.

The whole crew's was. But this was the same woman who had committed regicide and could laugh about it. While all rulers had their flaws, the last King Solaris had been generally regarded as a fair and fine ruler in all the history books Eira had read. But she had made a promise to someone not to attack Meru and seemed bent on honoring that… Perhaps there was something to Ducot's claims.

"Eira might not be the one at risk." There was a touch of chill to Lavette's usually calm and level words. "She might be the one helping the torture of others. Can you live with your magic being used for Adela's more nefarious purposes?"

Eira hadn't fully considered that notion. Though, it didn't change her plans. "I can't change how Adela will or won't use her magic. And she has a lot of means to hurt people as it is."

"But will you enable her learning new tricks—expanding those means?"

"I don't have a choice."

Lavette narrowed her eyes slightly. "We *always* have a choice."

Eira pursed her lips. What she didn't risk saying on deck with pirates—even with Ducot—was that her plan was to get her magic back as quickly as possible and then use it to flee at the first second she could, teaching Adela as little as possible. But Lavette was right in that she might not have the chance. In truth, just speaking through magical theories could've helped the pirate queen gain new and horrible ideas.

"Well, I like living, and I don't think me helping Adela or not will change anything about her terrorizing the seas."

"You're more heartless than I thought," Lavette said with a faint note of disappointment. It rubbed Eira wrong. *Who was she to judge?*

"I am trying to help us all survive," Eira said firmly. She pointed back behind the boat, back in the direction of Warich. "My family might still be out there. My uncle could be a prisoner of those zealots because they had already begun going after him as a result of *me*. My heart is with us and them and keeping us all as safe as best I can. I will do whatever it takes to accomplish that."

"There is more to this world than just your family and friends."

"Not anymore. You saw the royals' box. No one could've survived that." The words were like blades against her heart. She knew she was talking about her uncle as much as she was Vi or Lumeria. It was the folly of hope. Where logic and reason fought against what her better sense told her.

"Aldrik and Vi were powerful Firebearers; it's possible they could've manipulated the flames," Noelle suggested hopefully.

"They were flames made from flash beads," Varren said grimly. "That is not normal fire."

"Don't doubt the power of people's magic." Noelle clearly wasn't going to let herself be dissuaded.

"Yes," Lavette agreed. "Some could've survived."

"You're right. And I hope they did. I really do." Eira hoped her uncle had succeeded in getting people out. She'd seen him summon ice to defend himself from an avalanche that was seconds from toppling him. Maybe he did survive and saved others. "But, even if some did, not all of them made it out. Lumeria certainly didn't. She was too far forward. And she was the one holding together the Treaty of Five Kingdoms. Whether we like it or not…governments have fallen and the ones that survived are hanging by threads."

"You don't think I know that?" Lavette raised her voice slightly. It was uncharacteristic and that stilled Eira. "I also watched my father die that day. You aren't the only one who doesn't know where your family might be, or hopes against hope they're alive."

"Then you should want to do whatever it takes to get back to him, too." How was it they were so similar and yet not seeing eye to eye? If getting to her father meant working with Adela, then why not?

"If my father did manage to survive, he would want me to move forward, not back. I need to go home. Our people need leaders as desperately now as ever. They need the truth of what happened brought back to them from someone they trust—someone who was there, because rumors will no doubt spread. With the treaty falling apart, we will be vulnerable to Carsovia. And all that is why I can't look solely at myself. I must focus on the big picture and how everything I do will impact the world around me, intentionally or not." Lavette stood, looking down at her. "All your power… You could do so much good, Eira."

"I have always tried to 'do good,'" Eira said quietly, frustration seeping into her voice. And where had "doing good" got her? Never very far. "But I have no power right now. I can't do *anything* without magic."

"Your strength is, and always was, in more than magic."

"We can agree to disagree there." Eira smiled thinly. What did Lavette really think she could do without magic? What power did Eira have without it? Her magic was her bargaining chip with Adela; it was the reason they were all still alive. Her magic would be what ultimately ended Ulvarth.

Lavette continued to give her a hard stare for another long minute. Finally, she said, "I took you for better. But perhaps you really are the daughter of Adela. Because only a frozen pirate queen could be so callous and think only of themselves."

Before Eira could reply, Lavette stormed away. Probably for the best. It was taking all of Eira's control not to lay into her. Varren's attention darted between them. He sighed and shook his head.

"I'll speak to her." Varren stood. "She's just frustrated by feeling helpless for days on end. Not having any control over her destiny is hard for her." He left, following after Lavette.

"Never a dull moment with you, is there?" Ducot had a smile as Varren left.

Eira sighed, pinching the bridge of her nose. "Just for once, I wish there was."

"Y OU'RE NOT *REALLY* going to help Adela though, are you?" Alyss asked. The entire time Eira and Lavette had been at odds, her nose had been in her notebook. This was all, no doubt, giving her excellent ideas for drama in her "romance novel to end all romance novels."

"I'm going to do whatever I must, Alyss." Eira wished she could tell her friends all she was planning and thinking. She was well past keeping things from them. But, with how things had unfolded, she didn't dare risk it in the short term. Even if she could prevent the pirates—even Ducot—from hearing that she was planning to escape at the first possible opportunity, regardless of what she told Adela… Alyss might mention it to Noelle, who might mention it to Ducot, who'd be compelled to tell Adela. And, even if Noelle didn't, they might be overheard discussing it. Ironically, the only person she was somewhat confident could hold the information was Cullen.

Which, she needed to speak with him anyway…

"Cullen, may we have a word?" Eira gave him a pointed look.

"That's probably for the best." At least he realized it.

"Well, would you look at that," Ducot said awkwardly. "I think there's something important that needs my attention *waaaaaay* over there. For however long this is going to take." He stood.

"Wow, me too." Noelle stood as well. Alyss didn't move. Noelle nudged her with the toe of her boot. "Alyss?"

"Oh no, I'm fine." Alyss perched her journal in her lap.

"No you don't." Noelle lifted Alyss up by her arm. "They

need their space and you only *think* you want to be around. When the awkwardness sets in, you'll wish you were with us."

Alyss looked to Eira with hopeful eyes. Eira arched her brows and silently conveyed, *Noelle is right and you know it.*

"All right," Alyss groaned. "But, really, I *am* the resident expert on love and literally no one is taking my advice or welcoming my input on the subject. Which is a terrible loss for all of you." She sighed dramatically. "Still, I'll be here whenever you come around to realizing just how helpful I can be."

"Noted." Eira reached up to squeeze her friend's hand lightly. Alyss gave her a small but encouraging smile. "Thank you."

"I'm too good to you, but you're welcome." Alyss grinned.

"You really are," Eira agreed.

"What an unlikely bunch we are." Cullen had a gentle fondness to his words, directed at the three that were departing.

"That thought has occurred to me before." Though, not in some time. Eira had begun to see their team as an expectation, a given. But Lavette's outburst and Ducot's revelation called the perfect picture of their group into question. What would break the ties between them?

"Where would you like to start?" Cullen asked, picking at the scuffs on his boots. He wasn't looking her in the eyes, and rather than frustrating her…it merely made Eira sad.

"How are you feeling?" Eira asked, her words as heavy as the smoke in the coliseum that day. "Your father was there, too."

"I don't really know where my father was." Cullen shrugged and looked back in the direction of Warich. "Though, you're right, knowing him…he was probably in the thick of it. He could never seem to manage to get close enough to royals. Look at where that endless persistence got him, in the end. The cost of greatness…" He shook his head. "But I'm fine, really."

"It's all right if you're not." There was something strange about his tone. Something Eira couldn't quite put her finger on.

"I think that's what surprises me. I really am okay. I almost feel…relieved." The wind played in his hair as he wore a tired, but genuine smile. His eyes were sad, but his mouth was happy. He was slouched slightly, but for the first time he didn't look as though his shoulders were trying to eat his ears from tension. Or as though he were being crushed by the weight of the world. "My peace with whatever happened to my family and the citizens of Solaris that were there is part of what led to a recent quarrel between Lavette and I. She called me callous."

"*That* is why you're at odds? Not what I said before Adela took me?"

"Nothing ever really came to pass between Lavette and me. So other than her rightfully having affirmation that I am an ass— and admittedly being a bit shocked as to the scale of my poor decision-making—the revelation impacted her little."

And, yet, Eira was still wounded by his actions. He was right, it did show how little Lavette cared…and how much Eira had. Maybe still did.

"Not everything is about you, Eira." Cullen nudged her shoulder lightly with his. The gesture was friendly. And, though small, it somehow eased some of the tension she felt. "Though my heart sometimes tries to tell me differently," he added under his breath.

"I'm still going to talk to her about it all, when I have a chance." Eira glanced over her shoulder. Lavette was still in discussion with Varren. "I think I owe it to her."

"She'd probably appreciate that, knowing her. She's one to want to, respectfully, get matters out in the open." He glanced over his shoulder. "Though, you might want to wait until she's less generally on edge as a result of her circumstances." On that, Eira could agree.

"About your feelings for me… They're still there?" Eira folded and unfolded her fingers in her lap.

"I was ready to die for you less than a week ago," he said softly. "I'd say they're still there."

Eira nodded and continued to stare behind them. "Cullen, I… I don't—"

He rested a hand on her knee and shifted to look her in the

eyes. The setting sun was picking up the orange notes in his hazel irises.

"It's all right. You don't have to have an answer for me. So much has changed. *You've* changed—are changing. I'm changing too, or at least trying to. Who knows if we'll change in a way that brings us together, or pushes us apart." He wore an easy smile. As if, for the first time, he could say everything he wanted to. "But I do know I care for you still, despite all odds. I know that you defy logic and reason for me as much as you always have. And I know that I lost your trust, and possibly your heart. But I want to see if the man I'm becoming will manage to earn them again."

She couldn't stop a slight smile. There was an urge to kiss him. Even still, even now.

"My feelings don't make sense to me either sometimes," she admitted. "Sometimes, you're all I can think of. Other times, I want nothing to do with you."

"The feeling is mutual." He reached up and tucked a stand of hair behind her ear. His fingers lingered on the crest of her ear, trailing delicately down her neck as he pulled away.

"I fear I might be stuck with you forever," she admitted with a whisper. "In one way or another."

"I hope so. Right now, I still desire to be your lover. To be a man *worthy* of that love. But if it's not meant to be, I know I would be overjoyed to merely be counted among your friends." He chuckled and shook his head. "I would even bear it if you must call me your enemy… The only thing I wouldn't be able to stand is if we were nothing. Because then I wouldn't have even the slightest place in your heart. I would live with the knowledge that I never crossed your thoughts, and that would be a fate worse than death."

Eira sat in stunned silence. Her hand moved on its own, reaching for his that still rested on her knee. Their fingertips, just up to the first knuckle, slotted together. It felt like understanding. For the first time, they were on the same page. There were no more secrets. No more fears.

"What about the engagement?" she couldn't help but ask.

"Neither Lavette nor I have any interest in pursuing it. That much is clear." He shrugged. "Either our fathers are dead, and there won't be any pressure to honor it, or, even if they're alive, there are enough other concerns that I doubt they'll put up much of a fight. It's really up to us." He paused and then spoke before she could. Surprising her when he said, "Though I suppose it always was up to us. That was what you wanted me to see all along, wasn't it?"

"Yes." The word was part sigh of relief.

"So she will go back to Qwint as soon as she's able to find a way and, as for me…I'm not sure what's next, or what the future holds." He shrugged.

"I've never seen you so…" Eira struggled for the right word or phrase.

"Free?" Cullen smirked and leaned back, lounging as if for emphasis. Something about him on the boat looked right in a way Eira would've never expected before now. "Other than the guilt that surrounds the feeling—since it likely came at the cost of my father's life and my being a captive of the pirate queen—I have never been so relaxed. I don't have anywhere to be or any expectations upon me. I feel like I'm finally trying to embody the wind, rather than be the storm."

"What do you mean?"

"All my life, I was trying to exert force—or others were trying to do so upon me, or on my behalf. To make things happen. This is the first time I don't have a plan or direction. I'm just seeing what comes next and taking it one step at a time."

Eira leaned back as well and savored the easy silence. If only for a second. There were still more hard, necessary topics to discuss. But, for now, she enjoyed the sound of the boat cutting through the water. The cries of the birds as they pecked at the marsh minnows and worms in the nearby banks. The smell of a distant campfire where some traveler was roasting meat.

For a second, he was the wind and she was the current, souls dancing. They would see where fate would take them.

"When we get to Ofok, Adela is going to let you all go," Eira said softly, drawing Cullen's attention back to her. Everyone else had given them space—talking about lovers' matters had worked to drive any prying ears away and now was her chance. "She said she'll do so without harm to any of you. She should remove the shackles, too. But if she doesn't, I found out where she keeps the key—it's in an inside breast pocket of her coat."

"Eira…"

"I'm sure the *Stormfrost* is somewhere off the coast of Ofok. While I don't know where, given what Adela has said, she won't be coming back this way for some time—I believe she only came because of me."

"Eira," Cullen said more firmly. "What about *you*?" He saw right through her careful choice in words.

"I won't leave her side until I get my magic back," she said softly, weaker than she would've liked. "I don't know why it hasn't come back yet…but it hasn't. I do have confidence though that with enough time, she can do it."

"What if she's purposefully drawing out the process of getting your magic back?" His voice dropped to a whisper. He was looking out of the corners of his eyes as much as she was for any pirates who might venture too close or otherwise be listening in on their hushed conversation.

"Why would she? I'm more valuable to her with my powers than without. There are only so many hypotheticals of magical application we can explore with words alone."

"Unless she wants you at her side for *another reason*." Cullen didn't expand on what that "other reason" might be and Eira was glad for it. He understood strange and tense relationships that surrounded family. All the messy emotions that came with it. Mother above knew, he had those emotions himself.

"If that's the case, then I'd want to stay for it, too. Find out the truth."

"But—"

"My mind is made up, Cullen." That stopped his objections. "So if I don't get my magic tomorrow morning before Ofok, which I doubt I will, I'll have to stay with Adela. The rest of you need to leave."

"I'm not leaving you behind."

"Go while you can." Eira leaned over slightly, meeting his eyes. "This might be your only chance—if she keeps her word. I will try to escape later, as soon as I'm able."

He frowned slightly and his eyes took on a stern intensity. "You know that's not going to happen. Alyss and Noelle won't leave you. *I* won't leave you." She sighed heavily. It was his turn to speak over her protests. "Eira, all this time you wanted me to make a choice. To pick for myself and live in the way I wanted, not in the way others wanted for me. Well, now I am."

"You had to pick *now* of all times to start living life for yourself," she muttered, and shifted again, uncomfortable. He was right and she had to respect his choice. She had to respect all their choices.

"There's never a good time for hard decisions."

For a few minutes, they sat in silence. Just looking out at the world passing them by. She closed her eyes and sighed softly. After opening up to her friends, so much, it was becoming difficult to act without their support.

"She said she's not my mother," Eira whispered softly.

"Did she?" he replied, just as soft. Eira nodded. "Do you believe her?"

"Sometimes I do…other times I don't. Her power, Cullen, it's greater than any sorcerer I've ever imagined. She can do more than any Waterrunner I've ever heard—even dreamed—of doing. The more I learn about her, the more I think that her crew is right and she's telling the truth. There's no way I could be her daughter."

"Your power is astounding. *You* were the one who discovered echoes. Who had begun exploring widening channels. Don't sell yourself short."

Eira drew her knees back to her chest and wrapped her arms around them. "I never thought I would actually find her, but I dreamed that if I did, everything would fall into place. I would *know* that she was my mother beyond all doubt and she would be overjoyed to be reunited with me."

"Family never turns out how you think it will."

"It never does," she agreed with a heavy note.

"Earlier…you said you wanted to get back to your parents and uncle in Warich. That you worried for them."

Eira glanced over at him, trying to read where the remark was coming from. "I'm not heartless. Even though we were at odds, I wouldn't want them to die."

"I never thought you did. It's just…all this time you were fighting to get to Adela. Now, you want to get back to your parents."

"I want to make peace, if nothing else. We all handled things badly and, even if I don't know if I want them in my life forever, I want closure… I've gone soft," she said with a note of sarcasm, trying to inject some levity or jesting into the otherwise heavy conversation.

He ignored it, remaining serious. "You've found a more nuanced heart."

"Well, you're not the only one who's changing."

They shared a small smile. Things around him had somehow finally, *finally* become comfortable. Now that they weren't trying to be anything, ignore anything, or *not* be anything, it was as if they had the freedom to explore what they were meant to become and everything or nothing was on the table.

There was something exciting about the idea. Of meeting Cullen all over again. Learning who he was without everything else attached.

"Are you two done with your alone time?" Alyss said, coming up from behind them.

Eira gave Cullen a pointed look that said, *don't forget what we discussed.* He dipped his chin ever so slightly. She'd put her faith in him to seriously consider leaving when the time came, and encouraging the others to do the same. If they chose to stay… Eira couldn't do much to change their minds.

"I think so," Eira said. "Which is good because I want to hear everything you have in your journal now."

"I am not ready to share my work in progress." Alyss held the journal to her chest and patted it. "But as soon as it is ready, you will be the first I share it with."

"I better be." Eira had a sneaking suspicion that she had inspired a good portion of it.

"Dinner is ready." Alyss motioned behind her. The rest of them had metal cups they were picking food out of.

Eira and Cullen joined.

Lavette and Varren were off toward the bow of the ship, still keeping to themselves. But they shot glances every now and then in Eira's direction. Eira tried to ignore it. If—*when* Lavette wanted to talk, she was ready. But she wouldn't push the matter prematurely.

The meal almost felt…*normal*. Fen and Krut joined them while they ate. Pine sat off to the side, keeping to himself in his broody, disapproving way. But even he chimed in from time to time on the discussion, weighing in on the state of Meru's politics, or mild topics like the best port to get rum versus whiskey from.

By the time they went to the hold to sleep, Pine was the only one still up, seemingly keeping half an eye on them as he coiled the rope. Though his mild attempt at an imposing presence wasn't needed, everyone went to the hold willingly, as though it were a bedroom and not a prison.

Eira was surprised but pleased to see that the pirates had made it a point to make her friends comfortable. There were blankets of varying quality. Some threadbare, but others thick with fluff. A lantern held a faintly glowing rock that emitted shining motes behind the glass like fireflies. Eira stared at it in wonder.

Noelle placed a hand on her shoulder briefly and said, "Ducot said it's from the Twilight Kingdom." *His home.* "I hear the name is apt because it is never night, nor daylight—eternal twilight. Most of the light comes from the stars and constellations above the city, or lanterns like this."

"Useful on a ship." Eira thought to what Ducot had said earlier about fire and ships.

"I think fire would be fine," Noelle mumbled and dropped her hand from Eira's shoulder.

"Incredibly useful." Ducot yawned and crawled over to where Noelle was bundling herself. It was cold at night and damp in the hold. He placed an arm around her waist, pulling her back to his chest and holding her close.

Alyss had entered the hold and Eira glanced over at her friend, whispering, "*They* are the couple you should be using for your inspiration."

"Oh, trust me, I am," Alyss whispered back. "But they can sometimes be a bit…*boring*. Not enough drama to make an interesting tale."

Eira tilted her head to the side and narrowed her eyes at Alyss. The woman laughed and crawled over to her pile of blankets, peeling one away and handing it to Eira.

"Here you are."

"Thanks," Eira said, taking it and returning by default to the spot she'd first woken in. Everyone, save for Ducot, had kept to their same areas.

Which meant she was almost next to Cullen.

It wasn't until she lay down that she realized his face was a short stretch from hers. After seeing Ducot and Noelle, Eira was suddenly aware of just how cold the night was. How far he was and how good his body would feel.

Their eyes met as he lay down. Suddenly the gap felt larger and smaller all at once. Their words earlier had built a bridge between them. One she hadn't expected to ever be erected over the ashes of the old. Or perhaps that bridge had never truly burned down. There was something still to save, and fortify, if they wanted.

Eira shifted onto her side to face him and extended her hand, placing it between them. Cullen's hand crossed the gap. His knuckles brushed against hers as if to say, *I'm here*. Slowly moving her fingers, she slid them against his, weaving and unweaving. Coming together, apart, and together. Not entirely either, somewhere between.

Neither of them said anything. It was as though the spell would be broken with one word. So Eira continued to lightly brush her fingers against his and her lids grew heavy. His face was the last thing she saw before sleep claimed her.

· CHAPTER ·

TWELVE

THERE WERE MORE houses along the banks of the river the next morning. Gone were the flat, empty plains they had been winding through and in their place was a marshy delta. The river had begun to split, forking down like city streets underneath homes built on stilts overhead. In place of horse or carriage, people traversed on boats or suspended bridgeways that dripped morning dew as they drifted beneath. The citizenry oblivious to the pirates in their presence.

This must be the easternmost edge of Ofok, Eira realized. They would reach the coast before the day was up. The thought was so heavy she was impressed Adela could still carry her from one vessel to the other with ease. Her heart twisted as her friends were left behind.

She'd put her faith in Cullen to try and convince them to leave. But…what he'd told her…

There was no way they would go.

"You're distracted today." Adela folded her hands on the top of her cane as she sat in her usual chair opposite Eira. "Speak."

"My friends won't leave me." There wasn't any point in denying it. It'd be apparent soon enough.

Adela was as still as a statue. As unreadable as a book written in the ancient tongue of the elfin. Finally, she said, "Loyalty is a stronger force than even magic, is much harder to master, and wielding it requires far more responsibility."

Eira sank back into her chair. She should be working on getting her magic back. On doing everything she could to reclaim her power before it was too late…but she also knew, without all doubt, that she was out of time. There wasn't any way her magic would return in the next couple hours.

"I wish they would listen."

"Yes, well, loyalty can transform those you love into the most ardent, yet obstinate creatures."

Eira readily nodded in agreement. "What will you do to them if they refuse?"

"The same rules will continue to govern them—if they do as they're told and make themselves useful, I can find a place for them on my vessels." A thin, crescent smile arced across her lips. "I think motivating them should be easy enough. Seeing as I have you in my palm and *you're* the one they're standing by."

Eira's stomach clenched. She was the leverage Adela held over her friends. Both Eira's friends and her magic were the leverage Adela had over her. The pirate queen, unsurprisingly, was positioned as the one with absolute control.

"I have one more question."

Adela motioned with an open palm in a gesture that read as, *continue*.

"Are you genuinely trying to restore my magic? Or are you stringing me along?"

Her hand settled back on her cane. "What use are you to me as a Commons? There would be no motivation for me to keep you here without your magic. If I simply needed deckhands, I could find much better than you. And, if I were to set you free, it would be more advantageous for me to do so with you lacking magic, as then you could not use my name to your advantage. I would not be keeping you here, Eira, if not for restoring your powers." Adela's eyes shone. "I want to see you listen to these echoes for myself. And then, I want you to teach me mastery of them."

Eira nodded weakly, Lavette's objections about Adela's nature heavy in her mind. But what else could she do? Right now, Adela was her best chance. And…oddly enough…they might be safer with the pirate queen than anywhere else. At least, for now, she knew that the Pillars couldn't get to them. If there was one thing

Eira knew Adela wouldn't abide, it would be an attack on her ship and crew. She wouldn't allow herself to be made to look weak—a trait Eira found herself admiring.

"Then we should continue." Eira leaned forward, extended her hands, and braced herself for more hours of a chill that grabbed her very soul by the throat.

Eira stood on deck with Crow as the ship finally drifted to a stop alongside one of the many parallel docks that ran along the marshy banks of the center river of Ofok. It resembled the docks of Warich, but taken to the extreme. Like the houses that came before it, most of the small city was suspended on pylons driven deep into the wet earth. Some of the boats looked as though they'd been tied in one particular spot for years, the ropes dripping stalactites of algae as craftsmen and restaurants ran businesses on their docks. The stilted houses she'd seen as they approached Ofok were now dense, honeycombed together so tightly that one balcony became another's entry.

"Her Frostiness made it clear what she expected of you while we're roped up, correct?" Crow said curtly, looking out from underneath her hood.

Eira had also donned her cloak, per the pirate's instructions. She hadn't objected since her face was recognizable enough following the tournament and showing it was a risk not worth taking.

"Don't disembark. Don't go to the other ship. Stay in place and mostly out of sight," Eira tiredly repeated Adela's order. The attempts to restore her magic had exhausted Eira to her core.

"Good. The three of us are going to resupply." As Crow spoke, Puck and Zaila were shrugging on heavy coats, even in the heat of summer. Eira heard metal clanks and suspected there were daggers and other weapons stitched inside. "You stay in place and defend the boat if anything happens."

"With what?" Eira held out her empty palms. "I still don't have my magic."

"*Still?*" Crow seemed flabbergasted. "Just what have you been doing in there all these hours? Playing carcivi?"

"Maybe. Jealous I'm getting so much quality time with Her Iciness?" Eira arched her brows and Crow huffed. She'd long since picked up on how deeply Crow's loyalty and admiration ran for her leader. Eira dropped her expression, tone becoming serious once more. "I had a dagger among my things—gold hilt, a notch down the fuller. At least give me that?"

Crow must have been expecting the demand. Or she had already been told to give Eira the weapon, because it was waiting in the large pack she'd slung over her shoulder. Eira expected more hesitation before she handed it over. But Crow wasted no time.

"Here. But don't you dare get any ideas." Crow took a half step closer as she passed it to Eira, voice dropping to a whisper, side-eying the few people going about their business on the docks. "Adela might know better than to show her face, but if you cross her, don't think she won't freeze this whole city to the bone in an instant just to get to you."

Eira had no doubt that the pirate queen would, and could. "I know. She has my magic hostage. I'm not going to do anything that would risk her helping me."

"Good." Crow released the blade and stepped toward Puck and Zaila.

As the three of them exchanged quiet conversation, Eira unsheathed the blade, inspecting its edge. It was still wicked sharp. Being armed was a relief. Even if she could do little with it compared to her magic…it was *something*. She turned the blade over once and then sheathed it, tucking it into her belt and allowing it to slice through the helplessness she'd been suffering.

When she looked back across the deck, the other pirates were gone. Their silhouettes faded into the people passing through the docks. Well, it seemed like they trusted her.

Biting back a sigh, Eira walked to the opposite side of the vessel, away from the docks. Adela's other boat, with her friends, had moored up on the other side of the river. She leaned on the railing. Ducot was talking with Pine and Fen. Noelle was there, too. The competitors from Qwint crossed over. Alyss and Cullen wrapped up a conversation, and the former joined the group.

Cullen lingered behind, at the back of the boat. His eyes swept across the river and met hers. Even though it was impossible to make out his features, she could see the slight sag to his shoulders as he straightened slightly. Eira bit her lip to keep herself from calling out. She clasped her hands together, gripping them so tightly they shook.

If she called out to him now, he would stay. If she showed him even the slightest bit of need. He would stay for her.

The choice was his to make and she had to give him space to make it. She couldn't influence him. If she did, she'd forever regret it. She'd forever doubt his intentions.

So she waited, savoring what might be their last few minutes together, even though they were a river apart. The wind picked up, carrying on it the scent of rain. He stepped backward, and then away from the railing. He joined the rest of them.

Every, steady, even, step of his was a pound of her heart. Slow but relentless. It stuck in her throat. Eira tried to swallow it down, but couldn't. Nausea overtook her. She swallowed again.

Go, she wanted to shout.

Stay, her heart cried.

The pirates, Ducot, Alyss, Noelle, Lavette, Varren, and… finally…Cullen left the boat. They jumped the short distance to the dock and walked out of Eira's field of vision.

She waited, seconds ticking by. Half of her hoped that they would be back on board within minutes. Eventually, long after her fingers had cramped, she released her tension with a heavy sigh and hung her head between her shoulders.

They were gone.

Her friends had left. Eira wiped her face, half-surprised to find her cheeks dry. Nothing had ever hurt so much and yet felt so good at the same time. She pushed away from the railing and went to the bow of the boat, sitting. She imagined herself a figurehead, wooden and unfeeling. Trapped, but also free to travel the world.

Alone.

Was Adela in her room, still sitting at her chair, staring out the window? Eira imagined them as mirrors of each other. She closed her eyes and listened to the water lapping against the hull of the boat. Sounds of the docks faded away. Eira inhaled slowly, imagining Adela doing the same.

The pirate queen's magic was there. Adela was too powerful not to be constantly emitting power, especially if she was holding an entire island in her thrall. Eira's brow furrowed with focus.

Feel it, she commanded herself. *Find the magic, like yours, and feel it.*

If she could restore her magic now, then she could leave, too. Make a run for it while her friends were still nearby. Her fingers twitched. A drop of water.

Heart pounding once more, Eira scowled with focus. She could almost feel it there, like a current underneath a thick layer of ice. Her power churned, hunting for a way out. More water coated her palms.

Yes, yes! She was close. A little bit more and—

A distant rumble jolted her. Eira tilted her head back. Dark gray clouds were rolling in, blanketing an ominous orange sky. Fat drops plopped down on her forehead.

She hadn't been summoning her magic. It'd been raining.

Eira sighed and brought her knees to her chest, resting her forehead on them. Maybe it was hopeless. She would be better served learning how to live as a Commons than trying to fight to get her magic back.

Rain turned into a downpour. She allowed it to drench her,

making no effort to retreat into the hold. It was cool and fresh, washing away the exhaustion of the past few days.

She couldn't hear the footsteps over the pounding of the rain. It wasn't until she could feel the vibration of the deck that Eira realized anyone was there. All her focus returned to the here and now. She slowly reached for her blade. Crow, Puck, or Zaila wouldn't sneak up on her. Unless they were playing a joke? It did seem like something they might do…but probably not under these circumstances.

Drawing the blade, she feigned inspecting it. It gave away that she was armed. But it was worth giving away the element of that surprise—something a would-be attacker would've probably assumed anyway. Drawing the weapon had the added benefit of making sure she wasn't about to stab one of Adela's men as she caught a glimpse in the mirror of the blade.

The man was cloaked. Face cast in shadow but definitely not one of the pirates. He half knelt, creeping. Eira returned her blade to her lap and inhaled slowly. Did he notice she'd caught a glimpse of him?

Was it a Pillar?

She imagined her friends dead. The pirates slain. The Pillars were still hunting her and they'd caught up. It hadn't been exactly difficult to follow them along the river, given the steady and very slow pace they'd had.

The man was right behind her. Eira pushed backward. He was ready. A hand clamped over her mouth, the other around her wrist wielding the dagger. Eira struggled, trying to twist free. Thanks to the slickness of the rain, she almost had escaped his grasp when a familiar voice whispered in her ear, "I found you."

She inhaled sharply. Her heart stopped.

FEELING HER RELAX, he let her go. Eira spun in place and whispered, "Olivin?"

The elfin man gave her a tired smile. "I'm here to save you."

"Save…me?" She blinked, wiping away rain from her eyes to see more clearly. Her ears hadn't deceived her. It really was him. *Here*.

"Yes, come on, there isn't much time until they're back." Still holding on to her wrist, Olivin hoisted her up. Eira was too stunned to put up much of a fight. "What do I need to know? Who else is keeping you here?"

"Olivin." She ripped her hand from his grasp and shook her head. He stopped when she did.

"Eira—"

"Do you think if I wanted to escape I wouldn't do it when I was left alone like this?" She kept her voice low and shuffled her feet slowly, trying to shift the weight from toe to heel to prevent the boards from creaking unnecessarily. Adela was right underneath them and if she heard someone else on her boat, someone who wasn't supposed to be there…a chill crept up Eira's spine. "You need to leave. Now."

"I don't know what these people told you, but they are *not* your friends." He was clearly trying to rationalize her objections. "I have reason to believe they're—"

"Adela's pirates," Eira finished coolly. "Why do you think I'm here?"

Olivin straightened, squinted, and then his eyes widened, as if truly seeing her for the first time. "You…you're really her daughter…"

She strategically avoided answering outright. Instead, Eira insisted again, "Please, *leave*. Weren't you staying behind to save your brother? What about Yonlin?"

"I found him."

Three words shook her and flooded the cracks in her foundation with a relief and hope she didn't know she needed. If Yonlin had made it then maybe there was a chance for Fritz, her parents—for all their families.

But she shouldn't be so hasty. "Is he…"

"He's all right." Olivin smiled and gave a nod. "He's here. We've been traveling together, following the boats. He's not far, holed up and hiding somewhere safe."

"Good." Eira rested her hands on his shoulders and hung her head, basking in the relief as it washed over her in waves. It felt like as long as Yonlin was alive, hope was as well. She straightened, gathering her authority. The victorious smile slipped off Olivin's face as he saw her expression. "You need to go back to him and *stay* in that safe place for a good day or two." Enough time that she'd be long gone.

"Not without you."

"Listen to me." She gripped his strong forearms. His clothes were slick under her palms. They clung to the firm muscle of his chest. "I am not some damsel in need of saving. I am here because *I want to be*."

Olivin studied her. Rain ran down over his face. It pooled between them. "You're telling the truth."

"I know I am." Eira sighed. "Just like I know you meant well. But heed me when I tell you to go; I'm trying to protect you."

"I can be the one to protect you," he insisted.

"You can't help me in the way I need it. I lost my magic and Adela is the only person who can help me get it back." Every time she said it prodded the wound. But it ached less and less. Now, more a matter of fact.

Olivin's eyes widened slightly. There were a thousand

questions he no doubt wanted to ask. But he kept them, and any objections, to himself.

He hovered for another breath that was hot across her face, contrasting with the cold rain. He searched the depths of her gaze as she charted a course across his. There was so much more to this…he'd tracked her, followed their course on foot tirelessly.

Why do I mean so much to you? Eira wanted to ask. But doubted even he had the answer.

The coiled tension of his muscles eased. For a fleeting moment, the gray of the overcast skies became the night that blanketed Champion Village when they had first kissed. But, ultimately, Olivin gave her a light squeeze and released her.

Eira stopped herself from asking him to stay.

"All right, Eira. I trust you. I always have. I'm sorry for misunderstanding."

She shook her head. "You were looking out for a fellow shadow."

"I was looking out for *you*." He stepped backward. "If you change your mind, we're in the Rolling Pony Inn. That offer of spending the night in my bed still stands."

"Noted." Eira laughed softly. "I doubt I'll come, but maybe some other friends will cross your path."

He squinted slightly, tilting his head, and then the expression fell into a smirk. "All right, I'll keep an eye out." She always did appreciate how astute he was, how quick on the uptake.

Olivin turned and started back down the deck. His footsteps were heavier than she would've liked. But at least he was leaving. Even if Adela heard him now, he'd be gone by the time she bothered to emerge.

A faint smile crossed her lips as he made his way down the deck, the low light of town that glowed off to the side of the boat cutting his shape into a silhouette. The docks he headed toward were empty from the storm. But all she could hear was each one of his steps, louder than the last. Louder than the rain.

Louder than the rain.

Her head jerked toward the docks. The rain still pounded on them in fat drops. It was coming down so heavily that it was almost hard to see the nearest building across from them.

Yet the only sounds on the boat were his footsteps and the soft drips of their clothes.

"Olivin…" Eira whispered weakly. He didn't hear.

"Eira, you should have told me you were going to invite more friends," Adela said coolly. One hand on her icy cane, the other outstretched, clacking her nails against each other. "I would've prepared better for another guest."

The chill that had crept up her spine hollowed her throat with a soundless scream. Rain diverted over the boat as if dripping off an invisible shield. It streamed in rivulets down over either side, falling into the river.

"I can explain." Eira moved with slightly jerky movements. The muscles in her chest were wound tight, quivering with her breath. Was she being frozen over? Or was it sheer terror that had her fighting shakes throughout her body?

"Perhaps you should." Adela hummed, looking to Olivin. "He certainly isn't going to."

Eira's attention darted to her friend. Olivin was frozen, mid-step. Every instinct told her to run over to him. To check and make sure he was alive. But Eira stayed in her spot, not wanting to give Adela any reason to react in a more aggressive way.

Her head was splitting, trying to calculate every choice, weighing every option.

"He was coming to save me. I told him I didn't need saving," she said honestly. "So he was going to leave."

Adela walked over to Olivin, the tapping of her cane somehow louder than the rain. Every time it crashed into a puddle, flashes of ice crackled across the deck, hissing in the summer heat. She came to a stop before Olivin. Eira couldn't see his face, but she could see Adela's. The lines in her forehead deepened as she studied him, brow furrowing.

"Yet another at your beck and call."

"He's nothing more than a friend." Eira swallowed thickly; the words didn't taste entirely true. "Let him go, please."

"Fine. I don't need another mouth to feed." Adela waved her hand as she stepped to the side. Olivin jerked forward, gasping. His hands went up to his throat. Eira inhaled slowly, exhaling relief. Adela looked down at the elfin man. She wasn't particularly tall—Olivin could loom over her if he wasn't hunched. Yet, Adela stood as strong and ominous as a black flag. She leaned forward slightly to whisper in his ear—loud enough for Eira to hear while making direct eye contact with her. "If you tell anyone I am here, I will find you and I will kill you. I will slaughter everyone you have ever held dear. Do you understand?"

Olivin managed a nod.

"Good. Get off my boat."

He did as he was told, movements fluid enough to reassure Eira that he was once more in control of his body. She knew without doubt he was all right when he paused at the railing, looking back at her. Eira gave a small nod and he swung over, landing on the dock. The rain pounded his shoulders as he slipped into the night.

"Come, Eira," Adela commanded, starting for her cabin. Eira followed in a daze. As soon as she and Adela were inside, the rain began hammering the boat, the barrier dropped. When Eira crossed the threshold of the door, all the moisture was pulled from her skin and clothes, sucked back outside, puddling on the deck.

Eira inspected her suddenly dry cloak. "How much magic can you manage at once?"

"Enough." Adela headed to her usual chair, sitting in it heavily. The pirate queen did a good job of concealing any pain or hardship, but Eira had grown to suspect that her cane wasn't a fashion choice.

"When I have my magic back, will you teach me how to stop rain? How to manage many things at once?"

"What makes you think I have any interest in teaching you my secrets?"

"I already know half of them." Eira shrugged.

"Tell me, are there any more friends of yours I should know about?"

Eira noticed she'd changed the topic, but didn't call attention to it. Adela would share her secrets or not, when the time came. There was little Eira could do to force it now, or then.

"I hope not." Eira sighed, sinking into her usual seat.

"Good, I can only handle so many new mouths to feed at a time." Adela shook her head and flipped through a ledger, exchanging it for another. It was odd to see the pirate queen, the infamous Adela, poring over records while resupplying in port like a regular ship captain would. What little Eira had ever imagined of piracy was nothing but high seas looting and pillaging.

"Are you...*paying* for your supplies?" Eira couldn't stop herself from asking.

Adela glanced over her shoulder with a slight smirk. "You didn't think the pirate queen paid for anything, did you?"

"Well, honestly, no."

Adela closed the ledger and returned it to the shelf. "I'm sure you've well learned by now that we must pick and choose our battles. Is it worth it to me to risk exposure and the headache of fighting and running for a few bags of oranges? Is risking the lives of my crew worth such a meager reward?" She shook her head. "I have long since learned when to take risks and when not to, not just for my own well-being but on behalf of the people who trust me. I'll put their necks on the line when it really counts and they know it."

"You remind me of someone," Eira murmured.

"Let me guess, yourself?"

Eira snorted. "No, the Crown Princess Vi, if you can believe it."

Adela paused mid-step between her desk and her usual chair. It was a brief moment where her eyes went glassy. Eira resisted commenting on the change in demeanor. Adela clearly worked hard to cover it. But something about the mere mention of Crown Princess Vi had given the pirate queen pause.

Ducot had mentioned something about Adela intentionally avoiding Meru, as well as strict orders not to harm anyone or anything. Adela had always avoided elaborating on the decree. Could it have something to do with the crown princess? *No, the timing wouldn't work.* Adela hadn't been seen around Solaris or Meru for nearly twenty-one years. Which would be around the time of Vi Solaris's birth, but Eira doubted a baby was doing anything to threaten the pirate queen.

Perhaps Vi's parents? The birth of their children might have caused Vhalla and Aldrik Solaris to issue a clear threat. But then why also Meru? The treaties weren't in place that early…

Eira was going to make her head hurt with all the speculating. For the time being, she'd file the knowledge and oddity away. Something to test with a mention here or there, or perhaps connect future occurrences with.

"I cannot say I have had the pleasure of meeting Vi Solaris." There was no emotion to Adela's words. "But I imagine it is something that all rulers are familiar with. And I am the queen of the seas."

Right as Adela went to sit, she paused again. This time staying perfectly still. A scowl overcame her face. A low growl was barely audible in the back of her throat. Suddenly, the pirate queen looked like a feral animal, backed into a corner and ready to strike.

"I should have known this could not be done the easy way."

"What is it?" Eira stood as Adela straightened.

"Do you know how to use that?" Adela nodded to the dagger still wedged in Eira's belt.

"Yes. What's happened?"

"If I find out that it was your friend who alerted them to our presence…I will make you watch as I utterly destroy him." Adela took a step toward Eira. The pirate queen took up all the space, all the air in the small cabin.

"Olivin would never betray me," Eira whispered, not knowing if it was true. But it *felt* true…

Even though Adela hadn't answered Eira's question, she was beginning to piece together what was happening based on how on edge the pirate was.

"We shall see." Adela stopped at the door, her hand on the latch. "I will not go out of my way for you, Eira. Keep up or die." Somehow, it didn't sound malicious. It almost sounded like a test.

Eira drew the dagger Ulvarth had given her. The one that she was still determined to drive through his chest. "I'm ready."

"Good." A slight and wild smile crossed Adela's lips. Her eyes spoke of murder. Her movements whispered death. She threw open the door and magic erupted.

· CHAPTER ·

FOURTEEN

EIRA STAGGERED AT the initial explosion of flames. The whole ship was ablaze in an instant. She jumped, nearly bumping into Adela to stand in the cool shelter of the woman's presence. Just as fast as the flames began, they hissed, extinguishing into a thick mist that blanketed the vessel.

Adela cursed under her breath. Eira thought she heard the words "flash beads," but couldn't be sure.

Ice crackled across the deck, underneath fresh tongues of flame, as two mighty magics warred. Men and women leapt onto the vessel. Adela swung her arm. A sheet of frost covered the wood before their feet landed. Three of the four scrambled, falling back as the grips of their shoes lacked purchase. The fourth managed to find his footing but Eira dashed forward, tackling him to the ground. Even though the frost wasn't of her making, and even without her magic, she still understood ice and water as though it were an extension of her. An old friend that was eagerly awaiting her return.

The fourth cracked his head and blinked into the rain. Eira had his body to break her fall and she could recover faster, pushing onto her knees at his side. The man's eyes quickly regained focus as they met Eira's. She could feel his body tense beneath her, almost quivering with a sick excitement.

"It's *you*." The man wore a pin on his breast with three circles interlocked, stacked vertical. However, instead of one line connecting them, as was traditional for the symbol of Yargen, there were three lines—*the symbol of the Pillars*.

These people weren't fellow vagrants. They weren't the law

of the land who had uncovered pirates in their midst. They were Pillars. Even this far from Risen and Warich, the Pillars were here. They were organized.

And they were hunting her.

Eira had stayed her blade when she'd tackled him because she didn't want to kill one of Ofok's leadership or law. She wasn't a pirate; Adela had made that much clear to her. But a Pillar changed everything.

He opened his mouth to speak again. Eira moved faster than he could get a word out, drawing her blade across his throat. The man gurgled blood, hands flying to try and apply pressure. It was already too late, and she moved on to the next.

The woman hardly saw the flash of Eira's silver dagger in the rain. She swiveled and slit the woman's throat without a second thought the moment she saw the Pillars' pin on her breast, too. Blood splattered Eira's cheeks, washed away almost instantly by the thundering rain as she moved on to the third man.

But he had recovered enough to regain his focus. "*Mysst soto larrk!*" Light condensed into a dagger, parrying hers. Magic exploded behind them. "You're lucky he wants you alive," the Pillar snarled.

Him. Ulvarth.

"Yet another one of his many mistakes." Eira disengaged, dodged the wild swing of his blade.

"You'll go to him." The Pillar closed the distance again. Eira danced around the blade, parrying it with her own. "He has your uncle after all."

Her stomach dropped from her body. "Liar," she snarled. The Pillars would say anything to try and get her to go back.

"Is that a risk you'll ta—" He didn't have a chance to finish before Eira shoved her blade straight through his throat. Ulvarth should have killed her when he had the chance. Now she would leave a trail of bodies of his followers as she made her way back to cut off the serpent's head. If he really did have Fritz, or her parents, it would only make his agony that much worse for that much longer.

A flash of light. The ship crunched and exploded, lurching to the starboard side. Eira lunged for the port railing, grabbing on. The vessel stabilized, still at an awkward tilt. When Eira glanced back behind her, the river was a sheet of ice that the ship had been frozen into—the only reason it hadn't completely capsized.

Circles of light surrounded her hands. Eira let go right as the wood and deck exploded. That would've been her fingers if she'd waited another second. She slid down the deck, bracing herself for impact on the hard ice waiting for her below. To her surprise, the ice curved, making a chute for Eira to slide down and land easily on her feet.

Adela stood amid the pile of bodies that had slid off the deck and onto the ice. Their blood was striking against the sheet of white. "You're not as worthless as I thought."

"Just wait until I get my magic back."

Adela's other boat was a commotion as well. The deck was crowded with eleven people, all bustling about crates and sacks that hadn't been there mere hours ago. Eira recognized each of the faces—from the pirates, to her friends. Guilt tried to choke her, but selfish relief got to her first. They hadn't left her after all; and the Pillars hadn't managed to corner them in the streets.

"Don't delay now." Adela was already halfway to the other boat, running up a bridge of ice.

Eira raced behind. As soon as she was on the bridge, the ice holding the broken boat they'd just been on turned into water. The remnants of the vessel plunged back into the harbor, sending a wave across the docks, soaking the Pillars that remained. It then tipped back. The sounds of cracking wood and the cries of people filled the air. It was too quickly replaced by the calls of more Lightspinning.

"*Juth—*"

"*Mysst soto larrk!*" a male voice cut off the first speaker. Eira paused, two thirds of the way across the bridge. Her heart sank as the familiar sound drew her attention.

"*Mysst xieh!*" a young man shouted as he stepped in front of an attacking Pillar, holding up a shield of light with his fingertips alone.

Olivin and Yonlin. The two brothers had engaged the Pillars on the docks. Olivin was no doubt still nearby when he had heard the commotion. She couldn't imagine any world where he *wouldn't* run back. "Somewhere safe" for Yonlin must've been just out of sight, ready to support his brother.

"Eira!" Noelle shouted from the deck. Adela was just crossing the threshold of the vessel. She reached into her coat and handed a small key to Pine, who subsequently began going to each of the Solaris and Qwint competitors and unlocking their shackles.

"Get over here!" Cullen called as Pine was fumbling with the shackle on his wrist.

"It's Olivin," she shouted back. Cullen's eyes darted from her to the docks behind them and back. "If we leave him, they *will* kill him."

Perhaps it was Olivin the Pillars had been following the entire time—because of his sister, Wynry, he was equally a personal target. Wynry no doubt wanted to end their family line and finish the job she'd started years ago. Or they had picked up Eira's trail in Warich and had been hunting her. *We have your uncle.* The words haunted her. Real, or not? Either way, they wouldn't stop and this was their best opportunity to tie up a loose end with the other.

Cullen's expression was one of pure torture. Eira remembered the night neither of them could sleep during the tournament. *I can't stand seeing you with him,* he'd said. Wounds were still there. Tensions. Questions. But things had changed. They had all changed. This was more than complicated feelings; it was life and death.

"If we don't help them, their blood is on our hands. The Pillars want them dead as much as us." With those simple words, Eira brought Cullen back to the reality of the situation. She'd never felt more helpless. If she had her magic, she could go over there. She could make it.

Cullen ran to the opposite side of the deck. She didn't know if he was trying to get help, find a way over, or if he had abandoned her plea. If she'd asked for the one thing he wouldn't give.

Eira turned back to the docks where Olivin and Yonlin were fighting. She thrust out her hand, willing her magic to come. *Heed me*, Eira commanded.

It didn't.

She repeated the motion. With a shout and all her might, she searched the depths of her very being for power she knew was there. Still nothing. Shoulder aching, fingers straining from the tension of the movement, Eira resolved to make the attempt one more time. If not now, when her friends needed her, when? Taking a deep breath and gathering her focus, Eira threw out her hand.

And the ice moved.

The bridge shifted and stretched, connecting to the other dock. Eira stared at her palm. *Had she… No*. The bridge wasn't shaped like she'd been intending. There wasn't the same pull of power she was accustomed to when she used her magic.

A hand made of ice clasped her shoulder. "You are a hassle, girl, and a breathtaking trial of my patience."

"Adela?" Eira's voice had gone soft with shock at the pirate queen's presence, little more than a whisper.

"Well, then, let's get your friends. They seem useful enough to be worth the trouble of saving them. I can always use more powerful sorcerers in my debt." Adela looked over her shoulder and shouted to the crew, "Cast off! We'll rejoin you at the gate."

"Understood!" Crow shouted back.

"Eira." Cullen leaned halfway over the railing. "Please be careful…and good luck."

The words were like a beam of sunlight striking through the night. His worried expression tempered with confidence. The grim line of determination his mouth was set into. There was no guilt, or grief. No pained twisting of his lips. He wished her well. He supported her—even when it meant her running back to Olivin.

"I will be." She nodded, trying to exude more confidence than she felt. "You do the same, all right? Keep everyone safe until I get back."

"I'll do my best."

Eira didn't dare waste any more time. Adela was already halfway to the opposite side of the river. The pirate queen was truly a sight to behold. It looked almost as if she were flying. Her leg and arm of ice merged with the bridge, propelling her across.

The second I get my power back, I am learning how to do that, Eira vowed, and she began to run behind.

Adela made it to the opposite docks before she did, landing with an explosion of ice. The Pillars were ready, having seen them coming. But their Lightspinning shields did little against icicles that moved like sentient spears. Eira maneuvered around Adela, finishing off two who had managed to deflect the brunt of her attack.

Olivin and Yonlin stood in the center of a V of ice. Completely unharmed.

"Eira, what…" Olivin was at a loss for words.

"*This* is the friend you wanted to save?" Yonlin's attention darted from Eira, to Adela, to Olivin, and back. "The one from Solaris who was involved with the *pirate queen*?" He slapped his brother's shoulder. "Dummy. In what world would she need your help when she has *that*?" He motioned to Adela, who was making quick work of the Pillars without even taking a step.

Eira bit back a laugh.

"I am inclined to agree." Adela outstretched her hand, summoning her cane. Eira didn't miss how she had been swaying slightly before its use. Adela always seemed so strong and capable. Like she could conquer the world. But she was also at least eighty-five years old. Even if what Ferro had told Eira long ago was true—that Adela had elfin blood in her—that was still past middle-aged for most long-lived elfin and elderly for any human.

"You two need to leave," Eira said firmly.

"We came to save you," Olivin protested.

"Oh yes, saving *them*. We're doing a great job of it." Yonlin nodded sagely. Eira was surprised to find Yonlin had a marvelous sense of humor. Though, it was hard to be jovial when on the brink of death, and she hadn't seen him since his recovery. "I think they just saved us."

"Just, go." Eira turned to Adela. The other boat was already beginning to get speed in the harbor, no doubt thanks to some Cullen-supplied wind. "We have to get back to our boat."

"No. We're on foot and these two are coming with us." Adela started down the docks.

"I'm sorry?" Despite his objecting tone, Olivin did as he was told, following behind Adela with Eira.

"I'm the infamous pirate queen, not a charity." Adela glanced over her shoulder at the three of them and a scowl twisted her lips. She muttered under her breath, "Nor a bodyguard…"

Rather than be offended, Eira found amusement at the comment. The whole situation was surreal. Pillars were hunting them down. The only other boat they had was leaving without them. Olivin and Yonlin weren't supposed to be here at all. And the pirate queen, miraculously, was the one keeping them alive. Genuinely helping as she was able.

"What do you want from us?" Olivin stayed one step ahead of his younger brother, as if trying to keep himself between Yonlin and Adela.

"You are young and capable. I'm going to need your help with Ofok gate."

"Ofok gate?" Eira repeated.

Adela reached the top of a stairway and pointed. They stood high among the buildings of the tiered city of Ofok. Eira followed the river with her eyes. It was the largest gap between structures in the marshy city—a ribbon of golden haze from all the lamplights and storefronts that lined it. Where the river joined the sea was a massive gatehouse, nestled into a thick sea wall, that arched over the river's mouth.

The arch was the only structure made in stone. It loomed over the river with a raised portcullis that resembled jagged teeth.

"Look at my monument." Adela was full of bitter pride. "They honestly thought such a thing could keep *me* out." She scoffed.

Eira passed up the opportunity to further inflate the pirate's ego, instead asking, "What do you need us to do about the gate?"

"Open it," she said casually.

"It's already open," Yonlin pointed out.

"Your powers of observation are truly astounding." Adela began to walk again. "Best not to delay." She held up three fingers, not looking back. "Three."

"Delay what?" Eira exchanged a confused glance with Olivin.

"Two." Adela lowered a finger.

"Adela—"

"One." As Adela's hand lowered, so, too, did the gate. It came crashing down with a thunderous splash that seemed to rattle the whole city. Adela glanced over her shoulder. "You three had better hurry. If the boat makes it to that gate before you do, then everyone on it is going to be stuck in the river—easy pickings for the Pillars and guards."

FIFTEEN

THE SCENE OF what was to come played out in Eira's mind in conjunction with everything that was unfolding in the city around her.

The ship her friends were on was swiftly moving down the river, toward the closed gate. If the gate wasn't opened, they'd be forced to make a hard stop right underneath that towering archway where guards and Pillars could rain destruction down on Eira's friends. There weren't any docking points positioned that close to the gate—just high walls. Docking would be just as risky. And the ship wasn't letting up any speed. There was nothing but faith that Adela would see to it that they had a way out.

There were no other options.

Olivin and Yonlin rushed around her. They exchanged words between each other, plotting their tactics and approach. But it was just noise. She stared up at the pirate queen, glaring.

"You don't care about anyone but yourself, do you?" Eira looked Adela dead in the eyes. "You didn't have any intentions of keeping my friends safe. You were just holding on to them because Cullen could make the boat launch from a dead stop. Because Noelle is a good combatant and Alyss can repair the vessel." Eira thrust her hand in the direction Olivin and Yonlin had sped off in. "You didn't care about helping me save them; you wanted to separate me from my friends because you *knew* that if I was with you, if they saw me trusting you, then they would help your crew without question."

A slow, evil smile worked its way across Adela's lips. It split her face, the expression allowing the woman's true nature to shine in the lamplight as the rain soaked them both.

"Loyalty is a heavy burden, Eira."

A chill stole her breath, one that had nothing to do with magic. Eira's whole body was numb.

"I've been a tool for you, haven't I?" she whispered. "This whole time, I was a tool to help you figure out magic. A tool to hold my friends as leverage so we could do your dirty work for you…that way your hands could stay clean here on Meru. You're not the one attacking the gate, we are. You're not the one who's commanding a swift departure from the Pillars, I am."

"Very astute, Eira." Adela tilted her head slightly to the side. "Now what will you do with this information? Choose quickly. Your friends' lives are in the balance."

Eira had no doubt now that there was some kind of signal Adela could send that would cause her crew to kill her friends where they stood. They'd never suspect it. Perhaps Ducot was in on it…perhaps not. Either way, they were outnumbered.

"Fine." Eira took a step closer to the woman. Anger was lubricating her joints; hot rage fought against the cold horror that had tried to consume her. "But once we are in the ocean, no more stalling. You return my magic to me."

"We'll see."

"Swear to me."

"And what is my word worth?" Adela held out her hands with a shrug. "Trust me or don't. Help your friends or don't. It matters little to me. I know I'm not dying tonight."

Eira wanted to scream. She had known from the start that tangling with Adela was a dangerous game. But they hadn't had any other choice. The draw of the mystery of her parentage aside, there was her magic. And even if Eira could let that all that go… even if she could consign herself to being a Commons for the rest of her days…it was safer with Adela than out in Meru for them. The Pillars had already tracked them this far. If they'd been on foot, they probably would've already been dead.

"You might be wicked, but you're at least a wickedness I know," Eira said more to herself than Adela. She turned. But before Eira could sprint after Olivin and Yonlin—already lost to the night and the pounding rain—a frosty hand encircled her wrist. She twisted, meeting Adela's cruel, familiar eyes.

"I will see your magic returned," Adela vowed.

"More empty lies," Eira shot back, even though the words echoed with unexpected sincerity.

"No." Adela slowly shook her head. "You possess a gift, girl. A might that could make the world tremble if you learned how to wield it. It would be a shame to see talent like that go to waste. I will teach you, or kill you, that I swear."

Eira's heart pounded louder than the rain. Louder than the rising shouts and screams coming from the river and from the direction Olivin and Yonlin had run off in. Everything seemed still, suspended.

"*I swear it,*" Adela emphasized. "On all my treasure, I will return your magic."

"Swear it on the lives of your crew," Eira whispered. That was Adela's real treasure. They were the ones who did her deeds and guarded her name and wealth.

Loyalty has a cost, Adela.

The pirate queen's lips parted slightly and every carefully curated mask fell away. The tension slipped from the muscles of her face.

She smiled, and this time it was not sinister. This time there was almost a proud glint to her eyes. "You learn fast."

"When I must…" Eira swallowed thickly. "When I have a good teacher."

"I swear it on my treasure and my crew, Eira Landan. I will do everything in my power to return yours."

That was all Eira needed. She stepped away and Adela let her go. Eira shared one last look with the pirate queen. One stare to encompass the words: *Don't you dare betray me.* But the feeling seemed to be mutual.

Eira turned, and began to run.

Rather than taking the docks, she leaped from the high vantage onto a nearby roof. The docks were certain to be crowded, thickening further with people, as the commotion grew along the river and in the streets. The tightly packed rooftops, however, were completely vacant.

The thatching and wooden shingles had gone soft with the rain and Eira wobbled as she landed. With a pinwheel of her arms, she was able to find her footing again and she was a blur in the night.

Weeks of training, days of fierce competition, constantly looking over her shoulder, had all paid off. With every forceful landing of her feet against the rooftops, she felt nearly unstoppable, even without her magic. Jumping from roofs to balconies was almost effortless.

Confused diners shouted as she sprinted around their tables across a second-story balcony. She'd caught up with Olivin and Yonlin. They were in the thick of the market, slow to progress, as she'd expected.

"Olivin!" Eira shouted. His attention swung up to her, a flash of confusion and then a soft *ah* of comprehension. Eira pointed at a second-level doorway. "There!"

Further communication wasn't necessary. Olivin grabbed Yonlin by the hand and abruptly changed their course. He pushed his way through the crowd as Eira jumped from the balcony she was on and grabbed the nearby roof. With a swing of her legs, she was able to get a knee up and scramble on. By the time she made it to the gutter above the doorway, Olivin and Yonlin were there.

Eira stretched a hand down and Olivin swung up first. They both reached back and practically pulled Yonlin up with upper-body strength alone. Wasting no time, Eira began running again, the two men behind her.

They'd managed to catch up to the boat. An explosion of fire burst from its starboard side. Eira wanted to stop, to get a closer look at the combat unfolding. But she didn't dare slow her pace. The Pillars had no doubt engaged them. That, or the law of Ofok had taken stock of the commotion and were getting involved as well.

Or both.

Either way, her friends could take care of themselves. But what they couldn't do was open the gate looming ahead of them. A task Eira was left to figure out on her own.

"Plans?" she panted.

"Yargen if I know!" Olivin's dark hair was slicked against his face. He brushed it back, trying to get it out of his eyes to little avail. "Get in there, by force if we must, and make them lift the portcullis again." He glanced at her from the corners of his eyes. "Are you going to be all right doing this? Without your—"

"I'll be fine," she insisted before he could finish. Yes, her magic was gone, but she wasn't worthless. Eira continued before he could misplace his concern again, "Could you just shatter the iron with magic?" She had been feeling strong, until she tried to talk while keeping her pace. But Eira didn't let up.

"It won't work. Look—there—the joints. The arch." Olivin wasn't able to be very descriptive while running, but he didn't have to be. This close to the gate, she could see what he was pointing out.

"Runes." Yonlin could only manage the single word.

Eira remembered the runes in the coliseum—what was supposed to help strengthen, but in actuality helped bring the whole thing down. She doubted the same weakness was perpetuated here.

"Breaking through those will require an incredible burst of magic… You wouldn't happen to have any flash beads on you?" Olivin asked.

"Why, of course, I just keep a handful in my back pocket." Eira gave him a look to convey how ridiculous she found the question.

"The sarcasm is not helpful." Olivin jumped and extended a hand back for her. Eira wasn't too proud to accept the help. Their fingers closed around each other and he pulled her to him. The sensation of their bodies flush was emphasized by heaving chests and the sizzle of cool rain on hot skin. In a second, she was back against the wall in Champion Village. His mouth on hers…

Before the moment could linger, they split apart and both reached for Yonlin.

"The winch to lift it should be up there." Yonlin pointed to the top of the arch as he got his footing. They carried on. "Think of it like a spindle and thread, two chains attached to the iron grate. If we can get to it, we could alternate *kot sorre* to push the wheels that will make it rise. We'll also need to disable the quick release."

"I can do that." She couldn't help them with their magic, but she could at the least figure out how to disable the quick release… whatever *that* meant. "You seem knowledgeable about this."

"Weapons always fascinated me." Yonlin's breathing was becoming heavier. Luckily they were almost at their destination. "Any tools of war."

"Much to my personal dismay," Olivin muttered. "You make it hard enough to keep you safe."

"The shadow and the war expert, what a pair both of you are." Eira grinned at Olivin, who returned the expression. Though his fell some when he glanced back to Yonlin.

"You find odd hobbies with a background like ours." He seemed to very much wish that wasn't the case for his brother.

"Don't I know it?" Eira agreed under her breath.

"If only he'd let me help him more." Yonlin gave Olivin a glare.

"I never wanted you to be at risk," Olivin said.

"Good thing I'm going to be perpetually at risk from here on. The hero-ing isn't just up to you anymore." Yonlin didn't sound upset in the slightest.

Eira could feel Olivin's discomfort radiating off him at the idea. She could see it in the conflict on his face. He knew Yonlin was no longer a boy, but he would always see his younger brother as the child he once was.

Just like, no matter how much she grew or how capable she became, Marcus had always seen her as his younger sister. Someone to protect and take care of. Nothing in the world would change that, not even his better sense.

She wanted to reach out to Olivin and grasp his hand, letting him know that they would keep Yonlin safe, together. But there wasn't an opportunity. Yet, as they jumped again from building to building, his eyes met hers.

Time seemed to slow again in the way that only he could cause. He gave a small nod. She returned it. There was an unspoken understanding between them. Yonlin would be kept safe. No matter what happened, they would both look after him.

FORTUNATELY FOR THEM, it seemed like the guards weren't paying close attention to the trio running along the rooftops, instead focusing on the boat still drifting down the river. That meant they had the element of surprise at best. Or, at worst, a few extra moments.

"There's a door down there." Eira pointed to a door at the base of the archway that was guarded by a man and a woman.

"We'll be met with resistance on the inside route." Olivin took a step closer to her, holding out his hands. "There's a faster way, if I may?"

"Go ahead." Eira didn't even have to think about it; the only thing that mattered was moving as quickly as possible. She wasn't sure what he had been planning on doing, but she certainly hadn't been expecting him to sweep her off her feet.

Olivin leaned forward, wrapped an arm around her back and reached down behind her knees. Despite her surprise, instinct to stabilize herself kicked in. Eira wrapped her arms around his shoulders, holding on tightly as he straightened. The odd feeling of weightlessness settled into her lower stomach as he lifted her, adjusting slightly, settling her weight in his arms.

"I'm capable of walking, you know," she murmured. A crack of distant lighting lit up his profile in sharp outlines that quickly faded into the night. She shifted her grip. It somehow resulted in her being pressed even more tightly against him…not that it should have been possible.

"Not like this." Olivin shook his head and looked up at the

archway with fierce determination. He began running to the edge of the rooftop.

"Olivin?" Eira's voice grew somewhat shrill with panic. "What—"

As he jumped, he said, "*Mysst xieh.*"

Light spun from underneath his toes, forming a circular disk. *Mysst xieh—shield.* Eira had always known it for use in combat. But Olivin used it like a stepping stone, sinking into his right leg before lunging forward.

"*Mysst xieh!*" Another circle of light appeared, this time under his left foot. Olivin sank low again and then bounced upward.

Circle of light by circle of light, they made their way upward. Yonlin was behind them, doing the same. Eira was vaguely reminded of how Cullen could step on pockets of air to rise upward. But she had never joined him while he was performing the act.

She had moments of weightlessness combined with seconds where her stomach was in her throat before Olivin landed on solid magic once more and repeated the process. Again, and again, they rose.

Until a beam of light *whizzed* by Olivin's head. He swayed, falling to the side.

"Olivin!" Eira shouted. She was helpless to be of assistance. If she'd had her magic, she could summon a ledge of ice for them to land on. But all she could do was cling to him as they fell through the open air.

"*Mysst xieh!*" he shouted, almost deafeningly loud in her ear. A circle of light spun out beneath him.

Almost at the same time, Yonlin said, "*Mysst soto gotha.*"

Bow, Eira's mind filled in at the exact same time as the weapon condensed from strands of magic into Yonlin's hands. He drew back, and fired down at the people who had been shooting up at them.

"Get her up," Yonlin shouted between shots.

"Yonlin—"

"Go, Olivin!"

"I'll return fire when I'm up," Olivin called back, already working his magic to get them to a window at the top of the archway.

Eira's stomach had dropped out from her body since the fall. She continued to cling to him with all her might. "I'm sorry, Olivin," she whispered.

"Yonlin knows the risks, as do I." He seemed to shift his grip to hold her even tighter. Eira could see him swallow hard. "We're better off helping you, no matter the cost."

"I wanted to keep you safe." She'd wanted to keep all her friends safe, and only seemed successful at endangering them more.

"And I wanted to stay by you."

Loyalty has a cost. Eira pressed her eyes closed and drew a shuddering breath. She would pay any cost...but she wasn't ready for what it might cost to those around her. The people she cared about.

The people she loved.

As soon as Olivin landed by the window, Eira smashed it in with the butt of her dagger. He wasted no time and they tumbled in through the confetti of glass—enduring superficial cuts and scrapes along the way.

"Lumeria's murderers!" a man shouted, lunging for them.

Eira recovered faster than Olivin. She tumbled and jumped up, ignoring the pain in her arms and legs from embedded glass as she dodged the man's sword. Eira swung and dug her dagger into his chest.

Clumsy.

He half wheezed, half snarled, rearing back to attack her again with his sword.

"*Mysst soto tonc.*" Light flashed. A spear wielded by Olivin pierced the knight's shoulder, cutting through the soft spot between plates of armor. He dropped his sword and it unraveled into strands of light that faded away.

Eira freed her blade and jabbed it into the man's neck, ending it there. She panted, turning to Olivin. But he was back at the window already, returning fire so Yonlin could join them.

"I'm going ahead," she announced.

"Eira, wait!"

She didn't hesitate. Eira wouldn't allow the fact that she had no magic to hold her back, or be a burden to the people counting on her. Another gate guard in leather armor engaged her. He clearly hadn't had much practical application to his training as she managed to disarm and mortally wound him in a few blows.

But he didn't have a signet of a Pillar, so Eira left him to bleed. Perhaps he would die…or maybe he could hang on for help to arrive. Eira knew that it didn't make her any less guilty of attacking an innocent man. But hopefully he kept his life. Her qualm wasn't with the people of Meru, just the Pillars.

Bursting through a door at the top of an ascending hallway, Eira was faced with a mechanical room—blessedly void of any other knights. Panting, she took quick stock of the elements of the portcullis. As Yonlin had said, there was a spindle connected to two chains on the right. On the left was a lever connected to weights by more chains that was already engaged. *That must be the quick release.* Eira was still figuring out how it worked when Olivin and Yonlin arrived.

"You take that side." Yonlin pointed to the side closest to the door they'd entered in on. "We pull in three…two…one. *Kot sidee.*"

The two men worked in unison, standing before the massive spoked wheels that were on the ends of the spindle above the portcullis. The chains and spindle were so large it would take two or three grown adults, per side, to move the gate. As Yonlin and Olivin spoke, glyphs appeared on the opposite side of the wheels. The magic crashed into the spokes as it was sucked in toward their palms, pulling the wheels in the process. As soon as the magic met their hands, it vanished completely.

They repeated again. *"Kot sidee."*

As the gears turned, the gate slowly began to lift; hefty chain collected around the spindle. In tandem, the weighted mechanism connected to the lever she'd been inspecting began to move as well. With every turn of the gears behind her, there was a clicking of the winch behind the lever. As soon as the gate was up, she would find a way to disable it.

But in the meantime, Eira focused on the doors on the left and right sides of the room. There were heavy bars to the right of each of them that slotted into hooks on either side of the metal doors. The builders had planned for a potential attack and wanted this room to be easily guarded.

No sooner had she managed to get the bars in place than the doors began to rattle. A moment of silence. And then the whole door shuddered.

"We have to move." Eira turned back to them. The churning of gears and clanking of chain had slowed. Yonlin was breathless.

Sweat dripped off Olivin's nose. "We're going as fast as we can."

Eira stepped in for Yonlin, grabbing the wheel. "Take a break."

"It's too heavy."

"I can get a turn or two." She looked to Olivin. "On three."

Eira managed three turns of the wheel. Blood poured from around the shards of glass in her arms. Muscles threatened to give out. Her palms almost instantly became raw from how tightly she clutched the spokes. Gritting her teeth, she stayed focused, pulling as hard as she could while ignoring the pain. The screams and shouts outside were barely audible from within the stone room. But, in her mind's eye, she could see the boat making its way to the portcullis by the flashes of magic that sparked around it.

"We're almost there," Olivin encouraged. "A little bit more and the ship should be able to fit under."

"I'm going to disable the quick drop!" Eira crossed to the other side of the room, leaving Yonlin to finish the job. The stone around the doors was beginning to crack. The guards, or Pillars, were going to burst through soon.

Eira knelt by the lever and sucked in a breath, holding it. Her nerves were on fire. Hands trembling. If she got this wrong, the gate would fall immediately. The boat would be locked in. Or, worse, the portcullis would fall on the boat itself. Visions of it being cleaved in two, her friends on it, flashed through Eira's mind. She pressed her eyes closed and banished the notion, exhaling and forcing the wound-up tension in her muscles to abate. She had to think clearly.

There was a connection point between the lever and the locking mechanism that clicked with every turn of the wheels on the opposite side of the room. If she disconnected it here, then the lever would no longer undo the lock. Eira dug the side of her dagger into a pin holding a gear in place. She pulled. The gear popped off.

Nothing happened.

A small laugh of relief escaped her. The locking mechanism still clicked into place. But the lever was limp and useless.

"I think that's enough." The portcullis was two thirds up. But the doors on either side of the room were going to give in. With both men's attention on her, Eira pointed to the left of the lever—the one that overlooked the sea and a horizon that meant freedom. "Smash this wall."

"What? Why?" Even though Olivin was confused, he still crossed over anyway, readying his stance.

"How else will we get out of here?" Eira motioned to the doors and Olivin's expression flashed from exhaustion to panic, as if seeing the full extent of their current situation for the first time.

"After everything…I don't know if I have the power to walk us down like we got up here."

"Then we jump. It's a shipping channel, the water should be deep." Eira knew how quickly the drop-off was in Oparium by the docks so the large ships could get into the wharf. It was regularly dredged by Groundbreakers and Waterrunners to avoid ships running aground.

"From this high?" Yonlin looked warily out the window.

"Do either of you have a better idea?"

Olivin shook his head and his expression hardened into grim determination. "*Juth calt.*"

Yonlin joined him. "*Juth calt.*"

It was a race to see which stone wall would give first—the walls around the doors, or the one by the window. Which magic was stronger? She ran back to the opposite side as they worked, peering through the bars and out the window. The boat was just about at the arch.

They could walk, or jump down, and then Adela would scoop them from the water... *It would work.* It had to. A sharp crack and burst of sound accompanied the stone crumbling next to the window. Olivin and Yonlin had broken through.

"Let's go." Eira wasted no time wrapping her arms around Olivin's neck.

"You are *such* a demanding creature," he mumbled as he picked her up. She could feel his muscles tremble under her weight, but he steadied himself the moment she was enveloped in his embrace. Somehow, despite how exhausted they both were, Eira felt safe in his arms.

"You'd be much better off without me," she agreed, her words almost vanishing underneath the howling wind and rain.

"I never said that." His stormy eyes glanced her way. Time halted briefly, hanging on an inhale. *Kiss him; you're probably about to die, might as well.* The thought streaked through her mind, but he spoke before she could act on it. "Ready?"

"As I'll ever be."

"Let's go, Yonlin." Olivin jumped out into the air. "*Mysst xieh!*" He landed hard on a glowing disk. It wobbled underneath him.

Eira clutched tighter as Olivin regained his balance, not

wanting her weight to tip him more to one side or another. "We're almost there," she offered optimistically.

"I'm not sure—"

"Drop me, if we're going to fall."

"Eira…"

She met his eyes. "If we fall, go feet first. Drop me and make yourself as straight as possible." She'd learned a few things on the docks of Oparium.

He nodded and stepped off the glyph. "*Mysst xieh.*"

Yonlin was right over his shoulder. The ship was crossing under the portcullis. Noelle, Lavette, and Varren were at the stern of the vessel, returning bursts of magic with their own alongside half the crew. Cullen manned the sails. Alyss and Ducot managed to keep the ship patched as quickly as it was damaged. Adela was at the front of the vessel, stoic and poised, eyes turned to the safety of the sea beyond.

They were going to make it. It was going to work.

Everything seemed to slow as Eira met Adela's determined gaze. A slight smile crossed the pirate queen's lips. *Good job,* it seemed to say. Joy swelled in Eira's chest nearly to the point of bursting. For the first time in her life, it felt like she'd made someone proud—someone she looked to almost as a child would a parent.

It all happened so quickly. In a blink, there was an explosion high above.

Adela's attention jerked upward. Fractures spread across the archway like lightning bolts. The guards must've broken through the door with an explosion of their own…but they didn't know the building had already been weakened by Olivin and Yonlin smashing down the wall so the three of them could escape.

The archway crumbled. Light flashed. Chains snapped.

Eira inhaled sharply as the portcullis came rattling down. Olivin looked over his shoulder on instinct. His focus wavered and that was all it took for his magic to falter.

Eira, and everything else, tumbled down with deadly speed into the cold sea.

TIME FELT LIKE it slowed. Everything happened all at once.

A wave of ice rushed out from the boat on both sides. It crashed against the base of the archway, racing up like a pack of wolves on the hunt. The ice encompassed the falling stone and portcullis—freezing the latter in place, halting any drop. It packed so thickly that the top of the ship's rigging scraped against it as the boat continued to drift under.

But the vessel lost speed at the same time as Eira's descent slowed. An updraft rushed underneath her. She flipped in the air, arms flailing, as though she could somehow swim on the currents. The wind adjusted itself, trying to catch her—to pad her fall.

Cullen.

His magic shivered across her skin. It was a phantom feeling—the return of a familiar friend that she once knew well. All those afternoons working together. All those times it had tangled with her fingertips…

Eira twisted, putting her feet down and crossing her arms over her chest. He'd slowed her enough that she could get control of her fall. Eira was like an arrow breaking the surface of the water, plunging deep into the cold depths from the momentum. The chill tried to steal the air from her lungs. Eira clamped her jaw closed so she didn't let out a gasp.

As soon as she slowed, she began pumping her legs and pulling herself upward. Even without her magic, she was a strong swimmer. Being in the water—in the sea—was a natural state. It was as if her magic whispered from the recesses of her consciousness like a long-forgotten memory. A calling that beckoned like the pull of the tides.

The sensation was so strong that it gave her pause. Eira lingered, suspended in the chilling waters. She allowed the currents to envelop her, the cold to hold her. Magic flashed. The boat churned frothy waves. Rain thundered. And the sea stretched endlessly around her, encompassing every nightmarish memory of Marcus's death…and every hope she'd ever held.

Her power was her savior, but also her demise. It could do whatever she needed but never everything she wanted. And it was so close that she could almost—Eira stretched out a hand, reaching toward nothing but blind hope—*touch it.*

Out of nowhere, a rope whipped through the water as though it were alive. It wrapped itself around her waist and chest. She was pulled upward, her focus shattered. Eira let out an involuntary cry of frustration as she was plucked from under the surface and pulled onto the boat by the sentient rope. Eira coughed and sputtered, gasping for air.

The deck was utter chaos.

"We have to move!"

"Trying to!"

"They have a hook on us!"

"Get it off!"

"Wind to the sails!"

It was impossible to tell who was saying what. Eira propped herself up, looking to thank Alyss for the help. But her friend had already run off to the front of the vessel. Across from her was Yonlin, kneeling beside Olivin as Crow attempted to resuscitate the elfin man. Others were wounded and bleeding. The battle had more than taken its toll and, for the first time, Eira conceded with panic that they might not *all* make it out alive.

But amid all the chaos was a lone, calm, stoic figure. Adela stood with arms hoisted high, trembling, as though she were physically bearing the weight of the entire portcullis and shattered archway above them. Eira could almost sense the immense power radiating off her. The notion was certainly a fabrication of her mind—she knew Adela was exuding a lot of magic so she was telling herself that she could feel it.

Eira found her feet. The calls and shouts were a blur as she crossed to the pirate queen. This close, Eira could see every line of strain knitted between her brows as she focused.

"I'm a bit busy," Adela forced through clenched teeth. Wordlessly, Eira rested a hand on Adela's shoulder, standing just off to her side. "Girl—"

"Focus on your magic." Eira closed her eyes. Was it merely a fabrication of her tired mind, or could she really feel Adela's power? It was so much like her own...surely...

Wind dried the seawater on her face as Cullen forced another gust into the creaking rigging. Its sensation was slightly different. A new pull. The same shiver as when she had been falling. She knew him and his magic better than any other.

Currents were brewing within her. Churning. Calling.

Usually, to restore a sorcerer's magic, a Waterrunner would use a vessel of stored magic to guide the power back to their channel, reopening the flow. That was what Adela had been trying to do. She had been attempting to use herself as the vessel and the Waterrunner, guiding her magic into Eira, trying to pull her channel open.

But perhaps it needed to be a push. Eira needed to reach out to the power. She needed to be the Waterrunner and guide. She needed to know what to reach for.

"Cullen, do it again," Eira commanded. His eyes turned to her, confused and questioning. "The push of air."

He did it without asking for why.

Eira inhaled deeply as a gust of wind buffeted her face. *That was what magic felt like. Hold it, reach for it.*

The ship began to move once more. There were more shouts. Then, a burst of light.

Adela staggered back just as Eira's palm met her. Eira's eyes snapped open in time to see the fading glow of a light-spun arrow and a burst of blood. The pirate queen fell to a knee, her flesh-and-bone leg giving out. A grunt of pain escaped her clenched jaw, nearly drowned out by the cracking of ice above.

"Adela!" Crow shouted from across the deck.

"Get us out of here!" Adela snapped, pain marring her voice and arms continuing to tremble.

Eira was on her knees, pressing her hands into either side of Adela's upper stomach, where the arrow had pierced straight through. "We're almost free." But as soon as Eira said as much, the ship lurched, almost keeling over.

"Bastards!" Ducot shouted. He and Alyss were running.

Eira looked ahead.

They were so close. The sea was right there… But with hooks in the hull and magic on the sails, the Pillars tried to keep calling them back. A sheet of ice spread across the water, encompassing the boat. Adela dropped her icy hand and fused it with the vessel. The frost trying to claim them cracked.

"Girl." Adela swayed slightly. "There's something I need to ask of you."

"Ask me when we're out of here."

"There's a score on Carsovia I want you to settle for me… find…Salveus…"

"Find him yourself." Eira pushed harder on Adela's wounds. For as legendary as the pirate queen was, as mysterious her providence, Adela was still just a woman. A mortal woman of flesh and bone. Of blood that could be lost. "We're making it out of here, together."

Closing her eyes, fingers slick and warm with Adela's blood, Eira reached out with her mind. The power was there. If not her own, then Adela's. She just had to find it—to connect with it.

"Eira." Cullen's soft voice was at her side. "What do you need?"

She met his eyes, holding them, searching, silently begging for everything she didn't think he could give. "Open your channel to me," Eira whispered. "Like you did then."

With a solemn nod, Cullen let his eyes flutter closed. The sails filled with wind. The boat strained against all that was holding it back. Eira leaned into him, as if, by touching him, she could find the channel she'd hunted for during the weeks of the competition. Her fingers were hot with blood. Frost chilled the air around them.

Eira reached out…and held her breath. Like a bolt of lightning on a nighttime sea, a surge shot through her.

Open. Eira willed it for Adela. If not for herself, then to allow the pirate queen to access the unfathomable depths of her power.

Adela straightened slightly. The trembling in her body lessened. Ice coated her wounds, fusing with Eira's fingers.

A mighty shattering had Eira's eyes snapping open. But it wasn't from the ice overhead. That was as thick as ever. Instead, the ice that had been trying to hold back the boat exploded under an up-churning of currents. It splintered, fragmenting into thousands of pieces that fell like snow.

"Eira." Adela had never said her name with such warmth. "Help me guide us out of here. The *Stormfrost* is not far."

Freeing her left hand from Adela's front, Eira slowly lifted her palm. The rain slowed around her fingertips, hovering midair. Currents churned within her, breaking up the internal ice that had held her in stasis. Power tingled from the middle of her chest, radiating outward. It danced like the snow with the rain.

She could feel every drop of water. Every lap of the sea against the hull of the boat. The world was hers once more and she welcomed it with open arms.

The boat lurched forward and half the deck staggered; some of the crew fell to their knees. They began to speed ahead only to be pulled back with a sudden jerk. Through the changes in the rain, Eira could feel the last hook pulled taut on their stern.

"Go," Adela encouraged. "I'll be fine."

Eira didn't object or fight. She pulled her hand from Adela's and eased away from Cullen to run over to Noelle, helping her friend up. Noelle's right side was coated in small cuts and shrapnel. Whatever battle they had endured while Eira was working on the portcullis was severe indeed.

But there was no time to waste. "I need you."

"Good to see you," Noelle said sincerely.

Eira smiled and nodded, heading toward the back of the boat. Noelle's injuries either weren't that severe, or she was doing an incredible job of working through the pain. Unfortunately, Eira's gut leaned toward the latter.

None of them were escaping this without scars.

They reached the back of the boat in time to see the Pillars and guards readying another hook and chain. While Eira had been getting Noelle, she'd turned the rain hammering the chain holding them into a thick layer of ice.

"As soon as I shatter the ice, blast as much fire as you can—just past the boat, where the flames won't catch us," Eira instructed. Noelle shifted her feet, bracing herself. "Ready?" Noelle nodded. "Now!"

Eira swept a hand through the air, savoring the way the ice turned to water instantly, dropping off the chain. A ball of fire exploded. White hot. All the water and rain evaporated and the metal groaned, snapping from the sudden change in temperature.

The moment they were free of the tether, Eira shifted her magic and her focus. The sea rose to push them along the crest of a mighty wave of Eira's making. They were well out of reach of the other hook as it flew toward them.

Ducot and Alyss ran over, working on patching the ship. At this point, it was probably held together more by sorcery than construction. But all that mattered was that they were still afloat.

The ice that had been holding up the portcullis and archway finally shattered. It all came crumbling down, crashing into the sea and sending more waves that helped them slip farther and farther into the dark night.

Eira's breath hitched. She grabbed Alyss's elbow. "Adela is hurt."

THEY RACED BACK to the bow of the ship where Adela lay. Puck was already at her side, glyphs of light spinning underneath his palm as he moved it above her, murmuring Lightspinning words under his breath. Eira slowed, both her feet and her heart, as she saw that Adela's eyes were open.

Those frosty eyes turned to her. "You look worried."

"You looked almost dead." Eira knelt at her opposite side.

"Do you need any help?" Alyss asked Puck.

He shook his head. "But if you don't mind helping with the rest of the crew?"

"Not at all."

"Thank you," Puck said with a warm smile in Alyss's direction. "We wouldn't have made it without you."

"I know." Alyss grinned, but it didn't quite reach her eyes. Her shoulders were slumped as she went to attend to the other sailors. Exhaustion weighed heavily on all of them.

"It'll take a lot more than that to kill me," Adela said, and Eira's focus returned to her. "Better people have tried."

"I'm sure." Eira rested her hand on Adela's shoulder.

"I see your magic has returned."

Eira nodded.

"I told you I would see it brought back to you." Adela had an air of smugness that Eira couldn't help but laugh at.

"I don't think you did much other than put me in a dire state. Which is what my magic always seems to respond to." *That, and Cullen…*

Her attention drifted a moment, landing back on him. A breeze glided across her cheeks, as gentle as his smile. As if he knew without her saying a word. As if he was the one thanking her when she should have been thanking him.

"We'll work on that." Adela, oblivious to Eira's thoughts, sat straighter and Puck shifted to her back. "You will learn to be as in control of your emotions as you are of your powers. So much of our magic is wrapped up in our conscious and subconscious intention that it is natural for many to see it respond to such triggers. But to truly gain the mastery you want—that you can attain—you need to gain a firmer control of it."

It was surreal to have Adela be talking as plainly as Noelle might about magical theory and application. Part of Eira felt like the young woman she had been, getting a lesson from her uncles, or a tutor in the Tower. The other part was keenly aware that she was still on a boat with the pirate queen, speeding through a rainy night to the vast unknown. Yet...the latter bit didn't terrify her nearly as much as she felt it otherwise should.

"I'd like that."

"No doubt. Thank you, Puck," Adela added as he moved away. Puck gave a bow of his head went to check in with Alyss. "Now that you have regained your powers, we can begin to work with clearer purpose."

With the help of her cane, Adela rose to her feet. Eira did so as well, keeping an eye on the pirate queen. She still didn't seem as stable on her feet as Eira would've liked, favoring her icy leg that fused with the deck and relying more than normal on her cane.

"Once we get some rest," Eira agreed.

"The *Stormfrost* isn't far now." Adela looked to the bow of the boat. Eira could feel shifts in the water around them. She was reluctant to give up control to the pirate queen—as exhausted as she looked—but Eira relented. Adela had been at this far, far longer than Eira could imagine. And she no doubt spoke true about having recovered from much worse.

Like a ghost in the night, the *Stormfrost* faded into view. Its lanterns were the flameless sort, their pale glows illuminating the frosty haze that surrounded the ship and giving it a spectral appearance. The entire vessel was coated in ice. In the rain and lightning, it looked every measure of its namesake.

"I dreamed about seeing it," Eira said softly.

"That is not something I hear often." Adela chuckled.

"Seeing it meant I found you." Eira shifted, meeting Adela's eyes. The shade of blue that was so much like hers. Something in her expression gave Adela pause, her smile slipping from her lips. But only for a second, then it returned.

"Yet another thing I don't hear often."

Eira picked up on the clear clues that Adela didn't want, or wasn't ready, to readdress Eira's questions about her parentage. So, instead, she said, "Isn't that how you found most of your crew?"

"Are you saying you want to be a more permanent part of my crew now?"

Eira shrugged. "Do I have a choice? I thought I had agreed to as much in exchange for your help getting my magic back."

Adela merely hummed. The gleam Eira was familiar with was back to Adela's eye. But it didn't have the same sinister sharpness as Eira might have once seen in it. Still, she didn't press the matter. Being in limbo was better than being shackled again.

The boat slowed to a stop alongside *Stormfrost*. It towered above them—larger than any boat Eira had ever seen. Larger than she ever thought possible for a vessel. There had to be at least three belowdecks, if not four.

A rope ladder had already been unfurled for them, reaching the railing of their small vessel. Pine went up first, then Fen. After that Adela motioned to eight of them. Ducot squeezed Noelle's hand before he led her up, then the rest of the pack: Cullen, the two from Qwint, Olivin, Yonlin, until it was just Eira and Alyss.

Alyss stared up at the boat and made no motion for the ladder. She stood, hands limp at her sides.

Eira rested a hand on her back. "It'll be all right," she said softly. "I don't think they're going to hurt us."

"Oh, I know." Alyss glanced over at her. "That's just a really tall ladder and I am…very tired." She grinned sheepishly.

Getting her magic back had been a second wind to Eira. She knew the moment she sat, or lay down, it would all catch up to her. But, for now, she was able to keep going.

However, her friends did not have the luxury of regaining lost power to fuel their energy. They were coming off a hard-fought battle and narrow escape. Clothes still stained with blood and sweat, singed and pockmarked with magic. The six of them were slow heading up the ladder.

Eira couldn't imagine the amount of exhaustion Alyss felt. She had not only helped defend the boat, but also held it together throughout the relentless assault. She had been using her magic to an extraordinary degree for a length of time far greater than anyone could've ever expected of her.

"What's the holdup?" Adela asked as she made her way over.

"Alyss is tired; she's just catching her breath a moment." Eira stayed close to her friend and gave Adela a hard stare, silently challenging the pirate queen to say anything about Alyss's exhaustion.

But Adela continued to surprise her. "It's incredibly understandable, given all the magic she has exerted." Adela's attention shifted to Alyss. "I can help you up, if you would like?"

"If that's a genuine offer, I would be a fool to refuse," Alyss said with a tired smile.

"You would be." Adela smirked. "But so often I am astounded by the fools who end up in my company."

With a soft laugh and a nod, Alyss agreed. Eira had been expecting to see Adela use the same technique that she had implemented to transfer Eira between the two boats on the river. But instead, she used ice and not water to bring Alyss up to the main deck.

Adela pressed her frozen hand against the hull of the *Stormfrost*. The hand disappeared into the thick layer of ice that covered the boat. She sank her arm in, up to the elbow, as though it were sinking into the ship. At their right, a similar icy hand emerged from the frozen hull. But this time the palm of the hand was as tall as Alyss.

"If you please," Adela said with mock formality as she gestured to the waiting palm with her free hand.

"Don't mind if I do." Alyss played along and settled herself on the edge of the frozen palm, as though she were perching herself on a swing, kicking her feet with excitement.

"Now, don't get used to this." *There* was the usual edge to Adela's voice.

The hand slid magically up the side of the hull of the *Stormfrost*, carrying Alyss with it. She let out a surprised yelp that quickly became a laugh of wonder and excitement. She passed the others in a swift blur.

All the while, Eira remained focused on the magic at play. The whole of the *Stormfrost* was completely covered in Adela's power; it was as if the ship were more magic and ice than wood, rope, or tarp. But what truly amazed Eira was how seamlessly Adela could fuse different magical applications together. Everything she applied her magic to became one extension of her. One sustained, stunning act of control.

As soon as Alyss was deposited on the deck, she immediately leaned over the railing and called down, "Eira, you absolutely must learn how to do that!"

"I'll do my best," she called back. Eira didn't want to sound too confident, otherwise Adela might second-guess teaching her, or having her on board the vessel entirely.

"I did not realize that was an option." Noelle huffed from three fourths of the way up the ladder. She had slowed almost to a stop.

"You did not ask," Adela said as she withdrew her hand from the hull. "You cannot expect to receive if you never ask what you can get."

"Well then, will you take me the rest of the way up?" Noelle glanced over her shoulder.

"I think you're close enough to the top it would be pointless,"

Adela replied. Noelle made a noise that was halfway between a grunt and a groan, but she continued to climb. Adela glanced in Ducot's direction. "I can see what you see in her."

"She has a pleasant audacity to say the least." Ducot's voice oozed fondness to the point that Eira was surprised the *Stormfrost* didn't melt from the warmth that radiated from him.

"That's certainly a way to put it. She's much like every other Firebearer I've ever had the pleasure, or displeasure, of knowing." The last sentiment devolved into a mutter. Adela said, stronger, to the crew still around them, "Now, make sure everything that we need is off this vessel." Then she turned her attention to Eira. "What're you waiting for? I am not carrying you up there."

"I wouldn't expect you to." Eira began climbing. It was a long climb, but not a hard one, thanks to how the ladder had joined at points with the ice, making it fairly stable.

Eira savored how the ice no longer bit into her fingers with sharp shards or piercing cold. The wind continued to blow and rain pelted her. But no longer was it unwelcome. Every heavy drop was a kiss to her cheeks. Every curl of her fingers around Adela's ice radiated with a familiar power.

She joined her friends on the main deck of the *Stormfrost*. They were corralled into a group by a semicircle of pirates, waiting awkwardly. The drawn swords made it clear that they didn't have free reign of the vessel and still weren't trusted. But their postures also didn't feel hostile. If anything, Eira suspected they were simply awaiting orders—ready to kill or welcome them on a word.

But Eira took note about how none of them seemed particularly *surprised* to see them. Adela would've certainly communicated her mission before going ashore, at least to a certain extent and to some of the crew. So was the plan simply well-known among the crew and they expected Adela to take her "impostor" back aboard? Or was it common for them to gain new crew members this way? Given how the others of Adela's crew had spoken, she could guess it probably was.

Eira's assessment of their circumstances was brief. No sooner had she joined the group than Cullen pulled her into his arms. The embrace was long enough that she could hear him draw a shuddering breath, and exhale a sigh of relief that became a soft hum as his arms tightened briefly around her shoulders. But he let her go promptly. Though the slow pull of his hands across her back made it clear, if only to her, that he still wanted to hold tight.

"I'm so glad you're all right," he said. "When the pirates told us what Adela was probably sending you to do…I was worried you wouldn't be able to get back to us. I know by now I shouldn't worry about you. I know you can more than manage. But I worry anyway." Cullen gave a slight smile and a nervous laugh.

"I understand; I was worried about all of you, too. I saw the fighting happening from a distance…I'm sorry I couldn't help more."

"Getting that gate open was incredibly helpful," Noelle said. She turned to the two elfin brothers. "I suppose we have you two to thank for that as well."

"It's good to see you again." Alyss smiled warmly at them. Then she said, just to Yonlin, "And it will be good to have a chance to properly get to know you."

"Likewise, I've heard so much about you all that I feel like I know you already." Yonlin glanced up at his older brother with an expression that was only readable to Olivin, judging from the way that Olivin's smile dropped briefly.

"I wanted to make sure he knew of all the people who he owed his life to," Olivin said with a shrug, recovering his nonchalance in the process.

"Your brother did most of your saving." Eira tried to keep her voice strong and hide the guilt that still lingered at the role she might have played in Yonlin's misfortune.

She knew the Pillars were cruel, and it was likely that they would've put him through what he'd endured in that locked room, or worse, anyway. But she couldn't escape the idea that if she hadn't taken that key, then *maybe…*

She tried to force the sense of responsibility from her mind. Marcus had taught her that it did little good to focus on what could've been done, or what the outcome might've been if a different choice was made. The best thing she could do was to learn and keep moving forward.

"See, I told you I wasn't just ignoring your plight." Olivin nudged his younger brother, giving off the air of playfulness. But Eira could see the truth in his eyes—finding Yonlin in that state would be seared into him for the rest of their days. Even Olivin probably didn't realize how deeply that wound ran yet.

Their conversation was cut short when Adela came over the railing, frosty steps rising to meet her feet before disappearing, as though she were walking on the crest of a frozen wave. The ice merged back with the ship, disappearing save for Adela's cane. The pirate queen gripped her aid with white knuckles, leaning ever heavier upon it.

"Take them down and find them hammocks," Adela commanded.

"Among us?" one of the crew clarified. "Not in the brig?"

"Did I say to put them in the brig?" Adela's tone was curt.

"No." The pirate shook his head hastily.

"And someone clear this." Adela gestured to the skies. "Trim sails. Dog hatches. Weigh anchor." She began to head toward the stern of the vessel. Eira had seen the windows lining the upper portion of the vessel and knew from growing up in Oparium that the captain's quarters were always the best on the ship and usually in the back.

"You really expect us to just go with you?" Lavette was the one bold enough to step forward from among them.

Adela paused, half turning. The muscles in her face were tense, pulling her lips thin and eyes narrow. "Considering that you all now owe me your lives—"

"We fought as much as your crew did," Noelle objected.

Adela's lips closed slowly. Then curled into a dangerous smile. She slowly stalked back over, coming to a stop in front of Noelle, staring down at her. The younger woman failed to suppress a shiver. There were goosebumps trailing down her arms, visible from where Eira stood.

"Whose ship are you on?" Adela asked quietly.

"Yours," Noelle answered, finally, somewhat begrudgingly.

"Good. Now can you tell me, who sets the code of conduct on this vessel?"

"You." Noelle's stance was still defiant. She still stared up at the pirate queen with her chin extended slightly. But her tone was softening.

"That code of conduct has but one rule: what I say, goes. Don't mistake my charity for fondness." Adela leaned forward slightly. Eira didn't miss the slight wavering in her hands as they gripped her cane. "So if I say sail, we go. And if I say to my crew, kill…"

"I'm dead," Noelle finished quietly.

"Very good. The alternative is still shackles." Adela eased away and turned, starting back for her cabin. She commanded, far more harshly than the first time, "Now, get them out of my sight."

· CHAPTER ·

NINETEEN

A DELA WASN'T EVEN gone when Noelle looked over to Ducot with a wounded expression. Her hands were balled into fists, quivering. Though Eira suspected it was no longer just from fear or cold…now it was also hurt and rage.

Even though he couldn't see the details of her expression, Ducot must've sensed a shift in her. Or he was simply savvy enough to understand how it all played out. The betrayal Noelle was no doubt feeling in that moment.

Ducot stepped forward and said gently, "I can show you to your new quarters."

"Don't touch me." Noelle jerked from his touch as he tried to place his hand on the small of her back, down by her hip.

"Noelle—"

"You didn't even try to defend me, or back me up."

"She is my captain and this is her ship; I have to do as she wishes." Ducot's voice dropped slightly. "And she is like a mother to me. I knew she wasn't going to hurt you."

"That's not what she just said," Noelle hissed back, gesturing at Adela's back.

Eira had no doubt the pirate queen could still hear everything. And, even if she couldn't, half her crew was still lingering, watching with keen interest. No doubt eager to report back. Not that Noelle seemed to care. She had never really been one too concerned with privacy regarding personal matters.

"If she wanted to hurt you, she would've by now." Ducot tried to grab her hand.

Noelle was still having none of it. "Fen"—she picked him

out from among the group—"can you please show us where the hammocks are?"

Fen made a noise of hesitation but finally said, "Sure, I can do that."

"What're you lot still lollygaggin for?" Pine had stepped away with others on Adela's orders but had now returned, stopping as he was crossing the deck. "You heard the captain's orders. Go."

The pirates scattered. The decks were a sudden burst of energy. Rigging clattered. Coordination and commands were shouted.

Eira stepped next to Ducot as they followed Fen toward the bow of the ship. The rest of them were moving as well. But he continued to stand still, shoulders sagging. She rested her hand lightly on the middle of his back and he jumped.

"She'll come around," Eira said softly. "She can be like this."

"I know she can." Ducot sighed. Eira could feel the pulses of his magic underneath her palm. They stretched out, seemingly reaching for the woman walking away from him, placing tension between Eira's ribs. "But I wish she would trust me more."

"She does—"

"If she did, truly, she wouldn't keep doubting me. She'd believe I'm able to keep her safe." His tone wasn't angry. Merely hurt.

Eira could see both sides of the equation. Distance gave her some clarity. She could see how Ducot was caught between the only family he'd ever known, including the captain he'd sworn fealty to…and the woman he was falling in love with. She could understand Noelle, all too well, and the wish that his love would be enough for him to rally against it all and stand up for her no matter what. Eira's gaze shifted, briefly landing on Cullen's back. She swallowed thickly.

"It's not that she doubts you, it's just…" Eira trailed off, searching for words.

Ducot wasn't going to wait for her to find them. "It doesn't matter what she says. Her actions are of doubt and mistrust."

Ducot shifted the heavy-looking bag he carried on his shoulder. "Either way, we shouldn't dally. Let's get you belowdecks."

As they headed for the companionway at the bow of the vessel, a dull throb of magic had Eira skipping a step. She spun, looking for the source. But her gaze followed the direction the magic went—skyward.

A hole cleaved into the clouds, pushing them away. The sky parted, a curtain of rain dragging over the boat and away. Eira blinked at the starry heavens above them. Another pulse of magic drew her to the nearby railing. The seas were churning beneath them as the heavy clanking of the anchor chain filled the air. A small whorl opened beneath the boat they had left Ofok on, sucking it under the dark waves as it crumpled.

"The boat…"

"Adela can always get another boat," Ducot explained. "It's more dangerous for her to have things that could tie her back to this place and time."

"I see." *Get another boat.* The words stuck in Eira's mind. Even though everything was in flux, she was constantly thinking on what might be next for her and her friends.

Lavette and Varren needed to get back to the Republic of Qwint. She had to go back to Meru…hopefully with the means to end Ulvarth once and for all. Ideas had been forming in the back of Eira's mind during her time with Adela—theories for how she *might* be able to use her magic to end him if she could get back to him. Alyss, Noelle, and Cullen could choose their next moves for themselves and Eira could have the means to fulfill those wishes.

A short stair led to a salon that extended just below the main deck and back into hammocks suspended between the deck's supports. Before them, at the bow, was a galley and tables. At the very back was the head. The stairs looped down again to what Eira suspected was the gun deck, based on the anatomy of the ship that had been visible from the outside.

She wondered how many more decks there were and what they held. Some kind of jail, from what others had said. A hold of treasures, no doubt. One Eira would be keen to explore if she had the chance to sneak away.

"The open hammocks are back there." Ducot pointed. "I have some duties to attend to." He was gone before Eira could say anything else, heading back up the stairs promptly.

Eira briefly debated going back to her friends. They were engaged in a conversation with Fen and Krut, no doubt going over the rules. Olivin's eyes drifted in her direction and Eira gave a small nod. She stepped back for the stairs; he went to move and she shook her head. He stayed.

No one stopped her as she went back up on deck. The anchor had been hoisted, sails filling with wind given by sorcerers perched on the aft quarterdeck. The crew had people of all shapes and sizes. There were draconi working alongside elfin. Morphi shifted knots into ropes that humans fastened into place. Some were short and stout, others tall and lithe. Old and young. Eyes and limbs missing. Those magical and those not.

The Treaty of Five Kingdoms had been arranged to bring people together to work toward a common goal and it had been hailed as novel. *Nothing of its like had ever been done before,* was what they'd said. And perhaps it was true. Bringing five nations together was different than bringing a ragtag bunch of misfits into order…but Adela had somehow found something that the nobles and royals and leaders hadn't; she'd found a glue that had turned those people into a crew that the treaty hadn't come close to touching.

Eira walked straight back to a stately doorway that Crow was leaving from.

"Shouldn't you be belowdecks?" Crow asked curtly.

"I came to see Her Frostiness."

"Adela isn't taking guests." No sooner had Crow said as much than the door cracked open with a pulse of familiar magic. Adela was using the frost that covered the ship to have control of it—every part. She could no doubt feel where her crew was stepping.

So it came as no surprise when she called from inside, "Let her in."

It looked as though it took every scrap of Crow's self-control not to object. Her face flushed faintly purple with frustration. But she stepped aside, allowing Eira to pass. Crow closed the door behind her.

The cabin was a much larger and much, *much* more lavish version of what had been on the boat. The windows in the back were three times as tall as Eira. Bookcases lined one side with a long dining table positioned in front of them. Though, judging from the navigational tools and maps strewn about, it saw more use as a desk than for food. Two chairs were positioned back by the windows—currently black as pitch in the night.

To her right was a large bed, and that was where Adela lay. Underneath her thin blanket, her coat removed, nestled in a wall of pillows, Adela looked very little like the pirate queen and much more like a very tired woman.

"Speak." Her voice was as sharp as ever.

"Your magic is faltering, isn't it?"

"Bold as ever, I see."

"Not even trying to deny it is telling." Eira dared to approach, coming to a stop at the foot of Adela's bed. "I wonder if you're not because you know I can sense the flow of magic again."

"And what if you're right? Come to gloat?"

"I don't think you would've let me in if you thought that was the reason I came. I doubt you would've let me keep breathing, if that's what you thought my feelings toward you were."

Adela sighed softly and settled back into her pillows a little bit more. She was a stubborn, proud woman. Not that Eira could fault her. Her entire life had been one of power and terror. Of fearsome might and impossible feats.

"I think I can help you." Eira had been expecting to fight Adela on the notion.

So she was surprised when Adela motioned to the foot of the

bed with an open palm. "That much is obvious. Why do you think I've kept you alive for so long?"

"Because I thought that perhaps you were lying to me when you said I wasn't your daughter." Eira sat slowly at the edge of the bed. She didn't want to be standing for this. Her words were as weak as her knees. As weak as the fragile hope she'd been harboring despite all odds.

"Do I seem like a woman who would do that?" Adela arched her brows.

"Possibly. You're good at lying."

Adela snorted.

Eira continued. "You don't seem like a woman who would let someone see her in such a vulnerable state if not for a good reason."

"Is preserving my magic not a good enough reason?" Adela countered. Eira still wasn't hearing a no and it made her heart flutter. This was it…the moment where it all came together, or shattered.

"You could command me to help you and not allow me to see you exhausted in bed."

"My exhaustion comes from magical feats you couldn't fathom. There is hardly shame in it."

Eira agreed in principle, but Adela still seemed too proud for this to not bother her. She also still had yet to shoot Eira's theories of her parentage down a second time and that only made her heart race even faster. So fast that she couldn't handle it any longer. Perhaps it was the recent mention of her uncle, or just the desperation of the day, but if she didn't ask—didn't know beyond all doubt—she might snap in two. Or her heart would stop altogether.

"Is it because you are actually my mother? Did you push me away to test me—or to save me from the risks that would come with being your daughter? Is our magic similar enough for you to try to draw it out because we are kin?" Every word felt as though it was made of parchment-thin glass. Each required care to say.

Adela closed her eyes and exhaled heavily. When she opened them again, Eira knew the answer before the pirate queen spoke. "I told you quite clearly when we first met: *you are not my daughter*. I have no children. I have not lied or deceived you on that. It is the whole truth."

That was it. Hope broke with a sigh. Not a crash. Not with Eira's heart seizing and failing to start again. The end of her optimism was quiet, in a dark night as the ship finally began to move forward.

Eira stared out the back windows. Once more, she was adrift in dark water with no clear heading. She didn't know what was going to come next, nor the full scope of the consequences of everything she was leaving behind.

"Who are my blood parents, then?" The words were those of a lost girl falling into the chasm her parents had opened with their revelation. Eira balled her hand into a fist and it shook slightly.

"Does it matter?" Adela had an air of nonchalance.

"That's easy for you to say." Eira's attention turned inward once more with a flare of anger. "You probably know—"

"Who my parents are?" Adela arched her brows. "Child, do I seem like someone who would know who my parents are?"

"I just, assumed…" Who their parents were was just something most people knew. Something Eira had thought she'd known and taken for granted.

"I have a guess at who my father is, given that there were never many elfin hiding in Solaris at any point." Adela smiled thinly. "The Court of Shadows is to blame for my existence—a truth I'm sure they'd *love* to know—since to the best of my research it was one of their spies sent to keep an eye on the Crystal Caverns who unknowingly sired me."

"Why, then, is our magic so similar?" Eira knew she was grasping at straws. But she couldn't stop herself.

Adela shrugged. "Perhaps because we are both from Oparium and there is something in the water? Perhaps we're some distant relation without knowing it—as I never bothered to find out who my mother might be."

"But I was left with your mark on my parents' doorstep."

"I thought you didn't know who your parents were?" Adela hummed.

"I don't know my blood parents. But the people who raised me…"

"It sounds as if, to me, you have been searching for something that you had all along."

Eira grabbed her upper stomach, balling a fist into her clothes. "My parents did the best they could, yes. There were good times, and bad, as I'm sure any family has…" Eira trailed off, thinking of all the conflicting feelings she still held toward them. Feelings that couldn't be glossed over by the worry of their fates alone. "But from the moment they told me the truth, I've felt like something is missing. Like there's this vast *hole* in me, filled with nothing but unknowns and questions."

"That sounds like a problem you will have to fix for yourself. No person—blood parent or otherwise—could do it for you."

"But if I knew—"

"If you knew, you would still have to come to terms with the unorthodox circumstances of your birth. You would have a face to the person who willingly *gave you up*. 'Good' reason or no, that explanation is not simple to hear," Adela interjected harshly. Eira stood a little straighter, her grip slackening at the tone. "You are looking for someone else to end a war with yourself. No parents, blood or otherwise, could give you peace. That is something you must find for yourself."

Eira knew it was true. The pit had taught her as much. Why hadn't she thought that the same lesson she learned following Marcus's death and the peace she found there would apply to this as well? To all things that gave her turmoil?

"But my magic…surely my parents must be someone important…maybe they want to find me," she murmured. All the hidden thoughts she'd been clutching on to, secretly holding with her hope, were now slipping through her slackening fingers.

"Why must they be someone important? Exceptional people are born into unexceptional circumstances every day." Adela shifted, sitting straighter, even though it looked like it cost her much effort. She leaned forward, meeting Eira's eyes. "Perhaps that is the one way you and I are alike—*that* is the kinship we share. Not one of blood, but one of trial and triumph. That we are the extraordinary ones in a sea of ordinary."

Eira stared into Adela's eyes. Now that she was letting go of the hope that they were, somehow, secretly related, she could see the differences. Adela's eyes were slightly more narrow. They had a darker ring of blue around their outer edge. Her chin was a more squared shape than Eira's…

Her chest tightened. Eira had to break the stare, standing. "I should go. I'm sorry to bother you with this. It won't happen again."

"I hope it doesn't." Adela lay onto the pillows once more, settling the blanket around her. "If not for my sake, then for yours. You are only holding yourself back by trying to find someone else's shoes to fill. Who cares what name you were born to? Make your own."

"Why are you being so nice to me?" Eira couldn't help but ask. "You're not my mother…so why?"

"Perhaps it is because I see myself in you, girl. Or perhaps I merely need this skill of yours to open my channel wider so I can continue terrorizing the seas with my full might for at least a couple more decades." Adela grinned slightly. It brought a similar expression to Eira's lips. "Take the night and come to me in the morning. I'll let you and your friends live another day; you've earned it."

"How gracious," Eira muttered.

Adela heard and snorted softly. "Tomorrow we can figure out what we will do with you. With any luck, you will continue keeping your heads attached to your shoulders."

Eira nodded and drifted out of the cabin and back onto the main deck. Now that the ship was underway, it was quieter. The crew that was on deck moved leisurely, or perched themselves on crates, or the bold sat on the railings themselves. The sorcerers that had helped give wind and currents to get the ship moving were gone. It seemed, for now, the winds were on their side and they could be propelled by nature instead of magic.

She wandered up to the front quarterdeck, rather than heading back down to the crew's quarters. Her mind was too heavy to sleep. The hammock would collapse if she tried to lie on it now.

It seemed she wasn't the only one to have the idea.

Cullen leaned against the railing at the very front of the ship, looking as stoic as a figurehead. The wind pushed his hair down and away from his face as he stared out into the great unknown. She allowed herself to surrender to the moment. To admire him, feeling the breezes that, even now, seemed to connect them both.

"Do you remember the last time we were like this?" Eira said softly, trying not to startle him and failing. Cullen whipped around but instantly relaxed as his eyes landed on her. He leaned back against the railing but just with his right side, allowing her space at his left at the narrow point the bow made. "Risen was just out there." Eira pointed ahead, imagining the glittering city of Meru.

"And you wanted nothing to do with me."

"I wanted *everything* to do with you," she countered. "And that made a difficult time harder."

"Sorry for that." He seemed sincere in his apology and that only made Eira smile.

"It was hardly your fault, that time at least. Though we've both done things we shouldn't."

"Or could've handled things better," he added. She nodded. A brief moment of comfortable silence passed between them. "You spoke with Adela?"

"Good guess."

"Not quite a guess. I ran into Crow when I came after you. She made it clear that under no circumstances would I be welcome in Adela's cabin."

"That sounds like Crow." Eira looked back to the water, the conversation with Adela still a fresh wound in her mind.

"Given the fact that you were welcome…were your suspicions correct? Was she lying to you to protect you?"

Eira shook her head slowly, still avoiding his eyes. "No. I'm not her daughter. If I'm related at all—which is probably unlikely—it would be some kind of distant cousin or niece through some branch of an unknown family tree I don't think I'll ever see."

"I'm sorry." Cullen rested both of his elbows on the railing next to her, staring out. Their shoulders were flush against each other and it was a relief to have him there in that moment. She had thought she'd wanted to be alone. But having a friend—or whatever Cullen was at this point—was a relief.

Even when the world pulled her to its vast reaches. Even when her heart was descending into a chasm of her own making. Her friends were still there. They'd never left her side.

The oceans they'd crossed together were thicker than the blood of any family Eira would ever know.

"It's all right."

"Is it?" He glanced her way.

She couldn't blame him for his skeptical expression. Eira shrugged. "It has to be, doesn't it?"

"You're allowed to not be okay."

"I know. But…" Eira sighed. "I feel like I am, but I also know I'm not. I think part of me knew this was coming. Another part of me didn't want to admit it. I think I'm in a place where I can accept it. But I also don't want to." She laughed softly. "I know the right thing to do is be at peace with it and keep moving. Accept it with grace. But…if I'm being honest, there's a part of me that still wants to shout and scream. That feels as though it is—*I am*—one cosmic joke."

"You're not."

Eira nodded. "The logical part of me knows that. I'll keep

myself together. It's just a moment where it would be so much easier to act like a child about all this."

"I can understand that." Cullen laced and unlaced his fingers. The nervous fidgeting almost had her reaching over to place her hand on his to reassure him. The urge was hard to resist. "My whole life has been learning how to suppress my emotions, despite whatever I want, whatever instinct tells me… You know, I was always so jealous of you."

"Of me?" Eira straightened slightly.

"You never seemed to care about what others thought of you in the Tower. Even after what happened, you kept walking with your head held high."

"I cared *deeply*. I just didn't let it show."

"I know that now." He gave her a small smile. "But, even if it was a facade, that woman was still you. The one who could act as though the world didn't matter. Maybe you need to summon her again, pretend until it becomes real."

The wind teased her hair. "No, I'm done going backward; I won't revert to how I was. I might not know where I'm heading yet. But, for better or worse, I want to keep moving forward. I know who I was yesterday, who I am today, and I'm ready to meet the woman I will be tomorrow."

THEY REMAINED ON deck for a while after their conversation died off, enjoying the quiet serenity of the other's company. The words stayed with her for the rest of the night—like a lullaby—as she made her way belowdecks to her hammock and fell asleep alongside the rest of them.

Unsurprisingly, she was the first to wake the next morning. Even though the slow and steady rocking of the ship had been a comfortable way to sleep, her mind was too restless to fall into a deeper slumber. She felt like she was at a crossroads—the future impossible to ascertain and yet she wanted, desperately, to grab onto it tightly enough to know it from her current vantage.

All the options kept her from falling back asleep as much as they pinned her to the hammock, their weight unbearable on her chest. Every thought and worry stacked upon the next. She used waiting for the others to rouse as an excuse to not be more hasty.

If Eira had been forced to guess who was going to be the second to wake, Yonlin wouldn't have been it.

She met his eyes and gave him a quiet "Good morning," more mouthing the words than saying them aloud.

He swung his feet over the hammock and kept his voice low as well. "Sleep well?"

She nodded rather than being completely honest. Yonlin didn't need to know all the things that kept her awake at night. She wanted to protect him from those harsh realities as much as possible. Eira grimaced inwardly. She was becoming her older brother. Olivin had rubbed off on her too much, because all she could see in Yonlin was a younger sibling in need of being protected. Which wasn't fair to him. Yonlin was a man grown and she wasn't going to coddle him.

"You?" Eira asked as he stood and stretched. She knew the answer before he said it, given how he had been sleeping with his mouth hanging open, snoring faintly, in an adorably similar pose to his brother when she returned.

He nodded as well. "I'm going to go one deck lower to see the heavy guns. Puck promised to take me this morning. If Olivin wakes up and wonders where I am, will you tell him?" The young man's excitement at seeing the larger cannons was palpable.

Even though she wanted him involved in the forthcoming decisions on what was to come next for them, she didn't want to hold Yonlin back from something he would so clearly enjoy. Moreover, she didn't know when everyone else would wake. So she said, "Certainly. Go and have fun."

He practically skipped over to Puck's hammock. Without the slightest amount of fear, Yonlin woke up the fearsome pirate, who—to Eira's surprise and delight—agreed with much grumbling fanfare to take him right then. Adela's crew wasn't nearly as bad as the stories made them out to be.

Or perhaps this "soft spot" Adela had formed for Eira ran deeper and was far more sincere than she expected.

The clanking of wooden bowls and utensils in the galley at the bow was what ultimately began to wake the rest of them. Seeing her friends stirring, Eira made her way over to the galley where breakfast was being passed out by a pirate she didn't recognize. It was a grain porridge that had been cooked a previous day and rewarmed by Firebearers, likely hastily, given how inconsistent the heat was. Some sections of the porridge were so cold it was in globs. Others so hot it burned her tongue.

None of the pirates she knew made their way over to her, allowing Eira to claim one table in the corner for herself. She wondered if it was out of consideration because they knew their unlikely guests would want to sit together. Or if it was because they were still wary of growing too close to people whose fates were still unclear.

Olivin was the first to make it out of his hammock. Sitting across from her on the bench that was bolted to the floor, he swung his feet over and adjusted his positioning, spoon poised above the bowl.

"Tell me this is shockingly good and I'm going to be surprised at how well Adela's crew can cook."

Eira hummed, making a show of thinking for a moment. "You're certainly going to be surprised." She swore she heard a hasty prayer to Yargen before he took a bite.

Olivin chewed slowly, his nose scrunching in a look that accurately reflected the texture of the meal. He swallowed hard. "I'm surprised it doesn't taste worse; I'll say that much."

"Bland, but there are far more foul things," she agreed.

Olivin tilted his spoon, allowing a lump to *plop* wetly into the bowl before bravely taking another bite. Eira did the same. Adela had made it more than clear that on her vessels they should be grateful for whatever they were given. So Eira ate like it was the only meal she was going to have that day.

"Oh, Yonlin is down with Puck looking at the guns."

Olivin nodded. "I heard him pestering Puck about it last night. If my brother blows us all up with his fascinations, I am very sorry."

Eira chuckled. "There's a dark comedy if, out of everything, what does us in is a friendly accident."

"You're not wrong."

"I so rarely am," she teased with a grin. Olivin snorted.

"So far the rumors of the pirate queen's bloodthirst seem to be overrated."

"She has made it a point to regularly remind me that she is, graciously, *letting* me—us—live."

Olivin chewed for a long minute. "'Letting' you live? Would she really kill her own daughter?"

A sad smile crossed her lips. But it *was* a smile. She would grin and bear her pain—smile away the bitterness, anger, and frustration. However cathartic it would be in a moment to rage. It wouldn't change anything.

"She's not my mother."

"What? But I thought you said on the boat…" Olivin tailed off, blinking several times as if the truth was coming into focus. "On the boat *I* was the one who said she was your mother and you never denied it."

"Sorry for the deception." She forced another spoon down, grateful for how long the gruel took to chew. "I didn't want to lie to you—even a lie of omission. But I was worried that you wouldn't leave if you knew the truth and I wanted to keep you safe. And we both know I am not the exemplar of safety."

Olivin let out a rumbling chuckle that reached deep into the lower registers of his voice. It shifted her smile into something far more sincere. The sound of him was like a cup of honeyed lemon tea. Sweet and warm. Light.

"Well, here I am, wrapped up in it."

"I know and I am sorry." Her smile wavered as guilt washed over her.

"You did try to push me away." He lifted his eyes from his bowl, meeting hers, freezing her in place. Holding her in thrall.

An insatiable urge to reach over and take his fingers in hers, squeezing them, overtook her. It nearly moved her limbs like a puppet on strings. Eira grabbed her bowl tighter, refusing to give in.

"Really, I suppose I should be thanking you."

"Thanking me?" she echoed with surprise.

"Ironically, Adela's ship might be the safest place in all of Meru's greater seas—so long as she's not trying to kill us. You might not believe me, but I might feel safer having Yonlin here than anywhere else. I know Wynry can't get to him." He glanced askance, leaning back and running a hand through his hair. A knot tightened in her stomach. "So, thank you, I suppose, for being someone I can't let go of. Even when I know I should."

A flush rose through her body, crashing down and pooling in her lower stomach. Eira didn't force a chill underneath her skin. She didn't fight it. But, rather, savored the sensation as it passed through her.

But, despite enjoying the emotions and feelings he filled her with, Eira didn't linger on the subject, instead asking, "Is it that bad on Meru?" He and Yonlin had been traveling by land; they might have more information than she did.

His expression hardened, eyes growing vacant. "Their network runs deeper than we ever expected in the Court of Shadows. They've made quick work unseating local leaders and constables."

"I guess I saw as much in Ofok."

"Every town we passed while tracking your boat—from the smallest to largest—was like that."

Eira wondered just how much she'd missed of Meru from the relative safety of Adela's vessels. But her musings were cut short with the arrival of Noelle and Cullen. The former sat at Eira's left hand, the latter at her right.

They all willfully ignored the slight tension that immediately took up residence in the silence between Cullen and Olivin. It wasn't anything overt, but visible in the slight glances they gave each other from the corners of their eyes. The way Cullen greeted Eira and gave Olivin little more than a nod. While she appreciated they weren't acting out like children, she would've preferred if this awkwardness wasn't there at all.

But ending it resided with her. She was keeping them in limbo with her words and actions. If she'd done a better job of making it clear to either one of them—or both—where she stood, it would end. But just thinking about it made her chest ache and throat tighten. They both had brought her safety and joy. Companionship through hard times. Things that made the idea of giving either of them up after she'd lost so much even more unpalatable than their breakfast.

"How did you sleep, Cullen?" Eira asked, trying to ease the

discomfort. If she couldn't—wouldn't—outright end it at the moment, the least she could do would be making it more bearable for everyone.

"I slept well, thank you. And you?" When he asked, his eyes searched her expression, no doubt thinking back to how he'd left her last night.

"Well, also." Eira was saved from having to think of any more safe topics when Lavette and Varren arrived and all the morning etiquette repeated itself.

Unsurprisingly, Alyss was the last one to join them. The last person to get out of their hammock for the whole ship. Noelle ended up dragging her over so she didn't miss breakfast or the conversation that she really needed to be a part of. Alyss's delay turned out to be oddly well timed, as it gave Yonlin the opportunity to rejoin the group—brought up by Puck—so he didn't miss breakfast either.

As soon as all eight of them were crammed onto the benches around the small table by one side of the hull, Lavette wasted no time getting right to the point with the air of authority she usually had around her. An air that Eira had noticed was only growing with time.

"What did Adela say?" she pointedly asked to Eira. "Are we prisoners, forced crew, or guests?"

"I don't think Adela does 'forced crew.'" Eira had to consciously stop herself from bristling slightly at the implication of *that*. She knew the rumors that surrounded Adela and why Lavette would perhaps think that was a possibility.

"So we're walking dead or guests. Not liking our odds here." Varren poked at his porridge. It had begun to get hard as it'd grown cold.

"I wouldn't despair yet," Eira cautioned hesitantly. She wasn't sure how much of her conversation with Adela she wanted to share, especially since it ended with a lot still in the air.

"What did she say?" Lavette pressed.

"I didn't have much of a chance to speak with her about the

details. After the long day, she didn't want much to do with me. You know how she is." Eira knew Adela wouldn't appreciate her hinting in any way at her weakened state.

"I don't 'know how she is,' seeing as you're the only one among us who she spends time with." Lavette's expression was calm and collected, as much as her words, but there was an implied edge to them that had Eira bristling. Lavette didn't trust the connection. That much was still painfully clear.

"However," Eira continued, ignoring the remark, "I believe we're going to speak this morning."

"Just you, or all of us?" Lavette asked. Eira raised both her hands with a small shrug. Lavette folded her arms and leaned back with a sigh. "I'll just assume it's only you, given how things have been thus far."

"I think that is a fair assumption," Eira reluctantly agreed. It was clear that Lavette was viewing herself as a sort of stand-in delegate for Qwint and Eira didn't want to offend her. "And Adela could always surprise us...but, in case my suspicion is right, I wanted to speak with you all first thing." Eira swept her gaze across the table and returned to Lavette first. Hopefully it would signal respect. "I'm going to assume that you want to go back to Qwint as quickly as you're able?"

Varren started to speak, but Lavette got in a word faster. "Yes. Absolutely."

Eira didn't miss Varren's moment of tense hesitation. Or the way he looked at Lavette from the corners of his eyes. But he ultimately said nothing and gave a small nod.

"Right, then..." Eira turned to Olivin and Yonlin next. "I assume you both want to return to Meru?"

The two brothers met eyes and exchanged an entire conversation with gestures, shrugs, nods, humming, and short grunts. It brought a small smile to her lips. She remembered the days of terrorizing her parents with Marcus using plans coordinated without a word. Corroborating alibis with mere glances to get each other out of trouble. The brothers' presence in their group filled her with a sweet ache. For once, thoughts of Marcus weren't agony, but an almost dreamy nostalgia. Good memories that she'd suppressed alongside the bad because she didn't know how to untangle them from the trauma when thoughts of her brother returned to her.

"The most important thing," Olivin began, "is that we stay together and I keep Yonlin safe."

"I can look after myself," Yonlin muttered, clearly offended.

Olivin continued as if his brother said nothing at all, "If I'm being honest, I don't know if Meru is the safest place for us right now."

"But your sister—" The words slipped from Eira's lips before she could stop them. Olivin's sudden fixation on his empty bowl at the mention of his family's horror and shame had her hot with guilt at the omission.

Ultimately, he relaxed and said, "The moment I have the chance to go after her, I will." He threw his arm around Yonlin's shoulders. "But I almost lost Yonlin once because of her. I won't risk losing him again."

Even as certain as Olivin sounded, Eira saw his hesitation. The words were slightly strained. Movements tense. He meant what he said…but a part of him still yearned to go after Wynry *right now*, a part Eira understood all too well.

Thanks to Ferro, she knew what it was like to watch family die before your eyes and then what it felt like when the murderer walked free. Making any kind of real, long-term peace with that was an impossible emotional demand.

"However, with all that said…I don't want to run forever. I will have my vengeance. If you are going back to Meru to fight the Pillars then I will fight at your side. If you are returning to Solaris, then we'll seek to return to Meru before then." Olivin folded and unfolded his hands. He seemed to be filled with eagerness at the prospect of finally evening the score with Wynry.

The mention of her home, and her plans, shifted Eira's focus to her friends. "What are you three thinking? Back to Meru to fight, or Solaris for safety?"

Alyss surprised her when she said, "Or somewhere else entirely?"

"You don't want to go back?"

Alyss settled her chin in her palm and tapped the table, staring at nothing. "It's not that I don't *want* to go back. More that I don't think I *need* to go back yet. All my life, I have read stories and lived through the tales of others." She dropped a hand to the satchel at her hip and pulled out a familiar notebook. "I am determined to write my own story now. And I feel like I won't be able to do that if I spend my entire life in the comforts of everything I know."

The discontent—the hunger for more—that Eira saw in Alyss in that moment was new, different, and filled her with pride. She didn't want to linger on it and risk making her friend uncomfortable. But it was noted and warmed her from head to toe.

Instead, Eira turned to Noelle next. "And you?"

"I should think it's obvious," she said, "given that the man I am courting, however frustrating he might be in any given moment, is on this ship. I'm not going to leave until I know how things between us end."

Alyss stared at Noelle as if she were the moon and stars. In a flurry of movement, eyes wide, Alyss had her journal open, furiously grabbing for a pen. Noelle tried to wrest it from her grasp.

"Don't you dare!"

"But, Noelle, it was so beautiful!" Alyss objected with aching sentimentality. "How could you deny the next great storyteller such inspiration?"

"I am not your inspiration." For all her annoyance, Noelle was still smirking with one corner of her mouth. If there was one thing Eira was fairly confident that Noelle would enjoy, it was the idea of being immortalized in some kind of written format regardless of how flattering or unflattering, or vulnerable, the portrayal might be.

"So, yes." Noelle's tone turned serious as she looked back to Eira. Alyss's pen darted hastily over the page when Noelle's gaze was off of her. "I don't want to be gone from Solaris forever. It will always be my home and at some point I *will* need to go back—or at least get word to my family so they know I'm all right. My father might slay me if I don't return the rubies sooner over later. But, for now, I'm still seeing where the winds of destiny blow from, and am riding their currents."

Alyss continued writing. Noelle was playfully batting at her hand and then correcting the notes, to, at the least, "get the quote right." They both groaned and laughed at each other, bringing a smile to Eira's lips.

One that was short-lived as she turned to Cullen. "And you?"

He was silent for a long minute, and when he finally went to speak, he had to clear his throat twice, as if it was hard for him to not only find but form the right words.

"I've given it some thought, and come to the conclusion that what I *want* to do and what I *should* do are two different things." He clasped and unclasped his fingers. "I *want* to stay on this ship and sail past the edge of the map. I want to go into that distant unknown and feel these winds of destiny Noelle is speaking so eloquently of."

"I am never saying anything again." Noelle folded her arms in a mock pout as Alyss triumphantly scribbled.

Cullen chuckled, then continued. "But doing that would feel a lot like running. Running from who and what I'm supposed to be. I need to stop taking the easy way out and face these things head on, regardless of how uncomfortable it might be or how afraid of it I am."

"Good for you," Lavette said with an approving smile, stealing the words from Eira's mouth. For the first time in a while, Lavette displayed what looked like genuine, outward warmth for Cullen. It was an expression of understanding shared between two people born and raised to assume the mantle of leadership. Something

Eira might never be fully able to understand, and the streak of jealousy that arose at the notion surprised even her.

Eira forced the conversation to continue moving. "So you want to go back, then? To Solaris, or Meru?"

"I wouldn't say I *want* to, but, like Noelle, I do think I have to, eventually. Or at least get word back to Solaris," he said, still reluctant. "I need to go to Meru. I need to see if my father is alive. I can't abandon him. Not to mention, it'd feel like a slight against Empress Vhalla if I didn't try and help make things right after all she's invested in me and taught me. I can't abandon her, or her family, in their darkest hour."

"I understand." For the first time, it seemed as though Cullen was making a decision for himself. Even though he was factoring in and heavily weighing others' wants, perspectives, and opinions, the decision was still for himself and what he felt he needed to do.

"What about you, Eira?" Lavette asked. "Now that you know where we all stand."

Eira shifted uncomfortably in her seat, the weight of their stares pressing down on her shoulders so heavy that it put pressure on her hips. She agreed with all their sentiments in different ways. They convinced her of different things, she agreed with some, and she objected to others. But, much like Cullen, after considering everyone else, she had to make the choice for herself.

"I will go back to Meru," she said finally. "I swore to myself and Ulvarth that I would end this—I wouldn't let him run free." Eira's attention landed back on Olivin and the knowing that filled his gaze. "Like you, I know I should let it go. I should go back to Solaris, or somewhere else, and keep safe. But I can't. I will never know rest until I end him."

DELA SAT QUIETLY as Eira gave her the summary of where everyone stood and what they wanted to do next.

The pirate queen hadn't talked much this morning and Eira wondered if her relative silence was related to their conversation the night before. She wouldn't be surprised if Adela felt a margin of shame for having been seen in a weakened state—not that she *should* feel shame. But such emotions were rarely logical.

When Eira finished speaking, Adela lifted the delicate teacup off the table next to them, taking a thoughtful sip. She stared out the windows at the churning blue and white waters the ship left in its wake.

"You think you will be able to defeat him as you are now?" Though fair, Adela's skepticism was still a glancing blow.

"Perhaps not as I am now," Eira admitted. Cullen's words from the tournament cautioning her against killing Ulvarth—the risks that'd create of another taking his place, of turning him into a martyr—had lingered with her. "But I have an idea of how I might be able to use my magic to get the upper hand."

"Which is?"

"The echoes." It was a far-fetched idea and Eira knew it. "Though, I admit, it hinges on theories you sparked in me that I don't yet know if they're viable or not."

Adela seemed to preen at that. But her expression turned serious once more. Whatever curiosity she held toward Eira's plans, she kept it to herself, for now. "Regardless of if you have the means or not, I am the pirate queen, not a delivery service. Moreover, I will not be returning to Meru."

"I understand." Eira had expected Adela to say something of that variety and had been preparing her response. "None of us expect charity."

"Then what is your barter?" Adela turned her cold stare to Eira. "Do not forget that you already owe me for the restoration of your magic."

Eira refrained from pointing out that Adela hadn't really done anything to return her magic. It had more or less returned on its own. Though, she didn't have proof that what Adela's actions over the days before hadn't helped her. And…Adela had kept her word that her and her friends would stay safe. They were fed, sheltered, and still weren't shackled. It wasn't worth splitting hairs over the details.

"I will help you work on any magical techniques you desire, as well as show you my own…and I will open up your channel as I'm able." Eira thought that was all she'd promised. Which felt like more than enough. But any deal with Adela was going to have to favor the pirate queen if it was to be successful. "We understand our help on the ship covers nothing more than our room and board, and your good will—if that much. So we will work hard to make ourselves useful and follow your and the crew's orders. What we ask for is that you grant us a vessel of our own once we have earned it."

"Excuse me?"

Eira couldn't decide if the surprised expression that Adela wore was a good sign or not. She continued, "Ducot mentioned that it is easy for you to acquire boats when you need them. I'd imagine, as the pirate queen, you have many at your disposal. Or know of a few ways to get one. We would like to find a way to earn one. Then, you don't have to 'deliver us' anywhere. We can sail ourselves to where we need to go and, in the process, remove ourselves from being a burden on you and your crew."

"And you think that you have the capacity to sail yourselves?"

"With the right boat, yes." Eira nodded. "I grew up in Oparium; I would work on ships in the summers when they were in port."

"Coiling some rope or scrubbing the deck of a ship in a wharf and managing the sea are different beasts."

"I realize. But we'll have time to learn on your vessel—and we don't need anyone to teach us; we'll pick it up as we go. We also have the exceptional talents of a sorcerer of each affinity, two Lightspinners, and two runic sorcerers from Qwint. I think we can manage whatever comes our way." Eira leaned back in her chair. "What happens to us wouldn't be your concern. We'd be well out of your hair."

Adela rested her elbows on the armrests of her chair and steepled her fingers in thought. She pressed the edges of her index fingers to her lips and hummed thoughtfully. "There is a vessel I could get for you. One that's nimble, easily managed by a smaller crew."

"And what do you want in return for this vessel?"

Dropping her hands, Adela smoothed her palms over her thighs. Eira noticed how her left hand massaged just above her knee—the leg that was missing and replaced by ice.

"The ship I will grant you is currently in Carsovia. And to get it, I want you to help me get something in return."

"What is that?" Eira dared to ask, even though the malicious glint in Adela's eyes already assured her that she wasn't going to like what was said.

"The head of Salveus D'Astrov."

"And he is?"

"The overseer of the flash bead mines of Carsovia."

It wasn't until later that evening that Eira had a chance to relay Adela's information to her friends. She had spent the day in Adela's cabin, working with the pirate queen on the art of channel manipulation. But rather than feeling exhausted, Eira was invigorated.

"Impossible" didn't seem to be in the pirate queen's vocabulary. Everything could be done, if one was clever and strong enough. Unlike her parents, who always seemed to shy from Eira's magic—a mystery long solved, or her uncles, who disregarded many of her theories because they were nervous how Eira's pursuit of them might impact her, Adela wanted to pursue every avenue. Debate. And discuss openly.

But Eira's enthusiasm quickly waned as she reported back to the group on Adela's demands. Specifically as Varren's face fell. His stare became as vacant as the ocean they'd been sailing through all day.

"We can't attack Carsovia—especially not the flash bead mines," Lavette said when Eira finished. "She's sending us to certain death."

"We're not attacking Carsovia, or the mines, really. We're going after one man."

"The overseer of the mines is handpicked by the empress herself. There are few things more precious to the empire than flash beads," Lavette said gravely.

"I know their power…I can understand why they'd be so precious," Eira admitted. "But we don't have much of a choice. Look at it as going in, killing one man, and getting out. Nothing more."

"We're going to die," Varren whispered. "No one makes it out of that place alive."

"You did." Lavette wrapped her arm around his shoulders and turned back to Eira. "Qwint is in a precarious enough position as it is with the treaty falling apart. If they see us infiltrating their mines"—she held up her wrist covered in runic bracelets, as though that would be enough to signify their origins—"Carsovia will use it as an excuse to attack."

"I understand," Eira said. She didn't know enough about the politics of Qwint and Carsovia to object. Though, everything she heard made Carsovia out to be a monstrous empire with little regard for the sovereignty of others…much like Solaris was under the first emperor.

But Eira also suspected that their hesitation was about more than political reasons. Varren continued to stare past the table. She didn't know his full story and wasn't about to pry, but whatever surrounded a past escape from Carsovia for him…she could tell wasn't a matter that should be pressed.

"By that logic, should we be worried about how this might reflect back on Solaris?" Cullen mused.

"We'll change our clothes and dress like pirates. No one from Carsovia was at the tournament so they won't know us by our faces; we'll just be Adela's crew," Eira said.

"Assuming Carsovia didn't have spies at the tournament." Olivin tapped the table in thought. Lavette made a humming noise akin to agreement.

"It's possible," Eira relented. "But are they really going to be looking for us all the way in their land? And even if there were spies at the tournament, that information likely wasn't reported to this overseer. They might not have even made it back alive."

Olivin tilted his head left and right, then shrugged.

Yonlin leaned forward. "I, for one, am ready to attack this overseer."

"You just want to see how flash beads are mined and refined." Olivin sighed. "You are twisted, brother."

"I am a man of science *and* magic."

"You should be nowhere near those mines." No sooner had Olivin said the words than Yonlin was giving him a cutting glare. The two had a staring contest that the rest of them readily left them to.

"What about you two?" Eira looked to Noelle and Alyss.

Noelle cracked her knuckles, sparks flying with each *pop*. "Kill one man? I think we can manage that."

"It'll be good experience for when we go after Ulvarth," Alyss agreed. "We could use all the practice we can get when it comes to cutting off the head of a snake."

"Then the six of us will go." Eira looked to Lavette and Varren. "You two can stay on the *Stormfrost*."

Lavette nodded. Varren inhaled deeply. She expected he was going to caution them a second time about marching into the mines. But he surprised her when he said, "If you're going there, you'll need all the information you can get."

"Varren," Lavette said softly. "You don't have to do this."

"I know." He lifted his chin with a determined gaze. "I might not be ready to confront the monsters of my past, but I can tell you all about their cages. And, with any luck, you'll finally kill the man we called 'nightmare wielder.'"

Over the next hour, Varren told them of the Carsovian mines. How the flash beads' discovery and refinement had changed the empire, giving it a unique military edge by overpowering most other magics, and arming Commons with powers that they weren't born with. He told them of an empire built on power and cruelty. Of extreme wealth and stunning poverty. *Small wonder the other kingdoms had tried to unite to stand against the tyrant that he made Carsovia out to be.*

But the parts that stuck with Eira, long after they'd gone to bed, were the parts that Varren didn't say. The moments his words broke and thoughts trailed off. The silence that followed the briefest mentions of life at the mines. Like the rest of them, he had his scars, and the monster behind them still reigned supreme over mines of flash shale and blood.

HOURS FLOWED LIKE the water around the ship that Eira dutifully tracked with her senses. Days slipped by like their feet across the decks during drills. Before they knew it, a week had passed as effortlessly as the wind between Cullen's fingers.

Their time was divided three ways: training, working, sleeping. Moments were slotted between where they began to learn the names of the crew. Where wary, sidelong glances turned to small nods. Gruff grunts and shakes of heads became brief conversations.

The sun beat down on their shoulders as they practiced combat. Salt spray coated them as they manned ropes and mended the ship. Muscles that had languished on the river on the way to Ofok returned with company.

With each passing day, they found themselves not only more in tune with their abilities, but with each other. Eira learned Lavette and Varren's rune spinning by the sounds of their bracelets clanking. Olivin, Alyss, and Noelle were already second nature and Yonlin didn't take long to learn. Cullen…she knew his body better than anyone else's.

Adela was always nearby. Even when she wasn't actively running their drills, Eira could almost always feel her sharp eyes turned from across the deck. Her guidance, though short and brisk, was invaluable. Nights were spent together debating theory and practicing the most far-fetched plan to bring down Ulvarth Eira could imagine.

"Remember, it is not about power, but precision. Not about

force, but control." She punctuated the statement with a tap of her cane.

They ran drills until they were heaving over the side of the ship. They coiled ropes until their biceps screamed and hands were bloody from blisters ripping open—magical assistance forbidden for many tasks to "build character." Yet, none of the struggle seemed to beat them down. They were all improving, little by little, day by day.

"Really come at me!" Noelle challenged. "I know you have more than that!"

Eira pulled back her hands and thrust them forward, and a spear of ice materialized that burst into steam the moment it met a shield of fire over Noelle's palm. With a flick of her fingers, Noelle had tongues of flame raining over Eira's shoulders. Which Eira deflected with a swipe of her hand and another hiss of fire and ice.

They went back and forth before rotating partners. Her muscles held a sweet ache from the intensity. Sweat trickled down her neck, but Eira ignored the encroaching fatigue and pushed her body to its limit as the golden light of sunset coated the deck.

She found herself face-to-face with Olivin. Eyes locked. A glint of mischief sparked through his cerulean gaze. Blood rushed through her ears as a crescent smile arced upon her lips. She summoned a sword of ice beneath her fingers and her blade met the one he held.

Every movement was swift and powerful. An electric current reverberated up her arm with each strike, coursing through her body, crackling in the air around them. As she parried and lunged, she couldn't stop herself from noticing the way his muscles rippled underneath his sweat-soaked shirt. She hadn't been the only one to find new strength over the past week of hard labor.

She spun, going for the determining blow, but he caught her hand. Her heart skipped a beat as they shared a breath, the intensity of his gaze nearly all-consuming. The moment held, longer than it should. Olivin drew a sharp inhale, as if he were about to say something, when another joined the fray.

Olivin released Eira as a gust of wind pommeled into him. Eira spun, having the benefit of knowing Cullen's magic, her senses alerting her to the onslaught a second before it happened. Losing her footing in the dodge, she scrambled, recovering faster than Olivin and heading for Cullen.

Cullen wore a lazy smirk, a mischievous glint in his eyes that told her he knew exactly what he was doing by interrupting their duel. But, rather than feeling petty, it seemed…playful? As if, with a stare, he held all the confidence in the world that boldly said, *That's it, come to me as we both know you will*. Amusement curled up within her and settled. What was wrong with her that she found this more delightful than frustrating? That his arrogance set her more ablaze than every time he had worked to accommodate her?

Eira lunged for him. Cullen caught her sword with his hand— the icy blade quivering against a pocket of air. His other hand grabbed her wrist as she went to attack.

"You look satisfied," she hummed.

"How can I not be, when your eyes are on me, and me alone?" He tilted his head slightly, brows darting up. "I told you, Eira…" His voice dropped low, barely a whisper and only for her. "Love me. Hate me. So long as I am in your thoughts."

She didn't have a chance to respond before Olivin had recovered enough to join back in, not to be outdone. Eira and Cullen broke apart. The three of them circled, magic and weapons at the ready. The weight of everything unsaid nearly broke the air in two. The tension in their muscles broke first.

Their three-way duel was frantic. Chaotic. And, yet, somehow, they seemed to know just how to move between each other. Magic sparked, steel and ice and light clashed. The men moved with the prowess of two great predators and Eira wasn't sure if they wanted more to consume each other, or claim her. Which only set her heart to racing even faster.

She was drawn to them both. Drawn to Cullen with a force that was indescribable and unshakable. He knew her. Every gaze felt as if it pierced straight through her clothes—straight through muscle and bone and into her very core.

The energy around Olivin was wholly different and yet equally undeniable. He was an enigma. Every time their shoulders brushed or bodies slammed into each other served as a reminder of just how much exploring there was left to do. How curious she was to find out how—*if* they could fit together.

She fought with all her might, emotions fueling each burst of power. They moved as if the end of this duel would hold the answer to the question none of them had dared to ask.

Finally, the three of them broke apart but didn't immediately spring back together. Breaths labored. Bodies threatening to give out with every tremble of their knees.

Olivin finally released his sword. It unraveled into strands of light, disappearing at the same time as Eira's blade of ice. Cullen leaned heavily against the railing for support, his back bending over it as he stretched.

As their breathing calmed, silence fell over them. Eira became keenly aware that the others had left at some point, focusing on random tasks. Some probably belowdecks helping prepare food. Perhaps they, too, realized that this was a breaking point between the three of them and didn't want to see who was going to emerge victorious, and who would be laid to rest on a battlefield of hearts.

Olivin was the first to recover. He stood a bit straighter, eyes darting between Eira and Cullen. With a few steps he closed the distance between them. Eira responded with her own movement. They all seemed to meet in the middle.

"I care for her, and if you—" Olivin spoke to Cullen, but the other man didn't give him a chance to finish.

"It's up to her." Cullen shifted and turned the focus to Eira. "If your heart is his, then I will gladly step aside. As fun as that little duel was, and as much as I'd gladly do it again, I'm not here to play petty games."

"Neither am I," Eira said hastily, hoping her next words didn't immediately contradict that. "But…I don't know how I feel," she admitted. "I know I care for you both, in different ways. But if you were to ask me to choose, right now, the answer is I don't know.

"I've been so focused on surviving, keeping everyone safe, regaining my magic, learning all Adela has to teach, figuring out what's next… My focus hasn't been on sorting through matters of my heart." Eira shook her head, glancing away. The brief shame of admitting it not just to herself, but to them, that she had been keeping them all in limbo, was almost too much. Yet, she forced her eyes back, anyway. They deserved that much. "I feel as though I've only just begun to get my footing enough again to *start* thinking about it. But I'm still learning who I am, and it wouldn't be fair to choose either of you as I am.

"I don't expect you to wait for me to decide, either," she added hastily. The words were flowing freely, riding on the currents of relief at being finally said. "I'm not asking that. But I'm not going to force myself into a decision, nor fall on a whim. Who I choose—if I choose love again at all—is going to be on my terms."

They both stared at her. Eira's attention volleyed between them, searching for any indication of justified anger, or brokenhearted hurt. But she found neither. Instead, a slight but tender smile curled the edges of Cullen's lips. Olivin's eyes looked like those of a cat's, staring down a challenging prey.

"That's understandable," Cullen said.

"Fine by me." Olivin nodded. The two men shared a brief and tense look. Yet, throughout it, grins split their lips. "You know I'm not going to make this easy on you, don't you?"

"I'm not going to fight you," Cullen retorted.

"Oh?"

"I don't think I have to." Cullen folded his arms.

Olivin tried to draw his height. Cullen didn't bother attempting to rise to the measure, instead looking even more secure.

A disbelieving laugh escaped Eira. "You're both…all right with this?"

"It seems a bit unreasonable, if you ask me, to put you on the spot and ask you to make this choice." Olivin eased away from his posturing with Cullen. His expression shifted into something more sincere. "Especially when you have so much you're sorting through."

"No matter who you choose, or when you choose, I want you to be certain," Cullen added. There was meaning layered underneath those words. *I don't want to rush into this again,* he said without saying. Eira remembered what he'd said when they'd first spoken alone. *I want to see if the man I am becoming will manage to earn your trust and your heart again.*

"I do want to make one thing clear, however," Olivin spoke. "Are there any rules?"

"Rules?" Eira echoed, confused, despite Cullen looking like he already grasped what Olivin was trying to say.

"Are we holding back?" Olivin cocked his head to the side, a lazy smirk gliding across his lips. "Or may we do whatever it takes—whatever feels right in a moment, to win your heart?"

Both of their eyes were on her, expectant. Eira swallowed thickly. They looked as if they wanted to devour her whole. A shiver glided through her. Part of her…wanted to let them.

"If we're all on the same page, and are all right with it…I don't know why we would hold back." Eira's voice dropped to little more than a whisper. There was a warble brought on by a shameful surge of desire that coursed through her. Unbridled fantasies, unleashed by their permission—their *enthusiasm*—raced through her mind. Every thought more scandalous than the last of what they might do to win her heart. Of just how fun the process of discovery could be for them all when there were no more barriers or questions.

"Excellent." Olivin shifted to face Cullen. "Then—"

Cullen stole his words before Olivin had the chance to finish. "May the best man win."

Eira bit the insides of her cheeks, keeping herself from reminding them that whether she chose either—or neither—she was fairly certain she'd be the one on top.

· CHAPTER ·

TWENTY-THREE

T HE WORLD WAS alive around her. The sea was a wellspring of power. Every drop of water in the air—from the salt spray to the clouds above—seemed to tremble as her magic washed over it.

Eira sat perfectly still on deck. Adela circled her like a hawk. Even though Eira's eyes were closed, she could feel the pirate queen's presence through the shifts in magic.

"More, Eira," Adela commanded.

Eira furrowed her brow. A bead of sweat rolled down her neck as her magic ran down the sides of the ship and curled with the waves. Adela's power pressed against her, as unyielding as the thick layer of ice that covered the *Stormfrost*. But there wasn't a trace of it in the seas.

She curled her hands into fists, as if trying to grasp the ocean itself.

Adela rapped Eira's knuckles with her cane. "No physical tells," she scolded. Eira relaxed her fingers. The tip of the cane pressed between her brows. "Here, too."

Eira bit the insides of her cheeks but forced her face to remain passive. She'd never had a teacher that had demanded so much of her. She'd had supportive instructors. Her uncles, who conveniently always told her to avoid pushing herself. But never someone who demanded more—who stopped her from holding herself back.

"Results, Eira," Adela sighed.

The water churned underneath the vessel. Eira caught on to the currents, shifting them. Relaxing wasn't just a function of keeping her magic a secret from her enemies. Once she stopped trying to exert force, controlling water became easier than she'd ever imagined. She had to move with it, not against it.

The ship groaned and swayed as the currents swelled around it, under Eira's control.

"A bit more to starboard."

Eira inhaled air and exhaled power. *Stormfrost* turned.

"Good," Adela praised. Eira opened her eyes to see the pirate queen lowering her compass. "We're back on track. Keep us there this time."

Eira caught the compass when Adela tossed it to her as she stood. "I'll do my best."

"I don't want your best. I want perfection." The sentiment could be harsh, but it came off as an expectation. Adela truly believed Eira could continue managing the direction of the ship. Her friends ascended the stairs and the pirate queen's focus shifted. "I appreciate your timeliness today."

"I believe yesterday I was late because I was providing wind to the sails." Cullen's lordly audacity had empowered him to have no fear when it came to sharing his every thought and opinion with Adela. A trait Eira found herself admiring. For once, he wasn't using his noble training like a shield to hide himself behind, but like a sword to be brandished.

"Ah yes, because I was entirely at the whims of the weather before you came along. However did I manage before Lord Cullen Drowel boarded my vessel and graced me with his powers?" Adela's tone was drier than the Western Waste.

The muscles in Cullen's jaw bulged slightly but he said nothing more. Noelle sniggered.

"And what is so amusing?" Adela turned to her. "I don't see you contributing much on the vessel."

"Just wait until we get to these mines." Noelle folded her arms. But there was no burst of flame. She'd already been scolded once for recklessly using fire on the boat. Even on a boat covered in ice, fire was still handled with extreme care.

"For your sake, hope you are more than talk when the time comes." Adela tapped her cane. "Now, if we are quite finished, I have more important things to do than wait on you all and make small talk with those I couldn't care less about."

Adela constantly reminded them of such, but Eira had yet to see it. Because every day she would wake and join Adela on the topmost deck and they would work together on Eira's magic. By the time the sun was high, her friends would join her. They would spar until they were too exhausted to move, Adela usually overseeing them. Sometimes Crow. Occasionally others. Sometimes they did it alone, knowing without ever being told that if they neglected their training, they would certainly hear it from the Pirate Queen.

Dinner was in the galley, together with her friends. After, Eira would always return to Adela for another hour or two of magical work and experimentation.

"You seem different again."

Eira was jolted back to the present at Olivin's words. She hadn't heard him approach, being too focused on maintaining her magic on the waters curling underneath the ship. The moment she turned her attention to him, her powers wavered. It was a subtle shift in the vessel, but a noticeable one—at least to her, and to Adela, since the pirate queen's gaze snapped her way. Only for a second. But long enough to assure Eira that Adela had felt it.

With a slow breath, Eira shifted her magic and the ocean moved in tandem. The vessel leveled out again. It was as though, in the back of her mind, she was carrying the ship within her own hand. Like a muscle she could never quite relax, but could forget how tense it was.

"Different *again*?" Eira repeated. He'd said that almost every time their paths had crossed over the past four days. "Goodness, I should watch out, or you might not recognize me by the time we make it to Carsovia."

"I've begun to think that's your intention." He shifted, hands in his pockets. They'd been given some additional clothing from the crew's communal pile. Olivin wore loose-fitting trousers that pulled in tightly around his ankles and tucked into his boots. His shirt was more of a vest, loose. Freer than she'd ever seen him during the competition.

"Perhaps, but I could say the same for you." Eira tugged lightly on the hem of his sleeve by his shoulder. "You're looking less like a lord of Meru and a lot more like a pirate by the day."

"Would you believe me if I said this is closer to how I would dress when I wasn't at state events?"

"Not in the slightest."

He chuckled. "Well, it's true. I might be a lord by title, but remember my family was on the cusp of disgraced. After the circumstances surrounding my parents' deaths, the assets were seized by the crown."

"I had no idea," Eira whispered. Her attention went to Yonlin, and then to Cullen. Their conversations during the tournament returned to her. *Things are not that simple, Eira,* Cullen had said. When she'd looked to him to make his own choice and stand up for himself, he had looked back to her in confusion. She'd had no idea, really, of the stakes that surrounded his family. If the truth of what he'd done in the East ever came out…would his family lose everything the crown had given them? It seemed too cruel for the Emperor and Empress Solaris…but Vi had shown Eira that appearances could be deceiving. Perhaps more was at stake for him and his family than just appearances. "What happened to you and Yonlin when it all was taken?"

"Lumeria is—was," he corrected with the slightest wince, "a fair ruler. She wasn't cruel enough to put two young men on the streets. But we were effectively under house arrest in a place of her choosing. We were supported by the crown, but nothing was *ours,* for a time." He sighed softly, shoulders sinking slightly. Eira wondered if they sagged from the relief of hardships long passed, or from the weight they still carried. "Once her knights had proof that we weren't involved with what happened at the Archives, they reinstated my title and some of our family's assets. But the damage was done to our reputation. The lands our family had owned had to be sold off as the coffers had mysteriously dried up. Our home was in ruins. There was nothing to go back to."

"How did you prove you weren't involved?" Eira didn't want to linger on damaged reputations or lost fortune.

"We didn't. Deneya did."

"And that was how you learned about the Court of Shadows," Eira realized.

"If they could get enough information on the Pillars to clear Yonlin's and my name, then I knew it was my best chance to find my sister. Deneya had been the one appointed to oversee our care while we were wards of the crown; I'd already known her." His tone turned harsh whenever he mentioned his sister. Eira wondered if he realized that he, instinctively, looked back toward Meru.

Was there anyone in the Court of Shadows that had been there purely for the sake of helping Meru? A true patriot? Surely someone, but it seemed as though everyone Eira knew had been there for their own gain as much as anyone else's. She'd gone to hunt down Ferro. Olivin was there to find his sister. Ducot went on Adela's behalf, and after Ulvarth.

They were all hunting down someone. Even now.

"What do you think will happen to the Court of Shadows?" she asked softly.

"It'll persist. I hope. Because they're going to be our best chance of getting a foothold in Risen. Or, at least facts about what happened and not propaganda. I wouldn't be surprised if Ulvarth has already seated himself on Lumeria's throne."

The thought churned Eira's stomach. She could only imagine how it made Olivin feel. "Do you really think we'll make it back to Risen, to Lumeria's castle?"

"No point in returning if we can't. We must to take Ulvarth down and actually make a world that will be safe for those we love." His tone was raw, determined. "But we'll tackle problems one at a time. Carsovia and these mines first, to get our ship.

Maybe we can also solve the mystery of who was supplying the Pillars flash beads. Cutting off their source will severely hamper them."

"Not a bad idea." Eira was surprised it hadn't crossed her mind yet. Ulvarth had already used the flash beads to his advantage and if he still had access to them, he no doubt would again. Especially now that his own powers were gone. Unless, he'd found a way to restore them…

"You two," Adela interrupted abruptly, startling Eira from her thoughts. "Would you care to join the rest of us in today's drills?"

"Of course." Olivin led the charge over. Eira nodded as well.

Adela murmured under her breath as she walked by, "If the ship veers off course once, I will have to reconsider you and your friend's lives."

"Understood." It was so common for Adela to threaten everyone that it hardly bothered her anymore.

"We're going to trade places tonight," Adela announced the moment Eira walked into her cabin, alone.

"How do you mean?" Eira crossed to her usual chair at the pirate queen's bedside. Crow no doubt had questions when she'd first begun putting it out. But Adela's handmaiden was discreet and had never said a word of it to Eira or anyone else. Which had led Eira to be equally tight-lipped about what went on during her evenings with the pirate queen. Moreover, she didn't want to give her friends false hope that her long-shot plans might work. Not until she'd made more progress on them.

"*I* would like to try opening your channel, instead of you opening mine."

Her nerves were ablaze at the thought and Eira pushed ice under her skin, forcing herself to remain calm. She'd already lost her channel once; putting it at risk again—for any reason—had her instantly uneasy. But Adela was a far more skilled Waterrunner than she was, even now after all their work together.

"To do this, I will first give you control of the *Stormfrost* so that I can focus more on you."

"Excuse me?" Eira blinked. The sensation of vulnerability was instantly replaced with responsibility.

"As I pull back my ice, you will replace it—until the entire ship is covered as it is now. We will start from the hull. If, *when*, your magic wavers, I will open your channel. But under no circumstances are you to stop. I will not have my ship exposed."

Eira supposed she should be grateful Adela had given her any indication of her plans. But the mere thought of what Adela was asking had Eira's throat tightening enough that she had to swallow to remind herself she could breathe, much less speak. "I understand."

Adela was full of continued surprises. With a terse sigh and small roll of her eyes, she leaned forward. Eira nearly jumped out of her skin when Adela rested her hand of ice on top of Eira's. The touch was gentle. Reassuring. In that frosty hand, she saw her Uncle Grahm's reassuring grip. She felt his cool hand on her forehead when she was a child, sweltering with a fever her magic couldn't abate.

It felt…like family. Like home. Even though Adela had sworn up and down that she wasn't Eira's mother—and Eira believed her—that made her contact no less comforting.

"Eira, listen to me, because I will only exhaust my breath on it once." *Ah*, the Adela she knew was still there. Sharp and pointed as ever. "You can do this. I am asking nothing of you that you're not already capable of."

"You think so?" Eira asked softly. She half expected Adela to scold her for her hesitation and doubt. Or rescind the vote of confidence.

"Your mind limits you before your magic does. Stop being afraid of your power just because some narrow-minded, weak fool somewhere in your history was intimidated and told you to hold back." Adela's fingers closed tightly around Eira's palm, as though she were trying to brand the words into Eira and make them undeniable.

It worked.

How many times had she refrained because someone had told her no? In the dim lantern light of Adela's cabin, Eira was transported back to another low-lit moment, before the tournament began. Before she was even on Meru.

Her Aunt Gwen had said something similar, back then. She had been the one to encourage Eira. To tell her *yes* when her brother and uncles were telling her no. And Eira had listened. She'd dared to take that chance. But…

"What happens if—when—I stop holding back and people get hurt?" The fear that had haunted her for what felt like her whole life returned. "Every time I've taken a chance on my magic, someone else paid the consequences." First was Marcus, and her family. Then the Court of Shadows. Had she also somehow doomed Lumeria and the royals for goading on Ulvarth? Eira looked to Adela for answers she knew the pirate queen couldn't have, but hoped she would anyway.

"You make friends with your failures. Continuing to push them away and fear them will only turn them into bigger beasts than what they already are." Adela leveled her gaze with Eira's. "Do not let your responsibilities overwhelm you. Let them focus you and move forward."

Eira gave a small nod. Then a stronger one. "I understand."

"Understanding and internalizing are two different things. Work on the latter." Adela leaned away and withdrew her hand. "For now, we will practice, together."

Eira nodded and allowed her gaze to go soft, blurring slightly. Her face was relaxed, as emotionless as she had seen Adela's countless times. Possessing deep focus without betraying such was certainly a learned technique. To be relaxed when every emotion, every strand of control was wound up tightly within.

Connecting with the magic around her was easier and easier

every time. Eira could feel where her friends still sat around the dinner table. The few crew that milled about on the deck. The majority that slept in the crew's quarters belowdecks.

Above, beneath, around it all was Adela's power. When Eira had first stepped onto the *Stormfrost* it was an overwhelming amount of magic. But now she had grown accustomed to it—had begun to untangle it enough that she could feel the difference in Adela's strong currents and determine what of her power went to sustaining ice not just on the ship, but in distant corners of the world. The pirate queen's powers rippled across the seas, using the salt water as a conduit to reach lands far beyond Eira's realm of comprehension. Though, there had been nights as she'd lain in her hammock that Eira had tried to follow those unseen currents with her mind's eye. To travel the world on the back of Adela's magic.

For now, however, she kept her focus restricted to the *Stormfrost* alone and felt the first moment Adela's powers began to unravel. It was an invisible handoff. The second Adela's powers left, Eira replaced them with her own. The ship thawed and froze again with a crackle that Eira wondered if anyone but them would notice. She tried to make the transition as seamless as possible, considering it a victory if there wasn't any disruption in the vessel.

Around halfway up, her magic wavered slightly. Eira took a slow breath, steadying the currents within her. She reclaimed her focus and continued.

Within what felt only like a few minutes—though she couldn't be certain it was such a slight amount of time—the *Stormfrost* was in her magical grasp from the lowest ridge of the hull to the tip of the tallest mast. There was an almost audible *pop* in Eira's mind as her power snapped into place, wholly replacing Adela's. It was an immense drain on her strength, but admittedly easier to maintain once the entirety of the vessel was in her hold.

"How does it feel?" Adela asked.

"Not as bad—" As if to spite her, the moment she went to speak, her magic wavered from lack of focus. Cracking and creaking could be heard throughout the vessel as the frost fractured.

"Keep it together."

Eira wondered how much of the ship was actually being held together by the frost. Now that her magic was on it, she could feel the scars of old wounds along its body—never fully patched, but rather mended by ice and long-ago rush jobs.

"Good," Adela murmured. "Now to make it a bit easier on you."

A chill like the first kiss of fallen snow landing on her cheeks after a long fall settled on Eira. The ship was in her grasp, and she was in Adela's. Eira shifted, bracing herself.

Adela wouldn't take her magic from her now. Though perhaps everything had been a ploy. Perhaps Adela had wanted Eira to regain her power only so she could help Adela learn what she wanted and then take it from her again.

"Your body grows hot. You fear me, still." Whether that pleased or frustrated Adela was impossible to tell.

Eira met her eyes. "I think I would be a fool not to."

"You are right in that." Adela leaned forward and reached out her hand. But, this time, rather than going for Eira's hands, she grabbed her chin. Inspecting her. "Do you think you could withstand an assault from me?"

"I will crush this ship if you try." Eira's voice was as low and dangerous as Adela's.

"The right answer." She smirked slightly. "Do not fear anyone, least of all yourself." Eira nodded, Adela's hand still holding her chin. "Now, let us see what the true depths of your power really are…"

An invisible, icy hand felt like it reached down her throat to grab her heart. Her chest seized. Eira inhaled sharply but kept her focus on the ship at all costs.

Adela broke her own rules, brow furrowing with focus. Eira remained poised and still. She still couldn't tell how much of this was a test, and how much was genuine experimentation on Adela's part. But she continued to give the pirate queen the benefit of the doubt and was rewarded for it as a wave of new power surged through her.

"That's it," Eira encouraged on instinct.

Adela's smirk grew, self-satisfaction abounding. "Keep steady, now."

There was another surge and then a sudden drop in her power. "Adela—"

"I said keep steady," Adela snapped.

Eira continued keeping her focus with all her might, furrowing her brow as well. The pirate queen had a hold on her magic, but it was a clumsy hand, still. No wonder Eira had managed to close her own channel with Ulvarth's when she had fought him, if this was how much finesse she had lacked.

Without warning, an invisible blow to her chest knocked the wind from her. Eira sagged, as if she'd been physically struck. She gasped, magic snapping and crackling around her. Frost fell from the ceiling like ominous confetti.

Adela staggered as well, blinking, as if whatever had struck Eira hit her, too. But there was no time to check on her. The ship hissed and popped. Frost dissipating. Eira thrust up both her hands, trying to regain control as the *Stormfrost* lurched.

They were under attack.

"**B**ASTARDS," ADELA GROWLED, and stood, exuding strength, but only for a moment. The ship lurched again, sending Eira tumbling from her chair.

Eira forewent bracing her physical body to brace her magic. She felt the moment of impact this time as some foreign object exploded against the side of the ship. The attack hit her magic—hit *her*, sending her reeling.

Her head spun and the hold that Adela had on her magic retreated, pulling up her stomach with it. Eira retched and braced herself against the floor. Though she didn't know if she was bracing for another dizzying attack, or if she was bracing for Adela's scolding. Eira was certain the rug she'd just ruined was probably very rare and expensive.

Icy fingers closed around her chin once more, wrenching her face up, ignoring the spittle. Adela's arm had magically extended to an inhuman length so that the pirate queen didn't even have to kneel to reach her. She looked down at Eira not with disdain, as Eira would've once expected, but determination.

"I will deal with these bastards personally," Adela vowed. "Until I return, the *Stormfrost* is in your hands. Do *not* let my ship go down."

Eira didn't have a chance to ask for details on what was happening. Adela left in a blur of hasty steps that crackled with power underneath her feet. She opened her mouth to call after the pirate queen when another explosion battered the side of the ship.

Digging her nails into the rug to steady herself, and her magic,

Eira weathered the blast. And then a second. She closed the holes in the frost on the side of the ship as they were made.

Eira pressed her eyes shut and drew shaking, shuddering breaths. She hardly had time to recover before there was another blast. The whole vessel groaned and tipped. Eira flopped onto her back, stretching out her arms and legs. Ice covered her, melding her with the ship.

The sounds of the chaos on deck faded away. People screaming. Heavy footsteps. Flashes of power grew distant from her awareness. Eira focused only on the *Stormfrost*. Her consciousness stretched around it, flowing through the ice, and reaching into the water.

She curled her fingers, magic crackling and charging through the frost. The sea swelled, pushing the vessel upright again. Eira withdrew her power and focused back on bracing for another blast. Just in time.

A scream raked up her throat and found no escape—frost had covered her mouth. Pain burned her side. It was as if she was the one being struck, rather than the vessel. As though her own flesh was being seared and carved away.

Eira thickened the ice once more. She wasn't going to let them win. Whoever "they" were. Be it the Pillars, a rebel pirate faction, or someone else long scorned by Adela…it didn't matter. It wasn't about them in that moment. This moment was hers alone, to prove to herself that the pirate queen's trust wasn't misplaced. That she had made progress on deepening her connection with her magic and learning new feats of power.

As the battle around the vessel raged, her awareness of her own body continued to slip away. She could feel the heavy footsteps of people racing about on the deck. She could feel the inconsequential pockmarks for magic bursts not even a quarter as strong as what was assaulting the side of the hull. Even though she wasn't battling alongside them, in her mind's eye, she began to construct the image of her friends.

And if she could see them, then she could help them.

Her muscles spasmed as she drew more power. Sheets of ice rose to block attacks on the deck outside. They served as shields for her friends to hide behind. Spears jutted from railings, skewering those she couldn't recognize. All the while, Eira continued to preserve the hull.

The tide of the battle turned, dictated by Adela's magic as the pirate queen gained the upper hand. Eira breathed a sigh of relief through her nose. But she didn't release her magic, not until two hands cupped the frost on the sides of her face and a distant voice called, "… back… Come back…"

Eira worked to relax her magic. Little by little, she released the magic making her one with the *Stormfrost*. The frost that had covered her cracked. Her ears were free and her consciousness slowly returned.

"What do you think you're doing in here?" Adela's cool voice demanded to know.

"What have *you* been doing in here?" Cullen, she could hear him clearly now. "What are you doing to her?"

"I have done nothing that she did not welcome enthusiastically and could manage beautifully." Adela's footsteps approached. Eira's eyes cracked open, finding Cullen kneeling at her side and Adela looming over. "Up with you. I will resume command of my ship."

Adela's lips were pressed into a thin line, the magic in the air around her writhing with agitation. And yet, there was a glint of what Eira would dare say was delight in her eyes. Was Adela impressed? *Manage beautifully…* Had there ever been two sweeter words said about her? The mere possibility soothed over the phantom aches that still riddled Eira sides and chest.

"Is the *Stormfrost* all right?" Eira croaked.

A long stretch of silence. Then, finally, "Passable." That was the best Eira knew she would get. But, for Adela, combined with everything else, she might as well have been singing Eira's praises.

"What happened?" Eira rubbed her stomach where she had

felt one of the blows. Her skin was intact. But that didn't stop her from lifting her tunic and searching for bruising. There was none. How had she felt so viscerally? What had Adela managed to teach her all these weeks without ever laying it out explicitly?

"Your magic? That was the natural evolution of seeing through the frost, as we had discussed. The attack? Come and see for yourself." Adela turned and then paused halfway to the door. She looked back to Cullen, any glimpse of approval in her eyes having vanished. "And you…should you ever enter my personal chambers again without permission, I *will* kill you."

Cullen frowned but had the good sense to say nothing. The moment Adela was gone, his arms flew around Eira's shoulders, pulling her in tight. Compared to the magic and the frost, Cullen was searing hot. She wanted to melt into him, to lose all shape of her own and rely entirely on his in an utterly boneless state. She couldn't resist the indulgence of his comfort for one sweet minute.

"Do you think you could stop terrifying me just once?" he murmured into her hair.

"Come now, if I did that, you would get bored of me." She inhaled his scent—sweat, salt, and the freshness of wind over snowcapped mountains. *Him.*

He chuckled and shook his head. "I could never be bored of you."

"Everyone else?" she asked.

"They're fine, everyone's fine. The other ship, however…"

"Good." Eira closed her eyes and took another slow breath. "Do you remember the last time you pulled me from a magical, frozen state?"

"As if I'd ever forget." Cullen's arms tightened briefly. He held her as tightly as he had that day in the room following the second trial, the day she had learned her parents weren't who she'd thought they were. "No matter how far you go, I will always be ready to pull you back the moment you need."

Her eyes fluttered closed and Eira sighed softly. A lifeline.

A North Star. Not a shackle holding her in place, or a high wall surrounding her, but a dotted line on a map to guide her from the brink—a tether to grab before she toppled over the edge of being lost forever.

Eira pulled away. Their eyes locked. Something had shifted—been shifting. Yet, in this breath, it was all the more palpable and real. His fingers pressed into her skin a little deeper. The air was a little thinner. Every swell of her chest against his reminded her just how close they were.

Kiss me, her heart whispered, loud enough that for a moment she thought she'd spoken the words aloud. His eyes darted to her lips, as if she really had.

"Cullen, I—" She didn't have a chance to finish, her words stolen with a kiss that sent a burning rush all the way down to her toes.

A gasp escaped her as the familiar taste of him consumed her senses. The feeling of him was like a return home at long last—somewhere she once knew, yet had been changed by time and distance. A place that she couldn't see quite the same as she once had, yet also remained imprinted on her heart. His hands moved to her face as her fingers curled around his clothes, balling into fists and pulling him closer, were that possible.

Time held its breath.

His lips parted, allowing her entry, and a gasp escaped. She wasn't sure who it belonged to, nor did she care. Cullen's hands continued to move; his fingers were now in her hair. Perhaps it was the rush of yet another near-death experience. Perhaps it was the tension that they had been building with every spar on the deck. With every look across hammocks in the dim light belowdecks. Every brush of their thighs as they ate… Building, and building, *and building*. All the way back to that night in Champion Village when it took everything they had to hold back.

But the things she would let him do to her now if he only asked…

He pulled away abruptly.

An unbecoming groan escaped her. "Why are you always the sensible one?"

"One of us must be." He tucked a strand of hair behind her ear, no doubt one that he had just pulled out of place. The movement was gentle, a stark contrast to him leaning to rasp in her ear, "I doubt Adela would want me locking the door and taking you on her floor."

A whole fresh wave of heat rushed through Eira at *that*. But it was doused by better sense prevailing.

Eira went to stand. Every muscle in her body was exhausted. Doing anything more than being putty in his palms and kissing was too much, given the pain that jolted between her joints. She stumbled.

"Are you sure you should be standing?" Cullen was at her side, one arm around her back. Gripping her arm closest to him to support her. "You could—"

"I'm fine, just exhausted." She gave him a weary smile in an attempt to reassure him. It was hard not to touch his face and get lost in his embrace once more. But... "I want to see what happened." She could only indulge so many seconds of escapism.

"I could carry you," he offered.

Eira considered it. She felt far shakier on her feet than ever before. She hadn't been aware of how much magic she'd been using in the thick of it. But now that it was gone, and the rush was leaving her...it felt like she had gone five days without sleeping, running nonstop the entire time.

"Just help me, I want to walk on my own as much as possible. I can do it," she decided. No matter how tempting the idea of being cradled in his arms was, she wanted to move on her own two feet.

If the roles were reversed, Adela would walk. So Eira would, too.

Cullen didn't fight her. He tightened his arm around her middle and she leveraged his support as they stepped out of Adela's cabin and onto the deck, covered in the aftermath of battle.

· CHAPTER ·

TWENTY-FIVE

THE FIRST THING her eyes were drawn to was an orange glow in the dark night sea.

The ocean was burning.

No… Not the ocean. The remnants of another vessel smoldered as it was slowly being consumed by the churning waves.

Opposite the entrance to Adela's cabin was a circle of pirates. Eira couldn't see what was at their center. But if Adela was among them then the situation was in hand.

Eira scanned the deck for her friends. She knew Cullen had said everyone was all right. She doubted he would've spent time kissing her if they hadn't been…but she was still relieved the moment her eyes landed on the small group that had become her entire world. She didn't have to go far to reach them; they were perched on one of the two staircases on either side of the entrance to Adela's cabin that led up to the quarterdeck.

They were bruised and scuffed. A thin trail of blood ran from Olivin's temple down to the tip of his chin. But he seemed more focused on Yonlin—who was pushing his elder brother's fretting away firmly enough that Eira wasn't concerned for his well-being. The one who seemed in the worst shape among them was Noelle.

She gripped her bicep at its top, almost by her shoulder, no doubt restricting the blood flow to a deep gash that ran from her forearm almost up to her fingers. She grinned through the pain, but Eira could see from the bulging muscles in her jaw just how tightly her teeth were clenched. Alyss was already working on mending the wound. Judging from the thin scars and deep pockmarks, she had been for some time.

"…be a hero," Ducot was saying as they approached.

"What can I say? Being the center of attention just comes naturally to me." Noelle leaned back into him as Alyss continued her work. She rested against one of Ducot's thighs. His arms were wrapped around her shoulders as if he could protect her from the pain.

"Well, make it stop coming naturally."

Noelle reached up and took his hand, guiding it to the forearm that Alyss had already healed. She ran his fingers over the flesh that was now raised and gnarled. The faintly glowing dots on Ducot's brow tipped upward in the center.

"My love…" he whispered. It almost stopped Eira in her tracks. She knew the two of them were close…but the way he spoke was with a whole different level of intimacy and understanding. It made her chest squeeze and her hand tighten slightly around Cullen's waist.

Noelle reached up and cupped Ducot's cheek. "Now you're not the only one with battle scars. We can both be 'monsters.'" The way she said the word betrayed that it was an echo of something he probably had uttered in quiet confidence more than once.

Eira had never seen Noelle look at anyone the way she looked at Ducot in that moment. They loved each other. Unlike Eira, Noelle had moved slowly, and with purpose. Ducot had remained steadfast at her side. They had worked through issues as they had arisen. Eira hoped that they were the ones Alyss was using as the muses for her story. They were the ones getting it right.

Maybe Eira could look to them as well. She was clearly more ready to start crossing lines again and exploring feelings than she'd previously thought.

"You will never be a monster," Ducot murmured, and kissed Noelle's temple.

"I'm quite all right with my enemies thinking I am."

He chuckled.

"Eira." Olivin was the first to notice her approach. He stopped pestering his younger brother and stood. "Are you all right?"

She nodded. "I'm fine, just tired." Perhaps it was due to the thoughts of relationships being fresh in her mind, or the tingling of her lips, but Eira had never been more aware of how close Cullen was to her. Of how tightly he was holding her. Part of her wanted to push him away…and the other part wanted to hold him tighter.

It was a reminder that, despite their patience and understanding, she needed to dedicate as much time to sorting out her heart as she was to her magic.

"What happened to you? To the whole ship?" Eira asked. "I was in Adela's cabin the entire time."

"Was she keeping you safe?" Lavette asked. No matter how much chaos unfolded around her, she was ever astute. Always looking for new information and important details. There was a time Eira might've found it annoying, but she'd begun to admire the other woman for it. Never missing a beat and always keeping her footing was a goal of Eira's.

Eira didn't see the point of lying. "I was helping her keep the ship together."

"Adela let you helm the *Stormfrost*?" Ducot's words were still soft, but no longer with tenderness. He was clearly struggling to sort out meaning that Eira had hardly had time to parse herself. Wonder and awe mixed with horror.

"It was just helping her thicken the ice on the hull," Eira backtracked slightly. But Adela had said… *Until I return, she's in your hands*.

"I see." Ducot seemed unconvinced as well, but a commotion from the circle of pirates behind them interrupted the conversation.

There was a burst of cheers and then a frenzy of movement. The pirates descended on whatever was in their center. The mass of people shifted—a tangle of limbs, grabbing and pulling—and when they retreated, a man was revealed.

He had been stripped naked and bound with a thick line of

rope. Raised markings—as much scars as tattoos—covered his shoulders, intricate line work that reminded Eira almost of Lightspinning, but the shapes were different. These weren't layered circles and delicate lines, but harder shapes. They looked like the runes from the coliseum and the gate had been imprinted directly onto his body.

He glared up toward Adela. And the pirate queen, in turn, looked back to Eira with a slight smile dancing across her lips.

"I think we shall leave it up to her," Adela announced. Everyone fell silent.

"Her?" one of the pirates asked, flabbergasted.

"Yes, she was the one who was the steward of *Stormfrost* during the attack." This announcement caused murmuring between the pirates. They shared uncertain glances that were turned back in Eira's direction.

She stood a little taller.

"This is a lutenz of Carsovia."

Varren sucked in air behind her as Adela spoke.

"Captain of the ship that attacked our vessel." Adela motioned to the bound and gagged man. "What would you have us do with him?"

What was the game that Adela was playing? Was she trying to make a wedge between Eira and the other pirates? No...that couldn't be it. If Adela had wanted the crew to dislike her, she would've never allowed Eira to hold any esteem in the first place.

"Kill him," Varren said coldly. Eira glanced over her shoulder. The man's eyes were haunted and as cold as his words. He stared at the man from Carsovia as though he wasn't even human.

The *lutenz*—which Eira assumed to be a term for some kind of knight or leader of Carsovia, given that Adela said he was a captain—for his part seemed completely unfazed by Varren's harsh reaction to the mere sight of him. In fact, a smile stretched over the top edges of his gag, curling around it as he bared the fabric in his teeth, spittle dripping off his chin. There was a sinister and cruel glint to his eyes.

He had to know he was going to die. How else could he be calm enough to smile, rather than beg, before Adela and all her crew? A dead man had nothing to lose—no reason to tell them any pertinent information. The look in his eyes reminded her of the Pillars. They, too, shared that same crazed and wild aura.

The likeness gave her the strength to stand a little taller. She was even more grateful that she hadn't accepted Cullen's offer to carry her. Men like this, even dead ones, were the last people she would show weakness to.

"Well?" Adela asked again, mildly impatient.

"We cannot use him in any way?" Eira doubted they could, but had to ask anyway.

"Wishful thinking, girl." Adela tapped her cane. "He is about as useful to us as a torn sail."

"The Empress of Carsovia doesn't make deals," Varren added. Eira glanced back at him. Lavette was holding his hand now. His face was still twisted with hatred. The closest she'd ever seen to it was when he had first told them about the mines.

She returned her attention to the bound man. If her assessment was right, and he was as loyal to his empire as the Pillars were to Ulvarth, the man would no doubt do everything in his power to kill himself before he could be used against his nation in any way. What made someone view their life worth so little and another's worth so much? And what type of place was Carsovia that it demanded this loyalty?

There would be no way he would join the crew, which meant he couldn't earn his place. All the resources on the *Stormfrost* were carefully allotted, and had to be dwindling given how long they'd been at sea. He wouldn't give them information…

"He dies." Two words summed up her conclusion.

"Yes, yes." Adela hummed, ever impatient. "We knew this. *How* does he die?"

Eira's curiosity toward Adela's motivations piqued further. What did the pirate queen presume to gain by deferring to her in this manner? Surely not the love of her crew, judging by their agitated and confused faces.

It dawned on her. *This must be a test.*

Adela was nothing if not overcautious. She calculated everything and it was clear she was at odds with Carsovia, given her demand for Eira to kill the man in charge of their flash bead mines. Adela must be wanting to ensure Eira didn't have any love for the other empire. It didn't matter to Adela that Eira claimed she'd never heard of Carsovia until arriving on Meru, when she had also proven herself during their many discussions to be well-read on matters of the world. Perhaps she'd been so successful that Adela wasn't truly certain if Eira knew nothing.

"If you wanted so badly to meet the Queen of the Seas, then you should die by her domain," Eira declared. The words were void of any emotion. Any guilt or remorse Eira might have felt had vanished, smothered. Her eyes met the man's. "Tell me, Lutenz, how good of a swimmer are you? How long can your magic hold up?"

His only response was a low chuckle, barely audible through his gag. Eyes aflame.

"Give him to the sea!" Adela declared.

Cullen gripped her tighter. "Eira, if he is meant to die then give him a quick death."

"A quick death is more than they deserve." Varren's tone grew more hateful by the second, his scowl deepening. "They do not offer clean deaths to the poor, the weak, the infirm. It is a luxury they don't deserve."

"I didn't say to do it out of kindness," he countered. Surprise brought her eyes toward him. Cullen's tone was shifting, a distortion of what she thought she knew. It had all the cunning of his careful plotting as a lord, but an ease with doing what must be done. As if he had finally been untethered. "What if he does survive? You see the runes on his body."

"Forbidden magic," Varren muttered. Though the sentiment

made Eira even more curious. *So the strange tattoos weren't just for show…*

"The last thing we want is to risk information of us getting back." Cullen locked eyes with her. "If it pleases you, let me do it."

She glanced back to Varren. He continued to glare at the lutenz, but he didn't make any movement or raise an objection to the notion of the lutenz being somehow able to survive. *If Cullen truly wanted to…* A dark and wicked streak in her wanted to see if he would—if he *could*.

"Do it," she said, mildly curious what he had in mind.

"If I may?" Cullen said to Adela.

"I left the choice to her."

Cullen reached out a hand and his magic swelled. His grip tightened around her protectively as the man began to sputter. The muscles in his throat bulged along with his eyes as his face turned purple. Eira could almost see a bubble forming around his face in the hazy currents of frost radiating from the deck.

She wasn't the only one who'd been practicing…Cullen was stealing the man's air.

The nameless lutenz kept his eyes locked with her, smiling his cruel grin the entire time. It grew more and more wild as his final seconds ticked on. As if he could somehow transfer death's gaze from himself, to her. Eira clutched Cullen a bit tighter.

The man's eyes rolled up into his head and he slouched.

"Get this garbage off my ship." Adela turned and slowly began walking back to her cabin.

It was Adela's words that spurred the crew to movement, carrying the man to the edge. They tossed him over the railing with the grace of a sack of refuse, casting him into the dark sea, never to be seen again.

· CHAPTER ·

TWENTY-SIX

EIRA LAY AWAKE in her hammock as the ship continued its course, plodding along toward a distant island—Black Flag Bay—that Adela had mentioned they'd be restocking in before continuing to Carsovia. But her mind was still in the sea behind.

The lutenz's eyes were seared onto hers. It didn't matter where she looked, or if she closed her lids, she could still see him and his cold, almost inhuman stare. What stripped a person so cleanly of anything that even remotely resembled a soul? What loyalty demanded the cost of one's humanity and why were so many willing to pay it? Those were the questions that kept her awake. She searched for an answer…one she wasn't entirely sure if she wanted to find.

Eventually, she gave up on sleep.

Eira swung her feet over the edge of her hammock and eased herself down. The creaking of the ship concealed her steps. But she didn't even check to see who else might have been awake. She wasn't trying to hide from them.

A few other pirates were up on deck, of course. Working. But they hardly had any reaction to her now. After the battle and surreal aftermath earlier, they had resumed their duties as if nothing had happened. Though, for pirates, sea battles and murdered prisoners were business as usual.

Still, there were questions left unanswered for all of them. Namely around Adela and Eira. She could hear their wonderings because she carried the same. The looks they cast her way were felt, more than seen. And the only person who had any insight into the game she was playing was the pirate queen herself. Who…wasn't about to tell.

So there was little point in her agonizing over it. Yet, agonizing was something Eira was very good at. And it had kept her alive by keeping her mind and feet moving, always one step ahead of the people who would kill her. So she wondered and plotted and planned anyway.

She made her way to the bow of the ship, determined to force herself to look forward, rather than back, and was surprised to find that she wasn't alone. Varren sat at the bow, legs over the edge, leaning against a railing. Had she been so wrapped up in her thoughts that she hadn't heard him leaving? Or had he never come to bed and instead had remained on deck as the night bled on, and she'd been too absorbed in herself to notice?

Varren acknowledged her with a glance and a small nod, one she returned. Taking his slight shift as permission, Eira sat next to him, but said nothing. She felt like his guest—one infringing on his contemplative solitude. She didn't want to be the one to break his thoughts and she had plenty to muse over herself.

After an indiscernible amount of time of Eira just letting her mind go blank, Varren said, "I'm sorry."

Eira was so startled that she nearly jumped off the ship. "Excuse me?"

"I shouldn't have put that man's blood on your hands or Cullen's; I shouldn't have told you to kill him."

She inhaled sharply, realizing what he was saying—what he thought. "It was *not* your fault that he died. I made my own decision, as did Cullen. And before you said anything, I'd already reached the conclusion that there was no point in keeping him alive. Cullen offered to end it faster.

"Carsovia wouldn't have negotiated for him, he wouldn't have helped us. And if he had any information, I'm sure Adela extracted it before she even asked me," Eira repeated all the things she'd been telling herself. It was odd that, despite having fought Pillars to the bitter end, despite having slain Ferro before men and women from around the world, *this* death was sticking with her…probably because it wasn't about the man at all, but about what acting on Adela's behalf had meant. Another step into a world that she was still figuring out where she stood within. "It wasn't on any of us, really. Circumstances unfolded. It is what it is."

"Still—"

"Varren," Eira interrupted him. She hated being firm with him when he was clearly agonizing over it. But she also needed him to understand he had nothing to worry about. So Eira held up her right hand, halting him. "We have all done things we might not be proud of to survive—things that haunt us. Don't let the ghosts win."

"Thank you for saying all that." He still seemed slightly unconvinced.

She dared to rest a hand on his shoulder. She hadn't exactly been close to Varren and didn't want to overstep any boundaries now. "I'm not just saying so; it's all the truth. I understand how guilt and doubt can make you cast unfair blame on yourself—make you second-guess your every action because it is *so easy* to think what you might have done with the luxury of hindsight. But please believe me when I say you have *nothing* to feel guilty over. I'm all right, Cullen—" She snorted. "He's sleeping soundly in his hammock. All is well."

He nodded and looked back out at the sea. Eira allowed her hand to slip from his person.

"If the roles had been reversed, he would've done the same to us or worse."

"I've gathered as much about Carsovia," Eira murmured.

"It's been years since I left the empire, yet their monsters still keep me up at night." He chuckled softly. "They live in my mind and never let me be, to the point that I've practically named them. I know them by the movement in the corners of my eyes, or the sound of a creaking floorboard. And you'd think, after coming to know them so well, having long accepted their presence, they would no longer bother me…"

"And yet they still haunt you as much as always," Eira finished.

Varren glanced at her. "The Pillars?"

She nodded. "I carry my own monsters. Whether I like it or not, they too will always be a part of me. Ferro's laughing eyes. The sound of Ulvarth's voice. The feeling of his sycophants beating consciousness from me will always be imprinted on my skin." Even now, as she said it, the phantom impacts were there.

"How often does it keep you up?"

"Only sometimes, now," Eira said with a note of relief. "I'm trying to acknowledge that Ulvarth is a part of me without giving him the power to define me. To varying success."

"Sounds familiar." Varren chuckled sadly. "But I don't think I've been as successful as you… The moment I saw the lutenz, I began to shake all over. All I wanted was to see him dead. And worse."

"What did they do to you?" Curiosity prompted her to ask before she could think better of it. She hastily added, "You don't have to tell me if you don't want to." He had told them very factually about the mines and the empire previously. But Eira had noticed, then, how detached it all felt. How he carefully avoided anything personal.

"I know, but part of me feels like I owe it to you for helping keep us safe and trying to get us back to Qwint." He shrugged.

"You owe me *nothing*."

"Fine. Part of me wants to tell you." He glanced her way. Eira nodded and remained silent, allowing him to speak uninterrupted. "I was born in Carsovia, in a small village not far from Qwint. Though I was mostly unaware of the two nations. Honestly, I lived most of my life without even really understanding what being part of an empire *meant*.

"We were fishers. But that was mostly food for us. The real treasure in the town were our pearls. The divers knew special rune magic that gave them the ability to swim deep enough to collect the rare spiked clams that make the golden pearls."

"Sounds beautiful." Eira thought back to the jewels Solaris wore at the opening ceremonies. The display of power took on a different meaning with the context of Carsovia having their own major trade of precious rocks and metals.

"They were. Some were as big as your eye." He smiled, but it didn't reach his eyes. Only the shadow of a joy long gone. "But all those were collected by the royal knights. They came twice a year to demand their share—hardly anything was left over for us to sell and earn an income."

"What did the knights do with them?"

"I heard the empress would take pearl baths, filling a pool the size of a small house with them, coated in precious oils and perfumes."

Eira tried to imagine it. The thought was incomprehensible. Even the gilded spires of Solaris didn't compare to that level of wealth.

"I never thought it was fair, even as a boy," Varren continued. "But I saw the way the elders of the village acted around those knights when they came into our town—the way my parents acted. I knew better than to say anything. I had a friend make that mistake once. The soldiers made his parents beat him."

Eira's mouth fell open.

Varren laughed bitterly. "Your face looks like what I imagine mine did the first time I saw it happen." He put his fingers under her chin, pushing lightly on her jaw. "Keep your face respectful, Mother told me. She explained later that parents always asked to perform the beatings because it would always be half of what the knights would've done. It was a kindness."

The circumstances were so far removed from everything Eira had ever known that it made her stomach churn. Her own parents came to mind. For all their flaws, they would never go out of their way to harm her. And the Solaris Imperial family would never expect a parent to do so to their child for merely speaking up—or asking a question.

Granted, dissonance against Solaris in modern times was rare. But it wasn't *forbidden*. Merely unpopular. She couldn't imagine what ruler would bring about a world that would make parents beat their own children.

"One year, the knights came an extra time. There weren't enough weeks between for the divers to stock up. So the knights took boys from the village to work the mines. My parents tried to flee—to smuggle me out to Qwint. But they weren't successful."

"That's how you know all about the mines," she said softly.

"Yes."

No wonder he had wanted to avoid them at all costs. Eira had never blamed him for it, but she had been curious. Now, knowing this full explanation, she didn't want him to even step foot on Carsovia.

Though, the full extent of the risk she and her friends were taking—what Adela was asking of her—was coming into view.

"How did you escape?"

"There was another boy, not much older than me at the time. The rumors were that he was born in the mines and grew up there—that was how he knew the tunnels so well. We called him Slip because he was always gone whenever the guards came around. Was like he vanished into thin air. I never knew what his real name was, if he had another name at all, but he didn't seem to mind Slip.

"Slip got people out as he could, one at a time. He never asked for anything in return and couldn't be bought or bartered. You never knew what was going through his head that made him pick some and not others…but one day, he showed up by my bunk and held out a hand. I'd been chosen."

"Didn't the guards ask questions about how people were disappearing?" Eira asked.

He shrugged. "We told them that the escaped person died in the deep tunnels. They didn't question us further and never searched for bodies. Why would they risk going into those hot, cramped, deadly places? We were little more than pickaxes to them—criminals of the crown don't last long in Carsovia. And since they never saw Slip, they had no reason to suspect anything else."

Eira was still struggling to fathom such a horrible place. Such inhumane treatment of "criminals," most or all of whom, by the way Varren told it, weren't really even criminals.

"So Slip picked you..."

"He came to me and guided me out of the mines through a labyrinth of tunnels far beyond any I had seen in my years there. The entire time, he gave me clear instructions on how to get to a nearby port. I repeated them after every time." Varren looked out into the night. His gaze had gone as soft as his words. "I ran through that forest as fast as I could. I gulped down the fresh, clean air as if it was going to be my last night alive. But when dawn broke, I saw the most beautiful sight I'd ever beheld:

"A horizon of unbroken water and a small village, not unlike where I grew up. Just as Slip had said, there was a ferryman who didn't ask questions. Who appreciated someone who kept their mouth shut, head down, and worked hard. It wasn't far from there to get to Qwint—just across a narrow strait under the cloak of darkness."

"Did you ever find your parents?" Eira asked softly, hoping that there would be one happy note to Varren's story.

He shook his head sadly. "I looked for them when I arrived in the republic. I knew, even then, they were dead. The knights don't let deserters live, especially not if they're deemed too old to work. But I tried to look anyway. I had to."

Eira nodded. She knew that feeling of wanting to find your parents at all costs. It was almost unbearable for her and she didn't even know who her blood parents were. Now, she had a new agony of not knowing if the parents who had raised her survived.

In a small way, she could empathize with him. But Varren's

turmoil ran deeper than Eira's worst imaginings. She wasn't going to lessen it by claiming she could understand that hurt.

"Lavette's father was overseeing refugees from Carsovia when I arrived. Even at her young age, she helped him."

"She seems like a natural leader," Eira agreed.

"Much like you." Varren surprised her with the sentiment. He must've seen as much on her expression because he added with a chuckle, "You and her are different types of leaders. She's very… by the book. It's easy to feel safe when Lavette is in control."

"And you feel in danger with me?" Eira grinned slightly. She knew the role she filled in their group.

"Maybe a bit more risks…sure," he admitted. "But, with you at the lead, I feel like anything is possible."

Eira was stunned yet again. She didn't think she'd made such an impression on Varren. Eira returned the focus to him yet again. "So you met Lavette through her work with the refugees?"

He nodded, finishing his story. "No matter what she says, I will always be in her debt. She found me shelter, food, checked in on me. Just like she did with all the others, time and again. Sometimes I think she spent more time in the refugee houses than her own home."

"She seems like an incredible woman." Eira meant it, too. Now wasn't the first time Eira could imagine it would have been for the best if Cullen had fallen for Lavette. But that was a different world. With who Cullen was becoming, now that he was free to explore his own path…Lavette only fit the lordly facade he'd maintained.

"She's always been like that. A goddess among men, really." Varren shifted, drawing up his knee to rest his forearm on it.

"Do you love her?" Eira whispered.

"Perhaps." He smiled faintly. "Or perhaps not… I never entertained it much. All I ever wanted, truly, was for her to be happy. With me, with someone else…near or far, it doesn't matter. Just knowing she's out there, thriving, is all I need." The words had remnants of what Cullen had told her—that he would be anything, so long as it meant he was on her mind. Eira's chest gave a slight squeeze. "I love her deeply as a best friend, a loyal soldier, or whatever words best encapsulate the immeasurable and unending wellspring of emotion that runs deeper than my magic."

The sentiment warmed Eira's heart. But, in all that, she didn't quite hear him saying that romantic love was *entirely* ruled out.

Without warning, he stood and dusted off his pants. "Thank you for listening to my tale."

"Thank you for sharing it with me," Eira said sincerely.

"I think my mind has settled enough that I'll go and try to get some sleep…and leave you both to it."

"'Both'?" Eira looked back over her shoulder to find Olivin waiting, intensity simmering in his eyes.

VARREN LEFT AND Eira was instantly aware of how empty the decks were. Only a couple pirates were awake and they were focused on their own discussion on the main deck below, barely visible from where she sat.

"I hope I didn't wake you when I left," Eira said. Though she had been gone for some time and suspected that wasn't the cause of his presence… She had to say *something* to break the immediate tension.

"You didn't."

"Good."

"I was already up." Olivin crossed over. The wind caught his dark hair, the strands highlighted by the stars. He knelt and her heart answered with a skip as his cool eyes shone in the silver moonlight. A contrast with the warmth of his expression.

"I'm sorry you couldn't sleep," Eira said softly, her words growing heavy and hard to say.

"You should be." Olivin's eyes traveled across her face before his hand did, knuckles brushing against the swell of her cheek and resting there. His lips parted as if he were about to speak, but he abandoned the notion, soaking in the moment. Just as she was about to ask him what he was waiting for, he found words. "I find I can't sleep as well as I used to."

"And why is that?" she asked.

"You know why." His attention dropped to her lips. "I've been here for weeks now, waiting for you to look my way."

"Olivin, I…" Words were harder and harder to say. A wave of heat rolled off him, enveloping her. The feeling of expectancy grew heavy in the air as his gaze became half-lidded. "I don't know," she whispered. "I still don't know."

There was so much tied up with those words. She didn't know where she was headed once they defeated Ulvarth—*if* they did. She didn't know who she'd be by the end of it. And didn't know who she'd want. It was all the words she'd said and everything she couldn't formulate into cohesive thoughts.

Somehow, he smiled in spite of her turmoil.

"You don't have to know everything." He chuckled deeply. Barely a rasp over the breezes. "You just have to know one thing…" He pulled lightly with the pads of his fingers. She straightened at what was little more than a suggestion. Eira's lids grew heavy.

"And what is that?" she murmured.

"In this moment, here, now, do you want to kiss me?"

The world went still. Even the ship seemed to pause and the creaking of the wood and groaning of the ropes fell silent. The wind held its breath and she held hers with it as the sides of their noses brushed together. Olivin brought her right to the edge, but no further. The pressure from his fingers around her cheek eased slightly.

Are you sure this is what you want? the movement seemed to ask.

Eira gave in to the pull of the currents between them. She closed the gap and her lips brushed against his. It was all the permission he needed.

Olivin's left hand found the other side of her face, pulling her closer. He tilted his head and she granted him access. His tongue slid against hers and a shiver coursed through her.

This kiss was different than the last time… It felt like it was the first time. When she'd kissed him in Champion Village, her heart and mind were a confused mess. Now…well, they were *still* a confused mess. But she was finding comfort in the chaos. In the unknowing. Gone were the expectations of order. The pressures of conformity.

Everyone knew where she stood—or, rather, where she didn't. There was no guilt or shame, just discovery. Opportunity for her, and for them. Besides…wasn't this sort of thing what pirates did? Explore? Pillage? Take what they wanted whenever they wanted?

A grin split Eira's lips as her hands balled into Olivin's shirt. She held on to him as though he were her sole lifeline in the current sweeping her away. He tasted like fresh winter snow, yet his body was as hot as fire, as hard as marble.

Olivin's hands took on a life of their own. They slid down her body and grabbed her hips. He eased back, pulling her onto him, their kiss unbroken.

His hair was spun silk between her fingers. She grabbed it as he gripped her rear, massaging the muscle there. A gasp escaped her lips, one he eagerly caught with his own mouth.

The kisses caused her to tremble with the force of her restraint. Her thoughts were blissfully quiet. The worries of the day smoothed away with the force of his caress.

Olivin nipped at her throat and Eira sighed softly into the cool night air, exhaling tension and doubt. He kissed and licked away any flashes of pain from his bites. Eira's fingers dug into his shoulders, holding him tighter, closer. Her hips pressed forward slightly and her eyes rolled back at the feeling of all of him so near and ready.

Nails digging into her back, he drew a shuddering breath against her flesh. "You are every nightmare and every delightful dream I have ever had wrapped into the shape of a woman. I'm damn near sure you will be the death of me, and yet I welcome you with open arms."

His words drew consciousness back to her, the heat of the moment becoming a simmer in the pit of her stomach. Eira met his eyes once more, hands shifting to caress his face. His strong jaw. The dark arch of his brows. There were scars that hadn't been there during the tournament. A nick extended from his temple to cheek, carving a thin, white line through his left eyebrow.

"Tell me, do you feel for me, Eira? Do you want me as I want you?" he whispered. "I can be everything that you need. Just say the word and I will remake the world in your image." He searched her expression. The fleeting moment of hesitation. And inhaled between his teeth. "Or…I can be nothing. But I must know at least if there is still possibility ahead. Because I see him with you, with his hands on you"—Olivin's fingers tightened at her waist, where Cullen had supported her earlier—"and my insides knot. I grow hot with a rage and frustration I've never known before." He shook his head slowly. "My emotions are hooked on your little finger."

"I'm so sorry." She pressed her forehead into his and shook her head. "I never meant to do this to you—to us. Things happened so fast and every time I think I catch my bearings, I'm gone again. A compass spinning with no headway."

"But there's yet hope?" he murmured, kissing her lightly between the words.

"One moment, I want his hands on me, holding me. The next, I meet your eyes and all I can think of is them staring down at me—you over me," she admitted. The confession should have felt more shameful. "You…him… I am lost."

"Then I will be lost with you."

Eira leaned away, studying his face. She smoothed her hands over his cheeks. An easy smile carved his lips.

"You look…surprised?" he whispered.

"I would've expected you to offer to be my North Star, my guide map." The side of her index finger ran up his earlobe and along the outside of his ear, reaching its point before slipping back down.

"Eira…" Olivin chuckled low. "You may pick the path, and I will beat down any who stand in your way. If you are mine, I will do everything in my power to ensure nothing will work against you."

She exhaled a soft noise that sounded like relief. It eased her back to him and Eira kissed him gently. Slowly and with purpose. No longer did she feel the need to rush. This wasn't the last time, but the start of many. His chest expanded to press against hers as he inhaled deeply—as if he were breathing in her worries. Taking them so she no longer had to carry them.

"When I am with you," she uttered against his lips, "I can't think of anything else. At first, I thought you would be nothing more than a distraction. An escape."

"I can be that, if it is all I'm meant to be."

"But…perhaps…I want more."

"Say the word, and I will give you it all." He kissed her again, pulling her lower lip between his teeth and biting gently. A moan escaped her. Loud enough that it brought the world around them back into focus. Even though it was night, there were still others not far.

"This is hardly the time or place."

A low growl rose in his throat, one he stopped, but it made her want to press her hips against his even further. His hand flew to the back of her head, gripping her hair. "When, then?"

"I don't know, but soon," she whispered breathlessly. "Very soon." The wanting would tear her apart. Knowing he desired her as much as she did him—that this fire was a mutual flame—would make their every interaction torture.

"And *him*?"

The cold of the *Stormfrost* reached her. The chill that permeated the air around it sent a shiver up her spine that had nothing to do with desire, or passion. *Him*. Cullen. The man she'd once fallen in love with. The man who Eira, for a blissful moment, had seen every day of her future with. A fantasy that now seemed like little more than the musings of a naive girl. And yet…

Yet…

Her heart couldn't let go of him. He was the measure of her. He was where the compass stopped spinning and she found a heading. Where Olivin was untamed, unending possibility, Cullen was order and purpose. They both held a piece of her that she didn't want them to give back.

"I'm not ready to let him go yet—I don't know if I want to," she admitted. Lying was going to get her nowhere. "I'm still learning who I am, and until I know that, I cannot tell either of you who or what I want."

"It's all right." He leaned up to plant an almost chaste kiss on her lips. If such a thing were possible, given how tightly her legs were wrapped around his hips. "I can share for a while longer."

"Are you sure?" she murmured, fingers trailing over his face, wondering how she'd struck such luck.

"These emotions are complicated. This decision is important—when you make it, I want you to be certain." Olivin locked eyes with hers. There was no doubt. If anything, understanding. As if he, too, had experienced young and great loves. As if he knew the confusion and enthusiasm of passion beyond just her. Relief flooded her at the understanding.

"Thank you."

He nodded. "All I need from you, is to still know you need me. All I want is your time, your smiles, your kisses whenever you might grant them to me." Olivin ran his fingertips lazily up and down her spine. "I don't need your forever. Not yet. Maybe someday we will be in a place where I would come to expect it—when I have earned you being mine, wholly mine. But, for now, just grant me tomorrow. Each day, I will show you why you should grant me the next day…and the day after that…"

"I think that much I can do."

"Good." He leveled his eyes with her. "Then, may I kiss you until dawn?"

A sly smirk curled one corner of her mouth. She repeated, this time far more coy, "I think that much I can do."

CHAPTER

TWENTY-EIGHT

THE NEXT MORNING, Adela didn't summon them for training. The day started almost leisurely. Eira had hardly slept more than a wink. But, oddly, she didn't feel tired. She expected she should have. Especially given all the events of the previous day—how exhausted she was following the battle with the lutenz of Carsovia.

But Olivin's hands—his mouth had given her life. The energy she'd lost had been restored to her and then some. Her skin still tingled from where he touched her. Even as the others began moving, she lounged in her hammock, blinking lazily into the morning's first light.

Her breath hitched when they locked eyes. Olivin gave her a slight smirk and said nothing, starting for the galley. Eira wore a smile of her own as she finally roused. It was as if she had a delightful secret meant for only her.

She spent most of the day on deck. When it was clear that Adela wasn't going to lead them in morning training, Eira took charge and guided her friends through their usual paces. No one seemed to question her stepping up to the task. Everyone did exactly as she told them.

After lunch, they continued along with regular tasks they'd been helping with. Eira was beginning to learn the ins and outs of the *Stormfost*. She was familiar with how the riggings sounded when the winds shifted and either the sails or magic guiding them needed to be adjusted. She could almost feel the slight groan, deep within the ship, as if it were in her own stomach, when the rudder met resistance from unexpected currents. Without thought, instruction, or permission, Eira exerted a little bit of magic to influence the seas beneath them and get the vessel back on course.

The day was sunny. Beautiful, really. The air out at sea was crisp and clean. The horizon seemed to whisper possibility no matter where one looked.

Yet…one significant piece was missing to it all. *Adela.*

So, as dusk settled and her friends were deep in a game of bones the crew had taught them—an absolute riot of fun—Eira excused herself. She was going to dare to head straight for Adela's cabin, but ran into Crow first. The pirate gave her a knowing look and Eira shifted course to fall into step with her as she crossed to a nearby railing.

Eira rested her elbows on the rail next to Crow. "Is she all right?"

Crow jolted upward, brow furrowing. "How dare you even suggest that she—"

"Fine." Eira held up her hands and took a step back, trying to signal she hadn't been looking for a fight—or to insult Adela. She leaned her hip against the railing and gave Crow a stern look. "I won't ask the obvious. Instead, I'll just wait for you to tell me the answers you know I'm looking for to the questions you're already suspecting I'll ask."

Crow snorted softly and shook her head, gazing back to the horizon.

"I'm waiting." Eira folded her arms over her chest.

"You really are a piece of work." Crow sighed. But there was a slight smile on her lips and a knowing look to her dark eyes when she turned them back to Eira. "You're just like her, you know that?"

Eira said nothing and waited. Perhaps she was channeling some of Adela's energy in that moment. But it yielded results. So she hardly had any reason to be discouraged from doing so in the future, despite Crow sounding frustrated by it.

"She's fine," Crow said, finally. "But yesterday was harder than expected on her."

"Alyss is a talented healer. She could—"

"No," Crow interrupted firmly. "Adela doesn't like an audience to her weakness."

"I can understand that, truly." Eira allowed some of her own insecurities to seep in so Crow would know she was being serious. It seemed to work. "But it's sometimes necessary to depend on the people around you, especially during the hard times."

"You try telling her that." Crow snorted.

"I will," Eira said quickly. "If you don't stop me."

Crow straightened, looking down the bridge of her nose at Eira. For her part, Eira simply waited, staring up at the woman in a silent challenge. She allowed her statements to speak for themselves.

A low chuckle rose from the back of Crow's throat. "Well, this was a fun talk, but I think I should go to bed now."

Eira glanced at the setting sun. It was far too early for bed.

"See you in the morning."

Crow headed for the crew's quarters. Eira took her leaving as permission. She went straight for Adela's cabin—none of the other pirates even so much as looked twice in her direction—and knocked on the door. There was a faint but dramatic sigh that was heavily forced to be audible through the door.

And then, "Come in, Eira."

The door swung open, pulled by the pirate queen's power. It was almost comical how well they knew each other's magic by now. All day, without consciously realizing, Eira had subconsciously noticed the absence of Adela's magic and had made necessary adjustments on her behalf. Just as Adela had known in less than a breath that it was Eira standing at the door.

Eira didn't bother with her usual chair. Instead, she crossed to the bed and boldly sat on its edge as the door clicked shut behind her. Adela arched a brow, but didn't object to the proximity.

"Is it magical, or physical?" She gave Adela a hard look.

"Because if it's magical, then I will assess. If it's physical, then I'm getting Alyss, and that's that," she said matter-of-factly, hoping to convey with her tone alone that it wasn't up for discussion.

"Looking after the pirate queen, are you? What would your empire think?" Adela adjusted herself in the bed, somehow seeming taller despite still lying down.

"I don't care." Eira shrugged. "For all I know, Vhalla, Aldrik, and Vi all died and the Solaris Empire is in chaos."

"They left their spare behind—what's his name?—Romulin, I think?" Adela mused, clearly trying to deflect.

"Magical, or physical?" Eira repeated, not about to allow Adela to distract them for long.

"Magical," Adela said with yet another dramatic sigh.

"Very well." Eira held out her hand over Adela's chest, as if she were reaching right for her channel. It hovered in the air. The pirate queen stayed silent, for once not scolding her for tying a physical act to the use of her magic.

Finding Adela's channel and manipulating it was now second nature. It only took Eira a second to have a firm grasp of it. A second more and she had it widened a little. Eira positioned her magic in such a way that it could be held open for a bit longer without conscious thought, and then retracted her hand.

Adela breathed a small sigh of relief. "Even if it's only a temporary fix, that is a significant improvement."

"Good, hopefully it can help restore your strength and be more than temporary." Eira remained seated on the edge of the bed. Adela stared up at her and she stared down at the pirate queen. Waiting. Expectant.

Another sigh. "Out with it, girl."

"How long have you been struggling?"

The second she said it, Adela shot her a glare. She shouldn't have overstepped. Eira knew it. And yet…she didn't feel panicked or nervous about doing so. Too many things had added up. She'd seen too much.

"I am not your concern." The statement was meant to dissuade her, of that Eira was sure. But it sounded tired, almost gentle. "I am the pirate queen—"

"And you are tired."

"I can rest."

"Fine, you're old." Eira smirked.

Adela blinked, snorted, and shook her head. "You really are a precocious child."

"Guess where I got it from?" Eira shrugged.

"I am *not* your mother."

"I've learned that blood has little to do with being a mother."

A slight smile cracked Adela's lips. "Perhaps, but who would want a crusty old pirate queen as their mother? I'm more likely to stab you than kiss you."

"Ah, good, you're just like so many I've known."

Adela snorted again. Even Eira smiled slightly. Then Adela's face relaxed and, possibly for the first time, the pirate queen looked every one of her years. The fine lines in her face seemed slightly deeper. Her eyes a little more sunken with all the weight of everything she'd seen.

"I thought that I would be young forever." Adela's eyes drifted toward the windows out the back of the vessel. "I thought the elfin blood was strong enough in me that I would live to a hundred, easily. A hundred and fifty, even, as they can.

"But time is an impossible mistress to read. One moment, she's off gallivanting. And then next moment she's knocking down your door, taking residence in your bones and haunting your dreams. She's sneaked up on me…" Adela sank farther into her pillows with a sigh. "Despite my best efforts to let the world believe the contrary, I am not immortal."

"I'm sorry."

"Don't apologize for the obvious." Adela rolled her eyes. "I was the one being unreasonable, looking for a way to make it so. I can freeze whole islands, but not time."

"How bad is it?" Eira's voice had dropped to a whisper. Adela had always seemed like a legend in the stories. More myth than woman. Seeing her as flesh and blood somehow made Eira feel vulnerable.

Adela barked laughter. "I'm not dead, yet, girl. A sentimental fool in my waning years? Yes. Does my back crackle like dried leaves every time I stand? Also yes. But dead? No."

Eira ventured a slight smile. "You'll be terrorizing the seas for many more years, still."

"People would kill you for wishing that."

"I don't care about 'people.'"

"I suppose you don't." Adela gave her the most genuine smile she'd ever seen from the woman and then looked to the windows. "But there is something about time, and age, that makes one… think. When I lost my leg, I didn't heal the way I used to. The call was a closer one than I've had in years. *I* made a mistake. And these questions began to haunt me… What was it all for? What will be left after I am consigned to little more than dust?"

"You will live on for centuries in myth and legend," Eira said softly. She didn't know what compelled her to do so, but Eira reached out and touched Adela's hand gently. The pirate queen, much to her shock, didn't retreat.

"*I* will. But what of the people who have given me their lives and their loyalty?" Adela continued to stare out at the vast ocean they were leaving behind. "What of my ship? Of all the treasure I have gathered? Was it merely for stories and tales that will disappear off the lips of people who are dead and gone after a generation? Do I want to leave myths and fear that fade with time? Do I want to have something else be my legacy?"

Eira didn't know. She'd never much thought of legacies or of what happened "after." She'd been so focused on surviving that it seemed foolish to worry about what she'd leave in the world when her final Rite of Sunset was performed.

Adela sighed in the wake of her silence. Somehow, she felt like she'd let the pirate queen down by not having a solution. But Eira didn't know what else she could've said or done. What more there was to offer.

"Look at me, growing sentimental in my age." Adela had a note of disgust with herself and withdrew her hand from Eira's, but surprised her when she patted Eira's knuckles. "For now, we focus on the task at hand. We continue training, you and I, and exploring our theories and plans." Plans that Eira still felt like were more wishful theories than practical. "We keep working. Seeing all you and your friends can do so that way I may properly exploit your powers. And in a few days more, we'll dock."

"At the outpost you mentioned?" Eira clarified. "Black Flag Bay?"

Adela nodded. "When we arrive, you and your friends may disembark and get anything you need. It will be our last stop before we arrive at Carsovia. As long as you are with my crew, no one will bother you."

"Understood."

"After, you will deliver me the head of my nemesis."

Eira nodded and stood, hearing the dismissal between Adela's words. When she glanced over her shoulder, Adela was back to staring out the windows. The words echoed in Eira's mind as she suspected they continued to in Adela's as well.

There was more to the pirate queen than the myths had said. She was not just a legend, a ghost, or a curse…Adela was a woman of flesh and blood. One with dreams—albeit bloody and questionable ones. But one who had also looked after her crew and built an empire of her own across the seas.

Looking back, Eira wasn't really sure what she had been expecting when it came to Adela. But she was glad this was what she'd found.

EIRA HADN'T REALIZED until a speck of land dotted the horizon just how long it had been since she'd last seen anything but ocean. At the first cry of, "*Land ho,*" they had all been on deck, blinking into the sunrise.

"It really is in the middle of nowhere," Lavette appraised. The eight of them—plus Ducot—were lined up along the bow of the ship.

"You said it was two thirds the way to Carsovia?" Eira asked Ducot.

His arms were loosely wrapped around Noelle's waist, holding her from behind. They rocked slowly with the ship. Noelle reached up and gently caressed his face with her now scarred and gnarled hand. They had grown more outwardly affectionate by the day. Perhaps it was something about being trapped together on a vessel that made hearts open. Eira's eyes drifted to Cullen and Olivin, snapping back when Ducot spoke.

"About that far…it's close enough to Carsovia that they tried one time to reclaim it from the pirates." Ducot smirked. "That went about as well as one might imagine."

"I am certain Adela's diplomacy was stunning." The way Lavette spoke, it sounded like a bad thing. But Eira admired the pirate queen for her shrewd and uncompromising nature—for taking what she wanted and needed and defending what was hers. If Eira was being completely honest with herself, it was something she wished to imitate.

"You said there was good food and drink on the island?" Noelle asked Ducot.

"Always. Being a common stop for us scoundrels means that there's always a fresh supply of loot, booze, and tasty morsels to devour." He leaned forward, nibbling at Noelle's neck while making chomping noises.

"Yargen bless, you two, get a room," Yonlin groaned. He looked to Alyss of all people. "Am I right?"

"I'm fine with them not having a room, more content." Alyss tapped her pen on her notebook as Noelle laughed.

"You would feel that way." Yonlin rolled his eyes, but wore an overtly affectionate smile. Eira caught it, but Alyss was too focused on her writing to notice.

"Will they have additional notebooks there?" Alyss had a singular mind.

"Have you already filled that one up?" Cullen tried to look over Alyss's shoulder. "Ready to let us read a bit?"

"Hardly, this is wholly research and planning. I've yet to actually begin penning the story." Alyss made a show of snapping the journal shut before Cullen could catch a single word.

"There should be some kind of notebooks there. But I'd imagine they'd be more like ship's ledgers, therefore less portable than what you have now," Ducot said.

"That's fine."

"I am glad to see that you lot are like the rest of my crew." Adela's sharp voice cut through their discussions. "Ready to spend the whole day lallygagging just because we'll be in port by noon."

"Of course not." Eira shifted to face the pirate queen. "We're ready to practice, aren't we?"

"Speak for yourself," Alyss muttered under her breath.

"Suck-up," Noelle mumbled nearly at the same time. The two shared a conspiratorial look and a snicker. Eira rolled her eyes and pretended not to hear.

"Then let's begin, we've a busy day ahead of us." Adela tapped her cane on the deck and they broke apart, resuming their usual places opposite each other for practice and sparring.

As Eira was taking her spot, Cullen stepped by and whispered under his breath, "Find me on the island."

Her heart skipped a beat. He glanced over his shoulder, fighting a smirk. The rest of them seemed to miss the brief interaction. But Eira wore it on the flush that crept up her cheeks and the untoward thoughts racing to the forefront of her mind.

The only instruction Adela had given them was to be back by midnight. Otherwise, they had free rein on the island to do whatever pleased them. And, judging from the stories on the rowboat over to the docks from the other crew, there was a lot to find pleasing on a pirate's paradise.

"I'm going to find new writing tools," Alyss announced shortly after disembarking.

"I'll join you," Yonlin said.

"Us, too," Varren added.

"Adela might have told us that there's an understanding among all the pirates on the island…but it's still an island of pirates." Lavette side-eyed the bustling docks. People of all ages, all shapes and sizes, went about their business. The *Stormfrost* was the largest vessel on anchor out on the horizon, but she wasn't the only one. Three other tall ships with black flags and scarred hulls were in port today.

"You'll be fine." Ducot patted her shoulder. "There's never fighting here. You'd be surprised how much better pirates are at keeping the peace than actual lawmen."

Lavette rolled her eyes.

"Truly," Ducot insisted. "Puck even has a wife with child here. Trusts her to be safer here than anywhere else while she's in her more delicate months."

"We'll see." Lavette still seemed skeptical, but slightly more inclined to believe him.

"Where are you two headed?" Eira asked Noelle and Ducot.

"There's a marvelous beach on the other side of those hills and cliffs." Ducot pointed. "It's a quieter side of the island because the rocks prevent it from being an easy place to dock. But that means it has great views and some secluded tide pools."

"Sounds wonderful, we'll join you," Eira declared for herself, Cullen, and Olivin.

Noelle was at her side, the men in tow, as they walked through the main markets. The town was somewhere between what Eira was familiar with on Oparium and the stilted houses of Ofok. Their roofs were thatched with large, woven fronds from the tall trees that swayed happily in the summer breezes.

"A moment!" Ducot shouted after them. Eira and Noelle paused in time to see him duck into a storefront, Cullen and Olivin behind.

"It was nice of Adela to give us some coin to spend," Eira mused. The intense stare Noelle was giving her had an awkward and uneasy sensation crawling up her back.

"Adela, *blah, blah*, yes, we get it. She sees you as a little murder-baby to mold in her image." Noelle tilted her head back and forth as she talked quickly, mocking the idea. It was comical enough that Eira didn't immediately object. Though she would have for the sake of keeping the conversation on that topic. "But what's actually important is what is going on between you and Cullen and Olivin?"

Eira groaned and shook her head. "I don't know."

"They want to get in your pants so badly they're practically tripping over themselves."

"Noelle!"

"It's true." She laughed. "And obvious. So I know you know, too."

"No, I do, it's not that. I—" Eira pressed her fingers into her forehead with a sigh. "I don't know what I'm doing with either of them."

Noelle's expression shifted, becoming more serious.

"I always thought that, when you fell in love with someone, you just...*knew*. You met them and they had your heart and everything slotted into place," Eira said softly as she watched the store for them to reemerge. "That's how it is in the stories, at least."

"You're around Alyss too much." Noelle grinned slightly, but it didn't quite reach her eyes and the expression fell off her face quickly, the muscles relaxing into something more somber and thoughtful. "Stories are simple *because* they're stories. But this is life, Eira. And it's rarely neat."

"I feel like I'm making a mess of it." She sighed. Her lips still tingled from Olivin's kisses a few nights ago. The feeling of his nails on her scalp sent shivers down her spine. The safety of Cullen's embrace. The familiarity of the taste of his mouth that made the whole world stand still. "When I'm around Cullen, I feel stable, safe. I look up to him greatly, in many ways."

"But?"

"But...he also drives me insane sometimes—and not in the fun way." Eira grinned. Noelle chuckled. "Though, he's working on it. He's trying to live for himself and it's admirable. He's genuinely...changing. And it's fascinating to watch. I'm more intrigued with him by the day. But that also means I can't be sure if I'll love the man he's becoming, or not."

"And Olivin?"

"Olivin is..." Eira paused, her mind back in the other night. "Like a dream that you wake up from and just want to fall back into."

"Dreams can be dangerous. They're not the real world."

"I know, and that's part of the problem." Eira sighed. "With Olivin, I want to explore, and discover. With Cullen I know what I have, I just don't know if it's enough."

"What do they feel about it all?"

"They're willing to wait until I know what I want. So far, at least."

"Good. They should give you room to explore and decide." Noelle nudged her shoulder. "And deciding should be *fun*."

"You make me sound so scandalous." Eira laughed, as if a dozen such thoughts hadn't crossed her mind already.

"Be scandalous. It's delightful." Noelle beamed at the mere sight of Ducot as he emerged from the shop. "If you're going to be stuck between two hard places at least they have very handsome faces attached."

"You are awful!" Eira slapped her friend's shoulder playfully. "What has Ducot done to you?"

"Made me a devious pirate." Noelle cackled.

"What about devious pirates?" Ducot asked as he approached. Eira noticed how Cullen and Olivin flanked him, no doubt to help him stay on the right path in the crowded market. His magic would surely have a hard time keeping up in such a busy area.

"That I love this devious pirate." Noelle kissed him on the cheek. "Now, are we ready to continue?"

"Essential supplies gathered." Ducot lifted the bag he was carrying, the neck of a bottle reminiscent of the liquor Adela had stuck out at an angle. "Let's venture onward."

Noelle and Ducot took the lead as they left the center of the small town. But Eira, Cullen, and Olivin stayed close enough that it felt like they moved as one large pack rather than two smaller groups. The foliage and dense underbrush of the jungle beyond town was just like the paintings Eira had seen of the North. Just like Alyss had described to her. She hoped her friend would venture far enough from town to see it. Though, it might just make her homesick.

Home… The word had a definition in her mind, but no meaning. Where was home for her? It wasn't Oparium. Nor was it the house she'd grown up in. The Tower of Sorcerers didn't fit, either—none of Solarin did.

Eira continued mulling over the thoughts as they crested the hill and walked down through small but rocky bluffs that stretched out into the sea. It was exactly as Ducot had promised—a beach secluded by trees and rocks. Waters as blue as the sky, gently lapping powdery sand of pale gold.

They set up a small picnic area and, while enjoying some of the local delights Ducot had procured them, Eira asked, "What is home?"

"Pardon?" Noelle blinked at her. The rest of them seemed equally confused.

"*Home*. When you hear that word, what do you think?"

They were all silent a moment.

"A ship on calm seas," Ducot said.

"A warm house not far from my parents. Maybe a little brood." Noelle grinned in Ducot's direction.

"Let's not get ahead of ourselves." He laughed, though wore an easy smile that told Eira he wasn't bothered by the idea in the slightest.

"Anywhere my brother is. Home is more people than place, I think. Home is what I can keep safe." Olivin couldn't stop himself from glancing back through the trees and toward the town where Yonlin was. Eira doubted he realized he even did it.

"The last place that felt like home..." Cullen's voice was wistful, deep with longing. "Was our home in the East, where I was born. When it was just my father, mother, and me. But, since..." He shook his head and looked to Eira. "What about you?"

"I don't know," she admitted, willing to help Cullen change the topic. His secrets were safe with her. "That's why I asked." Eira looked out to sea. "When I think of home...it's a sort of blank spot in my mind. I know what home is, or it's supposed to be. But I don't think I've found it yet. I'd thought that once I found my birth mother, I'd know—it'd give me all the perspective I'd need...but I still don't know who my birth mother is or what home looks like."

They were all silent for a long moment.

"Mother above, Eira, you can kill a mood." Noelle laughed. Eira joined in, as did the rest of them.

"Sorry, sorry!" Eira held up her hands apologetically. Noelle's remark shook her from the heaviness that had been settling on her shoulders. "You're right. We're in a beautiful place. And this might be the last opportunity we have for a while to just enjoy ourselves." Because Carsovia was waiting for them, just beyond the horizon.

"Bringing it down again." Noelle leaned over and pressed her finger into Eira's nose with another laugh.

"How much have you had to drink?"

"Enough that I think taking a dip in my smallclothes sounds lovely!" Noelle stood, pulling her shirt over her head. Her modest breasts were bound tightly. Underneath her loose trousers were a pair of small, thin shorts. "Are any of you coming?"

Ducot was already stripping down.

Eira shrugged and stood. Cullen and Olivin, unsurprisingly, followed her lead. She was keenly aware of every sidelong glance from them as she peeled her shirt over her head. After their morning training, she'd elected for a looser-fitting, sleeveless top under her outer shirt, one with a drawstring just under her breasts—more for sweat than support.

Cullen and Olivin couldn't be built more differently. Cullen was lean, but muscular. His tanned skin had a golden sheen from the day's heat. Thoughts of running her fingers over the divots in his stomach had Eira fumbling with the drawstring on her trousers.

Olivin, on the other hand, was lithe. Almost a pained frame. She could count his lower ribs when he inhaled deeply. But he was also a man trained for combat. Sinewy muscle cut against his pale skin, the shadows creating deep lines that accentuated every bulge and dip. He had narrow wrists and small hips, assuring her that his thinness was a result more of his natural frame than of poor nutrition.

Cullen was every image of a woman's daydreams. Strong. Full. Exuding the capability to sweep someone off their feet, if not by magic than with the bulk of his muscles.

But Olivin had a sort of otherworldly appeal to him. A number of odd angles and shapes that stacked up to make an unexpectedly handsome frame.

Eira needed to get in the cool water. Now.

She followed after Noelle and Ducot, down the hill and to the sandy beach. The rocky bluffs created a natural cove that broke most of the waves, creating cool, clear water. Noelle and Ducot splashed in, hands intertwined. But Eira glided effortlessly, the water parting and collapsing around her, as though giving her a hug.

"Showoff!" Cullen accused her, yet he jumped for the water but his feet didn't touch the surface. Instead, small pockets of air balled under his toes, pushing the water away as he took three steps like a skipping stone. Be it intentional, or his magic giving out over an uneven surface, he went off-keel and hit the water hard next to her, sending up a monumental splash.

Eira roared with laughter as he came up for air. "Graceful."

"Guess there's only room for one of us to be graceful," he praised her as Olivin, rather normally, joined the rest of them.

Noelle remained close to Ducot, always within reach, as they lazily swam around. Eira wondered if it was because his magic was disrupted in the water. Or so they could brush up against each other whenever desired.

Eira floated lazily on her back as her magic propelled her slowly over the surface of the water. She stared up at the sky, blinking slowly like a cat sunning itself. When was the last time she had gone swimming in the ocean? It wasn't the summer before the tournament's start…she and Marcus had been too busy with their various Tower obligations to make it back home that summer.

Which meant it had to have been at least two years ago. Two years since she had been back to Oparium. *Home?* She tried on the word again. It didn't quite fit, still. But just because it wasn't home didn't mean she couldn't look back on it fondly.

The faces of her parents flashed before her eyes. Eira's chest knotted and her magic faltered. Could she really be enjoying herself when they were possibly in the hands of the Pillars facing who knew what fate? Guilt put a chill in the water around her.

No… Eira swallowed down the feeling. She wouldn't torture herself when nothing could be done. Agonizing over their circumstances would only upset her—make it harder to focus and put more tension between her and her magic. She was helping them as fast as she could. It wasn't as if she asked to get wrapped up with Adela. Or for the pirate queen to be one of the safest places for her and her friends to be. And she was heading to Carsovia so Adela would give her the ship she could get back to her parents on, cutting off the Pillars' supply of flash beads in the process.

She was taking all possible actions to move forward. Worrying would give her nothing more.

"Hey, I think there are caves over here!" Cullen called, drawing their attention.

"Where's Alyss when you need her?" Noelle said, swimming over. "Where's the opening?"

"Down there." Cullen pointed. The water was clear enough to see a small opening all the way at the rocky bottom.

"Oh, *no*, no thank you, I am not going down there." Noelle paddled away.

"I've actually been meaning to try a new technique I've been working on." Cullen looked in Eira's direction. "Would you be willing to help me?"

"What do you need?"

"I'm going to make a bubble of air around me. I want to see how long I can sustain it for."

Marcus trapped under the water flashed before her eyes. She pressed them closed and drew a slow breath. "Why don't we try that in the open?"

"Because if I ever need it, I'll be in a dire situation. And dire situations are more like moving through a confined cave than a calm open sea."

Eira sighed. It did seem like a good skill for him to have, especially with them being on ships… "All right. But at the first sign of trouble I am getting us out in a blink."

"Of course." He beamed.

"We'll be back soon."

"Be careful." Olivin had a gentle smile. There wasn't a trace of jealousy or malice as Eira might have expected. If anything he looked…confident. As if his expression said, *Go ahead, go with him. You'll find out why I'm the one you'll want to come back to.*

She wasn't sure how much of that was his intention and how much was her imposing her own thoughts on him. But Eira was once more hot all over. She looked back to Cullen and quickly said, "Ready?"

He nodded.

Eira dipped underneath the waves. As her head lowered, the water cratered. Her magic helped push the water away, creating a bubble in which she could breathe. Doing so required practically no effort on her part.

Cullen had much the same, but rather than pressing the water away, he was holding the air to him. Eira beamed at him. He nodded and headed farther down.

It was easy enough to maintain the air around her head that Eira could put a little current behind them as they descended to the opening. Sure enough, it was a craggy mouth of a little cave. Bracing herself, she followed behind Cullen, quickly swimming into a deep blue of filtered and fading light.

Just when the water was nearly as black as pitch—just when Eira was going to suggest they turn around—another speck of light lit up ahead of them. Cullen continued to swim on and, despite her better judgment, she continued to follow. Her heart was racing and the air in her bubble was beginning to grow thin. How long had they been down? A minute? Ten?

She inhaled slowly through her nose. Panic would use up her air faster and then require more magic to keep the water at bay. This was not a frozen lake with a madman trying to murder her.

The tunnel—thankfully—hadn't branched; so if the light ahead of them was a trick of the water, they knew exactly where to go to get back.

But the light was real.

The tunnel opened into a cavern. Opposite them was a small opening to the water beyond. A small, narrow strip of beach had been pushed up on the far side. Sunlight bounced in and off the water, painting beams of light on the stalactites.

"We must be on the other side of the bluff." Cullen was breathless.

"Let's rest there before heading back." Eira pointed to the beach. He nodded and she drew the water around them just like Adela had done to transport Eira between the two boats. Holding Cullen in her watery grasp required a firm but delicate, giving yet confident touch—as if she were to try to hold sand in her palm and not lose a single granule. Difficult…but it worked.

"You're not the only one with new tricks." She grinned at his surprised expression.

Cullen chuckled, lying back on the sand. "I'm glad we both have used these weeks to our advantage."

"It'll be useful, being on ships. Developing that skill was good thinking," she praised.

"I didn't do it because we're on ships," he said with his eyes closed.

"Then—"

"I learned it for you, Eira. I thought, when this is all over, you might want to go swimming in the ocean together. Marcus told me how you and he would harpoon lobster in the late summer and cook it on the beach."

"He told you that, did he?" Eira wore a slight smile as she stared out to the sea through the above-water opening of the cavern.

"He said to never get on your bad side when you had a harpoon in hand."

"I never hurt him, I'll have you know."

"He never said you did, just that you threatened."

As the fond memories faded, she brought her attention back to Cullen in the here and now to find him staring back at her. "What?"

"It's been a long time since I heard you really laugh…since I saw you so easy and free." He propped himself up on an elbow.

"I've never been an easy and free person." Eira uncurled herself and lay back, hands behind her head.

"You should try it more often, it suits you."

"Maybe…when all our enemies are in the ground, our families are tucked safely in their beds, and there is nothing more to be done for empires or kingdoms, I will be." She gave him a tired smile.

Cullen reached over, gently pulling her wet hair to one side of her forehead. The pad of his finger on her slick skin was enough to give her a jolt. Eira was suddenly aware of how alone they were. How it was the first time they had truly been since the ball. They'd been around each other for months now…but it was always under the eyes of others. Always with pretense and concerns they couldn't escape. With people who could hear or see or walk in. With the weight of the world crushing them.

But here…this little seaside cavern felt like it was made for just the two of them. As if everything could be let go of with a soft sigh.

Without another word, he leaned forward, hazel eyes as intense as embers about to catch flame. Eira inhaled slowly, her chest filling with desire—with the smell of salt and taste of him.

· CHAPTER ·

THIRTY

S HE REMEMBERED THIS feeling all too well.

It had been imprinted upon her soul. Written by his lips and fingers and tongue. He tasted of the brine from the sea. Faintly of sweat that rolled off with the water. But there was more to him and more to this kiss. His hand shifted, fingers curling around the back of her neck.

Unlike when he'd kissed her in Adela's cabin—out of fear and desperation—this was slow and purposeful. Easy. Cullen kissed her as if to consume her whole, passion deepening, his tongue sliding past her lips and causing her whole body to tingle. She ran her hand up his arm, to his cheek, and then down his chest. The plane of unbroken skin reminded her of how the majority of their clothes had been left behind on the beach. How bare they both were. How the soaked scraps of what remained on their bodies left so very little to the imagination.

As if he read her mind, Cullen shifted and the slick expanse of his body settled along hers. Kissing him was like the first bracing breath of winter's air. It was the first drink after a hot summer's day. It was life and rejuvenation. It woke her body not with throbbing, restless need, but a steady pull of his strong hands as they slid down her sides.

Her nails dug into him slightly, scraping his skin as her hands balled into fists. Eira arched into him, clutching him with all her might. Knowing she had to let go.

Breaking the kiss, they shared ragged breaths. He pressed his forehead against hers. His wet hair fell around his face.

"What is it?" Cullen whispered, eyes searching hers. "What's wrong?"

"I…I can't do this with you." The words ripped through her chest, coming from the woman she once was. "You deserve better."

"It is not your decision what I 'deserve.'" He shifted to kiss both her cheeks and then pierced her with a hard stare. "I want *you*. As much—more than I ever have before. I have looked at you every day with yearning, watching in awe as you've transformed yourself into a new and stunning creature. Dying inside until I could find a moment to steal you away."

"You should be with a woman who knows what she wants." The dripping of water from the roof of the cavern was almost louder than her words. "I…still don't."

Cullen eased back, sitting on his heels. Eira sat as well, glancing down through the transparent water at the underwater cave they'd swum in through, thinking back to Olivin. She suppressed a shiver as the air suddenly felt colder.

"I'm sorry," she murmured.

"Tell me something." His words drew her attention back to him. Cullen still had that expectant, impossible-to-hide-from stare. "The part of your heart that loved me once. Is it there? Or has it completely withered beyond all hope?"

"Sometimes, I'm still so annoyed with you I'm surprised my eyes don't pop," she admitted and they both chuckled softly. "But, most often…I find myself admiring you. I look at you and I see the man I went to court with. Who was there for me after Marcus's death in ways no one else was. I see a man who makes me feel safe. Who's begun to fight for himself and makes me curious to see who he will become when all is said and done."

"But is it—*could* it be love?" He seemed like he was hardly breathing, hanging on her words.

"I think so," she admitted. "It's not the blind and dangerously fiery passion I once felt. But it's…deeper. Richer. I'm not blind to your faults and, somehow, I still want you. Even if I don't always understand why, and sometimes wish I didn't, I still want you near me. Touching me. Every time I look at you, I can't help but feel like there's so much left for us to explore together. You are equal parts known and unknown to me."

Cullen slowly reached out, his fingers closing around hers. He held her hand with both of his, guiding it to his face. He kissed the backs of each of her knuckles.

"Then nothing must change."

"But Olivin, he and I—"

Cullen shook his head. "I don't need to know. I understand and accept the position you're in. But I don't want all the details." He smirked slightly. "If you're willing to spare me those?"

"Of course." Eira could hardly believe what she was hearing. First Olivin, and now this? What about her made these men willing to hover in limbo?

"My offer to give you time to sort through your heart, and… his offer as well, I assume, did not have a short leash. These things need care and space. It's all right to move slowly. Really, it was foolish of me—of us—to think we could know the complete design of our hearts for what we wanted into eternity from a few months together. A few weeks, really." His eyes drifted up to hers with a soft chuckle. "If I am to have you for forever, then I want it to be a future you yearn for. I want you to look back and know, beyond all doubt, that *I* was the one."

"I want the same for you," she whispered.

"We share in that. I hope to find my own path, my own home, just as you are." He nodded.

The sentiment made her crack a smile that almost broke into tears. Not because it meant that there was a possibility of their lives charting similar courses. But because he was looking after himself. He was still dedicated to mending all the pieces within him that had been broken, dented, or ignored over the years.

"It only took taking you away from everything you've ever known and pirate kidnapping to make you begin exploring what you actually wanted for yourself."

He smirked. "Some of us are late bloomers."

Cullen shifted. He leaned over her, forcing Eira to lie back in the process. Her heart began to race again, faster than before. She had reinforced permission now to enjoy this. She could do so without guilt. No more hesitation. Only exploration.

He positioned himself atop her once more; this time the weight of his body pressed her into the sand. His warmth overwhelmed her senses, easing away all remaining vestiges of chill that had settled into her bones.

"I just want you to enjoy yourself," he whispered against the shell of her ear. "And I want to enjoy myself, with you. Maybe, if we're lucky, we'll have years ahead of us to continue doing so. But if it's not meant to be, then we will always look back on this moment with a satisfied little smirk."

He returned his mouth to hers. A deep, slow kiss. The world narrowed onto him. All thoughts vanished.

Every ache was smoothed away as he ran his hands over her. The wet fabric of her shirt clung to her breasts. His hot fingertips rumpling the liquid cotton made her whole body ache, tensing to attention.

Cullen kissed down her neck, to her collarbone. He kissed over her chest, his breath hot through the fabric. A whimper escaped her lips. It felt so good to be touched like this. To be wanted and needed. To not worry about the rest of the world for just a little while and lose herself in a moment.

Tension was already arching her lower back as he reached her bare abdomen. His fingers dug into her hips as his mouth continued trailing down. Fire erupted in her.

"Cullen," Eira said breathlessly. Everything else was vanishing from her mind. The only thing she could think was his name. "I… you…"

"If you want me to stop, I will. Say the word," he murmured across her flesh, kissing around and beneath her bellybutton. "But, if not…just relax and enjoy, Eira."

She did as she was told. She stopped fighting the worry and

concern that threatened to pull her mind back to reality and force her to overthink the moment. It all faded away as he reached his goal. She let out a sharp gasp, eyes snapping open. Everything was so vivid and bright. So beautiful.

His mouth and fingers drove her to new heights that Eira had never known. There were parts of her body that tingled and shuddered that she didn't even know existed. Her core had turned to churning molten, ripe with desire as he lavished his affections upon her.

Curling her toes, Eira pressed her eyes closed. She was a bow. Arching. Taut. Ready to snap and spring loose. The sweet, sweet release of breaking was so close. Cullen seemed to know it, too. Everything he was doing remained consistent and yet was somehow more.

Just when it was all about to snap, an unfamiliar voice echoed in to them, "You're sure they'll be here this time?"

CULLEN STOPPED HIS attentions instantly, sitting upright. Eira scrambled to get her clothes back in place. They both looked to the opening of the cavern, and then to each other.

"They won't miss another meeting. They're as invested as we are," the voice continued.

Eira grabbed Cullen's hand, pulling him with her into the water. She used her magic to allow them to sink in silently. There wasn't so much as a splash or a wave. Cullen followed, his trust implicit. Just as she was about to go under, she heard:

"How much is His Holiness demanding this time?"

"More than ever before, the heretics on Meru need a demonstration of his might. They still resist, eager to regroup around the tattered remains of their leadership. I hear he is asking for flashfires to help drive them out from underneath Risen and continue showing the city his domination over it."

Flashfires? Eira had yet to hear of such a thing.

"That would surely give our cause even more momentum—to think, arming those without magic. Putting power in their hands that is as mighty as the average sorcerer."

Eira slowed, staring at the opening to the cavern that led toward the sea beyond, rather than back to the beach they had come from. She glanced back to Cullen. He nodded, as if he could read her mind. Eira swam to the farthest point of the cavern, pressing into one of the craggy walls. Cullen stayed close behind her as Eira clung to the wet stone to keep an eye on the narrow beach they had just been lying on. With a wave of her hand, she sent the water onto the sand, smoothing away the indent their bodies had left.

Then she drew her magic around them. Between the sea, the moisture in the air, and the training with Adela, Eira had little issue crafting an illusion for her and Cullen. If anyone looked in their direction, they would just see stone and water. It was easier than she expected; even as they bobbed slightly, she was certain the illusion never wavered. Easy enough that she could also simultaneously adjust the ripples in the water coming from them to give nothing away. Turned out she didn't need Olivin's illusionary training, after all.

In the few seconds of waiting, it struck Eira how calm she was. During the tournament, when she had been sneaking around Pillars, her heart had pounded. She'd had her stomach in her throat. Anxiety would make her ready to fight or flee, like little more than an animal.

Fear is just inexperience manifesting in the unknown. It is little more than nightmares. What scares it away is experience, knowledge, and power. You do yourself a disservice by giving in to fear, for it denies you the strength you possess, Adela had said to her during one of their many nights of working together. The words had imprinted themselves upon her.

Eira wasn't afraid, because she knew she had the means to defend herself. To escape or to fight, no matter what it came to, she had the tools and strength to do what must be done. That meant there was nothing to worry about and she could focus with a clear head, ready for whatever came next.

Two men rounded the corner. There was nothing special about the way they were dressed. They looked like any of the other pirates she'd seen—a little rough around the edges. But nothing particularly alarming.

Except…

When one of them turned to face the opening of the cavern they'd just walked around, she noticed three vertical lines scarred into the back of his hand. There was no question as to what it meant: They were Pillars.

The urge to charge them ripped through her. She had the element of surprise. With a twitch of her fingers, she could skewer them on ice before they even had a chance to look her way. But Eira remained still, thinking rather than acting.

Why were they here? Who were they waiting for? And what did they want—flashfires? She wouldn't get her answers by killing them. Eira continued to wait, keeping her magic firmly in hand and her breathing shallow.

"How much longer?" the man with long, black hair asked.

The other man pulled a watch from the pocket of his loose-fitting trousers. "Should be any minute now." He glanced up. "*Ah*, that must be them."

A small rowboat drifted into the cavern. Eira pressed closer to the wall. Cullen stayed next to her. His familiar warmth reassuring her that, together, they could accomplish anything they needed.

In the rowboat was a single woman, who didn't even bother disembarking. Her tone was sharp, to the point. "There isn't much time."

There was a soft lilt to her words—an accent that Eira had never heard before, impossible to place. The woman had long, brown hair, woven into a thick ropelike braid. Bracelets like what Lavette and Varren wore covered her left wrist. She wore heavily tailored clothing of stiff silk and satin. A high collar, sleeveless.

The most curious thing about her was a rod of metal across her lap. It had a wooden handle on one end, slightly curved. Almost like a cane. But judging from the etched runes at its base…there was more to the object.

"We were wondering if you would come, given that the *Stormfrost* is in." The black-haired man reached into the rowboat, grabbing one of the heavy-looking sacks with a grunt.

"Adela knows the rules of Black Flag Bay; she won't attack us."

"We heard she took down one of your other boats." The other man pocketed his watch and began to help unload the bags.

"We drew first blood. One of my compatriots became a little too bold—a little too arrogant that he could take down the pirate queen with a pathetic little skiff and some emblazoned runes. If it had been one of our main fleet, it would've been a different story," the woman said confidently.

We…the way she spoke…this woman was from Carsovia. A horrible realization dawned on Eira, making her whole body feel clammy despite being mostly submerged in the temperate waters of the bay.

"Bold of the empress to begin attacking Adela."

"Empress Hannika has no reason to fear a pirate."

"Fear? No, no." The men agreed. Eira wondered if they really thought that, or were merely trying to avoid offense. "But Adela can pose an annoying problem."

"Leave our waters to us. And, as promised, we will leave Meru's to its own." There was forced politeness in her words, but the men didn't seem to notice. Or didn't care. Because they smiled and nodded, continuing to unload their sacks from the woman's rowboat until there were ten piled up on the narrow strip of beach. "I believe your lord has requested two more shipments."

They nodded.

"Very well. We shall meet again here in two months' time." With a spin of her bracelets, the water shifted around the rowboat, as though grabbing it and pulling it back. The woman took to the oars once more.

"Wait!" One of the men stopped her. She gave him a withering stare. "The wayward flock of Meru is putting up more resistance than we had hoped." Eira's heart continued to soar at any mention of the fight on Meru carrying on. "We might need more, faster."

"The mines can only move so quickly." The woman had a dangerous tone to her voice, one the men heard, given how they shifted their stances nervously. She tilted her head to one side with a sigh. "But I suppose I could see if there is a way to speed up production. There are always means to motivate the unmotivated."

"Perhaps the flashfires…" The Pillar eyed the metal rod in the woman's lap. *Was that what that metal rod was?*

She was silent for a long moment and then said, "You would do well to remember that Carsovia is aiding your cause out of our own generosity…it isn't good to test such kindness."

"His Holiness appreciates the continued support of your empress." The two Pillars bowed and the woman left. Black Hair turned to his companion. "We should get this to the ship."

They each flung a bag over their shoulder, starting out of the cavern. Eira waited a breath before easing away from the wall. Cullen grabbed her shoulder.

"They could be back any second," he whispered.

"I'll only be a moment." She reached up and squeezed his fingers. "I just want to confirm my suspicion, then we're leaving. You can go on ahead."

"I'm *not* leaving without you."

"Cullen, go. Warn the others. I'll be right behind you." He still looked unsure. Not that she could blame him, given her track record. Eira turned, propelling herself through the water to close the small gap between them, kissing him fiercely. "I know why you're worried. But I'm not that woman anymore. I'm not going to run off when you turn your back. So, go. Warn the others because I think we're going to have to move quickly."

The reservations left his eyes, replaced by steely resolve. Cullen nodded and dipped below the surface of the water, a bubble of air surrounding his head. Eira quickly glided through the water, propelled by magic. The wave she'd made lifted her up and deposited her onto the beach by the bags. Eira ran her hand over the one on top. She didn't need any more confirmation, but wriggled a finger into the opening at one end of the sack anyway.

The pad of her pointer finger rolled over a smooth, perfectly round ball. She'd been right. *Flash beads.*

The Pillars weren't working with a rogue operator to get their supply of the deadly material. They were working with the Empress of Carsovia herself.

· CHAPTER ·
THIRTY-TWO

E IRA DIDN'T HAVE time to process the full implications of her discovery. She had to escape, get back to her friends, tell them what happened, and then they all had to figure out a way to thwart what the Pillars were doing. Under no circumstances was she about to let the Pillars take these back to Ulvarth. But rather than attempting to dispose of the flash beads here and now, she started with the escaping part.

She had other ideas for how to make the Pillars pay and Eira was ready to play the long game.

Sinking back into the water, Eira didn't swim back through the cavern so much as rode on a current of her own making through. Cullen was just at the opposite end of the cave as she shot past. Hooking his arm, she pulled him up to the surface with her. The water swelled around them, taking them all the way back up the hill where their friends were waiting, thankfully already dressed.

Cullen landed more clumsily than she did, sputtering a bit. He no doubt inhaled some water with the surprise of her grabbing him. But he seemed to compose himself quickly.

"Could you always do that?" Noelle blurted. Even though her brows were high with surprise, her mouth had curled into a prideful grin.

"No, Adela taught me. But that's not what's important. There are Pillars. *Here*." It felt like Eira spoke a dozen words a second as her mind raced.

"What? Pillars?" Olivin was on his feet. "Are you all right?"

"Are you some kind of Pillar magnet?" Ducot asked incredulously.

"Sometimes I think I am. Sometimes I wish I wasn't. But this time I'm glad I have this streak of bad luck. I'm fine, but they won't be, soon." Eira was frantically pulling back on her clothes, tugging them into place. Luckily her friends picked up on the urgency without needing to be explicitly told. "They're getting a shipment of flash beads. There were six bags—no, seven."

"From who?" Ducot asked.

"I don't know who the person was, but they were definitely from Carsovia—the Pillars are getting flash beads on the order of the empress herself."

That stilled them all with shock. But only for a second.

"What are we going to do about it?" Olivin asked, a knowing gleam to his eyes. He could see her mind working.

"We can't let them get that much firepower to Meru," Eira said with nod to what they were all thinking. "Our options, so far as I can tell, are to try and stop them here and now. Or, we go back to the *Stormfrost*."

"Still amazed you didn't just stab them on sight," Noelle muttered.

"I certainly thought about it. And in thinking, I came up with a better idea to make them pay—but I wanted to solicit all of your insight. I'm not the woman who acts first and thinks later anymore." Eira grinned at her friend, too aware of her past faults to be offended.

"So you keep saying. Yet, every time I have proof, I'm astounded." Noelle's expression became serious once more. "But I think we should just get the bastards. Blow them up with their flash beads they find so precious."

Olivin hummed.

"You're not convinced?"

"Kill the men, and we stop *this* shipment. Sink the ship, and we probably slow a lot more shipments down the line, especially given the state we left the Ofok port in. This might be one of the Pillars last ships out, at least on this side of the continent. And bringing another around Meru will take some time. I say go for the ship." He put his hands in his pockets with a slight shrug. "But I'll do whatever you want to do."

"Cullen, Ducot?" Eira asked each of them.

"I'm following you," Cullen said without hesitation.

"I'm following her." Ducot tilted his head in Noelle's direction. "And she seems to be following you. But we're wasting time with this caucus."

"I know." Eira turned to Olivin. "You and I are of the same mind on this one. Cullen and Noelle—you two go over the ridge there and see where they're taking the flash beads. The rest of us will go and get the *Stormfrost* and come around this side of the island. When we're in sight, signal us, Noelle."

"What in 'I'm following her' made you want to split us up?" Ducot folded his arms. "I'm just going to slow you both down running back to the city, anyway."

"Then go with them, too." Eira nodded at Ducot. "You and Noelle can stop the people on the shore. Cullen, I need you to slow the ship itself if they try to get away."

"Understood." For once, there was no hesitation. No sideways looks in Olivin's direction. It prompted Eira to reach out and squeeze his hand.

"Good luck, you three," she said warmly.

"Move quickly," Cullen urged her and Olivin as they started down the path.

There weren't any words exchanged between her and Olivin. Their breathing was too labored from the aggressive pace they set back to town. The underbrush of the jungle attacked them anytime they veered a little too far off the beaten path.

"We're not going to make it back fast enough like this," Olivin panted. He was right. They were moving too slowly for her liking. Especially after the time they'd spent delegating. Eira didn't mind consulting her friends…but there was something to be said for rushing in when it came to matters where speed was an element.

Eira searched for ideas. Something to make them move faster.

Had it been wrong to have Cullen stay? He could've put the wind under his heels and she could've held the ship back with currents.

But Eira suspected Adela wouldn't move the *Stormfrost* for Olivin, Cullen, Noelle, or even Ducot. This was a favor she had to call in herself.

They blazed a trail through the town, pushing through to get to the docks. Of course, both of the *Stormfrost*'s rowboats were out in the sea, coming and going.

Eira turned, extending her hand to Olivin. "Are you ready?"

"For your marvelous madness? Always." His fingers closed around hers.

She couldn't stop a laugh from escaping as she sprinted toward the edge of the docks and jumped, Olivin at her side. The water rose to meet them, pushing aside tied boats and causing buoys to clank and thud together. Power surged through her. The currents swelled. Tiny geysers pressed under the balls of her and Olivin's feet.

Eira ran, leaping from one wave to the next. Olivin kept her pace, every stride in tandem with hers—identical, so she could predict the movements. He charged forward as fearlessly as she did. Trusting her magic to be there supporting him. Eira glanced over at him.

His expression was one of pure wonder, accented by a wide smile. "How are you doing this?"

"Magic, my dear."

They raced on water swells all the way to the deck of the *Stormfrost*. She could feel the impact on her magic. But it hadn't exhausted her in the way it might once have. By now, Eira was so accustomed to pushing her magic to the limits, and then some, that this was nothing.

"And to what do we owe the pleasure of that display?" Adela said dryly, a little curt.

"Bold to seem put off by dramatics when you're a woman who sails around in a ship of ice and mist," Eira retorted.

Adela's eyes widened slightly. Crow, at her side, looked

positively mortified by Eira's tone. Eira forced herself to grin through her nerves. She was on the high of power, the edge of worry with the Pillars, and the remaining restlessness that Cullen had worked into her with his tongue and fingers but never *finished*.

Fortunately, and by some miracle, Eira was on good enough terms that Adela chuckled.

She allowed herself a sigh of relief before blurting, "The Pillars are here. They're around the other side of the island getting a shipment of flash beads from Carsovia. They're going to take it back to Meru and I want to use the *Stormfrost* to sink their ship to really cripple the Pillars' influence."

Adela folded her hands on top of her cane and leaned back slightly, staring down at Eira.

"It's all true," Eira insisted to her frigid gaze.

"Very well then."

Crow balked. "Your Coldness?"

"The *Stormfrost* is yours for now, Eira. Enjoy your piracy." Adela started back for her cabin. Eira was too stunned to move for a moment. So she was still standing there when the pirate queen paused and looked over her shoulder. "But, remember, you are at the helm of Adela Lagmir's flagship. So if you're going to do this, do it right—completely annihilate them."

"Yes, Your Iciness," Eira murmured.

Crow looked between Adela and Eira several times. But Eira continued to focus on Adela's cabin, even after the door closed. The pirate crossed over to her, stepping in her line of sight.

"Your orders?" Crow's dark eyes met hers.

"Pardon?" Eira blinked back to reality.

"Don't we have a ship to sink? Your orders?" Crow's words took on an expectant tone.

Eira had a hundred thoughts all at once. How often did Adela just *give* over control of the *Stormfrost*? Would her crew even listen to Eira? Dozens of questions that might never be answered.

So there was no point in worrying about them.

"Tell the crew to raise anchor. Double time. Sails ready. I want every Waterrunner and Windwalker—or equivalent—getting wind and momentum behind the ship," Eira ordered.

Crow bustled off, barking orders on her behalf. Eira took a deep breath and walked up to the wheel on the quarterdeck. She ran her hands over its frosty surface, palmed the knobs that extended out from it. Olivin was still at her side.

"Olivin, help get the ship going," Eira commanded. "As soon as the anchor's up I want you to push the water." Her magic was already beginning to turn the vessel around the anchor point as the crew was getting the ship ready to sail.

Adela's pirates were well trained. They knew their roles. Didn't ask questions. Didn't even blink when it was Eira at the helm so long as it was a result of Adela's orders. And if Crow was falling into line, that seemed to be all they needed to know.

"Ahead!" Eira shouted as the anchor clanked with a dull thud at the top of its hoist.

The ship lurched forward, aided with the push of a monumental force of magic. A tall ship like the *Stormfrost* couldn't launch into motion. But the quick turn to sea was yet another testament to the sheer power Adela had at her disposal in the hands of her crew.

Eira guided them around the side of the island, by rudder and by magic. On occasion, she closed her eyes, letting her power slip over the sides of the ship and sink into the ocean below, looking for sandbanks and hidden rocks that might spell disaster.

As they rounded an outcropping, another, smaller vessel came into view. It was drifting just off the coast—no visible anchor— and a rowboat was being pulled up its side.

A tongue of fire shot into the air from the jungles on the nearby hilltop. A second tongue of flame crackled near the vessel, almost reaching it. But it was just out of Noelle's range. Hopefully it wouldn't be out of Cullen's.

Found them.

"Ready cannons!" Eira shouted at the top of her lungs. "Starboard side! Don't ease on the wind and currents!"

The other ship wasn't anchored and was already attempting

a getaway. It was smaller and no doubt faster, and the wind was coming from behind, so not much magic would be needed. Men and women were scrambling on the distant deck like little ants.

They'd have one good shot at the other vessel. Adela wouldn't allow her to give chase too far from Black Flag Bay, not with half her crew still on the isle, and Eira couldn't blame her. This moment was all or nothing.

"Fire on my mark."

"Fire on mark!" one of the pirates shouted down through a grate that went through to the gun deck. Eira could hear rattling and clanking from the depths of the ship. The cannons were being loaded with flash beads from Adela's own stash.

Eira could still feel the singe on her midsection from the assault of the explosions on the side of the hull. The pain merged with the hate she already felt for the Pillars. Fueling a wicked streak that she had less and less of a reason to hide the longer she was with Adela. She would unleash horror on them worse than what they'd brought to the coliseum. She would raze their desecrated temples and liberate their cities.

And it started with this. Here and now.

Magic flashed off the other vessel. The volley Noelle had initiated was returned. More magic exploded, its source from the hilltop. The Pillars were distracted and it slowed their getaway. The *Stormfrost* came alongside.

Eira projected her cold, bitter command. "Fire."

"Fire!" the pirate shouted belowdecks.

She crossed to the railing on the starboard side, feeling the cannons as they rattled the *Stormfrost*. Magic exploded with a burst of color and noise. The flash beads were as beautiful as they were terrifying in their destructive power.

The other vessel was turned into sawdust. Decks ripped apart. People flew.

Eira raised her right fist, as if she were holding an invisible shield. A wall of water rose from the sea, absorbing the brunt of the blast as the flash beads in the Pillar's vessel were ignited by the surge of magic. She gritted her teeth, sliding her feet apart. Bracing herself to hold the magic and the *Stormfrost* in place. But the vessel still tilted, wobbling to the side.

However, her barrier held, taking the brunt of the explosion and guarding against torn-apart pieces of the Pillars' ship. Ocean water poured down around them like rain, turned up from the explosion. Eira held her stance until the last of the water stopped pelting the deck. She relaxed her grip, slowly allowing the water to return to the ocean to not rock the *Stormfrost* too much. There was nothing left of the other ship beyond debris floating among scraps.

Eira straightened, her magic and muscles relaxing. She turned down to the main deck. "Can any of you get over to the island?"

A pirate raised her hand.

"Exceptional. Go to our allies up on the ridge, and let them know that we will be waiting for them back off the main docks."

"Understood." The pirate spun the bracelets around her left wrist and jumped into the water. The waves swelled to meet her and carried her across to the distant shore. It was a rudimentary version of what Adela and now Eira could do.

"All right, well done, all. Let's bring her back."

The pirates mobilized the second Eira issued her command. The corners of her lips curled slightly. Eira crossed back to the helm and lightly ran her hands over the knobs, not that she needed the wheel to steer. Helming the *Stormfrost* was conducting a symphony of magic.

Olivin was at her side without her realizing it. Between the explosion and the commands, she'd lost track of where he'd been standing. She could smell the seawater on his skin as he placed his hand on her hip, sliding close to her. It was a bold move, but Eira found she didn't mind being bold. Not when she was at the helm of the *Stormfrost*. A pirate would take as many lovers as pleased her.

"How does it feel?" Olivin asked softly, directly into her ear. "Stepping into Adela's shoes?"

Eira tilted her head slightly in his direction. Her temple brushed against his cheek, and her forehead. An almost wicked smile split her lips.

"Do you really want to know the answer to that?"

"I wouldn't have asked if I didn't," he murmured.

"Fine, the truth then. It feels…like I was born for this."

THIRTY-THREE

BLACK FLAG BAY was in the distance, fading away, collapsing into a caramel-colored sky. Eira was no longer at the helm of the *Stormfrost*. Adela had resumed her command and charted a direct course for Carsovia, their storerooms fully replenished. Oddly, despite the events of the day, Adela seemed to have no interest in speaking with Eira. There would've been a time when this had worried Eira, but, at present, she couldn't find it within herself to be bothered.

Her core was still molten, swirling at the lingering memories of Cullen and his mouth on her. Her hip burned with the feeling of Olivin's hand grasping it. To think, at one point she felt torn over these men. Over things like who was the best for her or who would make her happier. Torn over guilt for not knowing who her heart was drawn to more.

But in this moment…she was as free as the sea breeze. As bright as the distant sun. Opportunities were as vast as the horizon and her life as worth exploring as an uncharted course. She didn't need to have all the answers right now. It'd be doing them all a disservice to try. And she'd been completely honest with both men—with all her friends—on where she stood and what she didn't yet know.

Her whole life was still ahead of her. So much to discover once the Pillars were dealt with. And, after utterly trouncing their ship, even they felt surmountable. For the first time, Eira felt like she had all the resources at her disposal to bring Ulvarth to his knees and he wouldn't even know it was coming.

Eira rested with her hands on the railing of the back of the ship, reflecting on the events of the day. She didn't even notice Cullen approaching until he took a position next to her, their sides flush against each other.

"I think I owe you," he said, somewhat coy.

"I think you do," she replied with a chuckle. "I'm going to hold you to it."

Cullen laughed as well. "I hope you do. I hope you hold a lot more than that to me." He glanced in her direction with a smirk.

"I could arrange that, once we're no longer on a ship with everyone looking over everyone else's shoulders." She leaned away from the railing, drawing her height and power with it. The currents beneath them still responded to her whims, doing as she bid. "I'm afraid I don't feel inclined for an audience."

"Neither do I."

"Cullen..." Seriousness slipped its way into his name. "I've been thinking."

"Always a dangerous thing to do."

"Agreed. I've been thinking that once this is all over...once Ulvarth is dead, the Pillars are disbanded and nothing more than a few zealots clinging to a bygone ideal that whatever government Meru instates can deal with...once my parents are saved, the nations have peace, and Vi Solaris has her treaty..."

"Only a few things," he interjected.

"One or two." She shrugged as though everything she had listed were trivial matters. "I've been thinking that I'm not going to return to Solaris."

"No?" He shifted away from the railing, looking at her with a furrowed brow. Eira wondered if for the first time he was seeing her. Truly seeing her as the person she was meant to be. Probably because for the first time she felt like she could really *be* that person—or, rather, she had any idea who that person was.

"I want to see my parents safe and returned to their home, same with my uncle. But it is their place, not mine; Solaris is not my home."

"They love you, you know."

"I know." And for the first time she did. It was unequivocal, without fear, and no doubts or caveats attached. "They came halfway across the world to watch me compete. They left everything to be there, even though I wish they hadn't. I know they have been imperfect and, if I'm being honest, there are things that I will never quite forgive them for...but I know they're *trying*. And, to a point, that's good enough. Maybe not good enough for us to spend our winters together huddled around hearths, or summers on Oparium's beaches, but good enough to sit around the table whenever I'm in town and reminisce about when times were simple and good and easy. They loved me as best they knew how."

He was silent for a long time. Eira wondered if Cullen was thinking of his own father. Surely he too had wondered what had become of him...but Cullen had said very little about it, and it was something that Eira didn't feel like it was her place to push. Whatever he was working through was for him alone, until he invited her in.

"If not Solaris, where? What next?" he finally asked.

Eira shrugged. "I don't know where or what will happen when all this is over, assuming I survive."

"Of course you will survive," Cullen said firmly and quickly.

She gave him a small smile. "It was a wonder that we survived the coliseum. I have no expectations. I know what I'm going into. But," she continued before he could make another defensive statement, "assuming I do, I think I want to go and search for what home is to me."

"Where are you going to search for it?"

"Anywhere. Everywhere." The words were as light as the seabirds that followed the ship, gliding effortlessly. "Maybe my true home is somewhere out there across the distance seas. Maybe it's just over that horizon." Eira pointed to the distance. "Maybe it is still back in Solaris and I won't know that until I've explored everywhere else and have come to realize that nowhere fits me better."

Eira savored the feeling of the deck under her feet, a firm contrast to the gently rocking seas. A massive ocean that stretched far beyond her and yet that her power mingled with. The salt wind in her hair… There was a peace here indeed, somewhere she could stay until she found the place she was meant to be.

"I think I'm going to take the ship that Adela gives us and when all this is over, I'm going to explore as far as I can go—as far as the winds and currents allow."

Cullen was silent again. She gave him his space to process what she had just said. A knot twisted in her gut, wringing out the heat that had lingered from earlier. Cullen was finding himself as much as she was finding herself. But if any part of him was called back to titles, and courts, and balls…this was the end for them. Maybe not immediately, but eventually. Because, while Eira didn't yet know where she was meant to be, she knew it wasn't among the ranks of nobility. Hopefully, it wouldn't stop them from enjoying each other's company in the meantime…

"Well, if you're going to go as far as the sea allows, then having a Windwalker at your side would prove useful."

Eira's attention jerked to him. She could feel her lips part as her jaw went slack with surprise. She heard him clearly. And yet, she doubted her ears.

"Cullen…what you're saying—"

"I know what I'm saying," he stopped her there, gently. Cullen took her hand and laced his fingers with hers. "Every captain needs a first mate. Or, at the very least, someone who can make sure the wind is always in their sails."

"But your family…"

"My father is probably dead," he said softly. On instinct he turned back east, looking in the direction of Meru. "My stepmother, a widow, will have the sympathy of the court. She'll be fine. And I was never particularly her favorite to begin with… There's not much else for me there. Other than a life of contorting myself into the mold others have set for me. A mindless existence where I never stop to ask myself what I actually want in the midst of it all."

Eira silently admitted it sounded horrible…but that had been the life that he'd chosen—or at least accepted—until now. Could he really just walk away from it?

"Be that as it may, the life I want to live isn't one of accolades and ease. It will be hardship and hungry nights and cold days."

"If I hunger, it will be only for your kisses. If I am cold, it is only because I am waiting for you to come and warm me." He met her eyes, taking a half step closer. "Your home might be out there, somewhere…but I truly believe my home might be with you."

"And what if I choose someone else?" she whispered.

"Olivin? You can say his name." Cullen chuckled. "We're both well aware of the other."

"You never know, some other burly deckhand could sweep me off my feet and steal my heart." Eira slid her braid over her shoulder and glanced at him from the corners of her eyes.

"Fair." Somehow, Cullen still didn't seem bothered. "Eira, I know you can't promise how you'll feel, who you'll choose, if anyone. Just like I can't promise how I might feel in a year, five years, or beyond. Forever is a long time from now. But right now I understand that you need to find what you want, for yourself. Just as I am doing. So even if he's there at your side, too, even if you have a hundred lovers, I still want to go with you because I'm not going for him, or them, or anyone else; I'm going for myself and for you."

Shock crashed over her. The heat had returned, flushing her body from head to toe and filling her with yearning and admiration. With all the emotions that she hadn't felt toward Cullen in a long time, and perhaps never this sincerely or powerfully.

"Are you sure?" She tried to prevent her hope from slipping into her voice. This had to be his decision alone.

"If I change my mind, I'll let you know."

"But—"

"Eira, you kept telling me that I couldn't always live for others. That I had to live for myself. I took your words to heart. This is what I want for myself and I'm going in with both eyes open."

"Then…" Her fingers tightened around his. "I would be honored to have you as part of my future crew."

The anchor clamored with grinding metal and heavy clanking as it fell along the side of the ship and splashed into the water. In the distance was a strip of gray at the very edge of the horizon, where the hazy sky of dawn met the water. Thin enough that it was possible it was just an illusion. But Eira knew better.

It was Carsovia.

"Her Iciness would like to see you before you go ashore," Crow interrupted the brief conversation that they had all been having at the bow of the vessel, debating what fate held next for them. Trying to make what plans they were able. It seemed Eira would get answers for them all.

"I'll be back soon, I'm sure." She bid farewell to her friends and followed Crow down to Adela's cabin. Crow stood off to the side, as she usually did, allowing Eira to enter alone.

Adela was situated back at her usual table. But instead of sitting, she stood, poring over maps. Metal cartographer's tools glinted in the sunlight as they danced over the tanned and dyed leathers. The pirate queen hardly looked up as Eira crossed over.

"We are here," Adela said without fanfare, pointing to one of the coasts on her map. "The mines are here." Her finger slid back to the southwest.

"Why not dock off this port?" Eira pointed at a town adjacent to the mines, just southeast. It looked like it was the end of the closest road to the mines.

"Too many ships. We'll be spotted in an instant by Carsovia's navy. This is a harder route, but a safer one. More guaranteed that you'll get there, assuming your better sense doesn't leave you on land. Once you've done what you need to, go through that town and steal a boat to return here."

"Is this the boat that you promised?" Eira folded her arms.

"What? Not good enough for you?" Adela summoned her cane with a thought as she leaned away from the table.

"It just makes me wonder why I didn't steal a boat at Black Flag Bay."

"Because everyone there would've killed you for it. And, had you miraculously survived, you would've crossed the pirate queen, which does not promise longevity." She motioned to the maps with an open palm. "This way, you not only end up with a boat, but my favor."

"A valuable thing indeed."

"Glad you have enough sense to think so. We still have work to do, you and I." Adela paused. She added, "If something goes amiss, and your vessel is sunk in the process of getting it back to the *Stormfrost*—or it isn't truly seaworthy—I will ensure you get a proper one."

"Generous of you."

"I'm told I have a soft spot for you." Adela gave her a thin smile.

"And why is that?"

She chuckled, shook her head, and ignored the question, returning to the maps. "It should take you two days to get the mines from here. I'll move the *Stormfrost* on the night of the third day and hold my position for one dawn and one dusk. If you're not back by then, I'm leaving you for dead."

"Not that much of a soft spot," Eira said with a playful note.

"More than I would give most."

"Then I'm going to leverage your fondness and ask that those from Qwint be taken home if I don't return. My friends too, if they make it out without me." When the pirate queen said nothing in reply, Eira placed her hands on the table and looked Adela in the eyes. "Please."

"Granted," she said after a moment's consideration. "But I expect you to prove to me that all our training—all the investment I put in you—wasn't for naught."

"I'll do my best," Eira vowed and pushed away from the table. "If there's nothing else…"

"I want his right foot, as proof of his demise," Adela said coldly. "A foot for a foot."

Eira paused, staring at Adela's frozen leg. The pirate queen looked out her window with a sour expression, her gaze piercing Carsovia in the distance.

"I'll bring it to you." Eira had no hesitation.

"Good, I expect nothing less." Adela continued to stare out the windows as Eira took her leave.

Most of the crew had surrounded the small boat that was pulled up to the railing on the side of the *Stormfrost*. Her friends were already positioned in the vessel, along with Crow and Pine. To Eira's surprise, Lavette and Varren were included.

"Varren?" Eira said softly as she approached the railing. "What are you doing?" Her words had gone soft with surprise. With the answer she already knew.

"What does it look like I'm doing?" He forced a grin. So clearly trying to be brave. So clearly failing.

And yet, he genuinely seemed all the stronger despite it, from his windswept red hair to his ruddy, freckled cheeks to match. And that snaggletooth smile that kept on despite all he'd been through.

"You need a guide, and I'm the only one who *really* knows this land. I know the ins and outs of the mines. Plus, I have some unfinished business of my own there."

"You told us all the details; we will be all right." Eira had committed to memory every story of Slip and the mines that he'd imparted.

"Believe me, I made every effort to talk him out of this," Lavette said dryly. There was a sharpness to her gaze that radiated displeasure. "It's really up to you to tell him not to."

"I'm not going to do that; it's his decision," Eira said, ignoring the pointed look Lavette gave her.

"Good, let's shove off before I change my mind." Varren situated himself.

Eira boarded the boat. It was Varren and Lavette in the back. Eira positioned herself in front of Lavette in the same row as Noelle and Alyss. In front of them were the pirates, Ducot wedged between them. Cullen, Olivin, and Yonlin all crammed in the bow.

Crow called for the boat to be lowered and ropes groaned. It swayed slightly and that was the opportunity Lavette used. The one Eira could sense she'd wanted and had given her.

"If anything happens to him, it's on you." She'd leaned in to whisper to Eira, breath hot on the back of Eira's neck.

Eira glanced over her shoulder. "I'm not dictating what people can and can't do."

"That's your job." Lavette clearly didn't want Varren to come. She probably didn't want to come herself—and for good reason. Eira hardly blamed them and so she ignored Lavette's cutting remarks.

"My job is to keep everyone informed so we can all make the best decisions we can."

Lavette snorted and leaned away.

Eira shifted her attention to both of them, and before Lavette could speak again, she said, "Adela said she would bring you two to Qwint, no matter what happened to us."

"What?" Lavette and Varren seemed to say in unison. They both stared at her with wide eyes.

"I asked her to. I didn't think you were coming and I wanted to make sure that you would get home. If you don't want to come, I can build you a ladder of ice to get back up," Eira said hastily.

"Eira," Varren interrupted softly. "Thank you. But I'm going. I need to do this. Not just for you all, or to get back home, but for me."

She saw the resolve in his eyes as the rowboat splashed down into the ocean. Varren's determination and fear were equally palpable. So it wasn't just for her. Eira gave him a small smile and a nod, turning forward. Lavette might still blame her, and that was fine with Eira. She could handle the responsibility and the blame that came with it.

"Eira, if you please." Crow gestured to the mainland.

Summoning her magic, she called upon a swell of water. It collected behind the rowboat and they sped off, propelled by a current of Eira's making. It arced through the water, turning toward the shore. The sun was rising, illuminating the distant strip of land as it rose up from the sea the closer they drew. These weren't the sloping, gentle shores of the pirate island, but rocky bluffs more akin to the Solaris cliffs Eira was familiar with around Oparium.

"See that dark line in the rock?" Crow called over the wind. Eira nodded. "Go there."

She did as she was told. The line in the rock was actually a split between two cliffs, a crack that went all the way down to the ocean, where it parted in two with a breeze like a sigh. Eira slowed the current as they entered the natural tunnel. The rock here was different than in Solaris, a pale white and compacted together like columns.

"Did a sorcerer make this?" Yonlin asked. The stone looked too perfect to be natural.

Alyss reached out and ran her fingertips across one of the columns as they passed. "If so, it was a very long time ago…"

"You might not be able to sense anything," Varren said. "The cliffs have been around for eons. In Carsovia this region is called the Broken Wall of Thecules."

"Who was Thecules?" Noelle asked.

"A sorcerer so powerful that he created these sheer cliffs across the entire eastern coast with a wave of his hand to keep back the ravaging seas of the early ages that would've consumed the land of Carsovia." Varren spoke as though he'd had to repeat those "facts"—a generous term—many times. "He went on to become the first Emperor of Carsovia. It is said he lived a thousand years and bedded a thousand woman. He was the one to unite the far kingdoms under his banner. They called him the Lord of Endless Blood."

"Cheerful," Noelle muttered.

"It's Carsovia. If the history isn't written in the blood of the conquered, it's not worth sharing…" Varren trailed off. His eyes were haunted in the low light of Olivin's magic circle.

"Not sure how good the wall is at keeping out primordial seas. But it's pretty miserable at keeping out pirates." Crow grinned.

The tunnel opened to a small pool, surrounded by the columns like stepping stones. With no more water, Eira guided the boat to one of the lowest stone plateaus. Her friends needed no further instruction to disembark.

They got out one by one. Ducot, Cullen, Olivin, and Yonlin went first. Then Eira, Alyss, and Noelle. She reached a hand back, helping Lavette out.

Then it was Varren's turn.

He stood in the rowboat, perfectly still. Eira held the boat in her grasp with the water around it. Varren stared at the rock as if he were squaring off with the man who ran the mines himself.

"It's not too late, Varren. You can go back," Eira said softly.

"None of us will think less of you," Lavette added. The rest of them nodded in agreement. "If you want me to, I'll go back with you. *Gladly.*"

Varren looked from the stone up to Lavette. He held out his hand to her—to the woman who had guided and guarded him from the first moment he had left Carsovia. Eira stepped aside, giving them space. Lavette reluctantly took his hand and helped him out of the boat.

One foot. Then two. Varren stood, staring at his feet, then back at the rowboat. As if he couldn't believe that he had managed to do it. As if they'd moved on their own.

With a fire in his eyes, Varren turned back to them. His tone left no room for questioning. "Let's go."

· CHAPTER ·

THIRTY-FOUR

CROW AND PIKE wished them well—a kind gesture that Eira hadn't been expecting. It wasn't over the top. But their well-wishes betrayed more fondness than she'd thought had been fostered with the pirates.

The eight of them—her, Cullen, Olivin, Yonlin, Noelle, Alyss, Lavette, and Varren—made their way up the columns like giant stairs. When a height difference was too steep, Alyss lent a hand with her power, giving them actual stairs to get up. At the very top, they were met by idyllic, gently sloping plains. Tall grasses wafted in the breezes, dotted with wildflowers and buzzing with brightly colored pollinators that flitted on the breezes like confetti.

Eira was the first to speak after they took in the scenery. "I'm not going to lie, I expected something a bit more…bloody, after all the talk about the ruthlessness of Carsovia."

"It looks like the East," Cullen whispered. His brow had relaxed, eyes distant. The East, where he'd grown up. Eira wondered if he saw the distant lands of his forefathers. Or if he saw a memory of the pain he'd caused. One he'd rather forget.

"We should keep moving." Varren led the pack. "We'll look suspicious all out like this."

"No one's around." Noelle motioned to the general lack of anything.

"Not that we can see, for now. But there are often patrols, and I don't know what the color is right now."

"The color?" Alyss asked.

"In Carsovia, there are colors to define your status. Depending on where you live, the family you're born into, what you do…it all defines your color," Lavette explained. "There's a hierarchy among them. Red is usually at the top."

"Red, like blood, got it." Noelle rolled her eyes.

"You learn quickly," Varren appraised dryly. "But, yes, the other colors shift depending on who is in power based on the current moods of the emperor or empress. I tried to pick us clothes from the pile that were as neutral as possible—grays, black, white, cotton, tan—color voids that aren't in the hierarchy."

"The region with the mines should be orange, right?" Lavette asked. Varren nodded. Lavette reached into her pocket, pulling out three strips of burnt-orange fabric. "I grabbed these, just in case."

"I didn't see anything orange in the supplies the pirates offered us." Varren took them.

"They were mine," Noelle said. "Thank Eira for thinking to grab some of our clothes before we left Warich."

"Let's just hope we don't actually need them." Varren frowned and led the group.

They crossed through the empty field and down to a distant wood. It reminded Eira more of the tall pine forests at the foot of the Solaris Mountains, rather than the dense jungles of the island they'd been on the day prior. To think the terrain could change so much… Perhaps a sorcerer really did once cultivate the land by hand.

The trees were spaced out far enough that beams of light could strike through to the forest floor. It was shaded enough here that the grasses thinned, growing smaller. But there wasn't much in the way of underbrush, which made traveling fairly easy.

At least until noon.

A distant horn had Varren dropping to the ground. The rest of them followed. The man trembled like a leaf, but he kept his head up, looking around with wide eyes.

"That's the sound of imperial knights," he whispered. The rest of them were looking around as well, but it was impossible to see anything among the grasses and tree trunks.

"We haven't even seen a road," Cullen whispered.

"Alyss, Ducot, can you sense anything that might give us a direction?" Eira asked.

"Already working on it." Magic pulsed more rigorously from Ducot, filling the air. Alyss followed suit.

Eira waited.

"I think I have something," Alyss murmured. "It's faint, though."

Narrowing her focus on Alyss, Eira pushed away her senses of all others' magics. Where Adela's power was like a deep, underwater chasm, boundless and ominous, Alyss's was the valley between two mountains. Strong peaks. Impressive depth. And Eira would be the earthquake. She would rattle the foundations, creating new chasms that would allow untapped power to seep through. She would free Alyss's bound potential.

Alyss let out a soft gasp. Her eyes opened and swung to Eira. "Are you…"

Eira nodded with a slight smile. "Now, where are they?"

With a confident grin, Alyss closed her eyes once more. The tiny pebbles in the dirt around her rattled as her power swept outward with palpable force. Alyss's magic sank into the earth, running underneath root and plain until it was beyond the realm of Eira's sensing. But she continued to wear a look of intense focus on her face.

"That way." Alyss pointed to the west, southwest. "There's a small town there. I can feel the foundations of the homes. There are riders approaching it, coming from the north. It was hard to tell how many."

"At least six. Imperial knights never travel in fewer numbers than that," Varren said.

"I think we should go to the town," Eira decided.

"Why do you want to go into the town?" Varren balked. "Did you not hear me? There are *imperial knights*."

"I heard you. And agree that we need to be careful—not all of us should go in. But we don't have a lot of supplies." They were intentionally traveling light.

"I can go a night or two where hunger is my dinner," he said dryly.

"*And*," Eira continued, stressing that she hadn't finished in tone alone, "we should also ensure that this man is actually at the mines and not traveling elsewhere for some kind of business." She took Varren's pause to mean that it was possible for him not to be there.

"We can also make sure we're headed in the right direction," Noelle reasoned.

"I think we should scope it out," Cullen agreed. "*If* we can do so safely."

"I can always go in," Ducot offered. "No one will suspect a mole." The air rippled around him and the man vanished, contorting and folding in on himself in a blink until a mole was in his place.

"Just when I think you couldn't get any cuter, you remind me you can do this." Noelle scratched his tiny head with the tip of her finger. Ducot squeaked. "Don't fight with me, you are *adorable*."

Varren sighed. "I suppose the town is in the direction of the mines, more or less. As long as we swing wide…maybe we'll be all right." Another sigh, even heavier than the last. "This way."

They all stood but didn't get more than three steps before squeaking alerted them they were leaving behind a member of their party. Noelle paused, looking back at Ducot incredulously.

"You can't seriously expect me—"

More squeaking.

"Mother above." Noelle sighed dramatically.

Ducot darted over and circled around her feet.

"All right, fine." Noelle picked Ducot up and put him on her shoulder. "I swear you are so lazy."

"Can you really understand what he's saying?" Alyss asked with wonder.

"Not at all. He's just that easy to read." Noelle shrugged and they all carried on in the direction of town.

It was dusk by the time they arrived. Fortunately the town was nestled in what Eira suspected was a man-made clearing in the woods, given that the houses were made of the same timber as the pines. They were simple, log constructions. Wattle and daub, or clay, packed between to keep out the chill. Rather than having shingles or thatching, the roofs were covered in sod, the same grasses as the land around them.

They looked similar to Ofok, and yet had unique differences—like the stilts they sat atop, or how some of their second stories extended over their first. It reminded her of a child's drawing of a home, slightly askew. Out of perspective. But it clearly worked since they weren't toppling over.

"There, that's the main hall." Varren pointed at an oblong building at the center of town. "That's where all commerce will happen…and where the knights should be."

"So you should stay away from there," Noelle whispered to Ducot, still on her shoulder.

"He is right in that no one here would expect shift magic," Varren begrudgingly admitted. "He should be safe in that form."

"Ducot, go in and see if—" Eira didn't get a chance to finish. A commotion rose up from the heart of the town.

Two knights dressed in chain mail and leathers stained a deep crimson dragged out a man by the hair. Varren let out a cross between a whimper and a worried noise. He sank back slightly, flattening himself more into the grasses along the tree line they hid within.

Of course, the knights didn't see them. They weren't looking, either. They were focused on the man they had in their grip.

"What are they going to do to him?" Alyss whispered.

Varren didn't answer her. The knights did.

They took the man to the main gate of town, threw him to the ground, and while one began to kick and beat him, the other walked away. Eira felt every strike as if it were on her own skin. The hands of the Pillars were still upon her. Brutalizing her. She could feel blow after blow.

When the man was barely recognizable, the other knight returned with a length of rope. He threw the loops over the top of the main entrance of the town—two posts that were connected at their tops, stretching over the road. The first knight tied the rope to the man's ankles and then helped his comrade pull.

The man was hoisted into the air, barely moving. One of the knights pulled a long rod of metal and held onto the wooden part. With nothing more than a shift of his thumb, and the flash of runes, the man was blown away. A bloody hollow where a chest once was oozed onto the ground.

Noelle flinched at the sudden burst of noise, a whimper escaping her lips. Alyss looked on with a hardened stare. She had a stomach of iron from working with the clerics in Solarin.

Eira had seen cruelty in the hands of the Pillars. She'd seen what blind loyalty could drive men and women to do. The danger that came of one individual—a very mortal and flawed individual—defining what morality was for the group.

"What was that weapon?" Yonlin had a hard stare. "It was like a small hand cannon."

"I saw one on the island, though not in use. I think it's called a flashfire," Eira said. "But I know nothing else about it."

"Carsovia was always clever with their weapons of war," Yonlin said grimly.

"Flashfires arm Commons with the power of sorcerers," Lavette said in a slightly detached, matter-of-fact tone. "They're loaded with small flash beads and can be triggered even by someone who has no inherent magic due to a rune-infused ring, usually worn on the thumb. A small hand cannon is an apt name for it."

"More importantly, what did that man do?" Cullen whispered, horror deepening his words. "What crime did he commit to warrant such a punishment?"

"It's hard to say." Varren wasn't even looking down at the town anymore. He lay on his back, staring up at the sky. "Perhaps the man spoke out against the empress…or they just perceived he did. Perhaps he sold them a bad fruit."

"A bad fruit?" Cullen echoed.

"And they claimed he was trying to poison the knights of the empress for it."

"No…surely it was more. Surely…" Cullen trailed off. Eira looked over her shoulder to see his eyes were locked with Varren's haunted stare.

"No. It was nothing more. It never was. And it never will be."

They didn't end up going into town after all. They pressed on, through the woods, continuing until well after the sun set. One place was as good to sleep as any other, so they just picked a point where exhaustion had settled on enough of their shoulders that it warranted trying to sleep.

At Varren's suggestion, they all took watches. There were enough of them that no one had to be up too long at any point in the night. The timing was roughly estimated by moonlight, as none of them had a timepiece.

Eira was woken third of the group, taking over from Noelle.

"Hey, your turn," Noelle said softly as she shook Eira awake.

Eira roused quickly. It was hard to get that deep of a sleep in their current circumstances. "Any problems?"

Noelle shook her head. "All quiet. I think I saw a fox in the distance."

"Then let's hope Varren is right and there aren't morphi in the employ of this empress." Eira sat and stretched. Sleeping on the ground, especially after the comfort of a hammock on a gently rocking ship for weeks on end, was rough.

"Let's hope." Noelle stared off into the darkness that surrounded them. She had a haunted look on her face, the circles under her eyes made darker in the moonlight.

"What is it?" Eira rested her hand on her friend's forearm.

"I keep thinking about him."

"Who?"

"The man from earlier… Should we have done something? Should I have stepped in?"

Eira's fingers closed gently but firmly around Noelle's wrist as she tried to reassure her. "There was nothing we could do for him."

"That's not true, and you know it. We could've stopped them."

"And risked everything."

"What good is what we're doing?" Noelle turned back to her, fire in her eyes. "What good are we if we stand by and watch as innocent men are slaughtered?"

"This is a land we don't know, that we don't have a place in, or control over," Eira said slowly, emphasizing each word. "Varren knows this land and he says this is how it's always done."

"We could *change it*."

"Noelle, we are nothing more than a small group of strangers. We don't know how best to help or if these people even *want* our help."

"Of course they do." Noelle covered Eira's hand with her other one, leaning in. "You saw what they are forced to endure. How could they not?"

"We are not their saviors. We cannot be," Eira said softly. With her free hand she tucked a strand of Noelle's hair behind her ear. She'd never had a sister, and Noelle was the same age as her, but something about that moment made Noelle feel like a younger sibling. Someone to look after, take care of, and protect. Perhaps it was that unbridled idealism that Noelle pursued with unyielding passion. "You can't change something from the outside; the people have to want it enough to change it from within."

"You're trying to change Meru from the outside by killing Ulvarth," she countered. "Why couldn't we do that here?"

There were a number of ways Eira could've replied. She could've been defensive and pointed out how Ulvarth was a tumor feeding on Meru—that he wasn't the core of what Meru was. But he had gained traction. Followers. Momentum.

"Maybe Ulvarth represents the future of Meru," Eira admitted with the taste of bile in the back of her throat. "But I'm not killing him to change Meru. I'm killing him because it's *personal*. Because I must put a stop to this game of his that I'm snared in or I will never know peace." She leveled her eyes with Noelle. "If Meru changes after him, or not…is up to them. It's not my place. I hope they reject his ways, when all is done. I hope they chart a course far from what the Pillars have wrought. But it's not up to me. It's their land…and if they want to place another like him on their throne, that is their decision. Once Ulvarth is dead, I don't know if I'll ever go back."

"Of course you'll go back," Noelle said softly. There was a time that Eira might have readily agreed.

Eira took it as a victory that she wasn't focused on the man in the village anymore. "We'll see. But, for now, you should go to sleep."

Noelle nodded. "I'll try."

Perhaps it was how her shoulders curved in on themselves. Perhaps it was the dimming of her eyes. But something prompted Eira to reach out and grab her upper arm. To try to offer something that could be even mildly reassuring.

"We will help them, you know. Killing this man in the mines will certainly be of help. Think of how many might be able to escape in the chaos. How many we'll be able to free in the process. Moreover, we'll stop the Pillars from getting access to flash beads, which will help Meru, too."

Noelle nodded again with a slight smile. "You're right." She reached up to squeeze Eira's fingers. "Thanks."

"Of course. Now, sleep well."

Noelle tucked herself against Ducot. The man mumbled in his sleep, an arm slinging over her without him even waking. "You too," she murmured, eyes closing.

The words replayed in Eira's mind as she stared out into the empty forest. What good could they do? Was it even their place? There might have been a time where she would've been as idealistic. But now? All Eira wanted was to make it out alive.

THIRTY-FIVE

THEY ARRIVED AT the mines without issue. In trekking through the fields and forests of Carsovia, Eira was caught with a sense of the scale of the nation. For an empire that was touted as being large and rich with manpower, there were such vast expanses of nothing. Of course, there were some regions of Solaris with very little—such as the Western Waste. But even that had main roads cutting through it. Wells made and maintained by Waterrunners for the travelers traversing the dunes.

This was *nothing*. No more towns. Or roads. Or—*thank Yargen*—patrols. Which meant there was a lot more she wasn't seeing.

Carsovia was a scale unlike any she'd ever known, and it made the continent of Solaris feel so small.

Finally, in the timeframe that Adela had afforded, they arrived at the mines. They progressed slowly through the fields to a few boulders perched on a hillside. The cover would allow them to inspect the mine without risk of being seen from the patrols and watchtowers below.

Lavette stayed close to Varren, her arm around his shoulders. Without needing to be told, they all waited for him to be ready to peer over the boulders and get their first glimpse of the mines below.

The mines were a massive hole in the ground. It looked as though a star had fallen from the heavens and cratered the earth, down to its very core. The walls were stepped, descending far beyond their field of vision. It was difficult to make out details from their vantage, but Eira could see various towers positioned at different levels throughout. Plumes of smoke and dust rose from the work within.

"Well, that's it," Varren finally said. "The flash bead mines."

"If you don't mind sharing," Yonlin started, "how is a flash bead made? Does it come out of the ground as we know them?"

Varren shook his head. "It comes out as a crumbly rock called flash shale. We *carefully* break it down and then it's pressed into a powder, as it can be unstable in its raw form. Using magic runes that have been passed down in the imperial family, it's stabilized into flash beads—the little violent balls of raw magic you know. The whole process, beginning to end, is known only to the imperial family. Their most trusted lutenz and overseers take over at crucial steps, but the only ones with the full picture are the empress and her most trusted advisors."

"How do you want to proceed?" Lavette pointedly asked Eira.

"I don't think I get to make that decision alone." Eira looked to her friends. "What do you all—"

Lavette grabbed her wrist before Eira could finish, staring her down. "We are going to need a leader in there. Someone to make decisions if—when chaos inevitably happens."

"Everyone is perfectly capable of speaking for themselves and making decisions in good judgment." Eira had learned her lesson from making choices one-sided. She wouldn't be making that mistake again.

"Well, the first order of business would be getting in," Noelle said, moving the conversation along.

"I could make a tunnel," Alyss offered.

"They'll sense it," Varren cautioned.

"From here, how far is the entrance Slip used to smuggle you from the mines?" Eira asked him.

"It's down that way." Varren pointed down the slope of a hill. "Maybe an hour or two?"

"How many people do you think we could reasonably sneak in?"

"None." His expression lacked all hope.

Helpful. Eira looked back to the mines and talked through her thought process to give them all an opportunity to object if they so chose. "I think we should have some people on the outside. By the time we get in, it'll probably be evening. So those out here can position themselves closer once night falls. Moreover, I don't think we should try to risk bringing *everyone* inside."

"I should go," Alyss said. She pushed away from the rock, looking Eira in the eyes. "I can be subtle moving rock around. And, even if there's a risk of them sensing my magic, you need me there."

"I'll be good at suppressing fire," Noelle said. "I'll stay out here."

"Then Ducot and Noelle are offering support," Eira reasoned.

"I think you could use me to get into a tight spot." Ducot folded his arms.

"I didn't think you'd want to be separated."

He hesitated at Eira pointing that out, considering the implication.

"You should go," Noelle said softly. "I'll be fine. If everyone does their job well, I won't even be involved in the fray. You'll be at far more risk than I."

"If one of us is to be at risk…" Ducot murmured to himself.

"I want to go in, too." Yonlin stepped forward. "I want to see how the beads are made."

"No you don't." Olivin had a note of scolding for his brother.

"What if I could bring the information back to Meru? What if the minerals needed are in our home, too, and Qwint can help us make beads with their knowledge of runic magics? We could all stand a much better chance against Carsovia."

"I'm not letting you take that risk," Olivin declared.

Yonlin snorted. "That really isn't your choice."

"For what it's worth, I think you both should stay," Eira said. Separating the brothers seemed wrong. She couldn't—wouldn't make him choose between defending her and his brother. "Like Noelle's flames, Lightspinning is better for us at a distance."

After a bit more debate among all of them, the final parties were decided. Lavette, Cullen, Ducot, Alyss, and Eira were all led by Varren away from the rocky outcropping they'd been hiding behind. Noelle, Olivin, and Yonlin stayed behind to offer what support they could, assuming they could position themselves properly. The plan when they left was for them to take over the southmost tower—the one closest to the road—that way they could catch up with Eira and the others after fleeing.

But who knew what would happen?

That unknown was something Eira had to sit with as they made their way down through the woods. The landscape shifted, becoming rockier as they descended in altitude. The trees grew a bit smaller, struggling to gain roots in the hard earth.

Varren knew the way without hesitation or doubt, as if he had traveled it many times…even though he had probably never crossed through this forest from this direction. Fate pulled him back to where he'd escaped his worst nightmare.

Finally, he came to a stop before a cave entrance, chest heaving despite their walk being a relatively easy pace.

Eira rested her hand on his shoulder, patting it once. "Thank you for getting us here. You should go through the forest to the town. Get a ship ready for us."

"I'll take you inside." His voice quivered.

"You've taken us far enough," Eira said gently but firmly. "We're going to need that boat for when Adela comes to collect us by dusk tomorrow." She let her eyes drift to Lavette, hoping the woman heard her.

Go. If we're not back. Go and get yourselves home, was what Eira was really saying.

Lavette must have heard. "Thank you," she whispered. Then, stronger, to Varren, "I think Eira is right. And since she's letting us make our choices, I think we should go."

Varren still lingered. "Are you sure?"

He wanted to go. It was in his tone. His eyes. The way he held himself. But he still forced himself to stay. Varren must have been one of the bravest people Eira had ever had the pleasure of knowing.

"I am. We'll be fine," she said.

"That way." He pointed. "Head straight and don't look back. You'll get to the town without issue. We'll meet you all there."

She smiled and nodded one last time before the two went off into the woods.

"You sure that was wise?" Ducot asked softly. "He knows these tunnels."

"We have you and the most talented groundbreaker I know. We have a man who can sense the slightest of breezes. And my skills with ice. I'm not worried about navigating through a tunnel or sneaking through these mines." Eira exuded confidence. She didn't want her friends to be afraid or worried. The last thing they needed was hesitation. "So let's go."

"Now? Do you want to wait for nightfall?" Cullen asked.

Eira shook her head. "I might not be worried about navigating the tunnels, but I also know it might not be fast to do so. I'd rather get through and then stay hidden until night than risk being held up and emerging at dawn."

"Seems sensible," Alyss agreed.

"Alyss, you take the lead. I'll be right behind you. If I need to widen your channel again, I can."

"It'd be magnificent if you could do it permanently." Alyss batted her eyelashes.

Eira chuckled. "Perhaps someday." Adela could maintain sorcery across the known world with little more than a thought. Perhaps it would be possible for Eira to one day pin a channel open—or closed—with little more than her mind. "But I'm not there yet."

"I'll be waiting."

"Ducot, you'll be behind me. If we need you to scout ahead, you can get between our feet and then take front," Eira decided. "Cullen, the rear."

Alyss fearlessly led the charge into the vine-curtained and

damp cave. It was cramped and impossible to walk anything more than single file. The tunnel pitched down, and very quickly all light vanished.

"I'm going to make a sort of railing in the wall," Alyss said. She quickly lowered her voice as it echoed across the cramped space around them. "That way, when we have to rush back, we can use it as a guide."

"Good thinking," Cullen praised from the back.

Running her hands along the walls—her right in the divot Alyss was making and the other flat against the opposite wall—Eira sent her ice skittering over the rock with her left hand, quickly evaporating it so it didn't interfere with anyone else's power. She could feel the other pushes and pulses of magic as her friends worked to get their bearings. Alyss moved slowly and methodically. The ground beneath them groaned and shifted as she smoothed out any tripping hazards without risking the overall integrity of the cave.

Eventually, they reached a fork in the path. As they came to a stop, the sound of their breathing was loud in the deafening, cramped silence of the cave. All their magic continued to pulse.

"Thoughts?" Eira whispered when it seemed like everyone had stopped their inspection.

"We're too deep, still. I can't sense any fresh air," Cullen said.

"I *think* the vibrations are coming more from the right," Alyss reported.

"Ducot?" Eira glanced back, even though no one could see in the darkness.

"On it." A shift in the air around him. A pulse of magic. And the sense of his presence behind her was gone.

The sound of squeaking faded to the right. They waited with bated breath until he returned.

"Right's the way," Ducot reported. "Alyss, mind if I take the lead?"

"By all means."

Nearly three hours of slow going later, the first sign of light nearly blinded her. It was a streak of orange that bled through a crack in the wall ahead. The crack ran diagonally from the ceiling to their hip.

They each paused as they passed, peering through to get a tiny sliver of the room beyond. Crimson stained the walls, lined with chains, telling stories of horrors that none of them whispered a word of as they passed. Another room followed, a workshop of sorts with armor and flashfires laid out. Less bloody, but it still held hints that the laborers hadn't performed their work entirely willingly. Eira's stomach churned over, growing more ill with each glimpse they got of the mines of Carsovia.

Her thoughts lingered with the people cramped in a bunk room. They hung on the distant shouts and commands—unintelligible, but meaning still perfectly clear. She imagined a young man growing up in this brutal place, being born into it. Knowing nothing but these cramped tunnels and the horrors they held… yet wanting to help anyway.

Slip.

She'd been hoping they'd run into the man. But the tunnels were void of his presence. Perhaps he was so good at staying hidden, he could do it from them as well. Maybe at that fork in the road, the other path led to his personal home.

Maybe he'd finally left this place, claiming the freedom he'd helped so many others gain for himself.

Or…misfortune had finally caught up to him.

Yet, the thought of him and his resistance in these tunnels filled her with an odd reassurance. If the tenacity of hope could persist here, even among these people who—by Varren's accounts— were jailed and condemned to forced labor for little more than allegedly upsetting the wrong people at the wrong time…then hope could persist anywhere. Resistance against corrupt powers would always be lurking in the shadows, waiting for a spark.

After two more forks and much more arbitrary decision making, they reached an exit, at long last. They slipped through a crack into what seemed like a dead end of another tunnel, the entrance hidden in shadow. Alyss pulled her hand from where it had sunk into the stone, ceasing making her line right on the edge. Barely visible. But they knew it was there.

"If we need to get back in a hurry, find this spot and follow the line," Alyss whispered. They all nodded.

"What next?" Ducot asked.

"What do you think?" Alyss looked to Eira.

"For the time being, I think we should split up," Eira said.

"*What?*" The word was pure shock falling from Cullen's lips.

"I know, it's risky. There's strength in numbers. But there's also more of a chance for us to stand out. One or two of us can slip in with the rest of them." Eira had been debating with herself over and over what the best course was. "We just need to find the man in charge, kill him, and take his right foot back to Adela."

"Gruesome." Alyss grimaced.

"She always has had a thing for theatrics," Ducot said dryly.

"I do not care if I'm the one to kill him. This is all our task. If any of you have the opportunity, do it," Eira said plainly, continuing to glance up the tunnel to see if there were any signs of movement. "We all do what we must to survive and meet back here by dawn."

"And what if we haven't killed him by then?" Ducot asked.

"We should head back. I'd rather face Adela's judgment than Carsovia's, and the longer we stay here, the more at risk we are for it." Eira wasn't sure if she could convince Adela to help them if they failed in her task. But it was still the preferable option, given all they'd seen.

"You have a point," Ducot muttered. "All right. I'll go on ahead. Good luck." Ducot stepped and shifted into his mole form, scampering up the tunnel.

"We should probably stagger ourselves…I'll go next." Alyss went to leave.

Eira caught her hand. Alyss's bright green eyes swung back to her and Eira didn't want to let her friend go. She wanted to tell her to stay here and stay safe. But instead she said, "Please be careful. I want to read that story you have to tell."

Alyss nodded and put on a brave smile. "Trust me, I'm not letting it go unfinished."

With that, she was off.

"How long do you think we should wait?" Cullen whispered.

"Maybe a few more minutes." Eira continued to stare where Alyss had gone. "Do you think this is the right decision?"

"You're right to trust us all. We can look after ourselves. And…I don't think we have a choice." Cullen trailed his fingertips down her arm to take her hand in his.

She smiled slightly and leaned into him, leeching off of the brief second of comfort he could give her. Cullen wrapped his arm around her shoulders, squeezing her tightly.

"I hope this is the right approach." Lavette's final stare was scorched behind Eira's lids.

"We're going to be fine," he insisted. "Don't think like that."

Eira nodded. She knew such thoughts were unproductive. But doubt and fear were resilient foes.

"Besides…" His tone shifted, prompting Eira to pull away slightly and tilt her face up toward his. Cullen's hand gently caressed her cheek. "I won't let anything happen to you. Not now, not ever."

Rising to her toes, she pressed her lips gently against his. Heart in her throat, there weren't words in that moment. Even if his sentiments were nothing more than beautiful lies and they both knew it, they were what she needed to keep her bravery.

"Stay safe, Cullen," Eira whispered against his mouth. She leaned away, looking up at him through her lashes. "We have unfinished business, you and I."

He smirked. "I look forward to it."

Eira turned, leaving him behind and starting up the tunnel. It connected to another tunnel, no sign of Alyss or Ducot. She could head upward or down. Instinct told her to go up…logic told her down.

The way Carsovia was mining resembled a spiral, tendrils of tunnels spinning out from the main core—probing deeper for veins of their precious minerals. That meant the majority of the activity would be at the bottom. Her theory proved correct as she quickly heard the chipping of tools against hard stone.

Shadows moved on a far wall. Eira ducked down against a large crate, pressing herself against the side. Two knights passed, both armed with flashfires. Eira gathered up the dust and dirt, coating herself in grime before continuing. On the other side of the crate was a pickaxe. Eira grabbed it, slinging it over her shoulder.

She went in the direction the knights had come from, and eventually the tunnel curved around, opening to a large, flat cavern. One side was open to the giant hole they were digging straight into the earth. But she was so deep that she couldn't see the upper rim. The fading light hardly reached here.

Men, women, children, all labored in the smoke and dust of the cavern. Chipping at the walls. Clawing out thin sheets of rock—the size of a palm to a sheet of parchment—and delicately placing them in central basins on tracks that spilled over the distant, open edge of the cavern. Guards were positioned in the center of the room, overseeing the operations. Armed once more.

When they were looking in the opposite way, Eira scrambled down the side of the ramp that emerged from the tunnel. Rock and dust skittered down with her and she quickly turned toward the wall. Holding her breath. Waiting. Hoping…

A hand closed around her shoulder.

"I don't recognize you."

· CHAPTER ·

THIRTY-SIX

EIRA HAD BEEN expecting the guards to sound gruffer, harsher. So she wasn't surprised when she turned and found herself face-to-face with another young woman, rather than one of the knights. The woman was about Eira's height, slightly shorter. Her cropped, golden hair was gray from all the soot.

"Who are you, and why are you here?" she whispered eagerly.

"I…I reported to the wrong location." Eira looked to the wall, pulling back her pickaxe.

The woman caught it by the handle. "I wouldn't do that. While it usually takes magic force to trigger flash beads…strong enough brute impact can trigger the shale. And I'd rather keep my flesh on my bones."

Eira slowly eased her pickaxe down. She was solidly caught. Perhaps trying to get the lay of the land by assimilating herself was the wrong choice. But the woman hadn't reported her yet, so that was a triumph.

"I'm Mel. You?"

"Hannah," Eira lied. Giving her real name, even knowing it was extremely unlikely for anyone to have heard of her, felt far too dangerous.

Mel glanced over her shoulder and leaned in. "Are you with Slip? Did he send you?"

Eira had a second to weigh her options and, with barely any thought at all, she gave a nod. Thanks to Varren, she knew enough about Slip to craft a lie about knowing him. And Slip was on the side of those imprisoned here. So allying herself with him could be a boon.

"I knew he hadn't deserted us!" Mel kept looking over her shoulder, her words low and hasty. "We should keep working. Let's talk more when they take us back to the barracks."

Eira followed Mel's lead. The pickaxes were only used to carve out stone around the veins of shale. Once the shale was exposed, they carefully extracted it using only chisels and hands. Eira had to pry sheets free with her fingers. The thin layers of rock dug under her nails and cut into her skin. But she knew better than to cry out. Weakness would be met with cruelty.

When she delivered her deposits to the mine carts in the center of the cavern, Eira studied the knights from the corners of her eyes. But they paid her no mind. She was one of many. Another faceless, nameless worker. They didn't concern themselves with recognizing her or not. Her gaze shifted down the railings underneath the cart, over the lip of the open side of the cavern. Deep in the depths of the mine must be where the shale was refined into beads.

After about an hour, a horn echoed. None of the other laborers stopped, so Eira didn't either, until the knights begrudgingly shuffled into motion.

"Line up!" one of them barked, somehow both sounding authoritative and bored at the same time.

They did as they were told. One or two other prisoners looked twice at Eira, squinting as if they weren't sure if they'd seen her before. But the majority paid her no mind. It was reassuring, in a way, to know it was so easy to slip into the masses. She hoped her friends had been able to do the same elsewhere. But it was also an ominous indication of the truth of this place.

The people were treated like livestock. Interchangeable. There was no point for the guards to know their names or faces… no point for them to learn each others', either. A person going missing was treated with the same nonchalance as a new person showing up.

It didn't matter. None of this mattered…

Because they were all regarded as dead anyway.

Eira's hand balled into a fist as she shuffled off with the rest of them. She knew what she'd told her friends—what was true. This wasn't their place. Their fight. The systems that resulted in this brutality ran far deeper than they could touch. Even killing the operator of the mines wouldn't result in them stopping; another person would come in and take his place. The cycle would continue.

But that wasn't going to stop it from being immensely satisfying to cut the man down from the ankles up. And, with any luck, they could somehow cripple the mines in the process. At least for a little while…

Led through the tunnels, they joined up with other lines of prisoners as they continued downward along one of the pathways that lined the main hole. Eira found herself drawing in a slow breath with the rest of them as they emerged into the open air. Even though the cavern they'd been working in had been open on one side, the air within had hardly any movement. The hole itself wasn't much better. The heat of the day still clung to the back of her neck, settling in this forsaken pit. But seeing the stars offered marginal relief.

At almost the lowest point in the mine was a large plateau. This was where all the prisoners were shuffling. Eira kept looking for signs of Cullen or Alyss—she had little hope of spotting Ducot as a mole—but her other friends were nowhere to be seen. She scanned the towers above, specifically the southernmost one, but didn't see any indications of Olivin, Noelle, or Yonlin either.

They were fine, she insisted to herself. They were all capable. All well trained and had the sense to make the right decisions in any moment. They had put their trust in her, and she returned it by putting her trust in them.

The prisoners were herded into a large mass, walled in by knights around them. All focus was on a platform ahead where three men stood. Two were also knights, though they had long, red feathers sticking from the crown of their helmets. The man in the middle was dressed in a tightly tailored jacket and trousers. Both done in a satin as vibrant as a bloody sunrise. A silken black sash was pinned across his chest. His light brown hair and sharp eyes were a contrast to the rich colors of his clothing.

Her skin prickled into gooseflesh and the hairs on the back of Eira's neck raised. There was something deeply unnatural about having so many people standing so still. So silent. She found her own breathing was shallow. Her muscles tense from holding herself in place so that not even the soles of her shoes would disturb the gravel.

Without needing to be told, she knew that the slightest movement or whispered word would result in death.

"Her Imperial Majesty, holder of runic lore, keeper of sacred knowledge, defender of Carsovia, has informed me to commend you all on your recent successes," he said with authority. Eira suspected this was the Salveus she was after. "Your ability to double output of these mines is of great service to maintaining the safety of our lands from the brutal nations that claw at our borders and would seek to kill Carsovia's young with their viciousness."

Brutal nations? Did he mean Meru? Solaris? Before Princess Vi made proper contact with Meru, all the writings on the Crescent Continent—its former name for those on Solaris—were of how it was a backwards and untamed place. But the moment trade was opened, Solaris realized the truth of how wrong they had been. Eira glanced at the people around her, the tired faces.

Was this what they had been told their whole lives? These stories of how the outside world was determined to kill them? So far as Eira knew, Carsovia was the aggressor.

Unless…that too was a lie?

"Our great protector has learned of a plot for them to storm our beaches. To take our land. For this reason, she is seeing that we are well prepared. If you are able to triple the output, you will all have your sentences lessened by ten years."

A few gasps. Murmurs. The knights shifted, glancing at the

man on the stage, but the excitement seemed to be allowed. Eira could see the gleam in Salveus's eyes. He was dangling a false hope. She could see it because her body was not weighted with exhaustion; her eyes had seen the unbroken sun only a few hours ago.

But these people were blind to that truth. Too clouded by the dust and dinginess of the mines to see clearly.

"Now, even though you are disloyal and unworthy, Her Majesty is gracious and forgiving. Tonight you shall all receive an extra portion of bread to give fuel to tomorrow's labors." Salveus turned, starting down the other side of the platform. The knights condensed in front of it. Though none of the prisoners made a move for the man.

Instead, they slowly trudged to the back, where bread was being passed out. Eira followed the group, Mel still at her side. The line arced around the plateau and Eira caught a glimpse of the deepest point of the mines—where all the tracks led. Just as Varren had said, the flash shale was being broken down and refined. Two channels were built into the rock on either side of the opening and Eira caught a glimpse of a large metal door that could slide across the channels. Protection? Guarding from the elements?

She had to keep moving before she could inspect for too long. When they were up at the main table, they were each handed two scant pieces of bread. Hardly enough to even take the edge off the hunger that Eira was already feeling.

"This way." Mel guided them to the back wall, far from the knights. They sat on the ground, leaning against the cool stone. Mel's head tipped up toward the stars above. She spoke softly between small nibbles of the bread. "Are you really going to get me out of here?"

"I'm going to do my best." There was a twinge of pain in Eira's chest about the idea of lying to her. Perhaps she could get Mel out. Maybe more of them. She could tell her about the tunnel and maybe Mel could help Slip...though that might put

Slip at risk. Or, if Slip was gone, she could be the new Slip, if she wanted. "But first, there's somewhere I have to go tonight."

"Where?"

"A small errand," Eira said cryptically. She didn't dare say her true intentions, not even to a woman who should want Salveus dead more than Eira. "I need to make sure the way out is safe," she added so that Mel didn't suspect anything or ask too many questions.

"Of course. How many can you bring?"

"Just you, for now." Eira leaned in. "It's probably safest we keep this between us."

"Right. Right…" Mel looked up to the sky with a slight smile. She couldn't be much older than Eira. Maybe only by three or five years. Maybe she was younger and this place had aged her far beyond her natural years. "I've been here for six years now…I wonder if I'll even know how to live outside these walls. I wonder if Grendyl waited for me…"

"A lover?" Eira asked softly.

Mel nodded. "We were engaged to be wed, before I ended up here."

"What happened?"

"I was a baker, an artisan of bread at the imperial winter palace. I was one of the best bakers in all of Carsovia…I never found out how the poison got in the loaf for Her Majesty." Mel's voice hollowed. Her expression relaxed, going blank. It was impossible to read. Grief? Pain? Or…was she trying to hide her lingering joy and frustration at nearly killing the empress of this land but not quite succeeding or getting away from it? "All my assistants were killed. But my skills made me too valuable to kill. So, in all her *mercy*, Her Majesty sent me here for reformation and repentance with the hope of one day returning."

Eira chewed over the story, gnawing on the stale, hard bread with her thoughts. Varren had been wrongfully imprisoned here. Mel, on the other hand, faced a punishment for an actual crime. Eira couldn't imagine even Solaris would be lenient on someone who tried to kill the empress. Though, it didn't sound like Carsovia's empress inspired loyalty or love, only fear.

"Thank you for sharing." Eira ultimately returned to the notion that these weren't her struggles, so they weren't her place for judgment.

Mel shrugged. "Thank you for listening."

There wasn't time for further discussion. The knights blew their horns again and everyone stood. They continued their tired march into a large cavern that was used as the barracks.

The squalor was staggering. There were no beds, no bunks. People slept on piles of refuse. Scraps of clothing that Eira suspected were long without owners. The ceiling was singed by smoke from the braziers that burned in the center of the room.

Mel guided Eira to her place as a fight broke out to their left. Judging from the shouted arguments, the two men couldn't seem to agree on who had a tattered cloak the night before. They resorted to fists. No one stepped in. They passed countless people laid out, exhausted from the day.

A woman with sharp hazel eyes, almost yellow, stared at Eira with near recognition as she passed. She drew her scarred hands into her sleeves, narrowing her hungry gaze. Eira didn't allow her attention to linger, certain she'd never met the woman before.

They settled down on one side, by the wall.

"When night falls, I'm going to step away," Eira whispered. "But I'll come back for you."

"They're going to find you, if you do," Mel whispered back.

"I don't have one of these." Eira tapped the shackle on Mel's wrist and gave a slight smile. "I'll be fine." Her long sleeves hid the lack of magical binding.

"Right…" Mel glanced to the entrance of the cavern—a short tunnel that connected back to the main plateau they'd eaten at. "Let me at least make a distraction for you?"

"Mel—"

"Please?" Mel gave her a piercing stare. She had more fire to her eyes than Eira had seen so far from any of them. "I don't want to be a useless bystander to my own rescue. I want to help."

"All right." Eira sighed. She could sympathize with the feeling, it probably would help, and she couldn't exactly stop Mel without drawing attention to herself. "But please be careful."

Mel nodded.

The room settled to sleep. Eira lay facing Mel, wide awake even though her eyes were closed. In the growing silence, her mind wandered.

Where were the rest of her friends? A lump was growing in her throat. They were either all too good at being hidden…or something was going horribly wrong.

A tap on her hand had Eira cracking her eyes open, meeting Mel's.

"Now?" she whispered.

"Sure."

Mel gave a slight, eager smile. "Thank you for your help."

"Thank you for yours."

Mel pushed herself off the mound of clothes they'd been stretched out on and began making her way to the entrance, carefully stepping over the sleeping bodies of others. Eira rolled onto her other side so she could watch Mel, scanning those around her in the process. She'd draw her magic, go invisible and—

"Eira," Alyss whispered from seemingly nowhere.

Eira sat, looking around.

"Here." The voice was coming from the wall by her head. Eira lay back down. There was a tiny hole, barely visible in the natural curves and dips of the rough rock. Alyss's eyes gleamed up at her. "Were you captured?"

"No, I'm fine," Eira whispered back. "Relieved to see you are as well."

"Took a page out of Ducot's book and decided to be a mole." There was the hint of a grin in her voice. "It's been slow getting around though, making sure they don't sense me and I don't destabilize anything…"

"Any sign of Ducot or Cullen?" Eira asked.

"No." That could be good or bad. "Want me to get you out of here?"

Eira considered it. She went to look over her shoulder to see what Mel's status was on the distraction. At the same moment, Alyss let out a sharp gasp.

The long, cold barrel of a flashfire pressed against Eira's temple. A rune flared ominously on the ring the knight wore on his thumb—hovering just above what Eira easily assumed was the ignition point of the flashfire's handle.

A sinister smile curled his lips. "Don't. Move."

CHAPTER

THIRTY-SEVEN

THE MAN HADN'T seen Alyss, so far as Eira could tell. She suspected he'd be acting very different if he had. Which meant she still had an advantage.

"I will *go*," Eira said awkwardly, stressing the last part. In the corners of her eyes she could see the tiny crack in the wall shift. Closing. Eira held a sigh of relief. Now was not the time for heroics on Alyss's part. Her friend would be of significantly more help keeping herself hidden and striking at the right moment. "I'll go with you."

"Enough dawdling. Up," the man barked.

Eira moved as slowly as possible, trying to get a view of as much of the room as she could in the process. The people around her had scampered back. Most still slept, as if one of their own being manhandled out wasn't even remotely odd. Of course, none rose to help her.

When Eira was fully upright, the man grabbed her sleeves and yanked them up. The muzzle of the flashfire pressed further into her temple. He knew she had no shackle. She was as dangerous as he was.

More dangerous.

Eira made no sudden movements.

"Come with me." The knight forced her through the cavern. Two others were waiting at the entrance; each had their thumbs poised above their own flashfires. The barrels of the hand cannons pointed in her direction.

Eira kept her magic right under her skin. She'd only have a second to react if one of them got twitchy with the triggers. Could she encase herself in ice fast enough to withstand the blasts? Unlikely, given all she knew about the power of flash beads and their ability to cut through magic. The phantom sensations of the blows against the hull of the *Stormfrost* ghosted her midsection. It behooved her to see how all this played out, complying peacefully, for now.

She was escorted through the tunnel. There was no sign of Mel. Her stomach twisted…and then fell through when she emerged back onto the plateau to find Mel and another knight.

"Take me to see Salveus. Please. I have delivered to him one of Slip's allies. That is worth reward, is it not? Let me go back. Let me serve Her Majesty once more, *please*," Mel begged one of the feathered-helmet knights with wide eyes.

Eira swallowed down the taste of bile. She'd been betrayed. Outed. But rather than anger, she merely felt pity. What a pathetic existence to be groveling to return to the service of a ruler like Carsovia's—the same ruler that had condemned Mel here and probably hadn't thought of her once since.

Putting Mel behind, Eira focused on what was ahead.

The knights led her down the winding pathway on the interior of the mine, circling to one of the lowest levels and back into the heart of the stone. Every distant, faint crack of rock, every sigh of earth and plop of a stone springing loose, had Eira glancing from the corners of her eyes.

Was Alyss following? The knights were setting a brisk pace so Eira doubted Alyss could keep up easily without giving herself away. Eira would prepare herself to be without aid for a short period while her friend caught up.

The end of the tunnel was barred off with an iron door and heavy padlock. There were chains on the walls and familiar crimson stains. Eira was already setting her jaw and rolling back her shoulders. Bracing herself.

"In," the knight holding the flashfire commanded gruffly with a nudge to her temple. As if Eira could've somehow forgotten he'd been threatening her life the entire time.

She stepped over the iron threshold, into the far back of the tunnel. Sure enough, imprinted on the chains were additional runes to remove magic. Which meant the moment she was shackled, she'd lose her powers. Eira glanced over her shoulder as the man moved her into place. There were two more knights behind the two escorting her, halfway up the tunnel, also with flashfires in hand.

If she moved quickly, she could probably take the two by her and then protect herself from any shots of those above. She could then get up to them before they had a chance to reload. Though it'd be better to assume they were all sorcerers and armed with more than just the flashfires…still, she could *probably* take them on.

Or…she could comply and let them take her magic away.

They would surely tell Salveus of their recent capture. Regardless if they believed Mel or not about Eira being involved with Slip, she was enough of an unknown that Salveus should want to see her for himself. He'd tangled with Adela, and Eira had long ago learned the resemblance was uncanny. If she went along with everything, they would likely bring him to her. And, if not, Alyss would find her and help her escape. Or she'd figure a way out on her own.

Eira remained the model prisoner and allowed them to place the shackles around both her wrists. She had a fairly long leash of chain, but didn't take advantage of it. She stood almost perfectly still, eyes following the knights as they locked her in.

"Still so defiant," the knight said slowly. "Such sharp eyes. I should be careful to look at them too long or they might cut me." He smirked. Arrogant with the power he thought he had. That Eira *allowed him* to continue thinking he had. "Now, I'm going to ask a few simple questions. It will go easier if you answer honestly."

Eira remained silent. Her stare seemed to unnerve him, as he took a small step backward. Perfect.

"Slip is dead and rotting, has been for two years. I was there when we caught the rat bastard. So don't tell me that you're with him or try to sell out a ghost." The knight chuckled. "Though, maybe you knew that and were trying to become the next escape master of the mines?"

Continued silence.

"All of this will end quickly if you show us the tunnels you used to get in and get people out. We will find them eventually, just like we did Slip. Tell me now and spare yourself some pain." The knight waited and Eira continued to simply stare. He took a step forward, looming over her. He was a good head taller, but Eira continued to feel as if she were the one looking down on him. The longer the silence dragged on, the more his face tensed, to the point that his eye twitched and his voice rose. "What is your goal here?"

Eira waited a breath, then said, as calmly as possible, "I have business with Salveus. Bring him here."

The knight nearly jumped out of his skin when she spoke. He snorted and shook his head. "You think you can command me? You think you can just demand to see the overseer?"

"I have a message for him, and only him."

"From who?" The knight was regarding her more warily now. As if he was finally seeing her for the dangerous creature she was, despite being chained.

"I have a message for him, and only him," Eira repeated.

"We have ways to get you to talk," the man leaned in and growled.

Eira merely smiled a silent challenge—*do your worst*—and also a threat—*and see how well it works out for you.*

"They all start out strong, but even the hardest stone will crack." The knight stepped away. "Let's see how long it takes you." He turned to his comrade. "Do not hold back."

She was bracing herself when his armored fist sank into her gut. Eira exhaled through clenched teeth and a wild grin, locking eyes with the first knight as the second reared back for another blow.

She leaned against the wall. Collapsed onto the floor. Blood streamed down the side of her face. It pooled around her shattered foot. Pain, bright and hot, flashed behind her eyes. Two ribs were broken, probably. Her ragged breaths were the only sound in the tunnel. The knights' footsteps had finally faded away but she had managed to keep her consciousness. Grim gratitude for what the Pillars put her through pulsed with every ache in her body.

"All right, Alyss, now is the time," Eira rasped. It was the first sound she'd made in what felt like hours. Time had stopped during her beating.

The wall across from Eira pulled back like a curtain, opening to the side. Alyss rushed out, eyes wide. She pressed her hands into Eira's sides and Eira let out a hiss of pain. But Alyss didn't ease up. Magic flowed into her and soon the agony subsided into the warmth of her friend's skilled hands as flesh mended.

"How did you know I was here?" Alyss whispered. "And if you did, why didn't you call me sooner? I was waiting for some kind of signal. Eira, I—"

"I didn't want you to come and help me," Eira said gently as Alyss moved down to her ankle. Her friend's eyes were already welling with tears that Eira didn't want to spill over. "Please don't feel guilty."

"Why?" Alyss shook her head as Eira gritted her teeth against the pain of bones knitting. "Why didn't you ask me to help? I should have—"

"No."

"I'm not useless in a fight, you know!" Alyss snapped. Her anger came from a place of worry.

"I know. Alyss, I am the first person to say that you are the most capable, the strongest, and best among us. There will be a time for you to fight, soon," Eira whispered calmly. "But I'm waiting for them to bring Salveus to me."

"What? How do you know they will?"

"A feeling."

"Or they will torture you for days."

"We don't have days," Eira reminded her. "I'm going to wait a bit longer. I suspect they're going to him now. After what I said—and all I didn't—he's going to want to come and see me for himself."

"And *then* we kill him?" Alyss moved up to Eira's face, cupping her cheeks.

"I'll let you deal the first blow if you want." Eira grinned slightly.

Alyss returned the expression. "I very much want."

"If the next time they come back, it's without him, we're breaking me free and running. If it is with him…break me free on my signal."

Alyss nodded.

"Have you seen the others?" Eira couldn't help but ask.

She shook her head. "This place is much too large…I admit, when I found you, I stopped exploring and stuck with you."

"That's all right." Eira squeezed Alyss's hand.

"Want me to get these off you now? Just to be safe?" Alyss touched the shackles.

Eira considered it, revising her plan slightly. "Can you break them?"

"Metalwork is more Noelle's realm of expertise. But maybe if I…" With delicate, small motions, Alyss worked a thin layer of dirt into the lock of the shackle.

It continued expanding and expanding as Alyss added more and more to it. The metal groaned and began to swell. Sweat dripped off Alyss's nose from her intense focus. The pressure on Eira's wrist was minimal. How Alyss was using some of the dirt as a barrier so it didn't apply pressure beyond the shackle itself was an incredible feat of magical talent. Not that she was surprised in the slightest, given her friend's skill.

The shackle on her right wrist cracked.

"You can stop there," Eira said.

"But—"

"The other one now." Eira glanced up the tunnel. There was no sign or sound of footsteps, but she imagined they wouldn't leave her alone for long.

Alyss repeated the process, stopping just before the shackle popped off. It held together. But barely.

"What are you—" Alyss was interrupted again, but this time not by Eira. There were the footsteps Eira had been waiting for.

"Go," Eira whispered as quietly as possible. "Hide."

Alyss nodded, scrambling back into her wall. As the rock closed, Eira saw the tiny slit—now knowing where it was—that Alyss left behind to breathe and peer through. Eira hung her head as the footsteps grew louder. She didn't move even as they came to a stop just outside the door. Even though her wounds were healed, the blood was still there, enough to give the illusion of injury should she sell it.

The padlock on the door opened. Two highly polished boots came into her field of view. Eira slowly lifted her head. There was a guard hovering just on the other side of the door—thankfully only one—but her focus was on the man before her.

Salveus had come.

"I hear we have business." His voice was all arrogance. He crouched down to her level, resting his hand on her head, balling it into a fist and pulling up her face the rest of the way. His fingers relaxed and his eyes went wide the moment he met her intense stare. "You…"

"Hello, Salveus," Eira said, as soft as the whisper of a dagger sinking between a man's ribs.

He released her, jumping backward. "No. No…" He laughed. He was so focused on Eira that he didn't notice the rock slowly crusting around his boots. "You look like her, I'll grant you. But Adela is dead."

Eira tilted her head and decided to play along. "Am I?"

"I killed you—killed *her* myself."

"Then perhaps I am nothing more than a ghost back for vengeance." Eira balled her hands into fists and lunged, tugging on the shackles. Her wrists strained, a moment of nearly unbearable pressure.

Shackles shattered. Time slowed. Eira's magic surged back to her the moment the bindings were fully broken. Her skin emitted a hazy frost into the air as ice coated her, shielding her.

At the same moment, Alyss lunged forward, emerging from the wall like a living golem and charging for Salveus's knight. She wielded a sword of stone, just like the ones Eira had seen her practice making during the tournament.

"Keep him alive," Eira said hastily. Alyss stopped, wide-eyed, mid strike. But Eira couldn't pay her any heed. Magic was alight under her fingertips. She would freeze Salveus in place. Worse. She would—

"Thank the Mother." Cullen's armored arms threw around her. Eira relaxed into him, but only briefly. Surprise struck her at the sudden realization that he was there.

"How…" Eira looked him up and down. *He* was the one in the armor. No wonder Alyss had halted. "Oh." They all had their ways and methods of maneuvering and Eira needed to focus on their singular goal.

She returned her attention to Salveus, still frozen under her control.

With a needlepoint dagger of ice in her palm, Eira tapped him under the chin. "I might let you live, if you tell me what I want to know."

"It…it is you…it's true what they say…Adela does not die."

"And I will haunt you into the next world." She pressed the point of the dagger into his throat. "Why are you sending flash beads to the Pillars in Meru?"

He laughed weakly. Nervously. Quivering and trembling. "If I tell you, I am dead. So I will not dishonor Her Majesty."

It was going to be impossible to negotiate with anyone from Carsovia with this zealousness. Eira gritted her teeth. She wanted answers, but one answer was probably as good, or as likely, as any of the others.

The empress was funding the Pillars to disrupt the treaty, as Vi had feared. Because she wanted to plant a friendly leader on Meru's throne. Perhaps Ulvarth was somehow related to her. The empress's motivations didn't matter in the end.

But it all came back to this man—and he was the only thing between her and the ship that would get them all back to Meru and beyond.

"Then die." Eira gave him a far cleaner death than he deserved. But as much as she would've taken her time, there wasn't time to waste. Eira dismissed the dagger, his blood splattering to the ground.

"You said I could deal the first blow." Alyss had a bit of a pout.

"Oh right. Sorry…" Eira rubbed the back of her neck. "The knight—Cullen—was a bit unexpected. But you can be the one to cut off his foot, if you'd like? We should get moving."

"It would be my pleasure." Alyss knelt and set to the task, her medical knowledge allowing her to make quick work of it.

But it took long enough that Cullen ran his hands over Eira's face, no doubt pushing away blood and gore. "I'm so sorry," he whispered. "I should have come sooner—when I heard they had you. I was trying to convince him to come."

"You did the right thing." Eira grabbed his wrists and closed her eyes as he pressed his forehead into hers. She was immensely glad she hadn't tried to dictate where everyone would be. Her friends' instincts were triumphant in the end. "Thank you."

"I wish I could steal the air from all their lungs for hurting you," he muttered.

"We need to focus on getting out of here." Eira shook her

head. "But your defense on my account is heartwarming." She smiled slightly. "When did you become so murderous, though?"

"You might be rubbing off on me." The corner of his mouth quirked slightly. The stolen armor suited him. Her twisted knight.

"All right, I have the foot!" Alyss stood up, holding the disembodied appendage with pride.

At that moment, they all heard a sharp gasp and turned to find another knight—a real one—farther down the tunnel.

"Oh, Yargen bless," Eira groaned under her breath as the man turned tail and ran, raising the alarm with a shrill whistle before she could fire off any magic.

So much for a quick, clean, quiet exit.

"WHAT DO WE do?" Cullen looked to her. Alyss as well.

"What do you both think?" Eira could hardly ask her question before horns blasted again.

"I can probably get us out of here undetected." Alyss moved to the wall, her focus drifting as she was no doubt charting a course.

"Ducot shouldn't have a problem," Eira mused. Knowing him, he probably was already scurrying back to their exit point.

"What about Olivin, Yonlin, and Noelle?" Cullen frowned. "Are they going to fight, or will they run?"

They hadn't gone over contingencies before entering the mines. Eira cursed to herself. Maybe Lavette had been right and there should have been a more dictated plan…

"Noelle won't run until she knows Ducot is safe." Eira landed on the thought and hoped one of them would contradict her. Neither did.

"Then we fight?" Cullen sought out agreement from them both. Determined nods were his response. Commotion was growing at the entrance of the tunnel that led to the prison. Knights were nearing.

"We're going out the front. At least until if—or when—we can tell the others to run," Eira voiced what they all seemed to have agreed upon. "And, remember, we're not heroes and this isn't a duel. Fight to kill by whatever means necessary."

"Eira, I've a man's foot strapped to my back to bring to the pirate queen. We're in a morally gray area at best; I'm not looking to fight fair." Alyss's grin suggested she wasn't upset in the slightest about that, either.

Discussion ended abruptly as a horde of knights appeared at the opening of the tunnel, rushing down toward them. Alyss wriggled her fingers; the rock around them popped and hissed. Cullen drew in a deep breath, as if he would suck in all the air from the entire world.

And Eira...

"These are mine," she growled softly and sprang into motion.

She raced upward toward the knights. Skidded to a stop. Thrust out her hands, fingers tense, like claws. Each finger was connected with a knight. They shuddered as her ice grew in them. Their hearts seized and they collapsed.

Eira didn't even look back, trusting her friends to keep up. She kept running and emerged from the tunnel as a *boom* echoed across the mines. Cannons shot down from the southernmost tower, blasting into the path along distant rock. Eira could swear she almost heard Yonlin howling with glee.

A group of knights in the opposite tower levied opposing fire. The smaller blasts from the flashfires broke against a massive Lightspinning shield. Eira could feel Olivin's magic cascading through the air as the shield broke into golden confetti, glittering down like a meteor shower.

"My turn," Alyss snarled, and planted her feet. With a fearsome grin, she grabbed the open air and yanked, as if pulling an invisible rope. The rock underneath the tower that was readying their next volley against their friends gave way, sending the tower careening into the pit mine and knights scattering.

A burst of magic to Eira's left was followed by the howl of wind. Cullen was a blur as he practically flew. His hand clamped over the mouth of one of the knights as he landed. In a blink, there was nothing more than wind and carnage where a face once was.

"That's new!" Eira shouted.

"You'll *never* believe who taught it to me." Cullen threw a smirk back over his shoulder. Gone was the perfectly polished Prince of the Tower. In his place was a man wielding power and death with the same ease as drawing breath. "Now, I have some business with the men who hurt you."

Another groan of rock was followed by the sounds of a second tower collapsing. Alyss panted, wiping sweat from her brow.

Fire erupted at the top edge of the mines, underneath the southernmost tower. There was Noelle, fighting from the top down to help clear them a way. Cullen's path would meet her halfway up. But Eira's attention was drawn back toward the knights collecting on the lower plateau. Then down, farther still, to where the knights were slowly moving the massive plates of metal she'd seen earlier to enclose the very bottom of the mine. Cart tracks crunched and broke off in their haste to shutter off the most valuable spot. Their frantic rush further reaffirmed that was the core of their refining.

Eira's attention volleyed between the lowest and highest points of the mine.

They should escape. She should get her friends out. But… if things had already gone sideways…why not *really* cut off the supply of Ulvarth's flash beads? More than a temporary delay as the empress appointed a new overseer for the mines, they could destroy the mines entirely. Then Carsovia would have to focus on their own borders rather than on Meru. They'd be too busy nursing their wounds to support Ulvarth, and that would give them time to take him down.

"Hang in there, Alyss." Eira squeezed her friend's shoulder and headed down to meet the knights rushing up toward them.

The mines were dotted with water—stagnant, shallow pools that had collected during the last rain, to condensation from the cooling air of night, to water that trickled through deep caverns within the earth. Eira gathered it all, collecting droplets over her shoulders that grew into heavy blobs. She strolled down as the knights ran up. They stopped, levying their flashfires.

"I'll give you one chance," Eira called to them. "Drop your weapons, leave, and I *might* let you live."

They leveled the muzzles toward her.

"Fine." Eira sighed dramatically. "I suppose nothing can be done with those who trifle with the pirate queen."

A few lowered their flashfires then. Their eyes widened. Eira could hear a gasp. A few recognized her with expressions of fear and confusion.

With a wave of her hand, the water she'd been collecting condensed into spears of ice, raining down on them, turning the men and women into pincushions.

More knights beyond regarded her with a mix of terror and rage.

She drew the water back to her and was on the move once more. Adela's training was in every fiber of her muscles. It lived in her thoughts. In her marrow.

Eira hadn't been crafted in Adela's image by the womb, but by the hand of the pirate queen herself. And she brought death to all those who stood against her.

With every progression to the plateau, she gained more water. More power. There was an ebb and flow to the battle. Shield. Retaliate. Attack again. Except Eira was in control of the currents and they were the ones who were helpless before her.

Her body was surrounded in a frosty haze that Eira used to blink in and out of perception as needed. Illusions with one hand. Daggers of ice in the other. She could manage it all.

Eventually, the last knight standing in her way fell and Eira was before the entrance to the cavern the prisoners were kept in. She walked in, knowing better than to think all would see her as a savior. There were those like Mel, those still loyal no matter how many times they were threatened, beaten, or worse.

"Those who wish to live, leave." Eira projected her voice from the pit of her stomach to the top of the cavern. "The era of the mines is ending at the hands of the pirate queen."

This was what stories were made of. How Adela's infamy and lore spread and grew. Even if she wasn't Adela's child, Eira was part of that story, now. And would be forever. This was the first time she was willingly using Adela's name and it would be to her full advantage.

She was the woman with the ice blue eyes and platinum hair. The woman who ended Carsovia's flash bead operations. The words of the Carsovia trader who had been delivering flash beads to the Pillars in the cavern echoed in Eira's ears—*Empress Hannika has no reason to fear a pirate*. Eira would see about that.

They stared at her. No one moving. Eira turned and walked back through the tunnel. The echo of footsteps was chasing her, hasty, sprinting. Then, more. Eira stepped to the side as the prisoners dashed for freedom, desperate and clumsy with their frantic haste. Cullen and Noelle had just reached the plateau and stepped off to the side.

Eira saw Alyss above, clearing a path to the top rim.

"What happened to no heroes?" Cullen approached.

"I don't care about being a hero. But I do want to hurt Ulvarth by cutting him off." Eira crossed to the edge of the plateau, looking down at the large metal doors that closed off the very bottom of the pit. "If these mines are operational, Carsovia and Ulvarth are both stronger."

Cullen followed her logic. "If they're gone…the threat is diminished, for a time."

"They'll just make a new mine, I know," she said grimly. "But I want to inflict as much pain as I can before we go."

"How do you intend to end it?" Noelle asked.

"Underneath that shield of metal is the heart of the operation. That's where they take all the shale and refine it into beads," Eira said.

"Then I suppose it's a good thing I came down." Noelle walked to the ledge. "You're going to need some strong fire to get through all that metal." She cracked her knuckles.

"We should find another way down—that door is operational somewhere. We don't want to set off the flash shale," Eira said with a note of caution.

Noelle shook her head. "There's no time and it probably can only be opened from within. I can keep my fire focused."

"You're sure?"

Noelle snorted. "Who do you think you're talking to?"

"I have faith in you." Eira patted her friend on the shoulder and stepped back to let her do her work.

A wave of heat had Eira and Cullen staggering. Noelle's jaw was set, a look of intense focus.

Another set of knights poured out from a side tunnel, like rats being flushed out with fire and smoke. Eira and Cullen wasted no time engaging them, giving Noelle the time and space she needed. None even got close.

Cullen's power swirled through the air against Eira's. Their magics were two hearts beating, pulsing in time with each other. They caressed, brushing like ribbons of silk. The air throbbed with raw power. Ice crackled. Linking her magic with his was effortless, barely a thought. Every movement was as natural as her own—as if he were merely an extension of her. The chaos of more towers falling, the stampede of prisoners escaping, and the roar of Noelle's fire all faded away.

For a moment, it seemed as though they had killed off all the knights there were. Noelle paused in the lull to catch her breath, breathing heavy. The world had quieted.

Then, the sound of a new horn in the distance.

Alyss slid down the side of the mine on a chute of her own making, arriving at their level. A mole was on her shoulder that leaped off and took the form of a man.

"There's more coming," Ducot reported hastily. "A *lot* more."

"How close are you to breaking through?" Eira looked back to Noelle.

"Close." Noelle nodded.

"We need to go, *now*." Ducot crossed over, grabbing Noelle's wrist. She spun with a smile, grabbing his face and kissing it.

"First I want to make these people tremble in fear at the might of Solaris," Noelle said. "You go up, help Olivin and Yonlin."

"I'm not leaving you."

"I'll be right behind," Noelle reassured him.

Ducot eased away, stepping backward as Noelle turned to the edge once more. The muscles in his jaw bulged. But he said, "You all heard the lady, let's go."

Eira hesitated. "Noelle, are you sure?"

"You know my family had mines for Western Rubies, right?" Noelle said without looking back. "Mines like this shouldn't exist."

Eira remembered what Noelle had told her and what she'd read in history books. She knew the stories of the conditions of the Western mines decades ago.

"This isn't your family's mines," Eira said. "This isn't on you."

"Go, Eira, I won't be far behind." Noelle glanced over her shoulder with a slight smile. "You're not the only one who wants to bring this place to its knees."

Eira relented. They'd come this far with her putting her trust in her friends; she wouldn't stop now.

The three of them began running—Ducot back on Alyss's shoulder in his mole form—leaving Noelle to continue blasting through the door. They sprinted up and up, toward the top rim of the mine to buy Noelle more time by thwarting knights along the way. When they emerged, it was to a wall of cavalry in the far distance. Olivin and Yonlin braced themselves.

"Are we leaving?" Yonlin called down from the tower where he was manning a cannon.

"Where's Noelle?" Olivin asked. Then, hastily when he saw the blood covering Eira, "Are you all right?"

"I'm fine. Most of it isn't mine, and what is, Alyss already healed." Eira glanced back down into the mines. "We need to buy her some more time."

"No... They're right, we need to *go*," Cullen disagreed, staring in disbelief at the distant riders. "This is beyond us. We don't have the element of surprise or tunnels to separate them out. We need to get Noelle and leave."

"Noelle made her choice and we should respect it," Eira attempted to say.

Ducot was already shifting back into his human form with a jump off Alyss's shoulder. "This changes things! Order her."

He was right. Eira could see it. But should she really try to order Noelle against her wishes? She looked back down, screaming, "Noelle, enough!" Her friend either didn't hear over the roar of fire, or chose to ignore the command. "Noelle!"

"I'm not leaving without her," Ducot declared, back in his human form. Worry was seeping into his voice. He stared at nothing, not the knights, and not Noelle. But his face was twisted with panic, as if by sense alone he knew how tenuous their circumstances were.

"We won't," Eira assured him.

"I'm going to get her," Cullen announced.

"Cullen—"

"I can help her get through the metal. Fire burns hotter with air."

"I should go; I can open her channel," Eira countered.

"They need you here for that very reason. I can only help her in this task. You can help everyone." Cullen took a step closer and grabbed Eira by the waist. He pulled her to him, hips flush, and kissed her in front of everyone. A kiss that tasted almost too sweetly of goodbye. "I love you."

"Come back and bring her with you," Eira whispered.

"You're not rid of me yet." Cullen grinned, and descended once more, the wind under his heels as he leapt into the open air.

Eira turned, eyes stinging, rage swelling. Suddenly her determination to end the mines had vanished. The knights were riding hard against the open plains to the northwest and all she wanted was to flee with the people she cared about most.

But Eira didn't let her fear and worry show. Instead, she

announced, "We're buying them time. And then we're getting out of here. *All* of us."

"Yonlin, I want that cannon at the ready!" Eira shouted, assuming the lead when they all looked to her. "Alyss, funnel them. We can't let them surround us!"

Fortunately, even as Eira barked her commands, a large swath of the knights was breaking away, riding off toward the mass of prisoners that were escaping into the woods. That'd keep some of them busy.

Alyss rubbed her neck, rolling her head. Eira knew the toll the demands were placing on her. Alyss was immensely powerful, and skilled, but her feats of magic weren't small.

"Hang in there," Eira offered some encouragement. "Do you need me to widen your channel again?"

"I'm fine, save your focus for yourself." Alyss grinned slightly. It wasn't as wide, or as confident as before. "There's magic enough in me yet."

"I have all the faith in the world in you."

Alyss stepped forward and lifted her left foot so high in the air that it almost threw her off-balance. She brought it down with a mighty stomp that sent shockwaves across the earth. The ground rippled like water. It cracked and split. Large boulders jutted from the earth as if they were crooked teeth in the maw of the world itself. Sharp points funneled the riders into the only place their horses could now go: a grassy V shape that narrowed to the point of Alyss's boot. The knights would have to come almost one at a time, or be severely slowed by the ledges, sharp rocks, and boulders.

"Cannon ready!" Yonlin shouted down. "I have three shots."

"Wait for my mark," Eira shouted back. "Olivin, Ducot, you take hand-to-hand here. Alyss, you keep shifting the landscape to keep them off-balance and assist me with range attacks as you're able."

The riders were nearly upon them. The knights were undeterred by their defensive efforts. They poured into the top of the funnel, cramping together. Leaders among them made their calls. Men and women shifted their horses, jockeying for the best position as Alyss's terrain cramped them against each other. There were about forty total…not counting the men and women that split off. Eira glanced over her shoulder. Noelle was making good progress; the door was almost entirely white-hot. It wouldn't be much longer until she melted through. They just had to hold out for a little.

"Yonlin!" Eira screamed at the top of her lungs.

The cannon fire set them all into motion.

Alyss stomped into the ground again, and magic reverberated like an earthquake; the earth churned underneath the horse's thundering hooves. Olivin summoned a bow of light and rained magic arrows. Ducot's magic pulsed out from him, the ground shifting into a pit right as the first riders were about to reach them.

And Eira…she took the water she'd gathered down in the mines and swirled it around the head of a knight, holding it there as he released his reins and grabbed at his throat. He clawed at the water, trying to splash it away. But Eira held fast. There was nothing he could do to stop her.

She could feel the moment the water slid into the knight's throat and sank into his lungs. The man fell off his horse, trampled by the stampede. Eira collected her water and moved on to the next.

They fought with every tool in their arsenal. Even though they were five against forty, they had the benefit of preparation. Of terrain of their own making. And raw power that Eira could tap into more of at will.

Just like Varren had said, sorcerers were less common here in Carsovia. There wasn't nearly as much magical firepower they had to contend with, and Eira focused on those that had runic bracelets around their wrists.

Once the first trickle of knights reached them, the fight shifted.

A woman leapt off her horse, rolling in little more than leather and chainmail. She was wickedly fast, spinning the bracelets on her wrists. Eira was upon her, sending her water to the knight and freezing the wrist before the bracelets could come up on the runes she wanted. But whatever Eira had frozen in place was enough for the woman to still be deadly. She reached out and pointed at Ducot.

The man went completely still. Rigid.

Eira raced past him, drawing her hand through the air and summoning a sword of ice. She lunged for the woman. That broke her focus enough that Ducot recovered.

The knight shifted her tactic, spinning to bring her frozen wrist into Eira's temple. Eira blinked away stars.

Ignoring the pain in her head, Eira pressed forward, collapsing the space between her and her enemy. A dagger of ice sank between the woman's ribs and life drained from her eyes.

Another deafening *boom* of the cannon. Another sorcerer spinning their bracelets. The five of them were nearly overrun. Panting, exhausted. But, somehow, they were still holding the riders off.

That was…until half of the first wave that'd gone after the prisoners reemerged from the woods.

Eira's heart sank at the sight of the onslaught. They'd done a good job picking off the first wave. But they were all injured and exhausted. It wouldn't be long until they began making mistakes. Deadly ones.

"To me!" Alyss shouted from the ledge. "All of you, to me." Eira, Ducot, and Olivin wasted no time. "Yonlin, hold your fire and stay!"

"What's the plan?" Eira panted. The hammering of hooves was relentless. There were just too many.

"Stay here…and when I say, dodge right. Ducot, dodge left with me." Alyss grabbed his hand. "But hold your position and look fearsome."

Eira glanced over her shoulder. Noelle's column of fire was white-hot with Cullen's air and magic fueling it. The steel plates the Carsovian mine workers had moved into position to close off the lower potion were sagging. The two of them were seconds away from breaking through to the heart of the operations.

"Ready?" Alyss said as the knights charged for them.

Olivin grabbed Eira's hand. Eira glanced up at him with a nod and a slight smile. One he returned. Somehow this felt like both the end and the beginning. If they survived this, nothing would be the same for any of them.

"Now!"

Right as the knights were upon them, they all dodged. The knights went to turn their horses, but the ground underneath cracked and gave way with a unified pulse of Alyss's and Ducot's magic. As if they were on a ramp made of gravel, the horses couldn't find traction. All remaining ten plummeted down into the mines, falling a distance no one could survive.

Still, Eira crawled over to the ledge to verify. If they were alive, then they'd need to get down there quickly to keep the knights from attacking Cullen and Noelle. Fortunately, there was nothing left of the knights but carnage and rubble.

Eira slowly rolled back, ready to find her feet. There were still more that had come from the woods on their way. They needed to—

An explosion that felt like it shook the earth to its core knocked the wind from her.

· CHAPTER ·

FORTY

HER EARS RANG with a deafening pitch. Eira slowly reached her hands up to them, touching the sides of her face, half expecting to feel blood dribbling from them. Her vision was blurry; smoke crashed over her, carrying ash that clotted her throat. Everything burned from heat, from the glass-like scraps of the flash shale that battered her, sliced her skin with burning edges and pockmarked tiny explosions on impact. She forced herself to breathe through the agony. To recover and stand on shaky feet.

What had happened? What had gone wrong?

Eira blinked through the haze, willing her eyes to focus. Her heart was in her throat.

Noelle had known the risks. She knew to be careful and was too good with her magic to have allowed it to get out of control. Unless Cullen fueling her fire had thrown her off?

Cullen. Eira's chest grew even tighter. She croaked, wordless as she stared down into the mine that was an inferno. Cinder and smoke continued to pour out, obscuring her vision further and making her eyes water.

"Noelle!" Ducot screamed. Her name had become the sound of a bone breaking. Of the world shattering. Agony incarnate set free with two syllables. "Tell me…tell me she's all right. I can't sense her. *I can't sense her.*" He was shaking Alyss. "What do you see. What do you see?"

"It's just…fire." Alyss's words were weak. They were all slowly recovering, crawling and stumbling toward the edge of the mines.

Cullen... Noelle... Everything seemed like it was happening very far away. This couldn't be—they couldn't be—

"There!" Yonlin shouted, nearly throwing himself over the railing of his vantage in the tower. Somehow it hadn't been toppled, but it looked far more precarious than Eira remembered. He pointed, squinting. They all followed his finger.

Far, far below, in the heart of the blaze, the flame moved unnaturally to form a small bubble. It was barely visible. But Eira could see Cullen and Noelle, back-to-back, holding the fire at bay. The air he had used to fuel it, he now was using to try to snuff it—to carve a hollow spot for them. Noelle took a step forward, sweeping her arms to make a tunnel. They stumbled and staggered, movements strained. But even though their wounds must've been far worse than the rest of them had endured, neither Cullen nor Noelle was giving up.

"We have to help make a path for them!" Eira shouted.

"I'm on it!" Alyss reached out, magic thin and wavering.

They were all at their limit. Eira included. She could either help batter back the flames or widen someone's channel. There wasn't enough strength left in her to do both. But the flames made the choice for her—the moisture in the air and earth had evaporated. Dredging up more would take a level of power she no longer had.

So Eira reached out to Alyss, wrapping her magic around her friend's and prying open her channel once more. Eira poured all the last vestiges of her strength into the effort. Cullen and Noelle were too far for Eira to open their channels confidently, especially with the magic-fueled blaze. But Alyss... She would give her enough power that Alyss would be able to do anything.

Two walls of stone rose on either side of Cullen and Noelle. Then one behind. The first two elongated up the crumbling ramps and smoldering remnants of the mines.

Cullen's magic shifted to snuff out the remaining flames and cool the stone enough for them to move. Eira debated if she should change to focus on his power instead of Alyss's once he was in reach. But Noelle was assisting him as well. The two of them moved as easily as Eira and Cullen had together. Their magic natural complements for each other.

"What's happening?" Ducot pleaded, his face rife with worry. "There's too much magic, I can't make sense of it."

"They're coming up. Alyss is making a path…" Olivin shifted closer to give Ducot the full explanation of what was happening. "Cullen *and* Noelle are working together. But the stone is cracking…"

Olivin spared no details. His words underscored the desperation of their circumstances. They highlighted every explosion that burst from tunnels to the left of Cullen and Noelle, battering Alyss's walls, as the fire that Noelle had triggered ran rampant through the veins of flash shale throughout the mines. The fire formed deep trenches as whole pieces of earth slid off, collapsing into the inferno. Eira wondered just how much of the path Noelle and Cullen were walking on was supported by Alyss.

"We need to move from the ledge." Yonlin was halfway down the ladder that reached up to the watchtower deck. "This whole area might go. Who knows how deep the tracts of flash shale run, and those other knights from the woods are nearly halfway here."

He was right. Eira knew it. But they had all come in together. They were all leaving together.

"We have to hurry." Olivin's words dripped with worry.

"We're going to get them, and then we're leaving," she declared.

"Eira…" Alyss said softly. Sweat poured down her face. It ran down Eira's as well, melting instantly through the ice Eira would usually keep under her skin. But she didn't expend her power on keeping herself comfortable, not now. "It's becoming too unstable for me to move too much rock. I'm doing all I can but—"

"They're almost here, Alyss. A little bit longer. You can do it. I know you can."

Alyss nodded and set her jaw in determination. Her magic

continued to surge. But it was beginning to waver, even as Eira tried to dredge up more.

Cullen and Noelle were over halfway up. They were racing as fast as they could. But the ground underneath them was giving way with almost every step. The mine was being consumed by magic fire—waves of power stronger than any Eira had ever felt before battered her with every burst of flame.

A fiery blast had Noelle tackling Cullen to the ground, her hand held out, elbow locked. Fending off the flames with a burst of her own magic. The explosion from the flash shale nearly won.

"Noelle!" Ducot shouted. "Hurry!"

She looked up, finally able to hear his voice. Awash in the bright red and orange glow, a smile crossed her lips. One of confidence, arrogance, of blind faith—everything that made Noelle *her*. She helped Cullen up and they began running again, magic flickering.

"Olivin, take Ducot and Yonlin, go for the woods," Eira commanded. "We'll have a better chance of losing the knights there."

"I'm not leaving!" Ducot snapped at her.

"This whole place is going down. We need to get clear. Go ahead," she snapped back. Then, softer, "Noelle and Cullen aren't far. We'll all be right behind."

Eira's eyes met Olivin's, focusing on him instead of Ducot. He gave a slight nod. But his expression was just as worried as Ducot's—except, he was worried for *her*. Not that she blamed him. Everything was crumbling beneath them and they were a breath away from it all tumbling down.

She gave him a slight nod, one he returned. Then, he started to move. She'd asked him because she knew he would. If there was one thing she'd learned, it was that he'd protect his brother at all costs.

"They're almost here," Eira encouraged, even though Alyss could see their status. Her friend's strength was nearly depleted.

"Eira, I can't..."

"You're doing amazing. A little bit longer." Eira placed her hand on Alyss's shoulder and squeezed, the contact deepening Eira's powers.

Between Alyss making a pathway, Noelle and Cullen fending off the flames, and sheer luck…

Cullen and Noelle crested the top of the mines.

Eira let out a squeak of relief as her hand slid from Alyss's shoulder. Every muscle in her body relaxed. Tears ran sooty rivulets over her cheeks. Cullen's gaze turned toward her and, in him, she saw the man that had hoisted her from the snow after her brother's death. The man who had been there in a night of chaos in the Court of Shadows. As the man he was now and could still become. He'd made it.

"We have to go." Alyss panted softly. "Now!"

They all began to run for the distant line of trees, following after Olivin, Ducot, and Yonlin. The knights were still slowed by Alyss's upturned earth—going around it would take them just as long. Hopefully the woods were close enough to escape into. Hopefully where the trees were meant the ground was too soft for the shale since their roots could penetrated. Hopefully they could lose the still-mounted knights in the dense and uneven woods. They'd find a place to hide.

Hopefully.

Blind hope had them all pumping their feet away from the upper rim, racing away from the still-blazing mines that battered their backs with heat and smoke. Behind them, explosions continued to ring out. The earth groaned and cracked; Alyss's magic wobbled, flickered, and then gave out. Eira looked over her shoulder when a spiderweb fracture shot between her feet. Geysers of flame erupted.

They'd done it. The mines of Carsovia were going to be no more…it'd take years for the empress to recover from this, and that would give them all time to prepare. She'd tell Vi what she found here—the princess was still alive, Eira refused to believe anything else. If Noelle could've survived this, then Vi and Aldrik, as the greatest Firebearers to live, had survived the explosion in the coliseum. Ulvarth would lose all access to flash beads. He'd run through whatever meager stock he'd have and that'd be it. They'd annihilate him, too.

Olivin turned back to face them. His eyes widened with sheer horror. "Look—" He didn't get more than a word in.

Everything happened almost at the same time.

All at once.

Painfully slowly.

Eira's head swiveled back around. There were three more knights emerging from the forest they were running toward, charging for them, still mounted. The group that had gone into the forest to chase the prisoners must've split once more and they'd gained the element of surprise. They'd hedged their bets, taking chances both on the wide path around Alyss's upturned terrain and on the terrain itself.

One knight struck Yonlin across the face as he rode by. An arc of blood streaked through the air as he spun and fell. Olivin swung with a scream, launching himself into a crazed frenzy.

Ducot skidded. Magic pulsed out under him and made a pit, catching another knight with a whinny and a crunch. But another two were riding toward them.

Cullen lunged, ready to take down one. But the third slowly raised her flashfire. Raw hatred furrowed her brow with ugly lines.

Eira tried to find water in the air, but it had all evaporated from the fire of the mines. None came to her hand. She tried to force it up from the earth. From the heavens above. From her own marrow if that's what it took. To be strong enough that she could will water into existence.

She wasn't strong enough.

Another explosion rang out from the mines behind them at the same time as the woman's flashfire burst with sound, light, and deadly magic. Eira dodged on instinct, bringing Alyss with her,

Eira's hand still on her shoulder. Cullen was already out of the way, the wind under his heels.

But Noelle…

As Eira rolled, sky turning to earth, and then sky again, she caught a glimpse of Noelle staggering back. Blood poured from the wound in her chest. It dribbled from her shocked, parted lips. The ground groaned, cracking under another explosion that was somehow softer than Eira's scream.

Noelle fell back, lifeless, as the earth under her feet crumbled and the blaze consumed her.

· CHAPTER ·

FORTY-ONE

EIRA'S SCREAM NOW felt as if it tore through the lining of her throat. Ice shot out from her in a burst of frost that coated the landscape, briefly snuffing the fires trying to break through the cracks in the earth, holding the remaining rocks together underneath her, Cullen, and Alyss. The ice coated every blade of grass, every grain of dirt, every inch of Eira's skin. It thickened over the two remaining horses and riders, turning them into living statues.

Hatred was cold.

It was bitter. It was numb. It was a midnight lake on a late winter's night. It was a pit where light couldn't reach. Not even the light of a magic fire stronger than any sorcerer Eira had ever known could touch her.

She slowly stood, shuffling over to the new edge of the mines following the collapse of a huge swath of the upper rim. Rubble had fallen into the vast pit. It was impossible to see anything through all the blazing orange and rippling magic. Tongues of fire hissed against her skin as they lapped against her, trying to consume her, too. Eira held out her hands and spread her feet.

Freeze. She willed it all to freeze.

The condensed, raw, natural magic of the flash shale fought against her. Steam rose into the air higher than smoke. It felt as if the fire was within. Burning her from the inside out. As if she were the one who had been cast into the blaze and not Noelle.

Eira let out a slow cry that built into a raw and animalistic scream. She poured out her magic as tears poured down her cheeks. She would destroy them all. Cast all of Carsovia and the Pillars and the whole bloody world into an unending tundra where nothing would exist but suffering.

"Eira…" a distant voice called. "Eira." Closer, now. Two arms circled her waist, trying to pull her back. When she didn't move, Cullen came to her. His front pressed against her back. He hissed softly, no doubt in pain from the biting cold.

He'd held her once like this before…or tried to. It was after the incident. So long ago, when things seemed so complicated but were really so simple. *Oh, that girl then knew nothing of problems and pain…*

"Eira, we have to go," he said softly, holding his position through what was surely agony.

"She's—she's a Firebearer. Fire can't hurt her…" Eira bit out. "If I can clear a path of flames… She… We can get her back…"

"You saw the hole in her chest, the fall," he whispered, temple pressing against her head. "I'm sorry."

"No. We—we're *all* going back. Every one of us," Eira insisted. More ice. More power. With enough power, no one she loved would ever die again. She was so much stronger than she had been when Ferro killed Marcus. This… "This should be nothing for me. I'm saving her."

"You can't bring her back."

"I will be so mighty that Death himself will fear me. I will fight him for her if I must," Eira bit out the words. They quivered around the tears.

"Eira…*we need you.* We need your help, or we're all going to die here."

The words jarred her enough that Eira looked over her shoulder. Snow and ash were falling, coating the world as an appropriately somber gray. The knights that had been pursuing them were all frozen, dead, in Eira's stasis. Olivin clung to Yonlin, inspecting his brother as he lay prone on the ground. Alyss clutched Ducot, who howled as if he'd lost a limb. If not for her holding him, he might have launched himself over the edge. He trembled, lunged, and rocked. It was as if his heart had been ripped out and the sound had even more space to echo within, magnifying, becoming heartbreak incarnate.

They needed her…

What had her help ever done for them? She'd lied to them. Hidden things from them. And when she had tried not to—tried to consult on *everything*. To ensure she wasn't unilaterally deciding…this had happened.

We are going to need a leader in there. Someone to make decisions if—when chaos inevitably happens. Lavette's words echoed back to her. Was all this because Eira hadn't made decisions for them?

Was it because of her that Noelle was dead? What else should she have done? Her head pounded; her heart was still.

"Eira, please." Cullen leaned away. His skin was blue and white from where he'd clutched on to her. His teeth were chattering.

Eira looked from him to the fire. To the inferno that continued to rage and smolder…perhaps these fires would blaze, fueled by shale, for eternity. Even in death, Noelle would burn brightly. She'd make her mark upon the earth well beyond her years. Eira eased away, turning, drawing her magic to her. The land was brittle and barren, frost-burnt.

She staggered away from the rim and every step felt like a betrayal. Part of her wanted to run back and try against all odds, even when hope was lost. Part of her felt like it was down in that blazing pit, clutching Noelle.

"We have to go." Her voice was detached, vacant, as she loomed over Ducot and Alyss.

Ducot tilted his head up at her. Eira knew what was going to happen well before it did. He lunged up, grabbing for her, balling her shirt into his fist. He reared back with his other hand and found his mark. Eira didn't fight. Not when he pulled back and struck her for the second time. Eira knew how to take a beating.

"She died for you!"

She didn't fight when the third blow landed.

"Because you let her!"

Nor the fourth.

But Eira stopped him the fifth time, her cheeks stinging as much as her eyes. Blood dribbled down her nose and split lip.

"I know." She held his trembling fist in her palm. "But this isn't going to bring her back. And we must keep going."

"Have you…did you even look? What if she's—"

"She's gone. I looked. I tried." But it took all her willpower not to run back and check again. Not to hope that Noelle would emerge, against all odds, with one of her usual, arrogant quips.

"I'd rather die with her."

"I know." And she meant it. But she didn't let him go and launch himself into the pit after her.

Ducot trembled and hung his head. He wept until his tears caught in his throat. Until he vomited.

Eira waited until he was finished. When he was, Alyss slipped her arm under his shoulders. She supported him with a strength Eira was in awe that she still had.

They left, starting for the woods and toward the distant town and the ship they were owed. That they had sacrificed everything for.

Noelle didn't have a proper Rite of Sunset.

There was no body for it.

But at least she had been immolated. So Cullen led the prayers that night from the deck of the boat Lavette and Varren had successfully procured. They stared at the shoreline of Carsovia in the distance, a bloody sky mirroring the fires that still burned in the distance—bright enough to light up a spot on the horizon when all else had turned to shadow.

There wasn't much talking after the prayers were over.

Ducot kept to himself. Everyone gave him space. Except Alyss. Even though, during their time at the clinics, Eira was the one who had dealt with the dying specifically, it was Alyss who went to check on Ducot. Eira was sure she was the last person he wanted to see. She felt like she was the last person whom any of them would've wanted to be around.

So even though he had the most experience sailing out of all of them, Eira didn't demand he help them with the rigging. With tacking against the wind. Or with finding the *Stormfrost*.

She'd asked enough of him…of all of them.

Eira continued to replay every word. Every decision and choice that she'd made or didn't make. Should she have ordered Noelle to come with her? If she had decreed that Noelle, Olivin, and Yonlin stay above the mines no matter what, they could've shaken the knights after Eira's capture, sneaked out quietly, and met in the forest.

There were a thousand ways she could've acted differently. Any of them would've saved her. All of them added up to, once more, she hadn't been good enough. She should have protected her friends better.

I did what I wanted.

Eira could almost hear Noelle's retort on the wind. Even knowing it to be true—Noelle was, *had been* a woman who listened to her own desires—that knowledge didn't stop Eira from laying blame at her own feet.

Two arms slid around her middle. Eira knew it was Cullen from the movement alone; he'd done it countless times now to pull her back from the brink. She knew him from the shape of his forearms. From the soft breath against her neck. She knew him almost like her own magic—as an extension of herself.

And she knew it was him because Olivin and Yonlin had made themselves scarce. Even though they'd respectfully joined in prayers, and offered some of their own to Yargen…neither of them had been as close to Noelle. This pain wasn't as deep for them. The mourning not as real. They'd gone off with Lavette and Varren belowdecks. Olivin had been even more of a shadow over his brother. The few shadowed glances he'd cast in Eira's direction had become harder and harder to decipher.

"I'm sorry," Cullen whispered against her ear.

Eira tilted her head slightly, pressing into him. "What are you sorry for?"

"I should have saved her. Should have done more."

"We all should have…and yet none of us could."

I made my choices, Noelle seemed to challenge again between the beats of Eira's heart. But it was hard to listen to the murmurings of a ghost when grief was real and present.

Eira pulled away from him, stepping to the side. "We should be respectful. Ducot just lost the woman he loved. We don't want to rub in his face that we still have each other."

"Of course," Cullen said softly as Eira went to leave so she could pretend to attend to something. "But Eira"—she stopped—"grief is a burden best shared. Don't go through this alone."

"I know," she said softly. If there was one lesson she'd learned following Marcus, it was that.

But, sometimes, grief demanded solitude and silence. And those were the private battlefields that Eira chose to fight her guilt upon.

FORTY-TWO

THE *STORMFROST* WAS anchored for two days. The smaller ship was tethered to it, its anchor not large or long enough to reach the depths of the ocean. The delay wasn't addressed outright. Yet Eira knew it was as a result of them.

Adela didn't seem the sort to stay in one place for long. Especially not when that place was relatively close to the coast of Carsovia. But the blow they'd dealt to the empire probably helped her decision. Carsovia had other matters to attend to, right now.

As soon as Ducot was on the *Stormfrost*, he wanted nothing to do with them. His crew—his family—welcomed him with open arms. Eira hoped they could help him in a way none of them could.

She had been bracing herself for the resentment of Adela's crew. After all, she had caused one of their own such pain. But nothing had changed. If anything, the crew seemed to regard them with a deeper sense of respect and understanding.

Every hour blurred into the next. Most of it was spent with her worst enemy: herself. Eira sat on the stern of the vessel and stared out in the direction of Carsovia, even though it was past the horizon now. If she closed her eyes and focused, her magic could be carried on the deep currents and crash against that distant shore. It could run through the rivers and underwater reservoirs in the earth all the way back to the fires that still, *still* burned.

Every hour, she looked for traces of Noelle's magic. Of a sign her friend survived.

Every hour, there was none.

Finally, on the third dawn, the mourning period came to an end with Adela's summons.

Eira went alone, as always. Crow didn't even bother guarding the door, letting her in, or threatening her. Eira helped herself into the chambers that had become familiar as if they were her own. Adela was in her usual seat, so Eira assumed hers.

They both stared out the windows at the back of the vessel. Silent for a long time. Eira bracing herself for whatever reprimands would rightfully come. She'd lost a member of her crew…beyond losing her treasure or disparaging her name, Eira could think of no greater offense to Adela.

"I have felt your powers these past few days," Adela finally said.

"I'm looking for her." Eira didn't bother to hide it. Though she did glance Adela's way, challenging the pirate to question her on it.

Adela didn't. Instead, she said, "Have you found signs of her?"

"No." The word was ash in her mouth—the taste of flash shale.

Adela hummed softly. "Neither have my men ashore seen any signs."

"You sent men ashore?" That brought Eira's attention to her in full.

"Of course I did. She was a member of my crew." Adela looked offended by Eira's surprise.

"Thank you," Eira whispered.

"The only thing more unforgivable than someone attacking me is a slight against my own." Adela proved Eira's suspicions right in a way she hadn't been expecting. "Perhaps the one lesson I learned from that damnable Tower of Sorcerers: you take care of your own."

Something Eira had failed at, time and again.

"Those men ashore have told me that there are endless rumors surrounding the Pirate Queen on Carsovia," Adela continued.

"Rumors that say Adela was the one to bring down the mines. That there are still scars on the earth from her frost."

"Rumors and frightful whispers seem to be your lifeblood," Eira said dryly. "What's a few more?" She wasn't going to cower in front of Adela, and she'd had enough guilt over the choices when it came to the mines. Eira wouldn't allow Adela to create more.

"The closest thing a person will ever have to immortality are stories on the tongues of others long after they're gone—stories out of fear and out of love." Adela finally brought her eyes to Eira, pulling them from the sea beyond. The world narrowed on the weight of the pirate queen's frigid stare. "Perhaps I should be thanking you."

"Thanking me?"

Adela tapped her frosty fingers on the armrest of her chair. "You are part of this story now, Eira. Part of this legend. And, judging from what I hear…you are honoring its viciousness."

Eira shifted in her seat. The praise was genuine. Adela wasn't one to say kind words for no reason. But now, of all times, it felt misplaced.

"Nothing I've done is worthy of honor," she murmured.

"You've inspired terror."

"I lost my friend." Vulnerability crept up in her. Faster than Eira could stop it. Adela was the closest thing she had to a figure of authority—someone whom Eira could trust. Who guided her… Someone—despite all Adela's claims to the contrary—like a parent. Just once, Eira wished she had someone in charge to lean on to lighten the load. "What's the point of all this power, all this skill, if we can't save the ones we love?"

A faint smile crossed Adela's lips. It was tired. Sad, even. Eira wondered just how many people the pirate queen had watched die across her years. How often had she suffered this? How much colder was her magic for it?

"It's just power. Not complete control over the world around you. Not immortality. It's a tool like any other. And while we can *sometimes* be strong enough to challenge fate…fate, in the end, will always win. Death will always come to collect his due."

Eira swallowed thickly, remembering how she wanted to become strong enough to challenge the shroud of oblivion. How foolish the notion seemed now that she wasn't standing on the edge.

"You know it to be true," Adela said softly. The words were almost tender when they could've been biting. Understanding when they could've cut deep. "Even if you do not want to."

Eira dipped her chin slightly. "I don't know how I can face them when they watched one of their own get killed because I wasn't enough." *Strong enough. Capable enough.* "I've hardly been able to be in the same room as them."

"They need you, Eira. Now more than ever. If you're not enough now, then become enough for yourself and for them." Adela's tone shifted. Firmed. The words stung in the same way a mending salve could on a fresh wound. Good…but still sharp. "You have entrenched yourself too deeply in your role to back away now."

"What is that role?"

"Lead them," Adela said simply, as if it were obvious. "Be their captain. See your plans through to the very end and then make new ones. You still have work to do."

"How can I lead them when I don't always know what the right choice is?"

"Do not dictate. But do not shy from being the final voice when it is needed."

"How will I know when it's needed?" Eira had a thousand questions and she suspected that the majority she'd have to answer on her own.

"Time. Practice. And mistakes that you will vow to never make again." The advice was cold, but earnest. "They will not move without you telling them to. If you abandon this post now, the crew you have assembled will scatter on the wind and, I assure you, will not be better for it."

"I know." Eira sighed softly.

"So we continue working on this plan of yours: the echoes that will undo him. Then, while you continue to hone your skill, you sail to Qwint and rally their banners. I suspect they will meet you with open arms—despite the rumors surrounding you. Once they hear of how you crippled Carsovia, you will be their ally. Gain the aid of Solaris—either through the princeling they left behind, or through the princess, who, like you, I'm sure survived and is somewhere on Meru wreaking havoc. Then, return to Meru and settle your business with Ulvarth as you have designed.

"Do not take no for an answer. Do not let anyone sideline you from your destiny. Do not hide your power. Show the world why they think you are my heir."

When Adela said it all like that, so plainly, so clearly, it seemed almost possible. Easy, even. Though Eira knew it'd be anything but.

"Prince Romulin might not help me, if I'm even able to get to him. And I'm not so sure Vi survived, if I think about it logically." Prince Romulin might not be willing to charge after the ghosts of his family.

"She's alive all right." Adela snorted. "If there's one woman who *could* fight Death…" Adela shook her head, dismissing the rest of the thought. "The question will be if you can find her. But, if—when you do see her again, put in a good word for me, will you?"

"Pardon?" Eira shifted to face Adela.

Adela smirked slightly. "Tell her my meddling in Meru was only to find you, and nothing more. That, should I sail close to those waters again, it would be for similar reasons."

Eira took a moment with the words, allowing the meaning to settle on her. Adela thought Eira would have some amount of sway with Vi. Enough to broker some kind of understanding, if the princess lived. But what her heart really settled on was the implication that Adela *would* go back to Meru again.

That she was looking after Eira.

"You'll return to Meru?"

"We'll see what happens." Adela glanced at her from the corners of her eyes. Slightly amused, but also cautioning not to pry too far into the hidden meanings of her words. "But, at the very least, I think there are some Pillar ships in the western waters that I can enjoy sending beneath the waves. And, you still need my help to draw out these echoes in the way you intend."

"What do you want in return for your continued aid?" Eira knew Adela too well to think anything was charity. Little was done purely out of the goodness of Adela's heart.

Adela exhaled the confident front she always wore, her shoulders sagging for a rare second of what almost looked like vulnerability. She stared back out the windows of the *Stormfrost*. But just as quickly, she looked inward, motioning to her cabin.

"As I said…power is not immortality. I cannot deny the ache in my bones. Or the wavering of my magic. Even a slip of a girl like you has felt it. While I think there are a good many years ahead of me, eventually, Death will come. And then what happens to all this? All I've built? My crew?" In tone alone, Eira knew the last one was the one Adela worried about most. "Was it all for naught? Will it fade into the sea? Will my crew squabble over my riches? Will one day the rumors of the Pirate Queen Adela stop living on the tongues of men? Will a dawn come where people do not tremble at the idea of my curse?"

"I doubt that could ever be the case in Oparium," Eira offered hopefully.

Adela shook her head. "All legends die, without magnificent and terrible deeds to offer new moments worth talking about."

The pirate queen shifted, crossing one icy leg over the other and looking pointedly at Eira. She leaned against one armrest, toward Eira. Her stare was pure intensity.

"So, what I ask for my continued aid is this: Once your battle on Meru is over, come back to the sea for good. Cast off your landbound tethers, board my ship, and take the Lagmir name."

"What?" Eira breathed softly.

"You still have much to learn, but there is time for me to teach you."

"You…want to give me the *Stormfrost*? The Lagmir name?" Eira whispered. Her whole body tingled with a rush of apprehension. With excitement.

"Should you continue to prove yourself worthy." Adela gave a slight nod. "You have exceeded my every test thus far. You would be a suitable heir, so long as you don't disappoint me."

"But I'm not your daughter." No matter how much time had passed, how long Eira'd had to accept the fact as truth, it still hurt to say. It still brought out the small part of her that was frightened. That was searching for a place to belong, desperate to find one beyond herself.

"You are not my blood. But that does not mean you cannot be my heir. Were I to have ever had a daughter, I would've hoped for her to be much like you." Adela continued to stare at her with the same intensity. The same ferocity. "Well, Eira, what say you? Will you continue to learn all I have to teach? Do you cast in your lot with this icy, salt-crusted pirate from here to eternity?"

Eira took in a slow breath and let the offer settle on her. Doing this would change her life forever. It would put her in charge of more people—more risks like Noelle. It would make her responsible for all of them. Their happiness. Their sorrows. She would have to grow, constantly, stronger than ever before. She would learn magic beyond her wildest imaginations.

And, when she thought there was nothing more in her, she would have to find more to give.

Eira exhaled with a nod and a single word. "Yes."

Eira's story reaches its epic conclusion in...

Learn more about A QUEEN OF ICE (A Trial of Sorcerers, #5) and grab your copy at:
https://elisekova.com/a-queen-of-ice/

Want to make sure you never miss a giveaway, cover reveal, or release day?

Sign up for updates from Elise Kova:
http://elisekova.com/subscribe

You can get a FREE GIFT on sign up!

ABOUT THE AUTHOR

ELISE KOVA is a USA Today bestselling author. She enjoys telling stories of fantasy worlds filled with magic and deep emotions. She lives in Florida and, when not writing, can be found playing video games, drawing, chatting with readers on social media, or daydreaming about her next story.

She invites readers to get first looks, giveaways, and more by subscribing to her updates at:
http://elisekova.com/subscribe

Visit her on the web at:
http://elisekova.com/
https://www.tiktok.com/@elisekova
https://www.instagram.com/elise.kova/
https://www.facebook.com/AuthorEliseKova/

See all of Elise's titles on her Amazon page:
http://author.to/EliseKova

MORE BOOKS BY ELISE...

a DEAL with the ELF KING

a MARRIED TO MAGIC novel

Stand Alone. Fantasy Romance.

Perfect for fans of A Court of Thorns and Roses and Uprooted, this stand-alone, fantasy romance about a human girl and her marriage to the Elf King is impossible to put down!

Three-thousand years ago, humans were hunted by powerful races with wild magic until the treaty was formed. Now, for centuries, the elves have taken a young woman from Luella's village to be their Human Queen.

To be chosen is seen as a mark of death by the townsfolk. A mark nineteen-

year-old Luella is grateful to have escaped as a girl. Instead, she's dedicated her life to studying herbology and becoming the town's only healer.

That is, until the Elf King unexpectedly arrives... for her.

Everything Luella had thought she'd known about her life, and herself, was a lie. Taken to a land filled with wild magic, Luella is forced to be the new queen to a cold yet blisteringly handsome Elf King. Once there, she learns about a dying world that only she can save.

The magical land of Midscape pulls on one corner of her heart, her home and people tug on another... but what will truly break her is a passion she never wanted.

https://elisekova.com/a-deal-with-the-elf-king/

Stand Alone. Fantasy Romance.

For romantasy fans who loved King of Battle of Blood, The Bridge Kingdom, and Crave. Step into a world of hunters, vampires, and curses that run deeper than blood.

On the night of the blood moon, the Vampire Lord must die.

Floriane's position as the forge maiden of Hunter's Hamlet is one of reverence, for it is her skill that arms and protects the vampire hunters. She knows her place and is a faithful servant to the Master Hunter and her community... until the night of the blood moon. Until her brother is dying at the hands of the Vampire Lord Ruvan.

Wanting to defend her home at all costs, Floriane fights the vampire lord, ready to give her life if it means taking his. But Ruvan doesn't want to take her life... he wants her.

Kidnapped and brought to the vampire castle, Floriane is now blood sworn to the vampire lord. She is bound in mind and body to her worst enemy. But Ruvan isn't the fiend she thought he was. She learns the truth of the vampires: They are not mindless monsters, but a proud people, twisted and tortured by an ancient curse.

Ruvan believes that Floriane might be the key to ending his people's suffering. All Floriane wants is to defend her home. Loyalties are tested and the lines between truth and lie, hate and passion, are blurred.

When her dagger is at his chest, will she be able to take the heart of the man who has claimed hers?

https://elisekova.com/a-duel-with-the-vampire-lord/

$\mathcal{A}$CKNOWLEDGEMENTS

Emily — I cannot express how appreciative I am of all you've done for this launch, and continue to do to keep me on track. Thank you so much for keeping me in order and helping with so much of the heavy lifting of getting my books in the world.

Rebecca, Melissa & Kate — This book wouldn't be what it is without the editorial help you all give. Thank you so much for your flexibility, hard work, and determination to see my books through to the end.

Robert — I'm not sure if this book would've made it out without your help. Thank you for all you do in the real world so I can spend my days in the fantastical.

The Tower Guard — Thank you all for being there, for stepping up, and for helping me spread the word. I cannot thank each of you enough for the help when it came to this particular release.

My Patrons — Caitlyn B., Carolyn H., Nikki B., Courtney C., Moa E., Laura S., Kiera J., AJ T., Aly N., Adrienne A., Ilse J., Joanna M., Kristýna E., Elizabeth H., Dyani S., Pauline, Chloe F., Nelle M., Jade, Hannah Montoya, Amanda C., Imzadi, Vixie, Caitlyn P., Kristin W., Rachael L., MasterR50, Rebecca R., Steffi aka. Lambert, Aniyue, Anne of Daze, Laura R., Missy Anathema, Sarah T., Nancy S., Laura B., Mandi S., Melinda H., Kayla D., Taylour D., Stephanie H., Nichole M., Sarah M., Gemma, Rose G., Karolína N. B., Laura H., discokittie, Teddie W., Dani W., Ayragon, Liz D., C Sharp, M Knight, Kate R., Jamie B., Jennifer G., Marissa C., Monique R., Ru-Doragon (Alexa), Claribel V., Sarah L., Nicole M., Ren, Lisa, Sorcha A., Tea Cup, Caitlin P., Bec M., Paige F., Bridget W., Olivia S., Sarah [faeryreads], Macarena M., Kristen M., Kelly M., Audrey C W., Amy M., Allison S., Donna W., Renee S., Ashton Morgan, Mackenzie, Kaitlin B., Amanda T., Kayleigh K., Shelbe H., Alisha L., Esther R., Brooke Elaine, Kaylie, Heather F., Shelly D., Andra P., Melisa K., Serenity87HUN, Nichelle G., Giuliana T., Chelsea S., Sisi, Matthea F., Catarina G., Stephanie T., Mani R., Elise G., Traci F., Samantha C., Lindsay B., Sassy_Sas, Karin B., Eri, Ashley D., Michael P., Stengelberry, Dana A., Michael P., Alexis P., Jennifer B., Kay Z., Lauren V., Sarah Ruth H., Sheryl K B., Aemaeth, NaiculS, Justine B., Lindsay W., MotherofMagic, Charles B., Kira M., Charis, Kassie P., Angela G., Elly M., Michelle S.,

Asami, Amy B., Meagan R., Axel R., Ambermoon86, Bookish Connoisseur, Tarryn G., Cassidy T., Kathleen M., Alexa A., Rhianne, Cassondra A., Sierra Fox, Emmie S., Emily R., and Tamashi T. — thank you for being among some of my most loyal readers and fans. It is a delight to share with you everything that I'm working on and I cannot wait to see what the next book holds!

To all the readers, reviewers, booktokers, bookstagrammers, book sellers, and everyone else who reads, shares, reviews, and talks about my books — I cannot do what I do without you. Everything you do makes a difference and authors like me truly wouldn't be able to survive without you. I'm sorry I don't always have the time to respond to each of you, but know that you are seen and appreciated. I cannot express the depths of my thanks enough.

www.ingramcontent.com/pod-product-compliance
Lightning Source LLC
Chambersburg PA
CBHW031001190726
48285CB00004BB/1421